FORGOTTEN ISLAND

Bob Ball

Forgotten Island

Published by WriterMotive
www.writermotive.com

PROLOGUE
ISLAND OFF THE COAST OF CALIFORNIA
1945

The convoy of military vehicles, 20 in all, were travelling to the little port of San Juliet, an Island 40 miles off the coast of California. It was carrying the last remains of a top secret air base on the Island, built there after the attack on Pearl Harbour, in *1941, which* was now being dismantled and shut down as if it never existed.

The base was never used for what it was intended, and that, was in the unlikely event the US was attacked by Japanese aircraft, or any other incursion, and was fully manned until the end of the war in 1945.

Now, the Base had come to the end of its usefulness, and was to be shut down and FORGOTTEN.

This was the last convoy to leave, and it was the most volatile, as it consisted of all the armaments that the base had, including small arms, rockets, and a lot experimental weapons plus explosives.

The whole lot was to be destroyed, or just to be made to vanish, and was now being spirited away, so no trace of the base would be remembered, or found, just FORGOTTEN.

They were making good progress, when one of the trucks broke down, the two airmen got out having a look, and seeing steam coming from the engine, they started to wave the other trucks behind them through.

A Flight Major came up and asked "What's the problem here?"

One of the airmen replied "It's the cooling system Sir, its overheating,"

The Major called out to two military police "You two come over here and stay with this truck until it's fixed, we do not want anything to go missing, as this truck is carrying very volatile material,"

The officers parked their bikes, and the rest of the convoy carried on, "How long will this take," asked one of them

The airman replied "Not long," one of them climbed back into the cab, while the other chatted to the officers. The airman came down from the cab with one hand behind his back and calmly shot both of them in the head, "Get rid of the bodies and the bikes, throw the over the cliff," and then, just as calmly, the other airman wheeled the bikes to the cliff edge, and pushed them over, then carried the bodies and once again calmly dumped the two unsuspecting officers on to the rocks below.

Meanwhile the other airman walked to a nearby barn, unlocked the door, and drove an identical truck out, the truck was loaded with a lot of scrap metal, to correspond to the weight of their own truck. The other airman drove the original truck through the trees to an concealed entrance, and drove as far inside as he could parked took out the keys and pocketed them, went outside and the two of them closed up the entrance. This was an entrance to a disused tunnel system that was part of the airbase, a secret system not well known, not even to the men manning the base.

All this time the airman had not said a word to each other, the whole scenario had been meticulously planned.

They both got back into the bogus truck and set off at a fast pace, as by this time the convoy had covered a lot of distance, and they had to make up the extra time, owing to the disposal of the two military police. They had planned for it, but were hoping that they were going to get an easier outcome.

They were travelling at a very fast pace, when for the first time one of them spoke "Don't you think you should take it a bit easier along this stretch,"

The driver took no notice just replied "Don't worry I know this road like the back of my hand," they took the next bend to fast, and the truck started to slide.

"Slow down!" Just as he said this, the slide got worse and the driver lost complete control, the truck just kept going right over the cliff edge to crash onto the rocks below, joining the bikes and the two police officers never to be seen again.

Back at the barn, a young lad was trying to work out what had just happened. He had been in the loft all the time. The barn was one of his secret places. He just made his way home and never thought of it again.

1

Present day
Tuesday

It was early morning, at a warehouse, just south of Santa Barbara. Angelo (Angel) Romano, a known drug dealer was supervising the loading of the three trucks belonging to the "State Marine Survey Agency Conservation Environment," but the contents did not conform to the requirement of a Marine Conversation.

Angelo (angel) Romano who on this operation was to be called No1, and all the men around him, would also have numbers or letters, his associate Carlo Bellini was No2.

No1 watched as a large digger was manhandled into the back of one of the trucks, along with two forklifts, and various tools. Another truck was being loaded with electrical equipment; neither truck was your normal marine apparatus. The third truck was carrying earth moving Machinery, plus a large quantity of dynamite. On a bench two men were checking their weapons, including a hand held missile launcher.

No1 came over to inspect the arsenal, one of the men G1; the main guard, asked if all this fire power would be necessary, No1 replied "I hope not, but if we have to use it, we will,"

G2 a guard, started to load the armaments onto the third truck, all the men ten in all were all ex forces, drug enforcement thugs, or just engineers. One off the men was an Ex, Air Traffic Controller?

Once the trucks were loaded and the men assigned their vehicles, they set off for the ferry port 15 miles south, each man looking forward to a large payday for a week's work, all realising that their particular skills may be needed including what most of them were good at, Killing. The convoy consisted of two Range Rovers, and the three trucks all with the State Marine logo along the side, a legitimate agency connected to the California University. But the logo, hijacked for this operation.

They were heading for San Juliet, a small Island about forty miles off the mainland, that was served by a once a week ferry, that had been booked for that morning. The convoy arrived at the port at

6am, and waited to board the ferry, No1 making sure that all weapons were concealed.

"The Islanders unaware what was heading their way?

While at 6am on San Juliet. The day had started like any other day; David Croft had got up at his usual time, and immediately started out on his morning run. David was a stickler for routine having been in the army, but now, he was a small time farmer, and a part time teacher, in a small community, on a small Island, called San Juliet, off the coast of California. His life had dramatically changed after he had decided to leave the army. Having been in it since he was seventeen, he was now a very fit 39 year old, having been out of the Army for three years, but he still kept himself very active, although, only for him. The rest of the Islanders just took him for a small farm owner, and a not a very fit person, he always wore baggy clothes, not wanting to let other people to know that underneath those clothes was a very fit and muscular ex special forces soldier. That was the past and he did not want to be reminded of it, although it was always in his head. The people he had killed. And the friends, that had died around him.

He was coming to the end of his six mile run when he saw another runner, the girl from the Marine life Laboratory, he quickly reversed his path so as not to meet up, he liked the dark skinned girl with her beautiful Latin looks, they had even been out for a drink, but had never met up on his punishing fitness runs, or his workouts in his gym.

He arrived back at the farm just in time to put on his baggy clothes and perfect his innocent and slightly defeated look, a look he had maintained since he came to the Island, three years ago.

Chloe came running into the yard pass the sheep and geese, scattering them all over the place, "Sorry about that," she cried as David tried to calm his flock down,

"Don't you worry your sweet little head I wanted a bit of exercise," he said, puffing and panting.

"You should come on a run with me, you are so unfit," she laughed,

"No I'll leave that to you silly people, why would anyone want to kill themselves by doing all that unproductive work,"

Chloe looked around "Where's your Dog?"

David glanced over towards the house "He's feeling a bit poorly today he didn't even eat his breakfast,"

Chloe sat down on the grass and caught her breath, "Will it be too much for you to offer me a drink, or is that too much work for you?"

David pulled a funny face "No I think my body could just about manage that," he went into the house.

Chloe thought to herself "He must have been doing a bit of work as he was all sweaty and hot," she put to the back of her mind, "Maybe I'll find out a little bit more about him if I ask him out again,"

David came back with two iced drinks, "How often do you this running lark," he asked with a smirk on his face, she stuck out her tongue, finished her drink, and went on her way, again scattering the farmyard animals, and she gave a cheery wave as she run down the hill.

David watched her go "I'm going to like that girl," he said to himself. Since he had been on the Island he had not had any romantic liaisons, just keeping himself to himself.

He fed the geese checked for eggs found four, and then went in for a shower and a couple of his freshly laid eggs for breakfast.

San Juliet is as remote as you can get off the coast of California, it's just ten miles long, and five miles wide, and covers about 38 sq miles in total.

The Island consists of the South East, inhabited with the most of its 300 inhabitants; the South West is a rugged area due to storms coming in from the Pacific. The North, no one really knows, as it's a restricted area. It's hilly, but not mountainous. Most of the Islanders know, that years ago it was a military base, but that was all they knew, no one knows the true story.

The tiny harbour is the heart of the Island, with its smattering of shops, and stores. One hotel, that sees visitors on some occasion's especially when the whale spotting season is under way, There are no real beaches just a few sandy inlets where you can beach a boat but nothing large, so holiday makers do not visit, nor walkers as the Island is not large enough, or diverse enough, while the harbour with its small fishing fleet, was not large enough to sustain any sort of industry, as a remote Island it earns its name, but everyone who lives on the Island lives there for the remoteness of it, and would not have it any other way.

The Island is about 40 miles of the coast just north of the nearest larger Island of Santa Rosa, where most people go to get sand, sun, and sailing, but the Islanders do not like change, they enjoy their isolation away from the hustle and bustle of normal life.

One of the top moments of the week, is when the twice a week ferry comes into the harbour, its normally packed in the pretty little harbour area, with its brightly painted shop fronts and quirky quaint houses, as most of the residents live and work out in the surrounding area, it's a nice thing to do a bit of shopping and meeting your neighbours, the shopping consists of a supermarket, bakers, barbers that cater for both sexes, a drug store, and a few clothes and fashion shops, a small hotel with about six rooms incorporating a rather nice restaurant, all in all a lovely place but not much of it, the most important bit about the place is, it has a beautiful British pub. Sorry Irish. The pub is run by two Irish immigrants Sean and Mary O'Rielly put there by the few English men and their Irish partners, plus the Americans love all things British. There is also a gas station and a real American diner just on the outskirts of town, that's it. The cars on the Island you could count on your fingers. There are plenty of tractors and other machinery, but for the most part cars are not really needed.

Today the town was full to the brim, it is Tuesday, ferry day, David had come into town riding his buggy with a large trailer. He did not own a real car. He was there to meet the ferry to take back to his farm his latest purchase twenty Romney Marsh sheep, the same sheep he was brought up with, in his home town of Ivychurch in Kent, England, locally called the Garden Of England: He already had about twenty different kinds of sheep, but these came up for sale real sheep! And he could not resist buying them, they were very costly due to the distance but it will be worth it his Dad back in England had sent them over from his own farm in Kent.

There was quite a wait before the ferry docked so David decided to visit his best mate Sean at PP (Paddy's Pub)

David parked the buggy outside, and walked into the dimly lit pub, and strait away was accosted by a giant, Sean (paddy) O'Rielly a mountain of a man 6 foot six and sometimes looked as wide, "Davy boy!, how are you? Long time no see," giving David a big hug,

David found it hard to breathe in this big lovely mans arms, "I'll be fine when you let me go," he gasped,

Sean let him go, walked over to the bar and poured two large whiskeys, holding them up high in the air Shouting "Down the English, Up the Irish," David laughed out loud, he knew this was coming Sean always greeted him the same way every time for the whole three years they had been friends. Sean was the Dad of his best friend while in the army, and was the reason he had chosen this remote place to live and to forget those days, for all Sean's charms and jibes about England he was not fooled by the way they were uttered, deep down David knew, but was not sure, that Sean when younger, had been a member of the notorious IRA in Ireland, but would never voice his suspicions. He liked the 60 year old too much, and loved his wife Mary as you would your own Mum, and that was the way he saw Sean himself, as his Dad and would do anything for the pair, and he did mean anything.

David missed his own Mum and Dad badly, but all those things he did while in the forces meant he could not stay around, so found himself here on the little bit of land out in the Pacific.

They chewed the fat for an hour, Sean asked about the Dog, David explained, David rarely went anywhere on the Island without his Dog they had a few more drinks then David made his excuses and started out for the dock to his beloved sheep.

David and many other Islanders were waiting in anticipation for the ferry to dock, including the Islands Mayor, Peter Steinbach, David could not work out why with just a few hundred people living on the Island, they needed a town Mayor, but then again, there at to be someone in charge, so why not a Mayor.

At last the ferry docked with much hullabaloo, David looked on, waiting for the truck to exit with his sheep. But first off the ferry were two Range Rovers both looking brand new. And three really large trucks, David noted the writing on the side, State Marine Survey Agency conservation environment "That's a mouth full," he said out loud.

"I wonder who they are." Came a voice from behind him, David turned to see Chloe.

"You should know their part of your lot!"

Chloe looked puzzled? "They are not part of my lot, as you put it, I've never heard of State Marine," all of a sudden a livestock truck came rolling down the gangplank

"There she is," cried out David, as he started running down, to meet the truck.

Chloe was still looking at the Range Rovers, and trucks, trying to work out who they were, and what they were doing here on this Island. She and two other marine scientist had a facility on the West Coast, only a small place, where they were studying the sea otters, and how and why their population as gone up so much, "I must remember to mention it to the professor when I get back,"

David was overjoyed to see his flock of real Sheep; (David classed Romney sheep as real sheep) All twenty of them looked in good shape and fit, even after their long journey, he lost no time in loading them into his enclosed trailer and happily started on his journey back to his farm, he called it a farm but all it was, was a smallholding of about fifteen acres, but it was his and he was proud of that.

The Range Rovers stopped at the town Mayor s office, while the trucks continued through the town, two men went into the office presumably to report to the only official person on the Island, they were only in there for a few minutes, then got in their cars and followed the trucks, it seems that our Mayor was the only one that knew who these men and vehicles were.

The two cars caught up with the trucks and led the way through the tricky roads, especially the dangerous coast road, they did not stop until they came to a gate in the north of the Island, the part no one goes to, and no one is allowed to go into, the fence around this part of the Island is now in disrepair but it is still there and is still a sort of barrier.

Back at the Major's office the Mayor was looking pleased with himself whilst putting a large envelope in his safe, "That should do for starters," he thought to himself, not really understanding what he was getting into. And not spotting Mary his secretary looking puzzled. It seems the State Marine were not what they seem?

Chloe had finished her shopping trip, and was making her way back to the Marine facility that at the moment, was home, all three of them worked and slept there, Professor Lomax, Mike Phillips and myself, it was like a home from home, only not as comfortable, all

10

the way back the thoughts kept running through her head "Who are they? And what are they doing here?"

She pulled into the small car park, they did not need a big one as they just the one car the old battered land rover not a shiny new one like she just witnessed. She entered and went directly to Professor Peter Lomax's laboratory, "Good afternoon Chloe, did you get all the things?"

Chloe went up to him and kissed his bald head, "Yes, I even got you some very creamy cakes,"

Peter looked in the bag "I can't eat these they look very fattening," he said with a smile on his face,

"If you don't want them I can always feed them to the fish," Peter looked agarst

"How dare you try to poison our fish, I suppose I'll just have to poison myself with this awful delights," they both burst out laughing,

"You're a terrible man Professor, but I love you,"

Chloe looked serious "Peter did you know that another Marine life study was taking place here on San Juliet?"

Peter turned round "No why do you ask?"

Chloe looked a bit perplexed "While in town this morning I saw a number of vehicles with State Marine Agency on the side, and wondered if you had any knowledge of them coming here,"

Peter looked as confused as Chloe "No I did not know, State Marine? I've never heard of them," he turned back to what he was doing "No doubt they'll be in touch soon, even if it's just a courtesy call." They both put it out of their minds, but in hindsight wish they had checked it up at the time.

Chloe went down to her office that was also her own laboratory, the morning excitement forgotten; she started to deal with all the fish tanks feeding cleaning, and then would start on her thesis on Otters.

Chloe was a very bright and clever girl, also very beautiful with her dark Latin American looks. She had just turned 30 years a milestone for her. She had recently earned an award for her paper on habits of rare Marine life, around the shores of Florida, where she originated from.

Chloe's Father was an exile from Cuba, thrown out when Cuba started a war on drugs and gangs and her Father was involved in both, he ended up in Miami still on the wrong side of the law, still dealing in drugs and any illegal thing that would bring in money that he craved so much, he was gradually working his way up the criminal ladder when he got into a gun battle and died the way he lived.

Chloe did not know too much about his dealing just that they always had plenty of money; Chloe was fifteen when her Dad died, after that her Mum decided to move out of Florida to California, they settled in Santa Barbara, where they changed their names to Barnwell and Chloe changed her name from Maricela Rodriguez Ramirez to Chloe Barnwell. They both wanted to leave their past life behind them.

They had a good life style there, a large house, expensive cars, and she enrolled in one of the best colleges in the State, this is where she got her degree in Marine Biology, but her life was not easy coming from a broken home and being half black, she sometimes had to defend herself quite often against overwhelming odds.

Her Mum was a very beautiful woman when she was younger, that was where Chloe got her unique looks from, her Mum had pure blond hair, and a lovely nature Chloe often thought how on earth she ended up with my Dad.

Chloe's looks were sometimes a burden and sometimes really helpful, but in both circumstances she had to fight her way through everything, being brought up in a gangster environment she had learnt to look after herself, if you did not you were dead. At college she got into numerous fights but always came out on top, to help her on this she started kick boxing, and got pretty good and was asked to enter the ring, but her studies came first.

Once she had graduated she took up lots of different posts all over the world, learnt her trade and became a very young expert on Marine Life, and also become a black belt in a number of martial arts that were to become very useful in the coming weeks.

2
Tuesday

David could not wait to get home and let his sheep out onto the lush green pastures of his plot of land; the Island did get plenty of rain especially in February march, and as it was now coming into the springtime the fields were looking particularly good.

He stopped at his boundary gate jump out opened the flimsy gate, the gate and fence around his property was not like a fence really just white tape, but just enough to keep his flock from wandering off, he closed the gate then drove half a mile to the yard, as he entered a very large dog came bounding over with teeth showing and a look that said "Don't mess with me," it was a look that would send any intruder running for their lives. Since David had had the dog he had never heard him bark or growl? David got out and the dog came up to him so fast that he bowled David over and the licking of his face was just too much, "Down you ugly brute, back off and let me get up!" the dog obediently backed off, and just sat looking at him. The dog was a very large German shepherd named Shep, not a very original name but one that David could relate to as it was his call sign, Shepherd; whilst in the forces and he was always called Shep by his comrades, maybe this was due to his farming background.

David called Shep over and gave him a big cuddle, "It's just you and me buddy, and we're all we need,"

David had obtained the dog when he was on one of his very rare outings to the mainland.

"He was travelling back from Los Angelis, when he stopped at a roadhouse after driving for hours, he was feeling a bit tired, so a pit stop was needed, he stepped into the bar area ordered a drink, and a couple of burgers with chips, and sat at a table facing the door and window, a normal seat for him, always look out for trouble you never know when it will come so always be ready, his drink and food came and he wolfed it down not realising how hungry he was, feeling a whole lot better, he paid the bill, and asked where the toilet were, he made his way to the back door, once outside he heard a commotion, a dog going mad and men jeering it on, he walked up to them very

13

casually putting a glove on his right hand, he could see that the four men had hold of a very horrible scared Bullmastiff dog and was baiting a very thin what looked like an Alsatian dog, but the breed was hard to make out as it was in a terrible state, you could see the dogs ribs sticking out, and it's fur all matted, "Excuse me!" he said in a calm voice, "I don't think you should be doing that,"

The four men turned round utterly astonished that someone had had the nerve to talk to them, the biggest one, a large black man of at least six four "I think you should mind your own business mister" he said in a really threatening voice, David just looked at him, and slowly took off his glasses, David did not really need glasses but they helped him look wimpy,

"That wasn't very nice, did you know that I'm a dog lover, and I strongly object to what you are doing, in the sternest manner,"

The big guy looked at the others "Did you understand what he just said? I think he objects," he started to walk towards David with his fists balled up "I'm going to teach you some manners Limey," he came a little too fast, David dropped down onto one knee and as the big man came in range swinging the hand with the glove on, David caught him just above the his large belly perfectly aiming for the solar plexus, as the big man doubled up David hit him with his elbow on the back of his head, he went down never to get up for a very long time, by this time the second guy had picked up a plank of wood and was aiming at David's head, David ducked and as the wood went flying past and the man was off balance David swept his legs from under him and without any qualms stamped on his knee so hard he heard the bone snap, he turned to the other two with a look that said "Do want to have a go as well," the two guys put their hands up and ran away taking ugly dog with them, David looked at the two prone bodies and just shrugged, "Sorry but I did tell you to stop," and walked back into the bar putting his glasses back on, and taking his glove off, but first going over to see if the poor dog had suffered, he could not believe that someone could let a animal suffer like that.

Once inside he went up to the bartender and asked him, "Is that your dog outside?" the man replied

"Yes, what's it to you,"

David slowly put his glove back on. This man was not going to be very helpful; David put his nice voice on and asked

"I would like to buy it!"

14

The man looked at David his glasses and his baggy clothes and decided he was quite harmless so said in a very unfriendly manner "Piss off! He's not for sale!" David then knew that the men outside were part of his group, "Now if you don't leave right now I'm going to kick your arse," coming from around the bar, he was bigger than David, but seemed a lot slower, David in his pleasant voice repeated the question

"I'll ask you again can I buy him,"

"Maybe there's something wrong with your hearing" he was now standing right in front of David with a look of rage on his face, "Did you not get the message, piss off!"

David turned to leave and said "Then I'll just take him," David heard him coming up behind him, the barkeep did not realise he had been hit until his nose exploded, the hit had come so fast and unexpected, he hit the floor blood spurting everywhere David looked down "Sorry about that but I was trying to be nice," he left ten dollars on the bar went out untied the dog and carried on his journey. Saying out loud, "Eat your heart out Van Damme!" David always remembered his instructor.

GO IN FIRST, GO IN FAST, GO IN LOW, GO IN TO FINISH IT; NEVER HIT WITH YOUR FIST TO THE FACE, THE HAND IS FULL OF SMALL BONES AND COULD EASILY BREAK USE YOUR ELBOWS, FEET, BUT MOST OF ALL GO IN HARD!!"

David said "Come on you big softy we have work to do!" he unloaded the sheep and Shep rounded them up and drove them to join the others, Shep must be the only German Shepherd sheep dog in the land.

3
Tuesday

In the pub Sean was playing darts with two of his cronies, Darren and Scott, they were all about the same age round about 60. They had been friends since Sean had arrived on the Island thirty years ago. Darren was the owner of the only garage on the Island and was also the only mechanic, what he did not know about any kind of machinery you could put on a postcard, "Darren, you should do okay with that lot that came on the ferry today," said Scott,

"What lot?" Scott looked at him

"Those trucks and the Range Rovers that came off the ferry," Darren had no idea what he was talking about, so they explained,

"Well let's hope they need some work done then," replied Darren. Sean threw a double six and won the game

"Let's get another drink." They all walked over to the bar Sean went behind Darren and Scott sat on stools,

"Where did these people go then?" asked Darren,

"We think they went up north to the old restricted area"

Scott piped up "I heard the Mayor talking the other day while in the store, and it looks as if they have taken over the whole of the site up there, he seemed to think it could be good for trade," the others looked doubtful

"The amount of stuff they had in those trucks it could be a long time for them to need something," remarked Sean, the trucks did seem to be well laden.

They carried on chatting about nothing, both Darren and Scott were Vietnam veterans both serving their Country then being forgotten by their Country. But they were both proud men happy to have served, and still loved their Country and would do anything to help it, even to die for it. And as things later turn out they do have to fight for it, and maybe die for it.

The door opened and an old boy walked in, all three of them turned round, and there he was, the oldest person on the Island and was also the most liked, "Well if it isn't the most unwelcome person in the world walking into our pub," called out all of them at the same time, the old man went over to them and slapped each one of them round their face,

"I'm going to tell your wife's you are again being nasty to me," he said with a smile,

"I haven't got one," said Scott "so who are you going to tell," Ned winked at the others

"What about your mother, you know you're the apple in her eye," they all laughed out loud, for Scott was the only child and was always being put down my his Mum who was seventy nine years old, Scott fell silent.

"What brings you to town Ned," asked Sean

"I need some seed from the store so I thought I'd come in here to annoy you lot first," Sean poured him a pint and they all sat around for the next three hours, when Ned finally left.

Ned was the person to go to of you wanted to know anything about the Island, even what went on the Island years ago, for he had never left, not even for a holiday. In fact he had only been on the mainland a few times in all his eighty years. They would need some of his knowledge in the coming weeks.

4
Friday

The Island carried on as normal for the next two days, the excitement and intrigue of Tuesday forgotten, except for the professor at the Marine Centre, he had been online to find out who he was sharing his project with, on this remote Island, where all the wildlife had been documented and monitored for the last three years, but their facility was due to be closed down in about two months time. The first time of trying he had no joy finding the State Marine, he fired up the laptop again, put in the only info he had but once again and this happens very often on this remote place "No signal,," he put the laptop aside, and decided to take a trip up to the site to introduce himself, and to find out what they were doing and what their aims were, "I'll do that tomorrow," he said to himself, it's a bit of a cheek that another Marine outfit comes onto the Island and does not get in touch or even acknowledge they are here, he then went back to his work station and carried on cataloguing the latest population of the local sea lions, the Island had a large sea lion and seal population, plus an abundance of all types of sea birds most of these to be found on the cliffs at the top of the Island where the State Marine is conducting their new survey, whenever he or any of them had to go to this area there was a path that they could use that skirted the fenced off part. So they did not have to enter the restricted part.

The survey and the trucks were still stuck in the professor's mind for the rest of the day, he could not get rid of it, something somewhere was wrong, but he could not, for the life of him, think what it could be. He decided he would find out, and that, could cost him dearly?

5
Friday

Friday morning the Mayor was in his office when a car pulled up outside, he looked out the window to see one of the Range Rovers from the State Marine pull up, two men got out, and looked around in a very furtive manner. One of the men was quite tall, the other, short and fat, with dark features, and a rather large beard, both dressed in smart suits. They entered the building, "We've come to see the Mayor," the tall one said, he was a very abrupt and did not seem very pleasant, Susan the receptionist took an instant dislike to him, and replied in a not over friendly manner

"I'm sorry the Mayor is busy if you would like to make an appointment," she did not get to the end of her sentence as the two men roughly pushed past her and just walked into the Mayor's office, Susan was completely taken aback by this behaviour, as everyone she had ever came in contact with were normally only Islanders, maybe a few from the mainland but none as rude as this. She followed the men in and apologised to the Mayor, for letting them in.

"That's alright Sue, no problem, I'll see these two gentlemen," the fat man pushed her out the door and slammed it behind her, Susan sat down with a look of foreboding on her face

"I wonder what that's all about," she thought to herself, remembering the envelope. Nothing like this has ever happened in San Juliet before, mind you Susan was not the kind of lady you could scare or intimidate. She was definitely her own women and she never backed down on anything, so she would not let this go, she decided to find out what was going on, discretely of course. But it could be her undoing.

The two men were arguing with the Mayor, the tall man was the leader as he did all the talking, "We saw a bunch of kids up near our fence this morning, we had to stop them from trespassing onto the other side of the fence, I want you to dissuade your people from that area, we do not want anyone poking around do you understand," the Mayor sat down with a look of fear on his face for the tall man was very intimidating "Do we understand each other?"

19

The Mayor looked up and stammered "I've told people, that that area, as of Tuesday, is out of bounds to all Islanders and visitors what more can I do?" the short fat one put his face right into the Mayor's,

"If you don't stop people entering our area we will have to stop them ourselves and I promise you it won't be pretty," the tall man pulled him away,

"We don't have to get nasty, do we Mr Mayor, you'll do as we ask, won't you!" the Mayor looked absolutely dejected

"I'll do everything in my power, I'll put a notice's up," the tall man bent down and tapped him on the cheek,

"There's a good chap, I knew we could count on you," As they left the office Susan secretly took a picture of them, on her mobile phone

"You never know," she thought to herself.

Sean was in the hardware store when he saw the two men leave the Mayor's office and head for the hotel, as they passed the store Sean stepped out right in front of them, the small tubby man immediately stood in front of the tall man, and you could see that he was the bodyguard, "Can I help you?" he asked, Sean could see that the man had his fists closed and ready

"Are you from that place up north?" Sean purposely ignored the bodyguard and directed his question to the tall one, the fat one then took hold of Sean's arm and tried to steer him away Sean looked him straight in the eye and snarled "Take your arm away or I'll break in two," the fat one took one look at Sean and removed his hand,

"Can I help you?" said the tall one

"Yes you bloody well can," Sean did not have the finesse of most people; he was an Irishman from a very violent place, and era. The man did not flinch or raise his voice,

"How may I be of assistance," Sean was a bit taken aback, so tried to copy the man and curb his temper,

"My Grandson and a few of his friends were up your way this morning, and were threatened by four of your men, is all they were doing was going fishing in the lake up there, a place where they have been going for years," again the tall man said in a very polite way

"Yes! I'm very sorry about that, my men overstepped the mark, and should not have been so severe with the kids, please accept my utmost apology for any upset they endured, and I will instruct my men to be a lot more tactful," Sean was not satisfied with this reply and by this time had been joined by a few others,

"So what's so bloody secret that you have to scare a bunch of kids away with threats of violence?" the tall man started to walk away

"I'm sorry but I do not have to explain myself to you, if you have any complaints then I suggest you go through the Mayor's office," the two men then carried on to the hotel, Sean was fuming,

"The next time I see that jumped up little prick I'll flatten him and that fat little twerp," Sean went back into the store and reminded himself to ask his Grandson what happened, in a little more detail, and to have a word with David. It was a misconception on Sean's part, to think that the fat man was in fact fat, for underneath the smart tailored suit was a well muscled physique there was not an ounce of fat on him.

The two men entered the hotel, and booked in, and did not reappear until six in the morning, when they met a luxurious yacht down in the harbour. The yacht had birthed overnight, yachts like this were very rare on San Juliet, in fact any yacht was rare. So the night passage and the meeting so early in the morning would not raise too many eyebrows. The two men climbed on board, and were immediately searched for weapons, only then were they escorted to the main lounge, and there, behind the biggest desk the men had ever seen was a very good looking older man who just by his presence gave out a sense of authority "Good morning gentlemen," the voice did not fit the man, it was uttered in a very feminine way, the two men got over their surprise quickly and just replied

"Good morning Sir," this was the first time the tall man had seen his boss, he just knew him as "THE MAN" he waved them to a chair.

"Please take a seat," the two men sat and started to fidget "I hope my presence here is not upsetting you too much, but I decided to conduct this part of the operation personally, I hope you don't mind," the two men said nothing, just behind them they could see two enormous bodyguards both carrying guns that were purposely in sight, "Now down to business," said THE MAN, the two men gave their account at what they had achieved so far, "You have done good, when do the rest of the men and equipment arrive?" the tall man replied

"Today Sir," THE MAN nodded and seemed pleased with the detailed report,

"Gentlemen, I'm pleased with your progress so far, and can confirm that all the other factions of this operation are running as smooth as yours," THE MAN nodded to one of his guards, the guard left the room, and returned with two large suitcases and handed them to the tall man, "Thank you gentlemen I think that's all," and he waved his hand in a dismissible way.

The two men picked up the cases, and turned to walk out knowing that they had been dismissed, then THE MAN called out to them, they turned round, "Gentlemen those suit cases are very precious to me, so guard them with your life, and I do mean Life,"

The two men walked back to their car carrying a suitcase each, and then realised they were being followed by four other men, all four looked mean and frightening, the tall man knew that THE MAN was not taking any chances with the two suitcases, the other Range Rover with two of the tall man's men were waiting for them, the tall man got into one, the fat man into the other, there were now eight men returning to their secret restricted area, and that now made 14 men in total, and not one of them looked like a typical scientist or experts in marine biology.

6
Friday

At the small ferry port, south of Santa Barbara, the vehicles were lined up to board, there we're a number of small delivery vans, a few larger ones, and three more trucks, with State Marine emblazoned on the side.

They had chosen this ferry port, as it was the most relaxed in checking the outgoing and incoming of cars, and vehicles, along this coast, and as this small ferry port only served San Juliet it was not busy and also no customs officers.

"Good morning may I see your boarding tickets please?" the security guard asked, the driver of the first truck held out the tickets.

"Good morning to you, and a nice one it is," the security man inspected the tickets and handed them back,

"We will be boarding in about ten minutes," the man went to the next vehicle in line asked the same question, the driver handed over the tickets, he was foreign looking, properly from the middle east, thought the security guard.

The driver and his mate, rang the other trucks, to tell them that everything was going to plan; in the back of the trucks, were more diggers, earth moving vehicles, and a host of lighting and technical gear, again not the normal equipment you would necessary use for Marine study.

At last they boarded, and were told to park their trucks in the lower decks and proceed to the upper cabins, the main driver was not happy with this so, he designated one man to stay behind to keep an eye on all three trucks, and not to be seen doing it, the ferry put to sea in a nice calm water.

7
Friday

Chloe was on her early morning run, she had already completed four miles, and after skirting David's place, found herself running alongside the restricted area's fence, and could not help but notice that a lot of the fence had been repaired "That's odd," she thought to herself "It must be that Marine lot, not wanting any intruders, and wanting their privacy, but for what, what have they got that's so secret?" she carried on reminding herself to mention it to the professor when she got back, why she was bothering she did not know, as it really was, none of her business, but it still stuck in her craw.

She carried on running, until she saw to some men up ahead, she slowed down, wanting to ask the men what was going on, but then decided once again it was not her business, as she came up to the men, two of them blocked her path, Chloe changed direction to go round them, but as she did so, the men again stepped in the way, "Hello! Pretty lady," said one them in a Spanish accent, Chloe tried to pass once more,

"Good morning," she replied "Do you mind getting out of my way!" the other man, a rather large man with blond hair, said

"Now that's not very friendly is it, my friend was only trying to be nice," the two men were looking at her with a not to friendly look "Why don't you just wait up a minute and join us, we have some food, and a drink, that we would like to share with you," said the blond one, the Spanish looking one, walked around her eyeing her up and down, then said to know one in particular,

"Y puedes chupar mi cuca" Chloe being from a Cuban home knew what was said, but did not let on, the two men laughed, not knowing that this lovely woman in front of them, knew exactly what was said, Chloe was now on her guard, as the look on the faces of her two aggressors, were plain to see,

"I thank you gentlemen, but I have a very strict schedule to keep up, so if you don't mind," she started to push past them, the blond one put his hand out and grabbed Chloe arm,

24

"Now surely you could stay for a few minutes, we are very lonely up here," giving a wicked smile, Chloe gave the man a look that said, let go of my arm, then said looking at her arm,

"I think it would be a very good idea, if you removed your hand," and she said this with a touch of venom in her tone, the blond man smiled, and increased the pressure, then started to steer her over to the fence line. The one who Chloe now thought of as the Mexican, licked his lips in anticipation on what was to come, Chloe gave a resigned shrug, and started towards the fence, the blond man eased his grip on her arm, as he thought Chloe had given up, then in blur of movement, Chloe turned suddenly, the blond man lost his grip, Chloe grabbed the blond man's arm just above the elbow, her other hand grabbing his wrist, and with a quick turn not possible to see, the blond man, all fifteen stone of him, sailed through the air, and landed with a god awful sound on his back, Chloe did not stop turning, and as the Mexican came into sight she sent a full bloodied kick to the groin area, he fell into a heap holding his private parts, with tears in his eyes, still not stopping Chloe faced the third man, and he immediacy put his hands in the air and shouted,

"Whoa! I had nothing to do with this it was their idea," Chloe gave him a look of distain, looked down at the two men and to the Mexican said

"Your cock would not have been big enough," but said this in Spanish, so he would know that she understood what he had muttered earlier, she took one last look, and continued her run, vowing to complain to the Islands Mayor, also to have a word with David as to what just happened, and to what she saw as the other man put his hands up, a gun.

Chloe got back to the Marine facility, (Home) and related her experience to the professor, he was absolutely horrified, and vowed to take it up with the top authorities, when the Wi-Fi was again, up and running, but he knew that could be a long time as it often went off line for days. So he decided to take a trip up to State Marine, to find out what they were doing, and to complain about what happened to his assistant Chloe. He called the other office, and asked his other assistant Michael "Mike could you come up to my office, we have a very pressing engagement to deal with," The Professor needed Mike, as he did not drive himself. When Mike walked in he could see that Peter was visibly upset,

"Whatever is the matter?" he asked, Peter told him what had happened to Chloe, and to his misgivings, with State Marine,

"I would like you to take me up there In the morning, to see whoever is in charge, and to complain on Chloe's behalf, also to find out what their purpose is, on my Island,"

Peter replied, "No problem, I would be happy to give them a bit of my mind as well. Mike was a very fit thirty year old, about the same age as Chloe, and he was no slouch, he kept himself fit, visiting the Island's Seal, and Sea Lion colony, every other day, a six mile round trip, "What time shall we leave?" Peter replied

"We'll leave nice and early, see this Man, and then go into town, and use the stores computer, theirs is a lot more reliable that ours," they both nodded, and returned to their work, Peter looking forward to tackling this Marine Boss.

8
Friday

Meanwhile in the town David turned up at the school house just before 10am for his lesson at 10,30, he looked into the classroom, they only had the single classroom as there were only fifteen pupils registered, ranging from six years to fifteen, once the Islands Children reached sixteen they all went to college on the mainland and only came home once a month it was not easy being a Child nor was it easy being a parent but that was the way of the Island and all accepted it, inside the whole class were taking a maths lesson Danielle looked up and waved , and mouthed "Hi! See you in a minute," David went to their small office it was the size of a broom cupboard, David was taking the next lesson and that was English hopefully the Queens English David was trying to teach the kids to say Tomarto and not Tomato but he knew it was a lost Cause, he heard the Kids running out to the playground and shouted out "Stop running," Danielle came in

"They certainly take notice of you don't they," as the Kids carried on running, David looked up

"Someday I will earn their respect and trust," He didn't know how true that was going to be in the coming week.

The phone rang Danni as she liked to be called picked it up "Hi! Sue," she answered "What can I do for you this fine day?" she listened for a few minutes and then turned to David "I've got to go out for awhile can you cope?" David shrugged

"No! How on earth do you expect me, by myself to look after fifteen rowdy kids," David smiled "Go on I'll be ok,"

Danni walked over to the Mayor's office Susan was waiting at the door "What's the matter?" she asked "It sounded urgent," Susan related what had gone on earlier, "It does sound odd what do you make of it?" Susan looked confused

"That's the problem I don't know, but I do want to find out, I'm going to look into his safe," Danni looked shocked

"You're going to do what!" she cried "You can't do that, you don't have any proof that anything is going on,"

Sue gave her a look and said "That's why you're going to help me,"

Danni started to walk out of the office Susan took her arm "Don't go, we have to do this, something fishy is going on, and we have to find out what, those men were not nice, they were like gangsters, you have to help me," Danni sighed and came back inside

"What do you want me to do?"

Susan took her by the arm "The Mayor never lets me near his safe, but have seen him open it a lot of times, and I've got the combination, what I want you to do, is to keep a lookout," Danni did not look, or sound, convinced that this was a good idea.

"Where is he now?" she asked

"He's gone to the diner for breakfast he'll be back anytime, we must do it now before he removes any incriminating material from the safe," Danni gave her a puzzled look.

"What makes you think there's incriminating things in there?" She asked

"I don't, but that's why we have to look!"

Danni went to the door, and looked down the sidewalk, towards the diner; she called out "Good to go," Susan used her key to enter the Mayor's office and knelt in front of the safe and turned the dial hoping that he had not changed the code, the safe came open, she rummaged around trying not to disturb anything, so as not to alarm the Mayor, at the back she noticed a large envelope, she took it out and opened it, she could not believe her eyes "There must be thousands here," she thought to herself, Just then a loud shout came from outside "He's on his way back!" she put the envelope back where it was, shut the safe twirled the dial, and made a quick exit back to her desk, she managed to tell Danni what she had found; Danni went back to the school, ready to tell David what she and Sue had discovered.

9
Friday

Scott walked into the Diner with the fish he had caught that morning, "There you are," he cried "Fresh this morning," as he plonked the bag on the counter. The owner Julie, looked inside, went to the till, took some notes out, and gave them to Scott,

"Sit down and I'll make you some breakfast," she said. Mind you it was a bit late for breakfast, so Scott declined her offer, and shot off to the pub instead, he wanted to tell the boys what he had seen this morning, while on the pier, not knowing what had gone on in the town yesterday, again to do with the new people.

Julie thought "Funny Scott would not normally turn down a free breakfast," it must be something important for him to miss a free meal.

Julie was Sean's Daughter-In-Law.

Julie brought the diner when a secret benefactor, left her a lot of money, but the secret was not a very good one, she worked it out that David had given her the money. Where he had got all that money, she did not want to know, but to this day he does not know that she knows. That he was hers and her Dad's benefactor, for her Mum and Dad also came into a lot of money. One day she will ask but not now.

The pub had only just opened it was mid day Scott was one of the first in there "Well! Well!" called out Sean "Look who's first in here today," Scott walked up to the bar, Mary Sean's wife, said,

"Don't take any notice of him, the grumpy old sod, he's pleased to see you really," Sean put his hands in the air

"It's a pleasure to see you Sir," he said with a smile, all three of them laughed

"I'll have a pint landlord, and one of Mary's famous meat pies," Mary's meat pies were the talk of San Juliet I would say at one time or another every Islander had tasted one by now, Mary went into the kitchen, Sean pulled the pint,

"Where were you yesterday then?" he asked

"Busy busy," he replied, "But I do have something very interesting to tell you about that Marine lot," Sean knew that Scott had not heard about yesterday, so was quite intrigued to find out what he had to say.

Just then Darren walked in. They all had a drink, and their pie's, and finally got down to business, Sean told the two boys about yesterday's run in with that lot, "So what's your story?" turning to Scott, Scott started to tell them that while fishing early that morning what had gone on with the two men and the flashy yacht,

"Now that does sound a bit iffy," remarked Darren "First you, now Scott, there's defiantly something not kosher here,"

"Well done Einstein we knew we could rely on you," said Sean.

Darren asked, "So what are we going to do about it?"

"I know just the man," Sean replied, the boys looked at him

"Who's that then?" They asked together;

Sean lowered his voice a touch, and whispered "David" Darren and Scott looked at each other,

"What the school teacher?" they shouted together,

"Why don't you shout it so everyone can hear, yes the school teacher but he's not just a school teacher I'll tell you more after I speak to him," the boy's were not convinced as David looked to all the world, a rather dull, and wimpy, School teacher:

Back at the school, David was just finishing up his lesson when Danielle came back looking all flushed, "What happened to you?" he asked, Danielle told him all that had gone on the mayor's office "How much did Sue say was in the envelope?"

"She thought it was thousands of dollars," David scratched his head,

"Why would a so called reputable company, pay someone all that money?" Danni piped in

"We don't know if they are a reputable company?" answered Danielle.

David thought back to the day at the ferry when Chloe said, "She had never heard of them?"

All the school kids were going into the playground for their lunch break, Danielle was on play ground duty, so David decided to get another opinion, and the only one he trusted or could confide in, was Sean, the pub landlord, the only person on the island who knew David's secret past.

David told Danni where he was going, and headed off down to the pub. It would not be a normal visit to the bar, as he had more lessons to do so could not have a drink.

David entered the bar, and immediately, was accosted by three men, and escorted to the far corner, "I know you boys like me but this is just too much,"

Mary, Sean's wife, came into the bar carrying a full tray of food "Before you lot get down to changing the world, you had better get this inside you," she plonked three large portions of her latest Beef and Ale Pie in front of them "Once you've eaten that, then you can change things for the better!" The boys tucked in, eating it as fast as they could. They wanted to get to why they were there.

Once the food had disappeared, they got down to business, Sean went first, then Scott relayed what had happened down at the pier, then David told them about the Mayor.

"What do think it all means?" asked Darren, he was the only one who had not had any contact with this new bunch,

"I don't know," replied David "But I intend to find out," the way David spoke these words, bemused Darren and Scott, as this was the wimpy looking school teacher, so Scott said

"I'm not being rude but you're a school teacher, what can you do?"

Just then, the door burst open, and Chloe walked in looking for David, she came straight over to the table "David?" David stood up

"Whatever is the matter?" he asked, he could see that she was in a agitated state, Sean got up and got her a stiff drink

"Sit down and tell us what's bothering you," Chloe looked at the four of them, she had only wanted to have a word with David, David could see that she did not want to relate her dilemma to all of them, so he put his arm on her shoulder, and led her to another table, once she had told him what had happened that morning. He suggested that they went back to the boys table, and tell them, what happened, as things had progressed.

None of them could believe it, all of them except Darren had somehow had something to do with the Marine lot, David was livid after Chloe had told him of her encounter at the site, and wanted to go up there right away to have it out with the Tall Man. They were calling him the Tall Man as they did not know his name; likewise they called the other one the Fat Man for the same reason. But Sean the wise one said "Hold your horses we cannot go up there shouting the odds until we find out a little more about their operation," they all agreed, and sat down to plan their form of attack.

10
Friday

After his meeting the Tall Man travelled back to the site, he was not pleased how this trip to the port had gone, firstly the Mayor's office where he had had to threaten him, then the unruly fracas outside the store with an irate parent, "He will have to tell his men to be a bit friendlier," Then the meeting itself, with THE MAN who he thought was not really a man, especially by his voice , but knowing he was a very deadly man, having had dealings with him before, but this time, was the first time, he had actually spoken directly, to him.

The way back was uneventful. They came up to the gate house, a new addition to the fence, guards were manning it. The Tall Man knew they were armed, but no weapons were on show, they drove straight to the supposedly derelict buildings, and inside the largest one, from there, the floor of the building suddenly started to drop, the floor was a lift, the lift went down fifty feet, when they came to a large cavern of a place, with bright overhead lighting, and all about them, other vehicles ,including their other trucks, the Tall Man got out, and started to go to his office, when his number three, a very thin, but hairy man, came up to him with the three men from the fence incident, the blond man had his arm in a sling, the thin man explained what had happened, The Tall Man went berserk "You contravened my specific orders no contact with the Islanders and now this," you could see he was losing control, the Mexican who was the instigator of the attack tried to apologize

"I'm sorry Sir it will not happen again," the Tall Man snatched a gun off one of the men, and then calmly shot him in the head,

"I know you won't," turning, he shouted to all the other men in earshot "Do not talk to any of the Islanders, we must keep them onside for the time being, but there may come a time when cannot do so, when that time comes, it will come as a surprise to them: so there should not be any trouble unless someone on the Island makes it,"

11
Friday

The Tall Man, who did not use his real name, was called No1, and he had been planning this for a very long time. One year in fact. He is the main supplier of drugs for the whole of the west coast; his tentacles also extend to the other side of the Continent, his power in immense, but still he has to bow to that excuse of a man. THE MAN.

All over America, the authorities have been waging a war on all illegal drugs coming in, the avenues of transport were getting fewer and fewer, and that was putting the price of all their merchandise, out of reach of a lot of their customers, so all dealers were trying to find different ways to get the stuff into the Country.. The Mexican border was the easiest way to get drugs in. But that was now practically a no go area. The security and patrols had made this entry, a non starter, so all parties were trying to find other ways to get the stuff in. Then just by chance, he stumbled onto what he thought, was a fool proof plan, one that all the Agencies were oblivions of.

This came about, when he visited his dad in a hospice, his Dad now ninety two years old was not expected to last too long, and an old man in the next room to his, was also, not for this world for very long. One day, the old man told a story about a secret air base on a remote island off the California coast, where there was an airstrip and underground buildings that could not be seen from the air, and after all this time still no one knew they existed, No1's Dad had also been in the drug business, and related the tale to him, and also told him that the old man had plans and papers detailing the site and what was going on at the time, the old man had signed the official secrets act and was warned not to divulge any information about the airbase, or anything else that was going on at the base, due to the secret nature and the volatile materiel they were using, and was told, he would be charged with treason against the United States, if any such information got out, due to his indiscretions, or loose talk. The old man, did not really know the inns and outs of the real secret stuff, that was going on in the laboratories on the site, he was one of the planners and designers of the base, and dealt with the day to day running, although his role was crucial, it was not considered so important as the things going on, with all the scientists, and weapons, in the restricted areas of the base, he could not relate any of these things, but the construction, and the plans, were vital to No1, in the coming months.

The old man died quite suddenly, but he had told No1's Dad a bit more about the base. In all those years, the old man had not told a soul, not even his own family, but while on his death bed, and not of sound mind, he was happy to finally find someone he could confide in, he did not fully realise that this information was going to be used, as the person he was telling the story to was older than him, and most of the time he was out of it.

No1's Dad was in the hospice, but his mind was as sharp as ever, and he could see the possibilities that this information could have on the business, his Son was involved in, in fact, it was his idea that had started the whole operation getting under way.

After the old man died, No1 found out where he had lived, and later found a pile of papers, relating to the airbase tucked away in the attic, if the authorities had known about these papers the old man would have spent a long time in prison.

It took five months to organise a plan, and a further five months to implement it, but now it was coming together, and so far so good, but it had come at a cost, not only the financial side of it but the fact he had to include and collaborate with THE MAN, who he hated and told himself "At a later date, when this operation is over, I'll get rid of permanently,"

No1 continued to his office, as if nothing had happened, he knew by countless other operations, that you had to keep control over the men working for you, and most of the time that came from fear, fear of the consequences if you failed, or if you did not do as you were told, and if told, do not make the same mistake as the Mexican, what happened to him helps to keep the rest of the men in line, No1 was not a man to get on the wrong side of, especially as this particular operation was so delicate and important that if anything went wrong, his life and all his men could be at risk, as a lot of bad people were involved in this the largest of its kind ever to be tried.

On his way back to his what he called the office , he passed the trucks that were now empty, having been unloaded, and the building

35

plant vehicles that were in them, were now working nonstop above ground getting the runway usable and the perimeter fence secure, the area below was the size of a football pitch, with various passages going off in different directions, they had discovered the laboratories, and they had been destroyed completely, No1 often asked himself "Whatever had gone on in there?" but had no use for this part of the place, he was only interested in the airstrip and making sure none of the Islanders got wind of anything that was going on up here, and that was why he had to make that example of the Mexican, he did not want, and could not have, any confrontation with any Islander, and he would have a stern word with the men who came down hard on the kids yesterday, and make sure that if any contact was made, be polite, and do not antagonise anyone.

He was unhappy with himself, as to what had happened in town yesterday, it was unfortunate that he had had, that incident outside the store, with the pub owner, but he had kept his cool and apologised, so he hoped that the man would not dig into it any further.

The complex, besides the large area, where the trucks were parked, was home to a large force back in 1943, but now with just a few men most of it was not being used, just the living quarters, a galley, and the heart of the place, the generator room. One of the first things they had had to do, is to get the old generator working, so there had to be on the their team, an electrical engineer, his name was Stuart Collins, a twenty two year old, the youngest on the team, Stuart was fresh out of college and had come top in his class, and it seemed that he was a whizz, with any type of generator, No1 had searched him out as a possible member, when he found out, that his one bad habit even at his young age, was gambling, and was badly in debt, to one of the people No1 dealt with, he seemed like the perfect fit, to add to his team, and as it had turned, out all the hype about his knowledge on generators was proven correct, he had got this old world war two generator working, and working up to now, perfectly. Stuart was not told what this was all about, and why on this remote Island, is all he knew was that this was some highly secret thing, but he had no idea, what was being secretly flown in, but this was to be a big pay day for him, two weeks work, and one million dollars in the bank, plus his dept had already been cleared, at the moment his one job was to keep the generator working, so he did not leave the generator room to often, and did not communicate with the rest of the men, who to his mind, were nothing more that hired thugs.

He did not see the shooting of the Mexican, but was deeply concerned with the brutality of it all, he also knew that this thing was highly illegal, and was the start of something big, but for now he put it out of his mind, knowing that he was now involved, and was committed to the end, he did not want to end up like the Mexican, but his conscious could get the better of him.

12
Friday

Back at the bar, they all said their goodbyes, and promised to carry on the planning of what to do tomorrow.

David, and Danielle, went back to the school, Darren back to the garage, and Scott goodness knows, no one ever knew what he did with himself, except do a bit of fishing in the mornings from then on?

Sean and Mary shut the pub, and made their way down to the port, they were meeting the ferry. They had a very important delivery to collect.

The ferry was a little late in docking due to the extra cargo, mainly the Marine trucks, the trucks started to disembark first having been loaded first, Sean could not believe what he was seeing, one, two, three, extra large trucks with the State Marine logo emblazed on the side, "How many more do they need?" he thought to himself, there were various other vehicles all of them known by Sean, except for a small car carrying one passenger, Sean looked at the man as he passed by but did not take any real notice, only that he seemed to be foreign.

Sean saw the vehicle he was waiting for, and he and Mary, went to meet the large van, "Hello Pete!" he greeted the driver "Just drive straight up to the pub and we'll unload right away," Sean could not wait for the first view of his new toy, they both made their way back, and with a bit of help from other friends, they unloaded, put it all together, and then Sean and Mary stood back, and with pride, looked at their brand spanking new snooker table, "She is absolutely fabulous!" Mary nodded

"I just hope the punters appreciate it, they like their pool table more," Sean picked up a cue and took a couple shots,

"Now that's magic, I'm going to spend most of my remaining days, playing like Ronny O'Sullivan," Mary rolled her eyes and headed for her domain, the kitchen.

13
Friday

The three trucks made their way out of the town, heading towards the restricted area, they took it nice and slow along the coast road, as it was a notorious accident spot, as these trucks were a lot larger, than the previous ones, the drivers took extra care. At last they came to the gate. The gate, and the surrounding fence, was now quite a formidable barrier around this restricted area. The guards checked the trucks, and the men, and when they were satisfied, let them pass. Once again they drove into the largest building, and were transported to the underground cavern. You could liken this place to an aircraft carrier, just a few upper buildings, but all the important stuff was hidden below. They did not waste any time in unloading the three trucks, this was all overseen by No3. The earth moving equipment, was loaded onto the lift, and taken outside, to start the work of clearing the overgrown runway, one of the other trucks had a large quantity of explosives that were going to be needed again, to help with the runway and was to be put to good effect on another part of the area.

No1 came down from his office looked around and nodded with satisfaction "Good," he said to himself "Everything is now in place, nothing can stop us,"

14
Saturday

At the marine facility, Chloe was already on her way to her little bit of coastline, where the sea Otters lived and played, it was an exciting time for her, as this was the breeding season, and she had her favourite pair she adored, who were now, like her pets.

As she came down to the shoreline, she was a bit upset that her two Otters, were not to be seen, in fact, there were none on this little bit of the Island at all "What's happened?" she asked herself, Just then she heard an almighty sound, the ground under her shook, "What the hell was that?" she looked in the direction of the blast, and surmised, that it had come from the north of the Island the restricted part "What on earth are they doing up there?" she again looked for her Otters. And now realised why they had abandoned this part of the Island, the explosions had frightened them away, she hurried back to consult the professor, and then to go and fire up her laptop to find out a bit more about these people.

Chloe got back, and went straight to the professors office, he was not there, she went down to see if he was with Mike, he was not there, "Where on earth could they have got to?" she asked herself, she went out to the car park, and discovered that their car was not around, "They must have gone into town," She made her way to her office, and sat down in front of her laptop.

Meanwhile, the Professor and Mike were making their way to the Marine site, Peter, was still fuming about the way they had come onto his Island, and it seems, trying to undermine his work, plus the treatment Chloe had received in the hands of those men, could not go unpunished, he would insist on seeing the top man.

They drove along at a very sedate pace, as Mike was not a very competent driver, only passing his test one year ago, he never really had any use for a car, as his work took him all over the world, so a car would have been an extravagant expense, plus the fact he did not enjoy it. At last they came to the gate leading into the site, two burly guards came up to the car "Can I help you?" asked one of the guards,

"Yes!" said the Professor, "I want to see the man in charge of this facility," The guard gave a sniff and said,

"I'm sorry gentlemen, we do not allow visitors," and turned his back on the car,

"Excuse me!" shouted the Professor "I did not asked if I could see the man in charge, I said, I want to see the man in charge, so if you wouldn't mind getting him for us, it would be appreciated," At this point the Professor was trying to be polite, the guard came back over and leaned into the car and said,

"I think it would be in your interest, to turn this car around, and to return to where you came from,"

The Professor was not the type of man easily intimidated "We are not moving until we see the man in charge," he turned to Mike "Mike turn the engine off!" Mike turned the engine off, and they both sat there with their arms crossed, the Professor could be a very stubborn person, when he wanted to be.

The larger of the guards went to put his hand into the car to drag the Professor out, "You either move this car yourself, or I'll move you, and the car myself," he snarled, the other guard came round to Mike's side, and placed his face in Mike's face, you heard him, move! And move now!" Mike looked at the Professor,

"I think it might be prudent to leave," he pleaded, just then the Fat Man, who was called No2, came over,

"Is everything okay here?" he asked, the Professor looked him in the eye and asked,

"Are you the man in charge here?" the Fat Man put his hands up in the air,

"Alas no, but I can answer any questions you gentlemen have," the Professor started to get out of the car, one of the guards kicked the door shut,

"Please stay in the car Sir!" the Professor noted that when the guard kicked the door his jacket moved, and he was sure that he saw a gun, the guard was armed.

After venting his anger at the Fat Man's men, of the treatment of his assistant, and the insulting behaviour of them not letting him know of the intrusion of his Island. As his, was the only visa issued on the Island, to allow the study of Marine Life.

"I'm sorry, but we cannot divulge any information, about our presence here on this Island, and as for the matter of your assistant, the person involved in that unfortunate episode, has been dealt with," the man started to walk away,

"I'm going to find out what you are doing," the Professor called out to him, the Fat man walked back, and with a sigh

"Sir, the only thing I can tell you, is that it involves the Monterey Canyon, there has been questions about a possible fault, that could have a significant impact on Marine Life in this area," he again walked away the Professor called after him,

"Did you say the Monterey Canyon and if you did you are looking in the wrong place, as that particular Canyon is three hundred miles to the north," the man disappeared through the gate.

"Did you hear that," he said to Mike, "Now I know there's something fishy here, let's go straight to town and find some answers," Mike started the car, turned it around, and started towards the town.

At the site, No2 realised he had made a fateful error, he made a phone call.

They both remained silent on the way to town, both with their own thoughts, the drive was peaceful as there was not a lot of traffic on the Islands roads, they did not meet any other vehicles, Mike looked into his rear mirror and saw a large truck bearing down on them "The truck behind is going a bit fast!" he said to Peter, Peter looked round,

"Just slow down a bit, and let it pass, you know how dangerous this part of the highway is," They were on the coast road with a two hundred foot drop. Mike slowed down, and the large truck came alongside them, The Professor noted that the driver was one of the guards from the site. Mike concentrated on the road ahead, holding the wheel until his knuckles turned white, the truck kept pace with them, still alongside, when all of a sudden Mike heard, and felt an almighty bang on the side of the car

"What the hell!" he exclaimed, then, another bang, the truck had crashed into them again. Then the Professor heard a shot, glanced over to Mike and saw blood coming from his head, he realised that his friend Mike had been shot, looking back in front of him, the only thing he could see, was the sea crashing against the rocks below.

Back at the site, No1 was venting his anger on his number two, "You did what?" He screamed, No2 could not believe how mad his Boss sounded,

"I'm sorry, but there was no other outcome that would have fixed it, he knew we were not who we were trying to be, and would have blown the whole thing wide open," No1 calmed down,

"You made sure it looked like an accident?"

"Yes Sir, just a terrible accident!"

"If there's any comeback due to this, the Mexican may have company,"

15
Saturday

Chloe found out that Marine Life were in fact a boni fide company, and were part of the San Francisco State University, but she could still not work out what they were doing on this Island. Also she discovered that it was quite a small Company dealing with sea earth tremors, so how they come to quite so many trucks and bodies on this little Island really baffled her, "I think I'll go into town and try to find out a little more about what our friends up there are up to," she said to herself.

Chloe went outside, and made her way to the little outhouse near the car park, went inside and pulled the cover off her Piaggio Metro Scooter she called her Tinkerbell, as she was highly painted in fairies and flowers, to make her more girlie, although she herself was not a girlie person, but it made her feel good when she rode it, and it looks good. She adjusted her helmet and straddled the seat, pushed the starter, and lo and behold Tinkerbell started up straight away, it had been quite some time since she had been on the bike, but as soon as she got on the road she felt at home, then off she whizzed.

The journey to town was not a very long; in fact it did not matter where you went on the Island, as it's so small, that any journey would not take long.

The way to town took her along the coast road, a very dangerous road, as on one side there was a two hundred foot drop down to the rocks below, so extra care was always taken by any of the Islanders, on this particular stretch, she was riding pass a particularly black spot when she noticed part of the roads safety barrier between the road and the cliff was broken, "I wonder if there's been an accident?" she asked herself, Chloe pulled over to investigate, as she approached the barrier she noticed new tyre marks going from the road to the cliff edge, she tried to look over but edge butt is was a bit too unstable, she could just make out the rocks below and the waves crashing against them, she again looked at the barrier and the tyre marks, "It does look as if something as gone over here," she said to herself, "And it looks as if it happened this morning!"

She returned to her bike and carried on into town, "I'll go to the Mayor's office as soon as I get there just in case. Once I've look for the Professor and Mike, they must be in the town somewhere,"

She got to the main street, and started to look for their old battered Land rover, not finding it anywhere, she made her way to the store, the diner, and the pub, after the fruitless search and not one person had seen the Professor or Mike, she started to think about the broken barrier on the coast road. All of a sudden bad thoughts came into her mind, and she started to run down the road towards the Mayor's office she rushed in "Sue!" she shouted "I think there's been an accident on the coast road and I think it could be Professor Lomax and Mike,"

Susan did no more than rush to an alarm button and push it!, outside a siren started wailing, they had a small emergency unit in the town, that was manned by volunteers, Sean was the first on the scene, followed by two of the fishermen, and then Darren driving a small fire truck, Chloe related what she had seen. They all jumped onto the truck, and roared off, by this time the whole community was out on the street all asking the same question "What's happened?"

They arrived at the spot where the barrier was broken, Darren pulled down the ladder, and pushed it towards the cliff edge, positioned it so it overlapped the edge, and then anchored it down, he put on a safety harness, and gingerly edged out over the cliff, he edged his way back with a worried look, going over to Chloe he said "I'm sorry Chloe but it does look as if it is your car down there, but I couldn't get a clear look, but from the vantage point it did have, it did look like your Land Rover," Chloe's legs gave way, Sean just managed to grab her,

"We must go down there!" she cried "They may still be alive," Darren and the others rigged up a line, and as Darren, not the youngest of them, but who was the fittest, and the most experienced, decided that it was his job to abseil down.

Meanwhile, Chloe had got back her composure and volunteered to go down herself, Sean and Darren knew that she was possible the best one to do it, they both knew about her abilities, but they decided that she was too involved to do the job without getting to emotional.

They checked all the lines and when they were satisfied, Darren went down, Chloe got into the second harness just in case Darren got into any difficulties. The descent went without a hitch, but the sea was so choppy Darren had difficulty seeing but he did make out the logo on the side of the car, and yes it was the professors car, he couldn't get any closer, so could not see inside the vehicle, he signalled he was coming back up. Once on top he related what he had discovered, and they all agreed that the rescue would have to come via the sea, or wait until a proper rescue crew could be flown out from the mainland. The fishermen said they would put to sea as soon as the sea abated, they all started to dismantle the ropes when David pulled up, he was on his way to town, he jumped off his buggy the dog following him, he came over "What's happened?" he asked, Sean filled him in, "Leave that there," he said pointing to the ropes, He started to put on the harness "I'll me go down, I've properly got a lot more experience than you," looking at Darren "I may be able to find out a little more?" they all looked at David with his baggy clothes and his glasses, he did not look the type to throw himself over a cliff, after he convinced them he had the experience they relented and asked him to give it a go.

David let himself down very slowly until out of sight of the others, then just let go and shot down to the wreck, he did not want the others to find out to much about him as yet. The sea did seem a bit rough, but David had been in much more dangerous places than this, the car was utterly smashed up, but he did manage to get right down on top of it, and managed to see into the interior, he found Mike sitting in the driver's seat, he was dead, he looked around for the Professor but could not see him, he went back to Mike and inspected him in a little more detail.

He indicated that he was coming up, once out of the harness he explained what he had found out, there was no sign of the Professor and unfortunately Mike was dead.

By this time Chloe was beside herself, crying uncontrollably, Sean put his large arms around her "Come on let's go back to town, and get in touch with the authorities to get someone out here," Sean was the original gentle giant. They all got back on the fire truck and headed back; David said he would stay so as to have a good look round to see if he could work out what had happened.

Shep was prowling about and started barking, David went over to where he was sniffing the ground, David bent down and picked up a shell case, he sniffed it and satisfied himself that this shell was the remains of the bullet that was imbedded in Mike's head, after more scouting around they found bits of a car mirror and fragments of paint, David was sure that the Professor's car went over the cliff after Mike was shot, but not before it was rammed, and by looks of the tyre marks it seemed to be rammed by a large vehicle something like a truck. He sat on the side of the road trying to visualise the sequence of events, once he had it worked out in his computer like mind, it all came together, and it had to be the Marine lot.

"Come on Shep lets go," he called out; they climbed onto the buggy and continued their drive to town, David not too sure how to go about telling what he had discovered.

On the outskirts of the town David saw young Joe O'Riley, Sean's Grandson and David's best friend Sean Junior's Son; he was flying the drone that David had brought him?

When they got back to town with the fire truck, Sean went to see the Mayor as he was the only person who had the authority to call for help, Sean was a bit apprehensive about talking to him, as the past few days it has been clear that he was somehow involved with the Marine crowd, but this was a different matter entirely,

After relating all the details, Sean left and the Mayor said he would get in touch with the emergency services immediately, and we should get help quickly. The Mayor watched Sean go down the road towards the pub, then turned round and picked up the private phone he had been given by the Tall man, after a short conversation he put the phone down the Tall man saying he will sort it out.

16
Saturday

Sean arrived back at the pub, all of them were there Darren, the two fishermen, Scott, and Chloe who was sitting by herself her eyes red from her constant crying. The Professor and Mike had been her family for the last year it had been a terrible loss for her, Mary, Sean's wife was comforting her

Sean sat down and related what the Mayor had said about the emergency services, Mary went out into the kitchen, to come back with large portions of her famous pies, they all tucked in, except Chloe, she could not find the appetite for food the mornings event would stay with her for a long time.

David walked into the pub "How'd it go," asked Darren "Did you find anything out?"

All the way back David tried to make up his mind on what to tell them, he did not want to disclose the shooting at this moment, so he just said "Not really it just seems that Mike lost control somehow," Sean poured them all a beer, and they carried on for a while, then the two Fishermen left saying that they will put to sea in the morning.

Chloe could not stop crying "Why them?" she cried out "They were the nicest guys you could ever meet!" David went over and put his arms around her

"We will get to the bottom of this, I promise," David felt bad having to lie, but until they find out a lot more, it had to stay this way.

Mary came over "You can stay here tonight Dear, I'll make a bed up," Mary and Chloe went upstairs Chloe still sobbing. Darren took the fire truck back to the garage, and Scott went to where ever Scott went? Now they were alone Sean turned to David "What did you find?" Sean had read David's mind and knew he was holding something back, David checked that they were alone

"Mike was shot," Sean jumped up off his chair

"Shot, are you sure?" David waited until he sat down again

"Yes I'm sure, when I found him I could see the bullet hole in his temple he was shot whilst driving, then their car was forced over the cliff edge by a large vehicle, something like a truck," David had seen his fair share of violence back in the day, but to encounter this sort of an idyllic Island like this, it just did not make sense,

"So you think it was that Marine lot that did it then," David shrugged

"It does point to them yes, as they are the only ones who have, large trucks, but as we don't really know as yet; keep it to yourself for now, until we find out more."

Sean went to the bar to pour another beer each, David looked up at the wall behind the bar, to the picture of Sean Junior in his UNITED STATES MARINE CORP uniform, and just under that a box that took pride and place The Medal Of Honor, the United States highest award given to those who perform personal acts of valor above and beyond the call of duty "To be sure he was a fine lad," said Sean with tears in his eyes

"Yes he was and the bravest man I ever met, plus my best friend,"

David stood up "We'll meet tomorrow at eleven to decide what to tell the others and to work out some sort of plan," he said good-bye and left.

David did not have one of Mary's pies, so he decided to go to the diner to eat. Outside he called to the dog "Come on Shep food time!" the dog who was still sitting patiently on the buggy for his master to come out, jumped off and followed David down the road.

They walked into the diner and straight away were greeted by Julie, Sean Senior's daughter in Law and Sean Junior's Wife, Julie planted a kiss on David's cheek, "David Cross how long does it take you to pop into this fine diner, it's been at least a week since we have seen you!" David was just about to make an excuse when Joe her Son came running up, but Joe ignored David and immediately sunk to the floor to cuddle the dog

"Hello Shep where have you been?" Shep started to lick Joe's face, Julie shoed them away

"Take that horrible mutt outside, can't he read that sign NO DOGS ALLOWED" pointing to the sign, Joe got up and ran outside

"Come on Shep let's go and play,"

David looked at Julie, and what he saw was a very vibrant and beautiful woman who could have any man in the world, but her love for her husband Sean Junior, was real, she had never accepted his death, although it had now been three years, but hopefully someone somewhere will help her forget, but she still had it in the back of her mind that someday Sean would reappear somehow.

David wolfed down a bacon roll with a nice cup of tea "I'm sure I must be, the only person on the Island that drinks tea! That should keep me going for a couple of hours" he said. David started to leave when Joe and Shep came running up,

"David, can Shep stay here for the night?" David looked at the dog then at Joe and could see the pathetic look on both of them Joe having his arms around Shep,

"OK but don't feed him to much of your Mums food," David felt a bang on his shoulder

"And what's wrong with my food?" David turned round and veined an apology,

"I'm off," he shouted as he left in a hurry, "I'll see you three to-morrow" with a cheery wave, David shot off on his buggy, weaving from side to side Julie threw a kiss after him,

"Come on Shep let's get you some of Mums food,"

17
Saturday

After leaving Shep with Joe David, started for home, the day had been one of the most eventful days since leaving the Army.

David tied to put the killing out of his mind for now, but at the back it was a constant niggle that this was only the start of something big. David had been around killing for a very long time having joined the army when only 16 years old, and had killed his first at only 18, but this was different, those were when he was trained to do those sort of things, what if this all goes really bad and I have to resort to killing once again.

David mused over his days of fighting terrorists on the war of terror all over the world, and the days with Sean Junior at his side on most of the escapades they had been involved in, Sean Senior should, and was, very proud of his son, and of David his best friend and comrade, David and Sean had been in many dangerous scrapes between them but luckily and with plenty of skill came out on top until that fateful day in Afghanistan.

David had been lost for a long time, after Sean's death, as on all the missions they had been on together, Sean was always saying that it was him looking after the old man, but David always said his job was looking after the youngster; it was a standing joke between them, as there was only, three years between them.

David was coming along the coast road once again, so started to concentrate on the actual road. Coming up to the site of accident, he saw a Range Rover parked near the edge of the cliff, and standing around were three men, David pulled over intending to find out what they were doing, he felt it was a bit suspicions they would be at the precise spot of the accident, so he decided not to take any chances, he removed his glasses and put his glove on, and started to walk towards the men. The three men didn't look very friendly, and like professionals they took up positions surrounding him. One of the men was wearing a harness so David surmised he had been down the cliff face, they all looked like ex forces, "Can we help you?" Asked the man in the harness, David immediately took this one to be the leader,

"Yes I would like to know what you are doing tampering with an accident scene."

"We heard about the accident, and came to help, we all have experience on mountain rescue," he answered

"How did you hear about it, it was only an hour ago that we knew there had been an accident!" David now knew that this was not a team helping but a team trying to cover up a shooting, the Leader looked around but did not see any other person about, so decided he would have to do something about this little wimpy man, in his baggy clothes, he did not want him blabbing what he had seen here, David started to push past "I'll just have to see for myself what you have been up to," he said pushing the man to one side,

"I don't think I can let you do that," he replied in a very menacing voice," David took one step back and gave each man a stare that said,

"Do not mess with me," David dropped his right shoulder, and launched a vicious kick to the Leaders right leg just below the knee joint, the man went down his leg unable to support his weight, David did not see him crash to the floor as he was already turning to land a punishing elbow to the side of the next man's head, the side of the head is the best place to hit as the brain is more susceptible to a blow sideways, it causes the brain to bounce side to side so doing more damage, and to lose control, just then a forth man came up from the cliff edge and came running over, David then knew that this was not going to end pretty, three men he could handle but four? David landed a crippling blow to another one with his gloved hand before he felt his arms being pinned behind his back the forth man who had now joined in the fight hit him in the gut David nearly gagged, he could not believe that all four men were now on their feet, seeing as some of the blows David had landed would have put a normal person down for a very long time, David had been in this situation many times before, he leant back bringing his feet up in the air ,and with a twist of his body his arms were free, he ducked a right hand from the man in front of him, and brought his gloved hand up and caught the other man square on the chin, once again he was amazed that the man stayed on his feet, David felt an agonising blow to the back of his head, and nearly went down, his instructor always said to him "Stay on your feet," all four of the men were now landing punches, once again his arms were pinned back and now David did not have the strength to release himself, the Leader was setting himself up for the killer blow. David could see it coming but could not do a thing about it. Just then voice came from behind them,

"Excuse me, would you mind if I join in?" the Leader forgot David and turned to find a dark skinned man confronting him, that's all he saw, for the man hit him three times, before he had time to register that this man could be threat, he went down and this time stayed down, without breaking his stride the dark skinned man dealt with the next one with a deadly chopping motion, and he went down to join his comrade, while this was going on David had had freed himself, and in two seconds had taken down the other two, all four attackers were now laid out, David held out his hand to his saviour smiling

"Thanks for your help friend, but I did have it under control!" the dark skinned man smiled back,

"I could see that, but I needed some exercise, I hope you didn't mind?"

David offered his hand "David Cross," the dark skinned man took the hand,

"Abdul Abdullah at your service," David turned to look at the four prone men,

"Well we both got some exercise, but what do we do with this lot?" after a while they loaded them into their Range Rover, and drove to the State Marine site, David driving the car, Abdul on the buggy, they both stopped at the security gate, where there were about four men, guarding it, they dragged the bodies out on the car, and dumped them in the dirt "I think these belong to you!" David called out, David and Abdul just got on the buggy and drove off.

They made their way back to the accident site "I will have to see what they were up to," said David,

"I'll come down with you," using the equipment they appropriated from the bad guys, David and Abdul abseiled down to the wreak Mike's body was no longer in the driving seat in fact it was not in the vehicle at all the vehicle was now empty, they climbed back up.

Once they got out of the harnesses, David did not know what to tell Abdul about what was going on, and how he had found Mike with a bullet hole in his head, Abdul saw that David was struggling with what to say, as he seemed a pretty resourceful guy, "David," said Abdul "I don't know what's going on here, and it's probably none of my business, so you do not have to explain anything to me, I was just glad I could be of help, and stop those men giving you a real beating," he smiled as he said the last bit,

"Oh you didn't think I had it under control then?" they both laughed. "I'm sorry Abdul but I really don't know what's going on myself yet," David said with his hands in the air, "But we do have a meeting planned for tomorrow morning at eleven in the pub, if you feel you want to get involved, but as of this time, I do not know what we are involved in, but you are very welcome to join us, if you wish" Abdul smiled

"As I said I wanted some exercise so I might as well have a bit of excitement as well, I'll see you there," Abdul started to walk back to his car, David called out,

"By the way how come you were passing this way?" Abdul waved, and got into his car without replying.

David tried to forget his injuries on the drive back to his farm, once there he made his way to the gym he had built himself; he had plenty of medical equipment and every gym apparatus you could think of, including a hot tub and sauna, all these things came into use as he self medicated, in his former life injuries like this were common place, but now after three years of inactivity he knew that these would take a bit longer to heal, but after a couple of hours with the warmth of the tub and a good intake of food he decided he was not in bad shape at all.

18
Saturday

After David and Abdul had left the four men outside the gate, they were dragged down to No1's office, and to say he was fuming, was an understatement, "You're telling me, that the four of you could not see off a school teacher, and some foreigner?" he raised his hands in a mocking motion "Four highly trained former marines, could not take care of a couple of misfits," he waved them away "Get out of my sight before I do something I'll regret," the four men practically ran out of the office, not wanting to join the Mexican.

No1 had already talked to the town's Mayor, and asked who this man could have been, he also asked who the dark skinned man was, the Mayor could not think of anyone who could have done this, the only one who fitted the description of the man on the buggy was the local school teacher, but he was a part time teacher plus a farmer and to his knowledge could not punch himself out of a paper bag, the dark skinned man he had no idea?.

No1 decided to try to find out a who this school teacher really was, he now had a name, and he passed it over to his computer man to find as much information as possible, but for now he put it out of his mind, they still had a lot to do.

He walked out his office and made his way to the lift, going up he then made his way to the old airstrip where his men were hard at work, getting the runway ready for the aircraft they were expecting in a few days time, they had cleared about half if it so far, but as they cleared they then pulled movable pallets with earth and plants on them to disguise the fact that the airfield was getting near operating mode, not that they envisaged anyone spotting the runway but they did not want to take the chance that somehow, someone might see a fully functional airstrip, because up to this time know one here or on the mainland even knew that a long time ago a secret airfield was ever here.

He was very pleased on the progress the men had made this part of the plan was going as planned, but other developments were very upsetting, firstly The Man turning up, he was not supposed to be physically involved, he was just the finance side of the operation, but now his presence on the Island was a very disturbing faction, as he was not known for being very diplomatic when dealing with others and could easily jeopardise the whole operation if he decided to do something stupid as in previous dealings, that's why No1 had not wanted to use him on this, but the finance needed for this one No1 could not find himself, so sometimes who could not chose your bed mates and this time he dearly wished THE MAN had stayed out of it, he could see that somewhere down the line something was going to go terribly wrong.

He went back down below and made his way down a long tunnel to where there were a couple of men setting up explosive charges, "How's it going?" he asked

"Fine," came the reply "We should have it all set for when it's needed," No1 smiled

"Well done! once that's done set up the outside ones," he then made his way back to the office to find out if his computer guy had made any progress, walking into the office, one look at the man sitting in front of the screen told him that he had not been successful, "What did you find?" looking up "Absolutely nothing!" came the reply "I cannot find anything relating to a teacher called David Cross," No1 looked at the screen,

"Have you tried the armed forces, by all accounts this man knew what he was doing,"

"Yes, I've tried everything I could think of, but no joy, but I will find something don't you worry, give me time know one can hide from me!"

No1 decided to take a trip to town to track down this teacher for himself, and try to assess the man, but said to himself "That can wait for tomorrow, I need to get in touch with Columbia, to find out how things are going that end."

19
Saturday

Stuart, the generator engineer, was having something to eat in the canteen, and overheard the conversation about the two deaths, and the beating, four of their men had taken, he thought to himself "What have I got myself into here?" Stuart did not know why they were on the Island, and he did not care too much, he just knew he was being paid a lot of money to keep this old generator going, but this was turning into something else, people getting killed, first the Mexican, and now two perfectly ordinary people killed by us.

Stuart had been on the Island previously, about two months ago with the site manager, the thin hairy Man, the explosives man, and one of the guards; they had come as tourists hoping to see Whales and Seals. But in truth they had come to measure, take readings, and to sort out the generator, with the prospect of getting it up and running. They found they had trouble believing, that an abandoned secret airbase was here. What on earth was an old airbase doing on a remote Island like this, the No1 had not told them to much, in fact he had not told them anything, except to find out if the generator was viable, if not, they would they have to bring in their own, also, was the tunnels and the underground area still usable, the guard's job, was to scout around the perimeter, and to ascertain, if the old fencing surrounding the site, was still in place, and how much extra gear they would need.

All four men had specific jobs to do, and only had a long weekend to do it in, they did not want to make their presence on the island to memorable, especially as they were poking around the restricted part of the Island, but seeing as a lot of the keep out notices, were now, not readable. And they were not aware of any restricted areas, they were pretty sure they would not cause any one to doubt, that they were indeed, there to see the wildlife and unfortunately had strayed into this area.

Stuart got started straight away with assessment on the generator, and was surprised to find the thing was in remarkable good condition, he put this down to the thing being underground, and also one of the top models of its time, in fact it had some parts on it that had only just been put into practice on modern generators, he said to himself "Wow! This is one brilliant machine so far in advance of itself," Stuart marvelled at the machine, as it seemed to have different parts, from different machines, to make one perfect one, this was going to be fun. But on reflection he surmised that back in 1942 they must have had electric somehow? It took him only two days to get it running, but he only ran it for a few hours, as the fuel was a bit low, and they had not brought any extra with them, he wrote down all the things he would need, and it turned out quite a lot in fact, as on close inspection quite a lot of parts were not going to last, but with the love, and affection, he was going to lavish on the beautiful machine, he surmised it would last for another sixty odd years, but he was given specific instructions that it was to last six days then destroyed, but to Stuart's mind to destroy something like this, was amounting to sacrilege, so he made plans to make believe he had in fact destroyed it, but at a later date, come back when this "Whatever this is?" Is over, and to take it apart, and rebuild it somewhere like a museum or an engineering collage, but to destroy such a magnificent machine like this "No way!"

The so called site manager had done his survey, above ground and below, and had found just like Stuart, that the facility was in pretty good shape, the storage area, the airstrip and the personnel area were all usable with a little hard work, and he could not see any reason why their plans could not go ahead without too much trouble, and would be well within their six day time scale, the main thing was the generator, and generator guy had confirmed to him that that was all in hand and there were no worries on his part.

Down one of the long tunnels well underground, the explosive guy who was known as X1, was doing his sums, there was quite a lot of rubble to be shifted, as the previous owners had dynamited a large part on the tunnel system, but to his trained eye, his part of the operation was not going to cause any delay, he just had to make sure he had enough explosives to do the job, after inspecting the tunnels he concentrated on the airstrip, there were large boulders to be moved, and a bunker to be demolished, like everyone else he could not fathom out what had gone on here, but to his mind just like Stuart, and Site, everything could go ahead as scheduled.

Stuart did not know the names of the other three, and likewise they did not know his name, No1 had insisted, this was going to be so big, that he did not want any chit chat, or making of any friends, this was a one off job, so just get on with your specific jobs, and do not concern yourself with any others.

The other man the so called G1, guard one, portrayed the aura of a trained monkey, he was sullen, and Very Large, in fact they just took him for a hired thug, but like the others he was an expert in what he did, everything he checked out was all good.

After they had all compiled their own needs, they packed up and left the Island without anyone knowing they had even been there.

20
Saturday

Abdul Abdullah was sitting in his car, outside the hotel, after the excitement on the cliff thinking to himself, "That's the first time in three and half years, that I have done something for someone else, something good, something I could be proud of, plus I really enjoyed it" Abdul's face got a bit serious "I do hope that this man is not the man I'm looking for, as this is the first person I've liked, in a lot of years and would love to have him as a friend"

Abdul's mind went back, and contemplated what had brought him to this small Island, off the coast of America.

It all started three and a half years ago, in a village on the border of Afghanistan and Pakistan. At the time Abdul was an up and coming school teacher in his village, and one day in the near future was to be made head. Abdul had two boys in the school, one was eleven, the other nine, and they were his world, he also had a daughter Jasmine, but he left her to be taught and brought up by her Mother.

His boys were his life, they were both doing well in the school and the elder one was always top of his class, Abdul had high hopes for both his boys, but Azam was the one he was most proud of, as he was the first boy. His Sister Jasmine was also bright, but boys always come first, his younger son Parsa was more of a thinker, and Abdul thought he would grow up to be a great leader. He could never put into words how utterly proud he was of them both, for as well as their school lessons, they had private tutoring as well, like most children in this part of the world, there was not a lot of time for playing out, although Abdul insisted that part of the day, should be given for play.

The day was like any other day, except for a lot of excitement in the part of the village Abdul rarely visited, it held the stronghold of the local chieftain, who he knew was part of the Taliban, and had also turned the village into a strict Muslim enclave. Abdul was quite liberal in the teachings of the Koran, but the very strict laws they had to endure, sometimes, were not to his liking, but he never voiced his views, as that would have been met with possible death, or imprisonment.

He had been in his time, forced to watch beheading, and stoning. And so to protect himself, and for the protection of his family, he never spoke to anyone about his feelings.

The morning it happened, Abdul had been called away from school, one of the boys from the all boys school, had not turned up that morning, and Abdul, who had taken a liking to the boy was worried, as he lived near the stronghold, a very dangerous place, Abdul did not want to go there, but was compelled to help the boy, and to see if he was well. He was not afraid to go into this neighbourhood, as the Chieftain had given him safe passage where ever he wanted to go, as long as he taught the boys the strict Koran laws, and he himself adhered to them.

He found the boy surrounded by Taliban fighters; he pulled the boy to one side and asked "What is going on?"The boy explained what had happened, how they had found an American in one of the buildings, and about a drone that looked like a bird. Abdul looked around and all of a sudden gave a big shudder, and suddenly felt an overwhelming feeling of dread, he could not work out what had brought this on, but in his heart he knew it something to do with his sons.

He left the boy and started back to the school, the fear he was feeling got stronger, so he started to run, he was not a fit man but the adrenalin in his body propelled him through the streets like an Olympic runner, he was just two hundred yards from the school, when the explosion happened, he felt the shockwaves from where he was, he carried on running, and turned the last corner to be confronted with something that would stay in his mind for ever, his school and the surrounding area had been turned into a pile of rubble, with smoke curling up into the air, and flames burning fiercely, the site was so unreal, that Abdul could not take it all in, he sank to the floor, his hands holding his head, how could this be, my school, all the children gone, a place of learning a place where children played.

He started to wail uncontrollably, and called out his son's names, over, and over, again, unable to come to terms with what had happened. It was just an hour ago that he had left the classroom, where his sons were in front of him, he called out their names again, tears running down his cheeks. He felt arms taking hold of him, people had come to see, and to help, in any way they could, but the school had been completely obliterated, no one could have survived.

The emergency vehicles came roaring up, and started to tackle the flames, more family members had turned up, and the wailing had got so loud that all other sounds were blanked out, Abdul was not able to hear all this, is brain, had just shut down.

It was days before the bodies were able to be got out, and identified. Abdul's wife could not look, the bodies were so burnt, that identification, was very difficult, but Abdul's boys were identified, and Abdul and his family could mourn the loss of the one thing he treasured in the whole world. Azam, and Parsa, Is Sons.

In all, 100 children died that day, and 14 teachers lost their lives, but there was one thing that could not be explained, there were three vehicles, and a number of bodies in the ruins, and no one had any idea what they were doing there? It was a mystery that was never cleared up. What were the vehicles, and people, doing in the school? A mystery that was never, explained.

It took a further two days, to work out what had caused the explosion, most of the village believed it was a bomb, but now it had been confirmed it had been a missile, people had seen a vapour trail just before the school had been hit. And sifting through the debris, it was quite clear, that indeed, it had been a strike from a foreign country, and forensics had concluded, it was from an American source.

After the funeral of his beloved sons, Abdul swore on the Koran, that he, Abdul Abdullah, would devote the rest of his life to find the murderers, and seek revenge on all Americans, especially the two Americans that were responsible, for this repulsive and utterly repugnant act, of targeting, defenceless children.

He had sworn to Allah, and prayed to Allah, to find and destroy the men, and their families, the way they had destroyed his.

He joined the Afghan army. And had undergone hard training, and in pursuit of his vendetta, he had done things he would not have thought impossible, in his previous life, but the vision of the school, and the memories of his beautiful boys, drove him on. He had now become, a very accomplished sniper and assassin, he had been named, Assas Abdullah El Sin.

He had made many widows, but at the back of his mind, he was still a decent man, and one day, would go back to be a teacher. In all his killings he had vowed, he would not harm any woman, or anyone, who had children, so most of his targets were bad people, especially the Taliban, he still had an inbreed hatred for all Taliban, and he blamed them just as much as he blamed the two Americans and their Country. He had already taken out the village Chieftain, but could not find out who the Taliban leader was, the one who made that fateful visit to his village that day, and this was a thorn in his side that was to stay there forever.

And now after three years, his quest was finally coming to an end. The two men who were in his village that day, he know knew that these were the men who carried out this heinous act, he also knew that one of them lived on this Island, the other one he knew had been killed by the Taliban on that day, the man on this Island had enjoyed a life that he Abdul Abdullah had not been able to do, the time for revenge had at last come.

PRAISE BE TO ALLAH!

But the ending he had envisaged was not the one he got?

21
Sunday

Sunday morning David was woken up by his 6am alarm clock, the Geese, he had about a dozen of them, and as alarm clocks go, there are no better creatures on earth that are better alarms than geese, and as for burglar alarms, if you have geese you do not need any other outdoor device, you can't switch them off, you can't turn them off, you can't smother them, you can't placate them, the only way to get them to shut up is to feed them, or to send the dog in.

David looked at the clock they were bang on time 6am "Shep!" he called out "Go and shut those bloody things up!" no reply "Damm," he scouted out loud, "I forgot he's having a sleep over," David knew the only way to shut them up, was to get up and feed them, Once fed they returned to their pecking and fighting.

That done, he looked at the bruises he had suffered the day before, they were not too bad, after a nice hot shower and bacon and eggs for breakfast he started to feel like he always does in the mornings, fit, healthy, full of life, and ready for whatever the day may bring, and this day was special as it was Sunday, no school.

Then reality set in, this was not a normal Sunday, in fact it was not going to be a normal day at all, as he still had not made up his mind what to tell the others especially Chloe.

After dressing he looked at himself in the mirror, what stared back at him was a 39yr old who still had a good body, a mop of brown hair, but going grey at the sides, but, all in all, not to rubbishy. He did the rest of the chores, feeding the sheep and collecting any eggs lying around, and then got into his disguise, the baggy clothes, the glasses, and the defeated look he had perfected over the years, he indeed did look like a wimp, but it was a look that had taken some time to develop, being a very active man it was extremely difficult to keep this look going, but while at the farm he could relax, do his work outs, his morning runs all in secret, so keeping fit was not a problem, keeping others in the dark was!, maybe one day I can be me, but then again do I want to be the old me again? Reminiscing over he jumped onto his buggy and headed for town.

22
Sunday

In town, Chloe was waking up in a strange mood, firstly not knowing where she was, and then like David reality setting in. Now her mind was filled with the thought of not seeing Peter, and Mike again, her dear friends, plus the thought of them both lying at the bottom of the cliff, all alone, she tried to hold back the tears once again.

She showered, and put on the same clothes she had on the day before, "I must go home to get some clean clothes," she said to herself. Walking downstairs, she could smell bacon cooking, and suddenly realised she had not eaten for nigh on 24 hours, and now with this wonderful aroma coming from the kitchen, she could not get to the kitchen fast enough.

Mary and Sean were sitting at the breakfast table waiting for her to come downstairs, "Good morning my dear how are you feeling today?" asked Mary,

"Not too bad thank you" Mary could see that she had not had a very good night's sleep,

"I'll make you a nice cup of coffee"

"Thank you that would be nice" drinking her coffee Chloe started to feel a little bit better,

"Now it's time for one of my famous breakfasts," Sean rolled his eyes

"Everything she cooks is always famous, did you know that?" remarked Sean with a giggle,

"I've never had any complaints from you, you old goat," hitting him with her spoon. Chloe could not believe how much she ate, she did not know how she had the stomach to keep it all down, but as Mary had said, it was one of the best breakfast's she had ever eaten, if not the best.

Chloe said her goodbyes, and said she will see them here, at eleven. She retrieved her scooter from the garage, and made the journey to the Marine facility, her home for the last year.

23
Sunday

Darren was up at the break of dawn like any other Sunday. Sunday for Darren, was when he could get a lot of his work done, most farmers, and fishermen, did not do much on a Sunday, so it was the best day to have work done on their motors, and this Sunday would not be any different, except for the meeting at eleven in the pub about this Marine lot.

As he worked he started to ponder about what had brought him to this remote Island, where there was little chance of him finding love, or of earning a fortune.

He was now going on sixty one years, and said to himself "I think I might have lost my chance now,"

Darren was from a small town in Texas, what you would call a one horse town, in fact the horse ruled the town, not the car, Darren worked for his Dad in the only garage in town, this is where he learnt his trade in mechanical engineering, and that, over the years, had help him through his life. But sometimes that knowledge was put to criminal use.

One day, Darren's best mate, Steve, came in and announced that he was going to join the army, and as Steve was the only real friend Darren had, he decided to join up too, they went through basic training together, but then lost touch for a long time only to be reunited while in Vietnam, the two of them could not believe their luck being mates once again.

But it turned out short lived, their platoon found themselves in an impossible situation whilst on a mission, they were supposed to hold a bridge to keep it out of the Viet Kong hands, in the end they had to retreat, and as they did, Steve was shot. I got him in a shoulder hold, and walked out with our lieutenant ordering me to put him down, as it was endangering the other platoon members, but I was not going to leave my one and only friend to his fate in the arms of the enemy, so I refused, time, and time, again, until the Officer grabbed hold of Steve's head and announced that he was already dead, Darren gently laid his friend on the ground when he felt a tug on his arm "Come we must get out of here," came the voice of the lieutenant, Darren did no more that hit him not once but several times blaming him for Steve's death, the lieutenant fell to the floor. I was sorry it was not his fault really, I went to pick him up, and blood was pouring out of a bullet wound to his head, he had been shot, and it was my fault.

It was quite some time, before Darren was imprisoned for his attack on a officer commanding, and the charge was for manslaughter do to the fact that it was due to my attack, but he had no regrets as his actions on that day resulted on reinforcements reaching them, retaking the bridge and Darren able to get the body of his best mate back, to have a decent burial, but to this day he still felt guilty about the lieutenants death.

After he did his time, he was dishonourable discharged from the army, and that led him into a life of crime, stripping cars, stealing cars, and one time being a getaway driver, in all he spent fifteen years in prison, over a twenty year period, in the end he decided enough was enough, he still had a little money left, and saw this garage for sale on an Island he had never heard of, and as they say the rest is history.

24
Sunday

Very early that morning, the fishermen, as promised, put to sea to find out the fate of the Professor and Mike, as they approached the crash site they could see the remains of the car, the waves had taken their toll and there was not a lot of wreckage left, they scoured the cliff face using binoculars, but could not see anything or anyone, they then spent two hours searching the area, but to no avail, in the end they concluded that the bodies of the two men were going to remain in the bosom of the sea, and reported the fact to the Mayer's office, who related the findings to the rescue team, who on advice decided a helicopter search was on this occasion not warranted.

Now the job fell to Susan, to tell Chloe, and the others, the findings of the people searching, not a job she was looking forward to.

25
Sunday

Sean and Mary were not at all happy about the way things were going, they had settled on the Island nearly thirty years ago, Sean running a small bar and Mary running the diner, due to them having to leave Ireland in a hurry forty years ago.

Sean was a twenty year old Ulsterman, someone from Northern Ireland, and even only being twenty, was a member of the IRA. As some people would call it a terrorist group, but to its members a group trying for recognition and independence.

It was one day in 1972, that Sean, and three others, decided that they would help the cause, by ambushing a military patrol in broad daylight, so as the people of Ireland could see that it was a fight they could win, and that they were able to wreak havoc on all military establishments, at any time, but their plan was ill thought out, Sean being the eldest and the others, one was the same age as Sean, the other two, one was seventeen the youngest was only fifteen.

The day of their ill fated sortie into the world of armed conflict, started with them obtaining weapons from an IRA commander, who given their age, should not have supplied such weapons, although Sean had been in gun fights before, the others, this was something new, and they thought was going to make them real Irishmen, and hero's, to many, that supported the fight.

They laid in wait for the British patrol to come down the road, six armed men, three to each side of the road, when they opened fire, the younger boys did not really know what to expect and were taken aback by the guns they had been given, and could not fire them with any accuracy, one of the soldiers went down but the others were seasoned fighters, and soon had the situation under control, Sean and the seventeen year old managed to get away, the other two the twenty year old was shot dead, and the youngest the fifteen year old was captured, the leader of the IRA had not been consulted on this, and was furious that one of his commanders had given the go ahead for such a futile exercise, the commander was dealt with, and the two boys including Sean were spirited away on a ship to America, the IRA

69

not wanting the publicity that would be coming their way if the boys were captured, as their names had been posted, how their names were posted was not known, but it must have come from the fifteen year old who was captured.

Sean found himself on a ship with his pregnant girl friend, the IRA had relented when Sean refused to go without her, they had provided them with fake passports and they travelled as man and wife, that way it looked more plausible.

They settled in New York for a time, but there was always the threat of them being found, so they worked hard, and when they had saved enough money, changed their names again, and became Sean and Mary O'Rielly, and now with their Son Sean Junior, they travelled to the other side of America, and from there, to the this remote Island of San Juliet.

It was twenty years later that Sean heard about two British soldiers being prosecuted for gross misconduct in the interrogation of a young prisoner in 1972. It transpired that two of the soldiers that day, instead of taking him back to base as they were told to do; they took them to an abandoned warehouse, stripped him, tied him up, and subjected him to a verbal interrogation against all protocols, it turned out that the soldier who was shot was one of the men's best mate and in his defence said that it was grief that propelled him to do something so blatantly bad, it also transpired that whilst striping off his clothes, to their surprise his name was sown into the jacket, it was a school jacket, they then threatened him, his family, and all his friends, unless he told them the names of the other men, being only fifteen a child he told them the names, once they had the names they let him go with a warning, not to tell a living soul about what went on here today, if they hear that he had told anyone, anyone at all, they would go after him and all his family and kill everyone.

Now the two of them were frightened about any publicity this thing would bring although they knew about the good Friday agreement signed back in 1998, where all members of the now disbanded IRA were pardoned, but still neither of them knew what they were getting into, but Sean never in his life had he walked away from trouble if it involved him or his family, and this was going to bring lots of trouble to this Island that he and Mary called home, so he vowed no matter what, to help the others to save the Island and to save all the people on it, even if it means they get found out about their past.

26
Sunday

Once Chloe had changed into clean clothes, she vowed not to return to the facility again, it was too painful, the place felt empty and lost. She climbed onto her scooter, took one last look back, a whole year, that she now felt, was a wasted year, although all the work she had done was still in her notes and on her laptop, most of her work involved going down to the sea shore and meeting her beloved sea otters who she had got to know quite well.

Chloe tied a large box onto the back of the scooter, and said to herself "I'll arrange for the collection of all the data, and personal items, as soon as possible,"

She set of from the place she had called home for the last year, never to return. Chloe found herself stopping, as she came up to the crash site, she pulled over, and walked to the edge of the cliff, leaning over she nearly lost her balance, she felt a pair of hands grabbing her "Not a very good idea," said a voice, she turned, and there was David, with a concerned look on his face,

"I wasn't going to jump," David gently steered her away from the edge,

"I know but you were getting close to taking an unauthorized swim," they walked back to Chloe's scooter, and sat down,

"I loved them so much," she cried, tears streaming down her cheeks, David put his arm around her and tried to say things that would comfort her, but the words would not come out, as he knew that come later he would have to tell her the truth about the so called accident,

"I will find out who did this," he led her over to his buggy and placed her on the passenger seat; he still had the trailer on the back, so loaded her scooter into it, and carried on into town.

David left her with Mary and Sean, unloading the scooter and taking the box into the pub. He walked down the road towards the diner; it was now ten o'clock he passed the community hall, where Sunday morning prayers were being held, the Island did not have a church so used the hall as a place of worship, and for all other things,

71

like dances and town meetings, so was the main hub that made San Juliet a happy place.

He carried on walking thinking to himself "San Juliet was not going to be a happy place, once I disclose yesterday's findings," As her approached the diner, this big hairy thing came bounding out, David found himself on the floor with this big hairy thing licking his face, "Get off you ugly brute!" trying to push Shep off, but pushing four stone of Alsatian whilst on the floor, was nigh on impossible, Joe came running over and pulled the dog off,

"Bad dog," he said, with a big smile on his face, David stood up wagging his finger at the dog,

"That's it; I'm sending you to a doggy's home!" Julie had now joined them outside,

"Don't be so cruel," she said, Julie turned to look at the dog, he had dropped to the floor with his paws over his eyes and with a look of pure dread on his face, they all laughed out loud

"When did you teach him that?" asked Joe, David looked at his doggy friend,

"Okay I'll give you one more chance, you can stay," David said with a look of defeat, Shep jumped up and twisted around three or four times "Okay you can stop being clever now," David walked towards the diner "How about a cup of tea?"

After his tea, David walked back towards the pub passing the hall once again, the congregation were streaming out, David saw the two fishermen, went over to them and they related what they had discovered, the two men rejoined their families. The Islanders were a very religious people, especially the fishermen, as they would be going out early the next morning to their four days of fishing, over in the corner, David saw Abdul talking to the Pastor, "I wonder what's going on there?" he mused.

David walked into the pub to find Susan, talking to Chloe, he could see that she was visibly upset, and he surmised that she was telling her what the fishermen had found out. David went over and asked her if she was okay? Chloe wiped the tears from her eyes, they started to walk towards the others, when she caught David's arm, turning him around she asked,

"What did you mean, when you said that you would find out, who did this?" David carried on walking.

The pub did not open until 12, so their meeting would not be interrupted, they all sat down Sean taking the chair, those taking part were Darren, Scott, Chloe, Susan, Myself and Sean, then all of the sudden the pubs door opened and Abdul to walked in, "Sorry sir!" called out Sean, "The place does not open until 12" Abdul looked for David, David stood up and went over to Abdul,

"Ladies and Gentlemen, this man is with me, he saved my life yesterday, and he has volunteered to help us," the others all had puzzled looks upon their faces,

"What the hell are you talking about?" shouted Sean, and the others voiced the same question. David led Abdul to a chair, and related all that had happened the day before, and telling of their findings, including the real reason for the crash, Mike's murder. Everyone had a look of utter disbelieve on their faces

"How could something like this happen on a peaceful Island like San Juliet," asked Susan, David was bombarded with questions all of them coming at once,

"Whoa! Hold on, one at a time please," David tried to answer as much as he could, but he could only recount all the facts, but not the reason why. Sean being in hiding for a very long time, was always, suspicious of strangers, although it had been nigh on forty years since he and Mary had fled Ireland, he was still wary of anything out of the ordinary, he looked at Abdul

"We thank you for saving our friend David, but I'm not sure that we can trust someone, that just suddenly turns up at the right moment, and at the right place, and just happens to be able to see off four dangerous men," the others looked towards Abdul, realising, that what Sean had said, was quite reasonable, David also realised that he had asked the same question earlier, they all waited for Abdul to answer,

"After hearing all this, I can see why you are suspicious of strangers just turning up out of the blue, but I can assure you, I knew nothing about this Marine lot, before this meeting I had never heard of them, although, I couldn't help but notice there were a number of trucks, with that name on the ferry I came over on, and that was on Friday, I have only been on the Island two days," Sean remembered seeing a foreign looking driver coming off, Abdul continued "I was sightseeing before my meeting with a Mr O'Brian on Monday, when I came across these men beating up a man, who I now know as David, and although I'm not a very brave person, I could not just stand by and see someone who needs help, and me not giving it, so just helped out, and yes, I can look after myself having been in the Afghan Army for two years, also David invited me, I did not invite myself," Abdul took a breath "but if you are not happy with me being here?" everyone looked at Sean

"What the hell! None of us knows what's going on, so you may be of help," holding out his hand, Abdul took the hand,

"I'll tell you why I'm on the Island a little later, you have a lot more pressing things to discuss, but I will give you my card so you can check up on me if you so please," the card said, ABDUL ABDULLAH, EQUINE AGENT FOR PRINCE AHMED BIN ABDURRAHEEM, Sean passed the card around and all nodded

"Welcome to our Island," said David, looking around "There are now seven of us, and I want to be Yul Brynner?

After a long discussion they still had not come to any conclusion, on how to proceed, but they did concede that they could not solve the problem without proof "There has to be a way of obtaining proof," said Darren

"We go up there and take a look!" they all turned to look at Chloe,

"I may be talking out of turn here, but I think the lady is right, it does seem the most logical answer," Abdul remarked, they all looked at each other and all nodded in agreement,

"I'll go!" said Scott, David looked at Scott,

"That's very brave of you Scott, but it would be better if someone younger, and fitter goes, no disrespect," Scott looked crestfallen,

"Are you saying I'm not young and fit?" they all shouted

"YES!"

Abdul put his hand up "If I can help,"

"Thank you Abdul, but this is our problem, San Juliet is our Island, it's up to us to sort it out, but I'm sure we will be calling on your help, very Soon," said Sean.

David looked at Chloe "If we do this, the only people capable is Chloe, and myself, we know the area, and we are both fit, and can take care of ourselves," They discussed the matter further, and in the end, decided that Chloe, and David, were the best option.

The meeting broke up, Darren providing some necessary tools, and after collecting various items from the store, they had all the things they thought they would need, the two of them went back to David's farm, leaving the dog with Joe.

27
One week earlier Columbia

Two men entered the Columbian State Police Department, and were shown to a large basement, room with walls covered in charts and pictures, and what looked like large maps of Columbia, with banks, and banks, of computer screens, all churning out, reams of data.

A portly man of about Fifty came over to them, "Good morning gentlemen," with a cheery demeanour, and a large hand held out, both took the hand "I'm Captain Morella, It's a pleasure to meet you," The Captain pointed to a young man by his side "And this is Sergeant Durrell our computer expert," the two men shook hands with the sergeant, The Captain led the two men over to one wall, that was taken up by pictures of three men, all posing for the camera, "These three men!" looking at the two men, "Are the most wanted, and the most dangerous criminals, we have in our country at the moment, all three are the heads of different drug Cartels, and thanks to our informants, they are due to meet in the next few days, unfortunately we do not have a specific date, or time, at the present, but we expect to hear in the next 24 hours."

"Now this is of the utmost importance to us as is to you, this collaboration of different Cartels coming together like this, is unheard of, they are normally at each other's throats, so this indicates to us that something big is going down, for all three too be involved?" the Captain showed them pictures of aftermaths of gun battles, between the Cartels, and pictures of gang members, who had been shot by different gangs, and pictures of torture ordinary folk, who have betrayed them "This is the normal way things are done down here, and the information coming through is not consistent with this."

The two men asked a few questions, and went off to have a quiet chat.

The two men were part of the United States DEA department, (Drug Enforcement Agency) and were asked down here for the specific reason, that the Columbian Police, drug enforcement arm, were concerned, and convinced, that all this activity with Drug the Lords, and talk of a big deal going down, was of importance to the United

States, as their intervention in the drug smuggling operations around the Mexican border, and elsewhere, had dramatically stopped the flow of drugs into that country, but this development where all Cartels are cooperating with each other, makes us believe that this is big, and is highly likely to succeed.

The two men came back over "We have talked, and we both agree, that yes! Something big is definitely happening, as we have been getting whispers from our informants at home that triggered alarm with us, so yes, we will combine our forces, and try to find out more about these rumours and suspicions," they all shook hands, and started to work out what strategy they were going to pursue, "One question," asked one of the men, the Captain turned round,

"And that is?"

"Who is the main player here; do you know who made the first move to the collaboration of the Cartels?" the Captain looked at his sergeant, he nodded,

"Juan Luis Cordova!" the two men were taken aback, they had, had, Cordova in custody, only five months ago, but during a well organised prison break, Cordova had escaped, the two men could not fathom out, how he had got back into Columbia, and how he was again, head of the Cordova Cartel, and planning this big deal.

The escape was a huge embarrassment to the FBI; Cordova was being transferred by them, to a more secure prison, where he was to await trial, when it was attacked by a large force en route. Now many of Drug Lords had been captured and safely gone to trial and been convicted, but at the time they asked themselves why did Cordova matter so much that a full blown military style escape was carried out. It was now coming clear that the break out, was somehow, connected to this big thing that was about to happen, so Washington, the DEA, and the FBI, were going to have to work this together. In saying that, the two of them working together was going to be, one of the first.

Meanwhile, the CIA were conducting an investigation themselves, that would have implications, and add complications to the whole operation.

The two men said their goodbyes to Captain Morella, and were just being escorted out, when a shout from Durrell halted them, they made their way over to where Durrell was talking to someone on one of the secure lines, it was a few moments before he stood up a worried look on his face, "What's happened?" asked the Captain, Durrell looked at the two men and his Captain and said with a shaking voice

"This morning's raid on the warehouse has gone badly wrong,"

"How wrong?" asked Morella

"There were no drugs, no workers, and no guards, the place was empty," the Captain sat down with a thump,

"How can that be?" he asked "Surely we have had eyes on it, for a long time,"

Durrell replied "Yes we did, up until two days ago, when surveillance was taken down, and just a token presence was needed, we assumed that seeing as the site had been in use for a long time, it did not warrant a full blown operation, it was only yesterday after all these rumours that a full raid on the place was deemed necessary,"

One of the men asked "So what happened?"

"They do not know, the warehouse had approximately four tons of cocaine stashed there, we were waiting for the higher people to visit the place, then we were going to raid it, there's no way four tons of the stuff could have just vanished," Durrell again looked worried "The two surveillance guys were found dead, shot in the head," the Captain went over to the wall and looked for an item he had seen before,

"Look here," he cried "See this," the others looked, and there were two unrelated reports, from different area's that large quantities of drugs had literally vanished,

"I can see a pattern here," said one of the men, the others looked at him "Tons of the stuff goes missing, we have rumours that a large thing is going down, there's going to be a very large drug run, and it's starting right here, right now!"

They all looked at each other, then they all came to the same conclusion, but none of them knew, how it would affect a small community in, California so much.

The two DEA men left saying they would be in touch, Morella and Durrell poured over the Intel that was coming in, it did not make good reading.

The two DEA agents returned to their office, and reported to their headquarters in Virginia, they relayed what Captain Morella had told them, stressing the fact, that Cordova, was the kingpin of the obvious consignment of a very large quantity of drugs destined for either Mexico, or the United States.

They were told to cooperate, with the Captain, and assist with all the Intel they had at their disposal, and likewise, Captain Morella has been told by the President of Columbia, to do the same. The war on drugs, was a war, that all the agencies, were, destined to lose, but the flow of drugs coming into the United States, were at the lowest for years, due to the vigilance, and the network of agents, who had infiltrated, the heart of the drug world.

Columbia was one of the major cultivators of cocaine, and many other forms of drugs, but due to the intensity of the fight, the flow from this part of the world was at its lowest The cartels were always trying to find other ways to get the drugs to flow once more, and now the coming together of the three main cartels, was a frightening scenario, as it now feels as if, they have found some way, to achieve this

The two men sifted through all the intelligence they had, and found a similar pattern as Morella had found, tons of the stuff goes missing, but is it missing? Or being stock piled, for one enormous run, the phone rang, "Yes," answered the DEA man whose name was James

"We have had a break through," shouted Sgt Durrell down the phone; James put the phone on speaker,

"Go ahead," Durrell's voice could not hide the excitement of the information he was about to reveal,

"We were going through old reports, and came across an unrelated incident involving a truck carrying a consignment of coffee beans, to the port in Cartagena," James and Robert looked at each other

"And?" asked James,

Durrell carried on, "The truck was involved, was in a nasty accident, and when the contents were examined one of the containers was filled with drugs, about a ton of the stuff,"

James and Robert could not contain the excitement they felt, a large shipment by sea. There had been other sea drug runs, but the ports had beefed up security by so much, that a large consignment like this was nigh on impossible to succeed "Have you been in touch with the port authorities?"

"Yes and they are sending through all the sailings due in the next week or so, also, sailings that have left in the last few days," They heard Durrell talking to someone else down the line "Hold on." He called out, "There's a report coming through, that cartel members have been seen in Cartagena, I cannot confirm this sighting, but it does fit with the truck incident," another voice

"This is Captain Morella, I'm flying up to Cartagena in an hour's time, do you, want to join me?"

James replied "Yes I'll meet you at the airport,"

James got ready, and told Robert to inform Virginia with the new information, and to tell them to put all ports in Mexico, and the Southern States, on full alert, just in case.

The chief of operations put out the alert. But, if this does turn out to be reliable, it would be more than likely, that the suspect freighter, if any, would unload its cargo before entering any port, but how and when? The chief picked up the phone, to inform the FBI, about the whereabouts of their lost prisoner, Cordova.

One of the other agencies, the CIA, was also in a quandary, reports were coming through that a known assassin, had avoided security, and was now in the United States, as to what his objective was, was not known at this time, but the information coming through, was thought to be linked to the assassination of a high ranking officer in London, England. They are going through any operation connected with the officer in London and anyone of our own military forces here. But as of this moment we have no information as to his whereabouts, or of his identity, however we do have a photo of the suspect, be it not, a very clear one, so all air and sea ports have been alerted and been given the photo.

28
Sunday

Work at the site, started early on this Sunday morning, as they had only two more days before the merchandise they were expecting was due to fly in, the airstrip was near completion, although to see it, you would not know it, the vegetation was still very apparent, the movable pallets were doing a good job, the electricians were fitting the landing lights, and all other parts of the site were coming together brilliantly.

It was 6 in the morning when the No1 called all his men together, leaving THE MAN'S men on guard, two at the gate, and two patrolling the fence, the less they knew about our plans the better for No1 had specific plans of his own that he had not even told his No2. Once he had assigned his men to their tasks, he decided to do a tour of the facility, calling over X1 now the explosive man was called X1 his assistant was X2 all the workers on this project were given numbers, no one knew their real names, they all had numbers, or like the explosive guys, letters, the guards were G1 or G2 there was Stuart who was called GEN the computer man was TEC and so on, so when the operation came to an end, they could all go their separate ways, know one knowing who they had been working for, or with. It was a bit confusing at first, but now they were used to it. No1 had worked all this out in the last year he had been planning this, and now it was all coming together, barring the small hiccups we have been having, but he was sure all those things would be resolved before Tuesday when the plane was due to land.

X1 took him to the farthest tunnel in the system, "This one," pointing to a dark entrance, "We do not know where it leads to,, but looking at the angle, and the direction, it looks as if it leads to the sea, as you can see above you, there are still cables going beyond the rock fall, but as we will not be needing this part of the place we have not bothered to try to get through,"

No1 looked at the cables and at the rock fall and replied "Fine we do not need this area, take me to the place where you are working on at the moment," they travelled back along the tunnel, until they came to a large opening that had been dynamited all those years ago,

"Now this is interesting," said X1 "We do not know what's behind it, it has been extensively dynamited and to my eyes much more than all the others, but for your plans it was not necessary to explore further, but, with your permission, we would like to try to shift all the rubble, just to see what they were trying to conceal," No1 walked up to the rock face and touched it

"Okay I would like to see this for myself, but only after you finish the opening for the trucks," Over the other side of the underground facility, work was going on at a frantic pace, the trucks were getting new paint jobs, new pallets were being put into place ready for their delivery, and in the far corner X2 was putting the last charges to what looked like a very large opening,

"Fire in the hole!" came a shout, the explosion was not very loud, or very large, because they were in a very enclosed environment they could not use large amounts of explosives, so that was why the job of clearing tunnels, and entrances, was taking a lot longer than they first thought, but this was the final tunnel, also a vital one, as it should lead to the entrance that they had blasted yesterday on the surface, the smoke and dust settled, and on inspection they could see that this last charge had done the trick, they were through, over the next two hours the tunnel had been cleared completely, and after further inspection, found, that the path to the top, was now usable.

The whole complex was designed like an aircraft carrier, the few building up top, were the superstructures, with the airstrip as the flight deck, the platform the lifts, all to conceal, and to protect, the aircraft, so on the outside there was not a lot to see, just like this place, all vital operations were conducted below deck.

No1 shook X1's hand "You've done a brilliant job, once this has all been cleared and the last charges above have been done, you may look into the other tunnel,"

No1 went back to his office calling into the computer room, "Did you find anything?" the Tec shook his head,

"This teacher man, he does not exist," he replied

"I have not seen him myself, but I do assure you, he does exist, so keep trying," Tec went back to his screen.

No1 went topside and over to the main gate, where THE MANS men were talking, all four guards were there, "I need one of the bikes," he demanded, one of the guards shrugged his shoulders and handed the bike over.

G1 asked "What was that meeting about?" No1 was taken aback by the way the guard had asked,

"What do you mean?"

"Why weren't we invited to this meeting you had this morning, are you trying to hide something from us?" No1 did not flinch, he just went over, and hit the guard so hard, he fell to the floor unconscious,

"If anyone else is in any doubt who's in charge here now's the time to ask!" all the others stayed silent, "You can tell him when he comes round, that the meeting was about the airstrip, and the entrance to the tunnels being finished on time, nothing else, and no, I am not trying to hide anything from you, if the next meeting involves security you will be advised," with that he put on the helmet and took off.

Riding along the road, he was amazed how quiet the bike was, the bike was one of the newest electric one's, they had proven very useful in patrolling the security fence, they were not the quickest of bikes, but for what they had wanted them for, they were perfect.

He was on his way to the town but did not want to use one of the Range Rovers, as they were to conspicuous, he got to the town at 10am, and parked just on the outskirts, and walked the rest of the way, unfortunately, his height on this occasion, was not going to be useful to him, as he stood out like a sore thumb. He had no idea how he was going to find this elusive fellow, the teacher. So he just threw caution to the wind, and just walked into the main street, and to his surprise there on the other side of the street was the teacher just passing the church, he ducked in-between two buildings, and observed the way David walked, how he conducted himself, his posture, all these things No1 was adept at analysing, it was how he assessed all the people working for him, and he was really good.

He saw David go into the diner, and also noted the large dog, "That could be a problem down the line," he said to himself, although Shep looked voracious, nothing was more from the truth, because of the way he had been treated in the past, he was a pussy cat, and that was a fact, as a guard dog he was not very good, as a sheep dog he was brilliant.

The Tall Man waited outside the diner still concealed by the buildings, when he saw the towns mechanic go into the pub, then another man, then a girl he assumed was the girl the Mexican had accosted the other day, "How come they are all congregating over there," he mused, he had just started to walk towards the pub, when David came out of the diner, and started to walk towards the pub, also, he ducked back in, as David went past he followed, not knowing what he was going to do, He saw David stop at the church, and talk to the fishermen, then carry on to the pub.

He took up a post on the other side of the road with a good view of the door, "I wonder what's going on?" he saw another man walking towards the pub, this one was the dark skinned man his men had mentioned, he also went inside.

Making his way over No1 opened the pub's door a little, trying to hear what was being said, but he could not hear anything, walking back to where he parked his bike "It looks as if I will have to start stage two, a little earlier than I thought?" he climbed onto the bike, and started for the site.

After No1 had left the site earlier, leaving the guard on the floor, G1 went into the hut and picked up an encrypted phone; "Boss I think No1 is planning some sort of double cross," the other end of the phone went quiet,

"Keep your ear to the ground, I'm sending in some help!"

29
Sunday

David and Chloe moved with extra care as they approached the fence, David checked the fence for any alarms, or if it had been electrified, but found neither, using the long handled cutters, he cut a hole just large enough for the two of them to squeeze through, and once through,, they silently made their way to where they imagined the trucks, and all the other materials, were being held. Luckily, it was not a clear night, so the darkness was in their favour. They carried on for a long time, still not finding what they were looking for, "Where are they keeping all those trucks and other vehicles?" whispered Chloe, she could not see David's face, as the darkness, and the black makeup they were both wearing, blotted out any expressions, if she had noticed David's face it was the same as her's, with an extremely puzzled look on it,

"I was wondering myself," he whispered back, they carried on a bit further, and saw what looked like the derelict buildings that they knew existed, seeing them on some of their runs into the restricted area, but this time there was something different, the building were all lit up, and they could see armed guards posted around the perimeter, "That's not right," said David to himself, he indicated to Chloe to keep low, just in case they were spotted by the guards, David brought his binoculars up see get a closer look, just then he heard a crash, he looked round, and Chloe was on the floor,

"Sorry I tripped!" David looked down

"Shit!" he cried out "I've been out of this game to long:" Chloe picked herself up,

"What's wrong?" David bent down and picked up the end of a wire,

"We have just alerted the bad guys, you've just activated a trip wire," just then the night became day, as four search lights came on, "Down," David pushed Chloe to the floor, but too late they heard a shout,

"Over there!"

David grabbed Chloe's hand and shouted "I think it's time for us to leave!" they started running back to their makeshift entrance "whoa," David shouted, they were cut off, as flash lights were making their way to their position "Quickly this way," David steered Chloe into the thicker part of the trees, they altered course on numerous occasions, trying to lose their pursuers, but they kept coming, "They must be wearing NVG'S (night vision goggles") Chloe could not believe that David knew about all these things, "Come on," he said puffing and panting, and Chloe then felt the same way, she was panting, even though they were both extremely fit, this was different, they were running for their life, just then bullets flew over their heads, "Down!" they stopped to catch their breath, but their pursuers were still tracing them, "Don't worry they can only see us through their goggles, we are mostly a blur," the gun fire, is just to scare us,

Chloe thought "Well it's scaring me," they altered course once more, and continued running, hoping they were fitter than the men behind them, then all of a sudden they found themselves falling, and falling, they were picking up speed in a free fall that did not want to end, bang they landed onto a concrete floor,

David picked Chloe up "Are you ok?" he asked, their eyes meeting his arms around her body, then David felt a bolt of electricity serge through his body , and the way Chloe shuddered, David felt, that she felt something too, they stayed like that for what seemed an eternity,

"I think so," she answered, breaking away, and touching her legs and arms," I don't think anything's broken," she replied her voice shaking "But I'm sure going to have a few bruises in the morning, if we make it to the morning?" they looked around.

They found themselves in a large cavernous place, lit up with over head lamps, and a large expanse of water, "What is this place?" Chloe muttered, David did not answer; he had positioned himself at the bottom of the shaft, ready, if any of the guards found the shaft.

Up on top, the guards were running around not knowing how they had lost their quarry, one of them said "You go back and report, I'll carry on looking," The guard carried on looking, then to his surprise he heard voices coming from the ground, hunting around, he found the entrance to the shaft, and did no more than launch himself down, not knowing what he would find, but it had to be better than going back without the intruders.

Down at the bottom, David heard a body falling, one of the guards was coming down, David waited, the guard came tumbling down and landed in a heap, but he was up in a flash, but could not see a thing as night goggles are no use if there is light, he started to remove them as David came up behind him, one hand behind his head, the other holding his chin, then David gave a vicious twist, the guard's neck broke without a sound, David let the body fall and picked up the machine pistol the man had dropped, then proceeded to strip him of all the other weapons, he now had a machine pistol, a gun and a knife, plus the goggles, he held them in his hands, and decided, that after three years he had come home,

Chloe could not believe what she had just seen, this gentle school teacher had gotten us through a wire fence, evaded armed men, and has now killed a man with his bare hands, and is now handling weapons like toys, "Who the hell are you," she cried out, shaking with fear, David put all his weapons down, and put his arms around her

"I'm sorry you had to see that, but when we get out of this mess, I'll explain everything," he let her go after Chloe had stopped shaking, "Our first priority is to get out of this place as soon as we can, as more people are going to come down that shaft, only a bit more prepared,.

They explored their surroundings "What is it, and where are we?" asked Chloe; David replied

"It looks like a Submarine pen" Chloe looked at him

"What?"

David took a further look "A world war two Submarine base, I've seen them in the movies," Chloe looked completely confused

"Oh! Great now were the Dam Busters," David looked at her

"The Dam Busters was a plane movie, not about Submarines!" Chloe put her hands up

"I bow to your superior knowledge; I just hope this knowledge will get us out of this predicament, just like in the movies then!" David ignored her, they both decided to have a better look round, and to their surprise, over in a darker section of the cavern, Chloe shouted out, her voice not believing what she was seeing "David over here!" David like Chloe could not believe his eyes there sitting in the water was a submarine,

"No way!" exclaimed David, they walked up and down the length of the sub "I just can't believe a world war two submarine could just be sitting here like this," David held his head "This could be the sub in the film Run Silent, Run Deep," Chloe looked at him in amazement, after their shock find reality clicked in, "We will have to forget this for now, and find a way out, you look over that side, I'll look over here, try to find an entrance there must be one somewhere. After a fruitless search, they had to admit they were trapped, "Whoever this belonged to, they did not want it found, they dynamited all the openings so sealing the chamber off," stated David. They went down to the water's edge, and made their way to where the Submarine would have passed out into the open sea, David inspected it and came to the conclusion that this also had been dynamited. The place was defiantly sealed off, to the rest of the world.

"How come if this is a world war two submarine pen, there are still light on?" Chloe stated, David looked up,

"I would think that the electricity is somehow coming from those supposedly derelict buildings," They sat down, not saying a word, David deep in thought, he knew that the bad guys were going to come down that shaft in force, but had no idea what to do about it, he went back and checked his weapons "Here," he gave Chloe the pistol, it was a Sig Sauer semi automatic P226, "Do you know how to use it?" he asked, Chloe pulled back the cocking slide released the clip checked it was fully loaded and replied

"No,"

David looked at her totally surprised,

"My Dad was a Cuban Bandit, I was brought up with guns," they made themselves ready at the bottom of the shaft, David spotted what looked like a wooden cabinet over the far corner,

"Look over there" he said, pointing, Chloe looked "And see if there is anything that could help us!" she made her way over.

David carefully listening for any sound coming from the shaft, but knew it would be quite some time before anyone came, as it was not in the area of their camp, so they had to get equipment, and men, to the entrance.

Chloe shouted out "There's just some old diving stuff, it looks like scuba gear," Chloe came back over "It looks like some old scuba gear, not much good I'm afraid it's all rotted except for a few face masks," they just sat there completely at a loss.

Chloe looked at David as if he was a different man to the one she knew, "Tell me about yourself!" she asked, David looked at her, and decided, that he did owe her an explanation as to what she has witnessed in the last two hours.

"I will soon," he said

David wished he could fathom out how to get out of this situation they now found themselves in, then he noticed the water was making small waves, and to his surprise was very slowly rising, he took a better look, "Come over here," he called,

"What is it? She asked

"Look at the water do you notice anything?" Chloe looked, and looked,

"No, what about it?"

"It's risen up a couple of inches since we've been here!" Chloe looked bemused

"So,"

David touched the water it was cold and very salty "There must be an opening below the water line because the water has risen in line with the tide," Chloe could then see that indeed the water had come up, and David was right there must be some sort of opening to let the tide come through.

He thought to himself we have to do something and do something fast, "How good a swimmer are you?" he asked Chloe looked at him,

"I have worked and lived all my life by the sea, have you ever seen Dolphins swim? Well! They have nothing on me yes I can swim Why?" David pointed to the dark water,

"Because we are going to swim out of here," Chloe looked at the dark uninviting water,

"Are you mad," she exclaimed in a voice just above a scream, "No not that I've noticed, but one thing I have noticed, is that if we don't do something right now, we are going to get very dead," Chloe held the gun up

"We can use these," She said, "As they come down the shaft we'll just pick them off one by one," aiming the gun at the shaft,

"Well done," said David "Why didn't I think of that?" Chloe looked at him,

"Are you taking the proverbial out of me?" she asked David just looked at her, and smiled,

"When they come down that shaft, they will send down stun grenades first, then maybe a smoke grenade, then, fighters will come down in a rush, no! I'm not taking the piss I'm just saying it as it is, it's what I would do in the same situation," Chloe stayed quiet, "David lifted the guards body and threw it in the water, it sank at once, owing to the body armour he was wearing, "We don't want them to think we know what we're doing, so no body, no broken neck,"

They grabbed the face masks inspected them, the straps were not good, but would hopefully, last for their little underwater swim, David thought "hopefully a little swim:" David took his jacket and shirt off, and turned to Chloe, Chloe could not take her eyes of his body, he was built like Rocky Bilboa, David did not notice the look she was giving him, he was just making sure that everything was in order, they had found a small length of rope and tied themselves together. Once they were ready they gave each other the once over, no loose clothing that could get snagged, shoes round their necks and David with the guns tied up in his shirt and tied to his waist, they were all set to go, "GO!" shouted David and pushed Chloe in, and then dived in after her, once in the water visibility was not good, but they could just make out each other, David put his thumb up, they both took deep breaths, and dove down.

David led the way, David knew he could hold his breath for just over two minutes, having trained with Navy Seals, Chloe knew she was a pretty good underwater swimmer, having dived often off the Florida coast, so they were both confident, as long as the opening was not too long, David had estimated it, as about ten to fifteen metres long, considering the currant and the tide, so they were both capable of the swim.

They lost sight of each other, but owing to the life line, they knew they were both okay, David estimated they had swam just over ten metres, but the currant that was coming in, was more severe that he had first thought, and the progress they were making, was not good. David by this time was at his limit. Chloe behind, felt herself starting to lose consciousness, all of a sudden she felt a pull on the rope, and started to shoot through the channel faster, but the extra pressure was just too much, she had to take a breath, water gushed into her mouth, she was going to die, she knew it. That was the last thing she remembered, until she felt something pounding her chest, and a sensation of someone kissing her, David was giving life saving heart pumps, and the kiss of life, "Come on," he shouted to her "Take a breath" then all of a sudden, the water that had gushed in, gushed out in a steady stream, sputtering and coughing, she managed to sit up,

"I'm alive," she cried out, "Was that you pounding my chest?" David smiled, and held her tightly,

"Well I couldn't let my best partner die could I," he said, still smiling, Chloe smiled

"I've properly got a flat chest now," David looked at her soaking top.

"They look okay from this angle," he said letting her go, "Come on we have to find out where we are, and to get out if these wet things," They found themselves up against a rock face, to high and to wet to climb, luckily the waves were not to choppy, David had dragged Chloe from the sea, to a small sandy cove, and now the cliff towered above them. David once again brought his military mind to bear, he said out loud "Now the entrance to the Submarine pen is just around the corner, so at some point they had to have access from the sea, and down to this cove, "Are you okay while I look around?" he asked, Chloe looked up

"I'm fine you go,"

David made his way around the cove, hoping, upon hope, that his guess had been correct, Chloe found her feet and heard a shout "Over here," She made her way over, as it was still dark it was a bit tricky, plus she still hadn't got over nearly drowning, she found David with his head poked through a bush,

"What have you found?" David stood up and pointed,

"Steps that lead all the way to the top," the steps were overgrown, and were very slippery after all these years of neglect, the climb was very difficult, a number of times they both nearly fell to their deaths, but at last, they made it, with David helping Chloe, who was still struggling .

It took them two hours of walking, to get to David's farm house; both were on their knees by this time, "First things first," David said "You go up for a shower, I'll make a hot drink and some food, but first I'll get out of these wet things," Chloe went upstairs and found the shower room, David changed clothes, and made his way to the kitchen, and started up the coffee machine. A shout came from upstairs,

"There aren't any towels!"

David went to find towels for the first lady, to visit his house, he looked into the shower room, Chloe was still in the shower, "Your towels Madam," he called out, a hand comes from behind the curtain, "Thank you,"

David put the towels in her hand, then he felt himself being pulled into the shower "It seems a waste of water to have two showers, don't you think," Once again, David had wet clothes, but his time it was for a worthy cause.

It was about an hour later, that they sat down with steaming coffee, and hot soup, and then started to plan their next move, neither of them wanting to talk about what had just happened, it had come completely out of the blue.

Chloe wanted to know what David was going to tell her back in the cave, "Tell me about you, now that we're safe" she said to him.

They sat down, and David started to explain, and to tell Chloe, who against all the odds had come through this night so brilliantly, and was a great partner to have in a crisis like this, not since his last partner Sean, had he had to depend on someone so much, and as things were standing, he knew he had to depend on her and himself, in the very near future

He started to talk "Just over three years ago I was not a teacher, in fact I was a highly decorated soldier, and a member of the British SAS that's the same as your Delta force here, we were what is now called, Special Forces. We were the ones that had to do things that others couldn't do, or were not allowed to do, but something happened on my last mission, that made me leave the Army, and all that goes with it, and until this day, right now, this is the first time I have picked up a gun of any sort, after that last mission, I swore that I would not again hold, or shoot a firearm, and up to now I have kept that promise, although I have had to crack a few head in that time. But now I have been happy to be the Clark Kent of the teaching world, look soft, but underneath, still a tough, and hard, person, that would do anything for his country, or his friends.

Chloe found it hard to take all this in, but realised that all the things in his being and all the suspicions she had previously, and all what he had just told her, had to be true. Chloe put her arms around him "Thank you," she said, and she meant it, it must have been very hard for a man in such a high powered environment, and such a violent one, to do what David, and I suspect, a lot of other men have had to do, shut it out of their minds, and try to forget the past.

30
Monday

The guard who was sent back to get help, had came back with eight armed men, looking for the intruders and their lost man. After an exhausting search, they found no trace of the intruders plus no sign of their missing guard, they returned to the facility to find No1 had been told about the incursion.

No1 called all his men, plus the three guards together "Who can shed any light on what just happened?" he asked. "I want a detailed report, and now, would be a good time to give it,"

The guard related what had gone on, the tripping of the wire, spotting what looked like two intruders, them giving chase, when they lost them even though the guards were wearing their night goggles, "We searched for a long time, but with no success, then G2 told me to get help and he would carry on looking, I returned with more men, but we could not find any trace of the intruders, or of the guard, in the end I put more men at the gate entrance, and dispatched two men to walk the perimeter fence, to find out where the intruders had entered the site, they have now returned after finding the fence had been cut just enough for bodies to squeeze through, they also found where they had tripped the wire, and we have come to the conclusion that from their vantage point they could not see anything important except a few lights on the buildings, as of this moment, the function of the site, is still undetected, but we will have to find out who the intruders were, and if they found out anything, that would compromise the operation? Also we need to find out what happened to G2" the guard took a breath.

"That was a really accurate detailed report you did everything you could," he dismissed the men, making sure the extra patrols were going ahead "I could do without this," No1 walked towards his office with No2 tagging along "We have to find out who on this Island is capable of this," he said. Once in the office, he picked up the phone with the direct line to the Mayor, it took a long time for the Mayor to answer

"What hell are you doing ringing me up at this time in the morning," the Mayor shouted down the phone,

"Shut up and listen!" the Mayor went quiet, "We have had a bit of trouble here at the site,"

"What sort of trouble?"

"We had two intruders get through our defences, and one of our guards is missing," the other end of the phone went quiet once again,

"And how on earth do you expect me to help at three in the morning?" came the reply

"I want to know who on this god forsaken Island, is capable of something like breaking into a secure facility, killing one of my guards, and escaping with I hope, not too much intelligence," the Mayor could not believe that someone he knew was capable of doing something like this,

"You have the dossiers of all the Islanders in your possession, I gave you a long time ago," No1 was looking at the dossiers at the same time as talking to the Mayor,

"I'm looking at them at this moment," he replied "And the only one who stands out is the school teacher, what do you know about him?" he heard the Mayor thinking,

"Not much, he came to the Island about three years ago, and made friends with the people who run the pub, he has a small farm just below your place, where he keeps sheep, other than that nothing!"

No1 looked at the dossier once again "There were two intruders, any thought on who could be the other one?"

"No, and I'm not even sure the school teacher could do something like that,"

No1 cancelled the call, turning to No2 "The only other person is this biologist girl, the one who beat up the Mexican and G4,"

After a lot of thought No1 decided to send a couple of the guards to the teacher's farm, he called two of THE MAN'S guards, and as the guard who was missing, was one of theirs, these men would like to find the people who killed him, No1 was sure that the guard was no longer alive, "I want you to go to this teachers farm, and find out if he had anything to do with this incident, if he's there, find out what he knows, if not, search the house for anything relating to this place, but be careful we have no knowledge of this man's background, but I think he may be ex military so be wary.

David woke with start, not knowing what had woken him, he looked at the beautiful vision beside him, "That's what woke me," he decided "How lucky am I, she looks better than Julia Roberts (pretty woman) just then a awful racket came from outside, the geese were going mad, David shook Chloe awake "Get up quick we have visitors!" they both jumped out of bed "Tidy up the bed," they remade the bed as if no one had been sleeping,

"Why are we doing this?" she asked, David led her down the corridor "They will be looking for us, but when they come in we will not be here, and it will look as if we have never been here,"

"But we have guns we can kill them," David looked at her in amazement, just a few hours ago she was a marine biologist, now she's a killer, he led her to a cupboard at the end of the passage, he pulled the cupboard towards him and the whole thing just came away from the wall, he pushed her inside and down some steps, and she found herself in David's gym, "Wow!" she exclaimed her eyes popping out, "What a place,"

"Come on," he said, pulling her towards a door at the back, "No time to admire things," they found themselves outside behind the farmhouse, they made their way to where the geese were still making a noise, David had picked up the night vision goggles on the way out, and he saw two men approach the house, both had weapons trained on the door, one of them used a probe and expertly opened the door, then they both charged in, their weapons ready , David waited, with Chloe getting more frustrated,

"Why don't we just take them out?" David shook his head

"I've created a monster," he said to himself, "Just be quiet, we don't want to let on that it was us who got into their place and killed one of their men, this is just a scouting party trying to find out if in fact it was me, after the episode on the cliff the other day, I'm probably their only suspect," they made their way to where the men's vehicle was parked,

"Shall we let their tyres down," this time David smiled

"No we will not, we let them go back and report that they found nothing suspicious" the two men came out of the house, returned to the vehicle, and drove off, Chloe recognised one of the men as the blond one from her encounter whilst running the other day, they made their way back into the house Chloe making her way to David's secret gym, David grabbed her and dragged her back into the bedroom "Let's leave all that until the morning, I've built up an appetite,"

Back at the site, the two guards were giving their account of their findings, but neither could shed any light on if it was in fact the teacher, as the house was empty and a search of the place just confirmed that he was, just a teacher and a farmer, No1 dismissed them, and told himself to find out more about this mysterious teacher.

31
Monday

Early Monday morning, the four fishing boats were making their way out of the harbour, when they passed a large yacht coming in. They had to make a small detour as the yacht was taking up a lot of harbour space, the fishing boats finally made their way out, and would not be back for at least four days, depending on their catch.

The yacht moored up at the small jetty, where one of the Range Rovers was waiting, four men with large duffle bags exited the Yacht and climbed into the car, these were the extra guards G1 had asked for, the car moved off, and the yacht set sail at once, the whole operation took just five minutes, on the way back to the site the men did not speak at all, the four had been given strict orders not to talk to anyone except G1.

When they reached the site, G1 met them, and told them what he suspected No1 was up to, he deployed the men to different duties making sure one of THE MAN'S guards kept an eye on No1 at all times.

No1 came into the guard's room his face looked like thunder, "What's the meaning of the extra men you have just picked up?" he demanded "I did not ask for any extra man power!"

G1 replied "We have just lost one of our men; we do not want to lose any others, so I asked for extra guards, what's the problem?" No1 just shrugged and left.

He went to find his No2 "We may have a problem"

"What sort of problem?"

"I just found out THE MAN has sent four more of his men," they walked towards his office "We may have to alter the plan when the time comes," No2 looked worried

"You don't think he has got wind of our plans do you?" he asked worriedly

"Hopefully not, but we will have to be a bit more careful how we implement it, also we may have to do something about our town Mayor, he sounded very jittery on the phone this morning, I feel he may be getting cold feet, I think you will have to go to town this morning, to set his mind at rest, that it would not be in his interest to think about abandoning this project, at this moment in time, and to persuade him to keep to our agreement.

32
Monday

The Mayor of San Juliet, Peter Steinbach, had trouble focusing this morning, after the early call from the man at the site; he had a light breakfast, and decided this thing was getting a bit too dangerous for his liking. At the beginning, he just had to supply dossiers on all the people living on the Island, now he was being asked about possible killings, he reminded himself that he was being paid a lot of money to keep the Islanders sweet, but when you hear about bullets being fired, and men getting killed, one day they may decide to come after me? Steinbach had a small cruiser tied up in a boathouse just up from the harbour "I think it's about time for me to take a little holiday," he said to himself, he shouted out to his wife "Pack a few things by lunch time!" his wife came into the room,

"Are we going somewhere?" she asked

"Yes, I'm taking you away for a few days, to the mainland," his wife looked a bit puzzled,

"But we never go away this time of the year; In fact we never go away?" Steinbach put his jacket on and walked out saying,

"Don't argue, just do it, and be ready by 12 noon, I'll pick you up then," He left the house, and started to walk to his office, his wife could not believe, that her husband had spoken like that,

"Whatever has come over him?" she thought to herself, as she started to put a few things together.

The Mayor walked down the road very briskly, wanting to get there before Susan came in. It was still quite early, so he had plenty of time to arrange things, and to retrieve his money from the safe, get their passports, and to arrange a transfer from his bank on the mainland, to their new place that he had already brought, with some of the money the Tall Man had given him, in all he had received, $200 000 dollars, plus the money in the safe, a further $100 000, "That's plenty," he thought to himself, with his own savings, they could live a life of luxury in Israel, Peter said to himself "I'm finally going home,"

He opened the office and went straight to his safe, taking the money out, he decided to count it one more time, a lot of people on

100

the Island knew he was a very miserly man, he never joined in anything, except if it was going to benefit him, and never if it involved spending his own money, in fact, he was quite a wealthy man even before he came to the Island, but no one knew how he amassed his money, but most knew, he had a lot of it.

Susan entered to office bang on time, she was a very punctual person, and a very dedicated one as well, especially to her fellow Islanders. She sat at her desk, and started to sort out some paperwork. Looking up, she suddenly jumped, for there in his office was the Mayor, and at this time in the morning, she could not believe it, he had beaten her in, he never showed his face until at least ten, she knocked on the office door, walking in she asked if he was okay "Yes, Thank you Sue," he replied with a smile on his face, although it was a false one! "I needed some papers very urgently this morning, but I'm okay now,"

Susan went back to her desk, and carried on what she was doing, but keeping one eye on what the Mayor was doing "Something's up," she said to herself.

Peter Steinbach was not a very brave man, but then again he was not afraid of a little conflict, he had not made it big in business, without being a bit rough, and unscrupulous, he looked at his watch it was now ten, time for his morning walk to the diner for his breakfast, he was not particularly hungry, but he thought he should keep up the pretence that everything was as normal.

Once the Mayor had left, Susan picked up the phone and rang Sean, and related what had gone on, Sean dismissed it, suggesting that Steinbach really did have to get in early for some reason, as he had just seen him walk pass, on the way to the diner, "I'll tell you what," he said "I'll walk down there myself for a cup of tea, and try to have a conversation with him, and see if I can find out anything!" Susan put down the phone, but was still afraid that something bad was going to happen.

33
Monday

David woke up for the second time on this Monday morning, but this time is all he could see, and think of, was the girl laying beside him, her dark hair was covering half her face, he gently pulled it to one side, "How can something so beautiful, be in my bed," Chloe opened one eye, but quickly shut it again as David leant down to kiss her cheek, just as he moved in for the kiss Chloe quickly turned her head so as the kiss was on the lips, and not the cheek,

"So much better on that spot!" she said. Then just fell into one another's arms.

One hour later they were in the shower together, another hour went by until breakfast was served, "We must get into town as soon as possible," uttered David, with a mouth full of bacon, Chloe looked at David with a peculiar stare

"So how come it took you so long getting ready," with a terrible grin on her face.

On the way to town, they again passed the site of the killing "Can we stop," she asked, David pulled over, and let her go to the cliff edge by herself, after about ten minutes she came back with a look on her face that said volumes about her intensions towards those responsible, without another word, she just said "Let's go," They arrived in town to find Sean coming out of the diner,

"Ah! I have news for you," he exclaimed,

"And we have news for you," replied Chloe. Chloe and Sean walked back together towards the pub.

David went into the diner to see his dog, Shep. He had a cup of tea, spent a few minutes playing with him, and then he walked to the pub to join the others. Once inside they exchanged their news, Sean could not believe what the two of them were telling him,

"A submarine, are you sure?" David looked at him

"Yes! I'm sure, believe or not I do know what a submarine looks like, I saw Ice Station Zebra, with Rock Hudson!" Mary looked at him,

"What the hell is a Rock Hudson?" Sean stopped the exchange

"Never mind about what they were doing at that place all those years ago? We want to know what's going on up there now." David and Chloe exchanged looks,

"We did not get to see much, so cannot think of anything, we have both searched our minds but have come up with zilch," they discussed the matter at length, and in the end decided they needed to contact the authorities on the mainland, but who and what do they say,

"Excuse me! We have reason to believe, that something funny is going on here on our Island, but we don't know what? But we do have a WW2 submarine," said Sean. We have to find some real proof somehow, before we can get any sort of help," they decided to round up the others for a council of war.

34
Monday

The Mayor left the diner, and made his way back to his office, adamant, that the course he was considering, was the right one, he had to get off this Island, before those men, especially the fat one.

He walked into the office and called Susan over "I'll be gone for the rest of the day," he told her,

"Is there anything I can help you with Sir," she asked

"No I'm fine, I just have to do something that will take a few hours," Susan started to return to her desk, when the Mayor called out "Sue! Why don't you take the rest of the day off and close the office, there's nothing that cannot wait until tomorrow, so go and enjoy yourself," Sue could not believe that he had said that, as he never took a day off,

"Thank you!" she replied, ten minutes later as she was leaving the office, she saw the Mayor take a large briefcase out of his safe, and gave a furtively look around, but luckily she was out of sight.

Sue hurriedly ran down to the pub to report to Sean, and whoever else was there.

Peter Steinbach who was no longer the Mayor, walked out of his office, for to his mind, the very last time, he gave a very nostalgic look back, "All these years wasted, now I'm going home to Israel," he hurried towards the boathouse.

Back at Peter's house, his wife was doing a bit of ironing trying to decide what to take on their impromptu holiday, when a knock at the door interrupted her "Who could that be," she said to herself "We never get visitors," she opened the door to find a gentleman she had never seen before "Can I help you?" she asked

"Yes," said the Fat Man "I'm sorry to call unannounced, but I was hoping to talk with the Mayor," looking into the house he could see bags packed in the hallway "I see you're off somewhere," he stated

"Yes, we are just going on a little holiday," she replied

"How nice, is the Mayor here?"

"I'm sorry but you have missed him, he went to the office, then he was going to the boathouse to make ready our boat, for our trip," the man sighed

"Oh! What a shame, as it's rather important, could you point me in the direction of this boathouse I promise I won't keep him long,"

Thanking the Mayor's wife, the Fat Man made his way to where The Mayor had his boat moored.

The mayor was just putting the finishing touches to his preparations, when a voice came from behind him "Are we going somewhere?" Peter jumped, recognising the voice, turning rather to suddenly, he nearly fell over, "Here let me help you," demanded the man, grabbing hold of his arms with a grip that was like a vice, "We wouldn't want you to get hurt would we," in a tone that left nothing to the imagination "This is a very nice boat, it's yours I take it?" Peter by this time was shaking with fear

"I had a day off, so I decided to give the old girl a cleanup," he stuttered,

"That's very nice, and there was me, thinking you were getting ready to leave, but then again, you wouldn't think of deserting your responsibilities would you," pulling him away from the boat "It's such a lovely thing," he pushed Peter to the floor, and pulled out a very large gun from under his arm "I haven't fired this thing for a very long time pointing it at Peter's head, all of a sudden he turned and put four bullets into the engine, "Oh dear the thing just went off," Peter by this time was thinking this was his last day on earth, the Fat Man sat down beside Peter "Now Mr Mayor, you remember our little arrangement don't you, keep us informed of any activity on this Island that could be detrimental to our operation, you do remember that don't you?" Peter was sure he felt something running down his leg,

"Of course I would never abandon my obligations," the Fat Man patted his cheek,

"Oh! By the way I met your wife earlier, but she did not look to well after I left, mind you being tied to a chair and a hot iron near the side of your face would upset most people," Peter tried to get up,

"If you've hurt her I'll kill you, and you're Boss,"

"Yes, of course you would, but things do not have to come to that, just keep us informed, and do not divulge anything about us to anyone, and we all live happy ever after," with that the Fat Man picked up the Mayor's briefcase "You get this back when the operation is over, along with the rest of your payment," as he walked out of the boathouse not looking back..

Peter the one time Mayor, rushed home, ran through the house shouting his wife's name, "What's all the clatter for," his wife called, walking out of the bedroom, Peter could not believe his eyes he looked at her in such a way that she felt frightened "Whatever is the matter with you?" she asked. Peter sat her down and asked her about the man who called "Oh! That man, he seemed very nice, he said he wanted to talk to you, so sent him to your office, and told him if you were not there you would be at the boathouse getting our boat ready for our trip, he was very polite,"

35
Monday

David left the pub, and started to walk back to the diner, Chloe stayed at the pub to get changed, and as he walk down the road, he noticed a Range Rover and a man getting into it, the man said good morning, and David returned the pleasantry; he carried on walking, looking back at the car "It looks like one of the Marine lot's car, but without the sign writing on it," he put it out of his head for the moment, and looked forward to taking Shep back to the farm, although he knew he would have to return later for a full war council.

Shep and David arrived back at the farm to be greeted by a man, a very tall man, "Sorry to stop by unannounced," said the man, "But I understand that we are neighbours, I'm Professor Green from the State Marine site," holding out his hand, David took the proffered hand with trepidation, realising that this is the tall man from the site,

"Hello! I'm David Croft and this is my dog Shep," the tall man bent down to stroke the dog, but the hackles on the dogs back came up and a small growl came from within his throat,

"He's not too sure about strangers," said David patting the dog to calm him down "What can I do for you?" asked David, the Tall Man did not seem comfortable with his next question,

"We had a bit of trouble at the site last night, and I wondered if you heard anything, or saw anything suspicious?" David was not too sure how to answer, surmising that the man must by now, know that he was not at home last night,

"Sorry! But we spent last night in town," David did not emphasize further on the matter, The Tall Man who called himself a Professor replied,

"Not to worry, It was only that my men have seen you running near our fence line, and seeing as your farm is so close, you might have seen or heard something," he once again held his hand out "I wish you good day Sir, and I'm sure our paths will cross again," he said this last bit with more intensity than it should have been, David was sure it was said as a warning,

"I'm sure it will," taking his hand.

David could not help but notice that the Range Rover he was driving did not have any writing on it, just like the one in town earlier "That's odd," Come on Shep let's go and feed the animals.

36
Four days earlier

The DEA man James, and Captain Morella, were in Cartagena's harbourmasters office, going through all the sailings of the last week "Do all these ships have facilities for cargo?" Asked James,

"Yes most of them do, but seeing as this is only a small port, if any large shipment had been loaded, I would have known about it, and it would not normally go from here,"

Morella asked "If not this port where would you suggest we look?" the man pondered a bit and finally said,

"Cali or Barranquilla, those are the two major container ports, and would be the most likely ones, as they are large enough for your shipment to be loaded without being seen," The two men thanked the master, and started out of the office, the harbourmaster called after them "When you have the name of the ship we can find it, as you know all ships have trackers on them," the two men left, with a armful of document pertaining to the previous sailing.

Back in their temporary office, they went through all the information they possessed "I don't like saying this, but this has been a wild goose chase," the captain agreed with him

"So what do you propose we do?" James was just going to answer when the phone broke into his thoughts,

"Yes!" answered Morella

"This is Durrell,"

"I hope you have something for me!" said the Captain with a little desperation in his voice,

"I have something that should, cheer you up," Morella put the phone on speaker, they could hear Durrell tapping away on his computer "I do not have the name of the ship so far, but we have had a report in from the Columbian Army, a Major who led a raid on a large farm near Bucaramanga, they set fire to all the fields and rounded up all the workers, and the men belonging to the local cartel," the Captain cut in,

"And how does that help us stuck up here?"

"I'm coming to that, when they entered the warehouse where they had estimated tons of cocaine was being stored, is all they found was a few hundred pounds of the stuff, the majority of it was missing," Durrell took a breath, Morella and the DEA man James, looked at each other,

"Go on,"

Durrell carried on "Well this is the best part, the cartels top man had set fire to all of the paper work, but the Major managed to retrieve a small portion of one piece, and a very important piece it turned out to be, there was a note saying that the shipment should be ready by a certain date, and transported to Barranquilla, a port up north," the two men looked at each other and smiled,

"We're on our way!" the captain shouted down the phone,

"Wait there's more, the Major is at the moment interrogating a very high up member of the gang, and seeing that the Army's method of interrogating is not recognised by the Geneva convention, I'm pretty sure we will be finding out a lot more," the phone went dead, the two men packed up their stuff, and made their way to the airport.

Sgt Durrell put the phone down, and picked up another one, this time, one given him by an anonymous person, "They are heading for the port,"

The man on the other end of the phone smiled "Senor Cordova," he called out, Juan Luis Cordova looked up "That was the police sergeant, everything is going to plan Sir," Juan peered out of the grimy window onto an airfield that had seen better days,

"Good," he replied.

37
Two days earlier Columbia

The DEA man James and the Captain were getting nowhere with their inquiries, they had been in touch with the local police chief, and talked to many informers, but to no avail. All they had discovered was that a large shipment had left, but no one could say what, or when it had gone. The Captains phone started ringing "Hope this is better news than the previous," he shouted down the phone,

"I can assure you this is brilliant news," the Captain again put the phone on speaker,

"Go ahead,"

"We have had an informer come forward from the docks, the Barranquilla docks, with information about a container being loaded onto a ship last week,"

"And what did this man tell you," asked Morella

"He would not tell me over the phone, he wants to meet, and he wants two thousand dollars" Durrell gave the captain the address and they left straight away for the meeting down near the docks.

Entering the dingy cafe that the Dockers used, they spied their man just as Durrell had described him, a forty odd with receding hair and a large nose, with a scar along his chin line, he looked a bit like a crook, in fact he properly was a crook, he was sitting down near the window, they introduced themselves, and discreetly handed the money over, the Dock worker would not give his name, but did give the vital information, James had a sound recorder going during the meet, so all was now on tape, they were thanking the man, when the cafe's window burst inwards covering them in glass, and the man in front of them falling to the floor with a hole in his head, James and the Captain threw themselves to the floor, drawing their guns. After a few minutes they peered out over the sill, but no more shots were fired, they finally stood up and went to the informer, but he was dead, they heard sirens howling in the distance "Quick let's make ourselves scarce, I do not want to answer stupid question for the rest of the day," they retrieved the money, and left both of them pondering what had just gone on.

Once back at their temporary headquarters, they played back the tape "I was on night duty loading a freighter due out on the first tide that morning, when I noticed something strange about one of the containers, it had what looked like air bags fitted onto the bottom of it, I asked someone what they were and a large man told me to mind my own business, they were being particularly careful of the loading, to me, it seemed as if they did not want to damage the bags, I did not take any more notice my shift was coming to an end," Morella turned the recording off, "What do you make of it?" he asked

"The only thing I can think of, is that it could be a floatation raft fitted at the bottom, so as it could be dropped over the side, and then towed into some lonely beach, or a small out of the way, port," the Captain looked puzzled,

"Surely a container with tons of cocaine inside it, would be much too heavy?" The DEA man was looking at a computer screen,

"Look here," James showed him, "As you can see the Navy have been perfecting a raft to rescue downed planes,"

They continued listening to the tape "It was not until I heard that there was some sort of reward for information on container ships, that I put two and two together, so rang a number, and spoke to a Sergeant Durrell, and he arranged this meeting," Morella hurried him along "The ships name was the Bellamaria, a freighter destined for Galveston Texas," Just then on the recording they heard the window break and bodies falling to the floor, the tape came to an end.

Both of them started to talk on their phones, both to their respective agencies.

James phoned his partner Robert, and filled him in to what they had discovered, Robert was a bit sceptical on what was being said "I'm sorry, but all this you are telling me, does not fit in to what I'm hearing down here,"

"What do mean?"

"There is no talk from any of our contacts, about a ship going the United States, or anywhere else for that matter, the stories or rumours we are hearing, is about a large shipment being transported,. But it does not sound as if this shipment is going by sea, it looks as if it's by another means, and the stories I have personally heard, is, it is being flown from here to the US," James could be heard digesting all this,

"I have been wondering the same thing," he said "At every turn we have been led to believe that this particular shipment is going by sea, but supposing this has all been a smoke screen, diverting our attention from the real transporting mode," James was about to end the call when Robert stopped him "That raid you told me about involving the Columbian Army,"

"What about it?" James could hear Robert moving paper around,

"There was a raid, and yes, the fields were burnt down, but no prisoners were taken, in fact the farm was completely empty of personnel," James could not believe what he was hearing, all this time they were being led, firstly to one port, then to another, then a mysterious informer tells us about a ship being loaded with a special container, then this informer is shot just after telling us the name of the ship, "Robert find out as much as you can about this Sgt Durrell of the Columbian police force, the one we met the other day, I think there is something fishy about him,"

At the DEA headquarters in Virginia they were alerting all the ports, and the coast guards along the southern coast, and the war ships patrolling the Caribbean Sea and the Gulf of Mexico.

Over at Langley the CIA were having trouble with the suspected assassin in the country, they knew about a top ranking officer assassinated in London, but now they had a General from their own forces, found murdered in Maine, on the east coast, and it looked like the work of the same assassin, they were now trying to find a link between this murder, and the one in London, and as they had no mandate to operate in the United States, they had to call in the FBI for their help, so the two agencies who were notoriously competitive and normally would not share information, started to work together. And now all the Agencies were at work, and unknown to each other, or to themselves, they were all involved in what was going on, on a Forgotten Island, off the coast of California.

38
Monday

Abdul Abdullah (aka) Assa Abdullah El Sin, was making his way to the north of the Island, to the stables run by the parson, who was also a horse breeder and trainer, to look at a couple of thoroughbred horses that were coming up for sale, by being an equine agent for a Saudi prince, it enabled him to travel all over the world without any trouble, he was in fact a very capable equine agent, he knew a lot about horses having been an agent for nigh on three years, and was now respected all over the race horse fraternity, for his knowledge and his professionalism.

Abdul appraised the two animals he had come to see, and was so impressed that he purchased both of them on behalf of the prince, after completing the paper work, he made his way back to town, passing a Range Rover on the side of the road, the men from the car seemed to be putting telegraph masts up, he pushed it to the back of his mind, but vowed to mention it to the pub landlord at the meeting.

He let his mind wander on the drive back to his time in London, where he had assassinated the man responsible for the destruction of his school, then here, in the United States just a week ago, the other military man, who was also responsible, was murdered, both men were blown up just like his two boys were, but this time the two men knew what was coming. both men were tied to a chair with a explosive device attached underneath and both were told why they were being killed, they both pleaded for their lives saying that the target was not the school but a known Taliban leader, but the pleas fell on deaf ears, is all Abdul could see in front of him, we're the men who pressed the button that sent that missile to his village, and to his school, Abdul had killed a lot of bad people, but in the back of his mind these two men were not bad people, just the ones who killed his beloved boys.

It had taken a long time to find the names of the commanders of that ill fated operation; he had had to do numerous assignments without pay for the Afghan intelligence agency, for them to find the information he craved for. When at last he had all he needed, he set about this one last assignment. Then he promised himself he would return to teaching.

He reached the town and all the thoughts were put aside, and all the present day's thoughts were now in front, and he was ready to do whatever he could to help these people, as it felt so good to be doing something nice for a change, he walked into the pub, the rest of them were there.

David was talking to Chloe and they seemed rather engrossed, Sean was behind the bar pouring drinks, Daren and Scott were sitting at one of the tables and Sean's wife was talking to the girl from the Mayor's office.

"Would you like a drink" asked Sean pouring a beer,

"I thank you Mr Sean, but alas, I am not permitted to drink alcohol, but a small glass of juice would do fine,"

They all sat down, and started to collate all the information, once they had it all put together, they realised that they did not have any real prove, that something was going on their Island, that was illegal, except for the men with guns who decided to shoot at two intruders who had broken into a secure facility without permission, when put like this, the likely hood would be, David and Chloe being charged with unlawful entry.

"Tell us about this submarine you found," asked Scott, his face alight with wonder, David told the whole tale once again, explaining how he thought the submarine had been hidden since 1945.

The meeting came to an end with not a lot of progress, except for David coming up with an idea that would involve Sean's Grandson Joe. So he put this to Sean, and he agreed to it with some reservations, "You will have to run it pass Julie first," he said "And promise he will not be put in harm's way,"

Once outside, David asked Abdul how his meeting went with Mr O'Brian the towns Pastor, "Yes! Really good, I purchased both his horses, one of them should be ready to ship in about four months time, the other in a few days," David not knowing anything about horses, did not understand the time lag, but then again, David was afraid of horses. As a young lad growing up on a farm in England he was bitten by a horse, and now had an uncontrollable fear of them. So he turned the conversation to another subject. He explained his idea in as much detail as he could, Abdul looked impressed

"That's a really good plan; I hope the boy will do it,"

They got to the diner, and David ordered a tea, and Abdul had a black coffee, David first spoke to Julie before asking Joe, Julie was not happy with the idea of her son being in a situation, that could put Joe in harm's way, she rang her dad, and after a short discussion, decided she would leave it up to her son to decide.

Joe he was so enthusiastic about the idea, he wanted to go straight away.

They collected the things they would need, and David and Joe jumped onto the buggy, while Abdul went to retrieve his car, saying that he would meet them at the far end of town, they went their different ways. David starting up the buggy and moving off, not noticing a man sitting on a motorbike not a hundred yards away, the same man who had been hidden near the pub for most of the day, the man took out his phone and made a call, "He's on his way back, but he has a small boy with him," the person on the other end said,

"It can't be helped," the phone went dead,, the man started up the bike, and made his way back towards the site, the bike as silent as ever, without noticing, Abdul driving past, to meet up with David and Joe just outside of town.

39
Monday

As they came to the farm David got off the buggy to open the gate, and heard the geese making a racket, he looked around and motioned Abdul to come over "Something's not right," he said in a whisper, Abdul skirted around, and hidden in a small wood, was a motorbike the engine still warm,

"You have uninvited visitors," he said, coming back with the news of the bike, David put Joe in the car, and drove it down the road out of sight,

"Stay there," telling him to hide himself in the back "Do not move until we return," Joe looked a bit scared,

"Suppose you don't come back?"

David smiled "Don't worry I'll be back," remembering Arnold Schwarzenegger in the film, Terminator. David turned to Abdul, "As far as they know, I'm by myself. There can only be two of them, remembering, they came by bike, we can get into the house by a secret passage I had built a long time ago, and where there are a couple of guns we took, from the guard we killed, "Do you know how to handle guns?"

Abdul acted a little dumb "Yes, a little, I was in the army a long time ago,"

"Good let's go," they moved with care both men adapt at concealment, David was surprised at the fluency of Abdul's movements; he put it to the back of his mind. They managed to get to the entrance of the tunnel, the same tunnel that he, and Chloe, had exited just this morning; coming into David's gym they retrieved the weapons they had liberated from the site's guard, David taking the knife, Abdul the pistol "Do you want this," asked Abdul holding up the gun,

"No! You have it," they made their way to the secret door, David looking through a small hole, the same sort of peephole you get on outside doors, he did not see anyone near, so gently pushing the cupboard forward, it moved without a sound, David had already explained the layout of the house, so Abdul went to the left through

117

the bedroom, David made his way to the front, where he imagined the men would be waiting, Abdul made his way through the bedroom, to another door that led to the kitchen, he gently pulled the door towards him, when it crashed into him, knocking him off his feet, he rolled to one side trying to get the gun up, but a kick to the head stopped him, luckily he had just managed to turn his head slightly, so the blow was not to serious, he shot his legs up in a sweeping motion, and caught the man just below the knees, the man stumbled, but came back and aimed his gun at Abdul's now exposed body, Abdul saw his two son's as he waited for the shot that would end his life, when the man collapsed onto the floor with a knife sticking out from his neck. Abdul swiftly rolled over, as he heard the second man run into the room, the gun in his hand, started spitting out a deadly stream of bullets, the man was sent back with most of the bullets hitting his body armour, but one lucky bullet catching him in the throat. The house became quiet. Abdul turned and saw David pull his knife out of the man's neck, "Thanks!" he said, David and Abdul surveying the damage. They stripped the two men of their guns, and armour, and disposed of their bodies over a cliff behind the house, they tidied up before going back up the track to retrieve their vehicles, and Joe, who by this time, must have been going out of his mind.

Once back in the house, they went through their next step, "You realise that this is going to alert the people up there, that their cover is exposed," expressed Abdul

"We'll have to warn the others, about what went down here," replied David,

Abdul stood up "I'll go back to town and do that," David took them through the cupboard into the gym, and rummaged about in a large box, eventually coming up with something wrapped up in a stained cloth,

"This has not seen daylight for three and half years!" he stated

"What is it?" asked Joe, David gently unwrapped it, and to their surprise it looked like a bird,

"It's a bird," exclaimed Joe

"Yes, but not an ordinary bird," taking the covering off completely "It's a drone,"

Abdul nearly choked on the drink he was drinking, he could not believe what he was seeing, the bird was exactly the same bird that the lad in his village described to him, all those years ago, "This cannot be," he thought to himself "Not David," although in the back of his mind, he thought it was David, that he had come to this Island to kill, for the slaughter of his two boys. He still could not believe it, "Where did you get that?" asked Abdul

"It was made by a man I knew a long time ago, he was a genius at making things that worked," David replied, Abdul could no longer stay in the same room, with man who was responsible for his Children's death, he excused himself, and walked out saying,

"I'll go and warn the others!" David was taken aback by Abdul's quick exit, and shouted out,

"Don't you want to hear my plan?" but Abdul had already left, they heard a car start up and move off, "How strange!" David thought to himself.

Abdul could not think straight on the drive back to town, he looked at the speedometer, and realised he was going much too fast, he pulled over onto the side of the road, he got out of the car and sat on the grass for at least half an hour, trying to make sense of what had just unfolded. At last he got back in the car and carried on into town, still not having digested the full impact of his friend David, being the one who had killed his darling boys.

Back at the farm David had shown Joe the workings of the drone, and were now testing it, he had wanted Joe to fly the drone, as he had never flown one before, it had taken a long time for the bird who David called (Arnold Mark Two) to be charged up, so they scouted the perimeter fence that was not too far away from David's place, until they found a suitable place to fly the bird from. David would have liked to fly the bird from a longer distance away, but the range of the bird was not that great, once they had found a safe place, they went back to the farm to practice Joe's flying skills, and as it turned out, Joe was a natural, even better than the man who had made the drone, David's one time partner Sean Junior and Joe's Dad.

Abdul was in the pub telling Sean what had happened at the farm, "We need help now," said Sean,

"I don't think that would be a good idea," said Abdul "These people, at the moment, have no idea who is behind the killing of their men, let's keep it that way until we have more to go on," Sean thought about Abdul's reasoning

"No! We need to get help now," replied Sean, "I'll go to Peter the town's Mayor, to request help, but I'm not too sure if we can trust him?" Abdul did not know what to say, so decided to say nothing; he did not want any law enforcement officers coming to the Island just yet, not until his work is done, but he was still trying to work out what he was going to do about the man who killed his Boy's, David.

Sean made up his mind "I'll go see the Mayor," and started for the door,

"Wait," shouted Abdul, Sean stopped and turned

"What?"

"I forgot to mention this at the meeting, I saw men this morning, putting some sort of poles up, and they were all in one of those Range Rovers from the site," Sean did not know what to make of it,

"We'll talk about when I come back," he walked out leaving Abdul alone with his thoughts.

David and Joe, were hidden in a clump of bushes, on a small rise that gave them a view of the restricted area, it was not a very good view, but enough they would be able to see Arnold quite clearly "Let's do it," Joe settled himself down, as Arnold flew over the fence with David glued to the screen on his laptop, every now and again, giving Joe instructions on where to fly, the bird only had a short flying time, so after about fifteen minutes, Joe brought Arnold home, they packed up their things, and made their way back to the farm.

Once back at the farm, they connected the laptop to the TV, and reviewed the footage they had managed to obtain, David could not believe what he was seeing, "We have to get this to the others, and work out what it all means," they packed everything away, jumped on David's buggy, and roared off to show the others the footage.

Sean walked over to the Mayor's office, but it was closed, "That's funny," he said out loud. He walked back to the pub to find Abdul deep in thought, Abdul suddenly looked up,

"That was quick," he said. Sean picked up his phone to ring Susan,

"Great, he's taken the day off," Putting the phone down, "You were deep in thought when I walked in, anything I can help you with?" asked Sean. Abdul did not know how to approach the subject so he just came out with it,

"Up at the farm and on the cliff top, David did not act like a typical teacher, or a farmer, was in the military at some time?" Sean looked up at the picture on the wall behind the bar, and tried to decide what to tell this man, who he did not really know. He finally decided that David had shown the people around him, that he was more than just a teacher, so answered the question

"Yes he was, but he does not want people to know, it was a long time ago, and something happened that he was not proud of, so he left it all behind, and started a new life here, on the Island, to forget what happened, and before you ask, I don't know what went on for him to make that decision, but I do know, that it involved my Boy, Sean Junior," pointing to the photo.

Abdul decided to leave it there, he did not want to give any reason for Sean to be suspicious, by prying too much, but he now knew that David was the man who he, Abdul Abdullah, had sworn to kill.

Sean started to go out the door again "I'm going to see the Mayor at his house," he said walking out, the Mayors house was just on the outskirts of the town, walking up the pathway to the house, Sean could not help but notice the curtains were drawn, and the place looked deserted, he knocked on the door and called out the Mayors name "Peter are you there?" no reply, he knocked again, still no reply, Sean walked round the back of the house in case he was in the garden , the back of the house was the same as the front, curtains pulled and a deserted look "I wonder where he could be?" Sean started to walk away when he was sure he saw the curtains move in the upstairs bedroom, he shrugged it away and started to walk towards the boathouse where he knew Peter kept his boat.

Upstairs, Peter and his wife were looking out as Sean walked away," Why are we hiding from our friends?" asked his wife

"I'll tell you later, just keep all the things you packed away handy, as we might have to leave in a hurry very shortly,"

Sean got to boathouse, but could not see anyone around, the boathouse door was open, so Sean gently pushed it fully open, and with all that was going on he did not want to take any chances so decided to shout out "Hello is anyone there?" no reply, he slowly entered his senses fully alert, he called out again, Still no reply, He had been in similar situations as a boy in Ireland, so still being very careful he walked all the way in, thank goodness there was no one around, he saw the Mayor's boat tied up to the jetty and walked over to it, it was then that he saw that the engine had been completely destroyed by bullets, he shut the door, and made his way back home,

121

ready to tell the rest of them that their suspicion of the town's Mayor, were fully founded.

Sean walked into his place with a very worried look on his face, "What's wrong?" asked David who had just walked into the pub himself, Sean told them what he had found out at the Mayors house, and at the boathouse,

"He's in this up to his scrawny neck," stated Scott, who had joined them, "I never trusted that German," They waited until Darren joined them, before David gave a full account of what he and Joe had found out, David played the video for them all to see for themselves, once it had came to an end, they all started to talk at the same time "Whoa!" said David "Let's take a minute to reason this all out in a constructive way, not all shouting at the same time,"

The video showed that the site was being getting ready, for a plane to land, the runway was covered in what David thought was trees and bushes, but when the bird flew lower, he could see that these were just dummies, were removable objects, that could be moved aside and the runway would be completely usable for a large plane to land, in fact, the flying bird even picked out landing lights, "They are definitely getting ready to have a plane land there, and by the looks of things, in the very near future," said David summing up,

"What on earth can they be expecting," asked Darren, who had a small suspicion of his own,

"It could be a number of things," said David who seemed to have taken charge of the proceedings, and taken charge of the whole operation, Chloe entered the bar area from upstairs.

"You seem to know a lot about all these things," said Darren, "You're not just a teacher, are you?"

With all that was going on, on their tranquil Island at the moment, David thought, that now was the time to come clean, about who he was, and about his past, and also what he was doing on St Juliet, and how he became a part of the Island's life.

Sean knew that David was in fact an ex soldier, and served with his Son, but did know all the details, so he was intrigued as to what David was about to reveal, if in fact he was going to reveal anything at all, Sean, and his wife Mary, were like family to David, so now seemed the perfect time to tell them about their son Sean Junior, his Army Buddy,

David stood up "No, I'm not even a teacher, I falsified the certificates that stated, I was a qualified teacher, in fact I was a member of the British SAS, an elite part of the British armed forces, and a member of your elite force, Delta. That was where I met Sean and Mary's son, Sean Junior. We were partners, and did many secret operations together, until the last one, where unfortunately Junior lost his life," Mary gasped out loud and put her hand over her mouth, Sean put his arm around her, they both new that Junior was dead, but now out of this man's mouth has come the total realisation that he was in fact, dead! "I think it would be a good idea if you asked Julie to join us for this part of my confession," said David with a look of utter discomfort.

Julie came in, and David steeled himself to relate something that had remained dormant in his brain, for three and a half years. And now after all this time, he was about to get some sort of closure on his violent past, and closure on his guilt, at leaving his best mate in the hands of the vicious Taliban, in that village, in Afghanistan.

Chloe could see that David was not ready to do this, but now was not the time to stop him, he looked ready to tell all, so she went and stood next to him, and put her hand on his, and that helped David to carry on, he took a large breath and started to talk.

"It was the last op we did together, we had to assassinate the Taliban leader, Ali Masood El Jaffa, but it turned out bad, my partner Sean did not make it out. And the aftermath was so bad, that I could not, or would not touch, a firearm again, and up to now I have not had to use one,"

No one said anything, just waited for him to carry on,

"We were inserted into Afghanistan a week before our target was due to be at this spot, we knew it was going to be one of the toughest assignments of our life, but we had never failed in all the ops we have been involved in, and had no qualms about the success of this one. There were just the two of us, we were both fluent in Arabic, and with our beards, and clothes, we fitted in quite well, we had set up the hit well before the due date. When the Intel came through the target was on his way, I was posted just on the outskirts of the village, and Junior (that was his call sign) was at the militants, compound, it was heavily guarded, so we knew there was no way we could get anywhere near the target vehicles, so we had the idea to use a drone, the drone idea was Sean's, and it was designed by him, it looked and flew just like a pigeon, and it was so authentic, you could not tell the difference unless really close up, we were to use the bird to drop a homing device onto the target vehicle, it resembled Poo. It was a compound with magnetic components in it that would help it to adhere to the vehicle, and small transmitters to guide the missile this would enable command to identify the correct vehicle, so the guided missile that was to be deployed from outside the area, could, and would, hit it with unbelievable accuracy. These missiles were a hundred percent, as long as the target had been targeted correctly, so we had to make sure that this was the case, the planning and execution of the op, had to be done fast, and without detection,"

David had to stop for a while to collect his thoughts, and compose his self, this was the first time he had related the details to anyone, outside the military.

He carried on "Three vehicles entered the village from the East, and drove directly to the compound, once the vehicles were inside, the heavy gates were shut, and extra armed guards were posted, this leader was wanted by a lot of countries, so our job was vital. Sean was deployed high up with a view of the compound, not a good view, as he could not get any closer, but it would do. Once the target entered the building, Sean flew the bird, (Sean had named him Arnold,) The bird flew well, Sean had spent hours flying him back at camp, Arnold did a couple of fly over's, and even joined other birds flying about, when he was satisfied no guards were noticing an extra bird flying, he swooped Arnold low over the vehicles, and then back onto a nearside roof, everything was going to plan, but as everyone knows, plans can go wrong, Arnold again swooped down over the vehicles, Sean could see all this on the well disguised monitor that looked like a book, as Arnold passed over the first one Sean bombed it, then he moved to the second and third. Sean settled Arnold onto the roof of a nearby building away from the one he was in, but one where he could see the Arnold, plus his view of the compound,"

David took his time and had a sip of his tea that Mary had brought him.

"This is where it all started going wrong, Sean and I were in contact by radio, a totally secure one. The message came through.

"Junior calling Shepherd (Shepherd being my call sign) target sanctioned. It was my job to relay to command, when the sanctioned vehicles were leaving the village, we did not want the hit to take place where innocent people could be harmed, the village itself was a large one in fact here we would call it a town, the hit was to take place just outside, so as the ordinary people, and all insurgents, could see that wherever you are, you can be hit.

I acknowledged the call, and opened a secure contact with command, ready for the vehicles to pass my spot, then to order the strike, but it all comes down, to all other elements, to fall into place.

Sean was pleased with the performance of Arnold. He was just sitting there on the roof, with his camera on the three vehicles Parked in the compound. Sean knew, that the target vehicle the one with El Jaffa in it, would have to be bombed again, as like all convoys, the target always used different vehicles, so you never knew which one to target, and as all windows were blacked out, there was no way of knowing, unless you had eyes on.

The roof opposite was about one hundred yards away, so Sean could see Arnold quite clearly, he was ready for the bombing raid, (his words not mine) the target came out of the building and got into the last vehicle, Sean could see this with Arnolds camera. Then Sean flew Arnold over the vehicles, dropping the extra Poo onto the roof of the last one, this now had two droppings on it, and would be picked up by command, so as the correct vehicle could be targeted, job done! He relayed the information to me, and I instructed command of the success of the mission, so far, and to await confirmation, of vehicles passing my spot.

"This is Junior to Shepherd, vehicles en route, I repeat vehicles en route," the call came nice and clear, and precise, I waited for eyes on the vehicles, before sending call sign to launch missile. The missile would take ten minutes to target; I started to pack up my gear so as to make a quick exit, I did not want to be around when the explosion took place.

Sean had settled Arnold on the roof once more with eyes on the departure of Vehicles. That was when he sent the message. Sean was getting ready to fly Arnold to his nest, when he spotted a small boy of about ten years old, on the roof just behind Arnold, he could see that the boy was holding a large net with a long handle, he immediately realised what was going to happen, he had seen it before, kids or older people, trapping birds especially pigeons for food, Sean tried to get Arnold away before the boy could get to him, but to no avail, the boy had him in his net, Sean could see the boy inspect the bird,, he could also see the look of surprise on his face, then the boy looked up, and over, and unfortunately, Sean was in full view from the other roof, the boy went running to the stairs, Sean knew he had to get out fast, he called me and explained he had been compromised and was making a quick evac, Sean packed up quickly, and ran down the stairs, as he ran down he saw the boy gesturing to the armed men, and pointing to the building he was in, he ran faster knowing that it would be futile as there were still two floors to go, he made it to the door and peered out, and saw about twenty armed men with their guns trained on the door, and knew that this would be the same at the back door, he was trapped.

He called me up and explained what had gone wrong, and the last words he said were,

"I'm going to do a Butch Cassidy" OUT!"

By this time David had tears in his eyes, and Chloe could see that the memory of it all was so painful, she realised how much it had taken him, to tell this to a room full of people, especially Sean, Mary, and Julie, once again she held his hand.

David carried on talking, "How could this have happened, we had it planned down to the last detail, we had flown the bird five consecutive days, and every flight had been perfect, the bird had performed well, the plan was fool prove, but as our instructor always said, plans do go wrong, deal with it. As it turned out, not only did that go wrong, but the rest of the hit was compromised as well. But what came next was a lot worse that Sean getting killed, we both knew that at any time one of us was not going to make it, that was the nature of our work, and we knew that, and we accepted it without question

The three vehicles came into sight; the death of Sean was put aside. The mission had to be completed, there was no room for sentiment when on a mission, the hit had to be made, and command had to be informed.

The vehicles passed my position and at the same time, I made the call to launch.

Then the call came in, "Command calling Shepherd target acquired," command had launched.

"I never really heard target acquired, I was still thinking of my one true friend facing twenty terrorists.

(Ten minutes to target)

The vehicles carried on, and were just leaving the outskirts of the village, when it all started to go from bad to worse when I saw our target suddenly turn of the road they were on, it was now (five minutes to target) the vehicles raced up a side road, and pulled into the courtyard of a building, a building I knew quite well, as I had been in the same building previously, whilst reconnoitring the area, it was the local School, I quickly called up control, and explained what had happened, and appraise them that the target was secreted in the local school with young Children inside, so I shouted out "You have to Abort, the Mission has been compromised, Abort now!" (One minute) I shouted one more time "Abort, Abort," but no reply "I tried once more, then the missile struck, I felt the building shake."

"I knew that I had to get out, and get out fast, I ran; I did not need to see what I had done, as I knew how devastating these missiles were. I found our escape vehicle, and made it out of this godforsaken country, I will never got over that day, having to leave my best friend, and partner, to his fate in the hands of the Taliban, and for my part, in the slaughter, of innocent children, and the thought of the Taliban leader AL Jaffa, entering that school, knowingly using the children as hostages, It was the worst day of my life, I will never get rid of the guilt I feel every day, the memory will stay in my head until the day I die,"

David was exhausted, Chloe put her arms around him trying to comfort him and to let him know that she was there for him; the others were all just sitting there trying to digest what they had just heard, David looked around, stood up, and walked out of the pub, they all looked at the door, Chloe run to the door and rushed out to be with this man, who had given so much for his country, and had, endured years of torment. She had to find him.

Chloe found him outside sitting on a bench, his head in his hands, "I have to go back in there to explain why it has taken me so long to explain myself," Chloe kissed him on the cheek,

"They know!" is all she said.

Inside the pub they were all trying to digest the revelations, especially Abdul, for three and half years he has hated the two men responsible for his children's death, but now his mind was in turmoil, not knowing how to handle this news, and now knowing that the three cars in the ruins of the school belonged to a Taliban leader, made him hate the Taliban even more, if that was possible. He left the pub, and jumped into his car and drove off, to collect his thoughts.

40
Two days before, Columbia

Captain Morella was on the phone to the Barranquilla police force, trying to find out about the man they had interviewed in the diner that morning. He was speaking to a desk sergeant but did not let on that he was part of the Columbian Police Drug enforcement agency, like a lot of Police forces around the world, one force, did not necessary tell the other force, what they were up to, and the Captain was no exception, he did not bother himself with the daily grind of police work, his job was to rid Columbia, of all the drug trafficking, and to rid the Country of all the drug cartels.

He came off the phone with a worried look on his face "What happened?" asked James, Morella did not know how to start,

"The man we interviewed in that diner was not what he said he was, in fact, it turns out that he was not even a dock worker, he was a low life thief," James did not say anything "He was a docker a long time ago, but was sacked for pilfering, that was six months ago, the police talked to his wife and she told them that her husband said that their money worries were soon to be over, as he was about to earn some serious money," James nodded his head,

"I thought there was something fishy about the whole thing, when just after he told us the name of the ship, and the cargo, he was shot dead," Morella agreed by nodding his head,

"What do you make of it?" he asked

"I think we have been given the run-around, we have been on a wild goose chase all this time, and not looking for an alternative form of transport, my team have come up with some important information, about a cargo plane, being made ready at a airport in the south of the country, and we now believe, that this shipment is to be flown to the United States, not by sea," just then James's phone rang, picking it up, he listened for about ten minutes, his face getting paler, and paler, at last he put the phone down, "I think you had better sit down," he said to Morella, the captain sat, a puzzled look on his face "It's about Sgt Durrell,"

"What about him?"

129

"He's been the one that has been misdirecting all our operations, we started to investigate him when it seemed we were getting nowhere on the shipping thing, everything was to pat to be true, so I asked my partner to find out what he could about your Sgt Durrell, and he came up with a few startling things, firstly! he has a family, a wife, and two young girls who have not been seen for a month now, so we investigated into it a bit more, and found out that they had been kidnapped, someone from their neighbourhood saw the family being bundled into a car, but they did not want to come forward, as they were to scared, but once we explained the situation, they told us what they saw, the good news is that once we had this information, we were able to connect it to another investigation that was being carried out in another part of the city, and it turns out that the two were definitely connected, so we raided the house in the south of the City, and to cut a long story short, rescued Durrell's family, we arrested Durrell, and he is now cooperating fully, telling us the whole story, happy that his family is now safe," Morella could not believe what he was hearing, he had worked with his sergeant for two years, and in that time he had been a fine and honest policeman.

"We have to get back to Bogota immediately," starting for the door, the Captains phone rang, and he put it on speaker,

"Captain, this is the Columbian coastguard, we have intercepted the cargo ship Bellamaria, and there were no containers on the ship at all, they did not load any, in fact this particular ship did not have facilities to load containers, I hope that helps Sir!" Morella put the phone down,

"Come on," he shouted, rushing out the door while talking to the airport, ordering his plane to be ready.

Juan Luis Cordova was supervising the loading of the last of the bales of cocaine, onto the DC8 70 series, an older plane but able to carry huge loads, the plane was going to be dumped after the delivery was completed; in fact it was to be blown up, and just disappear.

Juan looked out from the large hanger door, and saw Captain Morella's plane take off with the DEA agent in tow, and gave a wry smile, "Everything is going as plan," he said to himself.

The plane was hidden out of sight, in the farthest hanger from the main terminal at Barranquilla Airport, the plane had been loading for some time as the largest drug run in history was about to unfold, the previous one was way back when Pablo Escobar was the King of all the Cartels in Columbia, mainly, the infamous Medellin Cartel, but now, Juan Luis Cordova was the King, and he intended to stay the King, for a very long time.

The flight was due to take off the next day, for a scheduled flight to San Francisco, with a cargo of coffee beans, all preparations were going well, and Cordova himself, would be on the flight, having to smuggle himself into the United States for a urgent business meeting, it was a very dangerous thing for him to do, having quite recently been in the governments custody, but this meeting had to be done face, to face, with his long term friend, and partner, THE MAN.

41
Monday

David, having collected his thoughts, came to the conclusion that he would have to do the unthinkable, and that was to get in touch with people he knew in his previous life, he had already set up a rerouted telephone line, a long time ago, but up to now had no use for it, until now, he made the call.

At the CIA agency in Langley, the man picked up the ringing phone, "Yes," a voice from the past said

"This is Shepherd," the man was so shocked that he nearly dropped the phone,

"David?"

"Yes it's me," answered David,

"I thought you were dead,"

"No I'm very much alive, and I would like some information with no questions asked, please!" David said the last word deliberately, stressing that this would be off the record,

"We go back a long way, anything you need I'm your man shoot,"

David got off the phone with all the information he needed, he now knew what was being flown to their Island, but how to stop it getting to the mainland, was another matter.

David walked back to the pub not knowing what to say to the others, and hoping that someone would be able to come up with a plan. He did not know the Island as well as them, they may know a way into that site, without a full frontal assault, he smiled as he said this, as they had no weapons, no police, and definitely no special forces. The others were still there; he just sat down and told them what he had discovered "Drugs! Are you sure," asked Darren,

"Yes, I'm sure," once again they all started to talk at the same time,

"Hold on," shouted Sean "Lets calm down, and think this out in a calm manner," they all agreed that they had to do something, "I'm going to see the Mayor again and break down his door if necessary," said Sean,

"That maybe a good idea," piped in Chloe "And if he doesn't tell us what we want to know, we can torture him to get the truth," David smiled,

"I've defiantly created a monster," Sean and Darren went off to find the town's Mayor, while David, Scott, Sue and Chloe carried on trying to find a solution to the problem of getting into the drug smugglers site, "Where's Abdul?" asked David,

"We've not seen him since you left, he went out straight after you," said Scott. Abdul, was in fact, just outside, having come to the decision to put his vendetta aside, for the moment, and concentrate on helping these people who he has come to like, including David, he walked in, David stood up and welcomed him, as did the others,

"You do realise this is not your fight," Abdul put his hands in the air "Yes I do: but looking around here, I do not see anyone capable of doing what needs doing," he said with a big grin, Chloe gave him a punch on the arm,

"Be careful Mr Abdullah, I'm a black belt Karate expert," Abdul cowed down on his knees,

"Please don't hurt me pretty lady," they all laughed, none of them had laughed in days, and it sounded good. Sean and Darren came back in,

"He's nowhere to be seen," said Sean, David sighed

"I guess It's up to me then, I do have a few connection left, I hope" he pulled out his phone and dialled a number just like the previous one, routed from one phone, connected to another, so as it was impossible to trace, "I haven't got a signal," he said,

"Try again," said Chloe "The phones do go off quite regularly here," after numerous attempts, still no joy, Chloe tried her phone "I haven't got one either," the others all tried, but again no one had a signal,

"Try the landline," said Darren, Sean tried the landline but still no connection, Chloe was connecting her laptop to the internet,

"That's funny I can't connect to the internet," Abdul stood up

"They are blocking the signal," they all looked at him,

"What do you mean blocking the signal," Abdul looked at David

"They have software that can block signals for miles around, we had it, and all government agencies have the technology as well, so it's quite feasible that these people have the same equipment" Sean turned to Abdul,

"What about those poles you saw those men putting up?"

"What poles?" asked David

"I saw some men putting poles up, I told Sean, but did not take that much notice,"

"That must be the way they are doing it," Chloe the Monster said, "I Know; we'll go and blow them up?"

"What a good idea," said Scott "If only we had some explosives, Sean have you any hidden in your cellar?" Chloe looked a bit sheepish,

"Maybe not then," After a lot more talking, but not a lot of progress,

"We have to find a way into that site," stated David, Scott jumped up into the air, startling the others,

"Old Ned"

"What our Ned?" asked Sean?

"Yes, his Dad has lived here a long time, in fact I do remember him slipping up one day, and saying that his Dad actually worked at the site when it was operational, but never gave any clue as to what was going on there, and Ned has never left the Island in all that time, and if anyone knows about that place, he would!" They all agreed, so Scott, who knew Ned the most, was selected to take Abduls car and try to get him to help them, but they all knew that he could be a cantankerous old sod when he put his mind to it, so they hoped that today he would be in a good frame of mind, but did not put a lot of hope in it, but then again, he loved this bit of paradise, San Juliet, so they had high hopes. "What shall I tell him?" asked Scott

"Tell him everything, right from the start, if we want his help he needs to know what he's getting himself into." Scott left, David and the others carried on working out different ways of getting in,

"Myself and Joe will go back up there, and fly the bird again, to see if there has been any more activity," Sean was not best pleased by this statement,

"I'm not too sure about my fourteen year old Grandson, being involved in this, it could become a very volatile situation, and not a place for a child," David did agree with this, but he knew that Joe himself was a very grown up fourteen year old, he was already very tall and had the build of his late father, (Sean Junior) and he would jump at the chance of helping his Grandad, and the people, and like his Grandad, and his Dad, he was fearless,

"I promise we will not be going anywhere near the site, and I will keep him out of harm's way,"

"I'll go with you," said Abdul "I may be able to shed some light on what shows up," David and Abdul went in search of Joe, Chloe wanted a few things from her home, the Marine facility she vowed not to return to, but there were things there that she knew she would need, if this was to get any nastier.

David and Abdul found Joe, whose real name was Joseph, but never liked anyone calling him that, in a workshop behind the Diner. David could not believe what he was seeing, the workshop was like a science fiction set, with computer screens, and every electronic devise you could imagine, even an old fashion radio set that looked older than me, "This boy is defiantly Sean Junior's Son," he thought to himself "Can you work all this stuff?" asked Abdul who looked more impressed that David,

"No, I just like looking at it," he replied, they could see that this was just Joe having a laugh at their expense, David could see that he was working on Arnold the bird,

"What's going on?" He asked, looking at the one thing that re-minded him of his friend Sean Junior, Joe looked up,

"I've been working on Arnold to make the flying time better, and I have just succeeded in doing just that," he exclaimed with a proud look, David took a look at his bird, it looked just the same as before,

"How long can he fly?" asked David?

Joe still with the proud look on his face, "Thirty minutes," he re-plied,

"Wow! That's amazing," putting his arm around his shoulder, "So are you ready for seeing if your revamped bird can deliver the thirty minutes in real flying time?"

"Are we going up to the restricted zone again?" he asked excited-ly

"Yes if you are up for it," Joe jumped up put Arnold in a box and started for the door,

"Well are you coming,"

"Not yet, we have to get your mum's permission first,"

42

Monday
The same day Columbia

The Captain and the DEA agent James, arrived back in the Columbian Capital, Bogota, early Monday morning, and went straight to the Police headquarters where they were keeping Sgt Durrell, "I want to see him by myself first," said Morella as they walked into the station, James put his hands up,

"Sure, you go for it," They were led to the part of the police station that doubled as prison cells, Morella looked through the glass partition at his Sgt who looked so dejected that the Sgt he knew was not the one behind this glass.

The Captain was shown into the interrogation room, and immediately went to his onetime colleague and put his arms around him, knowing that the thing he had been charged with was not of his doing, he was protecting his family, just like any normal person would do, but as police officers they were not considered normal, they were there to protect the people of the country, but that did not stop Morella from feeling for his Sgt, the interrogation went on for a very long time, although it was not conducted like a normal interrogation, more like a talk between two colleagues, when it had finished, Morella wished his Sgt good luck, and vowed to work on his behalf.

Outside, Morella and James listened to the recording through and through, and both came to the same conclusion, the ship story was a red herring; the drugs were definitely being transported by air. Is all they had to do was to find out where, and when, the one thing they did know, is that the shipment, had not yet left Columbia, so they still had a chance of stopping it! But both knew that they had to alert all the airports in Columbia, and all airports in the United States, they had one thing going for them, the size of the run! It was going to be one of the largest for many years, maybe the largest that had ever been attempted, so if this was going to go ahead the plane had to be big, so the number of airports were a lot fewer than if it was of a smaller quantity, they both went off to get in touch with their respective Governments.

James and Robert were both on phones to different agencies, James was conversing with his own agency, the DEA, Robert, was on the line to the FBI, and the Airport authorities to put out alerts to any airport, or any airfield, large enough to accommodate a large cargo plane, and one that was due in the next couple of days.

Meanwhile Morella was scouring his wall chart to see if there were any clues as to where the stash of drugs could be held, also he had another computer man, working on Durrell's computer, all of a sudden the man jumped up from looking at the screen, and shouted for the Captain to come over quick, the information that he had found was that all the disappearing drugs were making their way to the north of the Country, the pattern on the screen confirmed this, this was one of the things Sgt Durrell was keeping from the investigation, "Well done!" Morella said, and went to his wall where he had all the airports listed, he immediately eliminated all airports below their own, Bogota, and was left with just seven, including Medellin, the onetime Capital of the drug empire.

43
Monday same day Columbia

Cordova got off the phone, and was visible shaken by what he had just been told. His insight into the police drug enforcement office was cut short, his man, Sgt Durrell, was in custody, and was by now singing like a canary, but he thought to himself there's no need to panic just yet, as the informer did not know the whereabouts of the drugs, or of the way it was to be transported, only that it was not going by sea, as he was the one that was misdirecting his superiors to that fact, so as far as things were at the moment, he felt safe, but it would be prudent to try to bring the time line forward, and to get this shipment, and myself, away a bit sooner that we had planned, he informed his second in command, who then contacted the pilots, who then contacted Air Traffic Control, asking for a earlier flight slot, they said they would contact them as soon as they could rearrange other flights, but could see no reason why it shouldn't be possible, but due to the large number of flight leaving today, it would not be easy, but the extra money that the flight control supervisor had received, the pilots were confident that a earlier slot, would be found.

Back at the hanger the last bale of cocaine was being loaded, leaving enough room for real bales of coffee beans to be loaded out on the tarmac, to create the illusion that all the cargo was in fact coffee beans, not that anyone could see them, as this particular hanger was so distant from the main loading area, but no chances were being made, everything must seem as normal as possible, Luis had chosen this particular day as he knew that Mondays were the busiest day of the week for cargo transport, he also knew that today there would be forty flights taking off, and over twenty of them would be destined for the United States, so if by any chance the authorities did find out where they were flying from, by the time they had checked all the other flights we would be well on our way, and once in the air, they would not be able to detect us, that he was sure of.

44
Monday

Chloe pulled her scooter out of the shed, behind the pub, and with a wave to Mary, shot off to the place she had called home for the last two years. She knew that going back there would bring back the memories of the professor and mike, but there were certain things she thought she would need, like her wet suit, and spear gun, you never know David might want to go back into that cave again. On the way she saw two men near a rundown barn, and one of the Range Rovers parked, she thought to herself "I wonder what their up to? They're up to something," but decided not to stop, and carried on.

Once at the facility, she gathered all the things she thought she'd need. She took one last look round, and said goodbye, never to come back, but then she reminded herself she had already said that once, she started for the door when she heard a noise from outside, looking out from the window she saw the two men who had been near that old barn, Chloe also saw that the two men were armed, one of them with a semi automatic gun. She went down to the lower level of the facility to a door that led out the back way, quietly opening it a tiny bit, careful that one of the men had not come round to cover it, with a furtive look round, the coast looked clear, but to be on the safe side she pulled out the spear gun checked it, and loaded a spear, then ventured out still very mindful that these men were professionals, and she was a scientist.

The two men one of them No2, were approaching the Marine Laboratory with care, as they remembered that the woman who saw them near the barn, was the same one that beat up two of their best men, so they were not taking any chances, "You go round the back," said No2, the blond man remembering what this woman has already done to him, held his gun well out in front of him, ready to kill her if necessary, creeping through the trees he saw the back door open and the woman come out carrying a holdall, and what looked like a fishing rod? He followed her, keeping out of sight until she came to a small clearing, then with a authority voice, told her to drop whatever she was carrying and turn round, training his gun on her all the time, she dropped the holdall and all her training at the dojo came into being, she turned so fast and her hands holding the spear gun were a blur of lightning, she pulled the trigger and the spear ended up protruding from the blond man's chest, at her dojo in Santa Barbara they often practiced finding the enemy when you could not see them, just by the sound of their voice, so as the blond man uttered those words Chloe had known just by instinct, where he was standing.

Chloe looked at the man she had just killed, and started to shake violently, her hands dropping the gun, she knew her father had done this many times, but not in her wildest dreams, did she ever think that one day she would follow in his footsteps, she tried to calm herself, saying that this was different, this was life or death, and he was, a bad man, all these things went through her mind in a instant, but the reality of it was not one guilt, but of sorrow that she had killed someone, be it a bad man. She was brought out of her daze, by the sound of the other man coming out from the back door she had just exited from, and instinct prevailed once again, she picked up the spear gun was about to pull the spear out of the blond man's chest, but could not do it, she was still repulsed at what she had done, picking up her holdall, she quickly made her way towards a small beach, down a path that was partly hidden from view, knowing that there were caves there, that she could hide in, if the other man came after her.

45
Monday

David, Abdul, and Joe, made their way to the same place from where they flew the bird the last time, only this time, they could do a lot more flying, they took a lot more care this time round though, as the people at the site would be more alert now they knew that something was up. By now, they must have realised that two of their men were missing, they settled down, David on his laptop, Joe at the controls of the bird, and Abdul standing guard.

Whatever Joe had done to make Arnold fly better, was defiantly working, he flew with great dexterity with Joe at the controls. They travelled all round the perimeter first, to see what sort of security was present, but not seeing one guard on duty was worrying, "Where are all the guards?" asked David, talking to himself "lets fly over the buildings but not too low," Joe manoeuvred the bird to a hovering position over the main building, David who's eyes were glued to the screen, could not believe what he was seeing, he called Abdul over "Look at this," what they could not understand was two of the trucks coming out of the seemly derelict building "How on earth could they come out of there!" David remembered the submarine pen that he was in with Chloe, just the other day, "It's underground," Abdul looked confused,

"What's underground?"

"The whole of this place is, or was, a secret base, probably from the Second World War," Abdul looked even more confused,

"You can't be serious," he said. David looked at the screen again and there it was, Proof! As another truck came out of the wide door of the building, "There must be some sort of lift in there," unable to take his eyes off the screen, "It must be a very large area down there, to accommodate all the trucks that have come over since this thing started," David agreed, Joe who was giving his full attention to the job of keeping Arnold in the same position, did not have a clue what these two were talking about, secret bases, submarines, and now large trucks coming out of a building that only looked big enough for one truck, and now they had seen three exit from this crappy looking place, he informed David that the time was up, and Arnold has to come home,

"We'll do, one more sweep of the area, near, and around the building" he told Joe. Once Arnold had done the last sweep, Joe brought him back. Arnold had done his job and there was no indication that he had been spotted, and all indication that the camera on board was working well, and the recording would be good, the three of them packed up their things, and made their way back to David's farm.

46
Monday

Chloe had been in the cave for 30 minutes before she had the nerve to venture out, and carefully made her way up the slope trying to be as quiet as possible, keeping away from the overgrown path, she finally came to the spot where she had killed the blond man, seeing the blood stained grass, made her shudder, and the sight of him with the spear sticking out of his chest, flashed through her mind, not being able to hold it back, she shuddered once again and the vomit just rushed out of her mouth, it took her a few more minutes to regain control of her insides, but once she did, the sight of those two men with guns gave her the courage to pull herself together, and to say to the grass, "Good riddance"

Chloe made her way to where she left her scooter, but nearly cried when she found it, her pride and joy had about ten bullet holes, in, and around, the engine, it looked as if the other man had gone berserk with rage, and because he could not find me, just took it out of my bike, Chloe pulled herself together once more, and tried to think about how she was to get back to town, she certainly would not be able to carry what she had come to the faculty for, "It looks like I've got a long walk ahead of me," she said to herself, and started to collect the things that really mattered, and then an Eureka! moment happened, she dropped what she was carrying, and ran to the shed where Mike kept his bike, rummaging around, she came out with a shiny new push bike, she stood back and admired this beautiful thing, digging around a bit more she found the small cart that her friend Mike had made for his two wheeled wonder, looking at the bike and the cart, her mind wandered off once more, to the great times they had together, nothing romantic, just really good friends, and the sight of the blond man with the spear sticking out from his chest vanished from her memory forever.

Putting all her belongings in the cart she started her long cycle ride back to town, once again saying farewell to the place she called home.

143

47
Monday Earlier

After No2 had confiscated the Mayor's passport and money and threatened him with all sorts of things, he made his way back to the site, having said hello to the school teacher, who apparently had no idea who he was,

Once back to the site, he immediately reported to No1 and showed him what he had taken from the now defunct Mayor, "We don't have to worry about him anymore, but if we do need him, I'm sure I can get him to do as he is told," No1 nodded his approval. "Now we come to the problem we have with the two men who did not come back from their visit to that teacher's farm house? Have you sent anyone to find out what happened?"

"No, I thought it prudent not to go there again" No2 looked perplexed

"Then how are we to find out what happened to them?" No1 could not answer this

"We will just have to leave it for now; I do believe though, that they will not be coming back at all, their dead," No2 took a seat

"If that's correct, we are now down four men, you do know that losing four men, could jeopardise the whole operation don't you," No1 nodded

"I have been in touch with our contact on the mainland, and four more men will be coming over tomorrow on the ferry, I was going to ask THE MAN for men, but thought better of it," they both agreed that they did not want any more men that were not loyal to them, "Now due to our men not coming back from the farm, and the problem of the town's Mayor, I'm going to instruct the computer man to instigate the phone blocking programme, I have already sent men to disable the landlines, so from now on we will only be able to use our secure lines, make sure you let everyone aware of this," No2 got up, and was about to leave, when No1 stopped him "As you are aware the plane is coming in early tomorrow morning, so I want our plan to be in place before that, I want you to take one of the men to the place we have picked for the drop, and make sure It's secure and private,"

"Right I'll go now, I'll take G3, he's the only one we can trust at the moment, but we will properly have to cut him in," No1 replied,

"Do not tell him too much about the plans, only that he will become a very rich man, that is if I let him live?"

No2 left the office, No1 was trying to decide what to do about the school teacher, when his secure phone rang, he immediately knew it was THE MAN, as this particular number was only known by THE MAN, "Sir," he answered, during the call the phone seemed to be getting hotter, and hotter, or was it No1 who was getting hot? THE MAN on the other end of the phone was not happy, in fact he was fuming, a number of times No1 held the phone at arm's length due to the torrent of abuse he was being given, but still THE MAN carried on, until he ran out of steam, NO1 said "I take aboard all what you are saying Sir, but be assured all the issues you have just highlighted, will all disappear once the package is delivered, we are still on track with the runway, we have electrified the perimeter fence, and have now cut off all communication from the Island to the mainland, Sir you have nothing to worry about, we have now got this all in hand,

"What are you going to do about this teacher, and the girl you mentioned,"

"They will be eliminated if they become more of a problem," THE MAN cancelled the call.

No1 left his office, and went to find No2 to inform him of the call from the Boss, but No2, and G3, had already left, do deal with the first part of their plan, to steal the money, using the two suitcases THE MAN had given them whilst on the yacht, the plan the two of them had worked out, was a little complicated, but seeing as there was two hundred million in the two cases, they thought it worth the risk.

No1 did a tour of all the different sections of the facility, the trucks were undergoing their new paint job, the perimeter fence was working fine, although Gen1 was unhappy about the amount of juice it was using, to keep it alive, "I'm sorry but the generator was not up to run the fence as well has everything else, we may have to turn it off periodically, to save energy and fuel, but at the moment things are running smoothly,"

No1 went into the communication room, the man at the bank of screens was studying, one particular screen, "Is everything going as planned,"

"Yes Sir!" Came the reply, No1 put his hand on his shoulder,

"Keep monitoring the whole island, we do not want anyone to be able to contact any other person on this Island, or on the mainland,"

He travelled the two hundred yards from one end of the facility to the other, checking and congratulating all the men he came in contact with, his Dad always said "Keep the men under your command happy, and give them encouragement when earned, but never loss control, always show them you're the boss,"

He ended up with X1, the explosive man, who was part of the hijack plan, "Is everything in place?" X1 showed him the charge he had just placed,

"Yes it's all ready to be blown!" No1 started to walk away then turned as if he had just remembered something,

"What about the other thing?" X1 smiled,

"All ready fitted," he replied,

"Well done, be ready for my signal," No1 was pleased with himself as he walked back, all things considered; the whole operation was still on track?

He visited one last person, a carpenter who was constructing a design No1 had designed himself, "Is it ready?" he asked,

"All ready to go Sir,"

The guard who has been keeping an eye on the No1 for his boss G1, reported back.

48
Monday

Scott who had been sent to recruit Old Ned, was just pulling into his rundown farm, Ned called it a farm, but now it was just a rundown collection of barns and stables, Scott looked around "I bet this place was brilliant years ago," Scott could make out the way the farm was set out, and admired some of the buildings; one or two of them were still quite good, BANG! A shot rang out, "Who's there," came a shout,

"It's me Scott, you old goat," Old Ned came out of the house carrying a shot gun, "You could have killed me!" shouted Scott going over to him, trying to take the gun off the Old man,

"Don't touch the gun son, there's still one shot left, and it has your name on it if don't leave right now," Scott sat down on a bench and put his hands in the air,

"I surrender!" Ned looked at him and started laughing,

"I knew it was you, I only shot into the air to scare you," Scott lowered his hands,

"I knew that," they exchanged pleasantries, and Ned invited him into the house, once inside Scott could not believe the difference between the inside, and the outside, one was like a dump site but this was a palace, everything was spotless and shiny, "WOW!" Scott could not stop himself from admiring the place "This is absolutely fabulous," he said looking all round and trying to take it all in,

"That's enough of that, what do you want?" Scott stopped his admiration of the place, and got down to the reason he was there.

"We need your help," said Scott, Scott filled him in with all that had been going on. Ned got up and went to a door that led into a basement, after a few minutes he came up with a large box covered in dust, "This was my Dad's," he said, putting it on the table,

"What is it?" Scott asked, Ned opened the box after wiping it down, inside were papers marked Top Secret "Wow! Scott exclaimed once again "Is this what I think it is?" He asked, Ned took one page out with the heading JULIET ONE, and quickly put it back in the

box, picking the whole box up, they headed for the door, in the car
Ned said,

"Put your foot down young man, we have an Island to save,"

49
Monday

Scott and Ned were heading for town along the coast road, Chloe on her bike, was also on the road, as was David, Abdul, and Joe, all converging for another meeting, of, the Save the Island Committee.

David and the others were the first one's back, David and Abdul went straight to the pub that had become their focal point, and war cabinet, Joe went home to the diner, he and his Mum lived behind the diner in a small bungalow, where Shep started licking his face uncontrollably.

Chloe meanwhile was still on the road when Scott and Ned came up behind her, "Is this your new health kick?" shouted Scott, Chloe got off the bike rubbing her backside,

"No, My scooter broke down," she exclaimed, "Can you get me and my bike in there," pointing to the large trunk, "My butt cannot take anymore of this totally excruciating torture," Scott laughed, got out and manhandled the bike and the cart into the back, while Chloe made herself comfortable on the back seat, still rubbing her backside, "Hello Ned! What are you doing here?" Ned turned round,

"I'm now part of your assault team," he stated "Your Commander In Chief requested my presence," Chloe was a bit taken back, what's with this assault team stuff? And who in the hell made one of us a Commander? And what on earth could an eighty odd old man do? Scott got back into the driving seat, and they carried on into town, Chloe rubbing her butt all the way.

The pub certainly resembled a war cabinet room, Sean had put a chart up on one wall, with all manner of writings were on it, Chloe and Scott were astonished by the amount of work Sean had put into it, there were times, faces, places. And a whole lot of facts displayed in an almost perfect chronicled order.

"You've been busy while we've been away," remarked Scott,

"While all you lot have been on your holidays, me, and Sue, have been slaving over this fantastic war chart," it sounded good that they could all laugh and make jokes, even though the situation they all found themselves, in was not a laughing matter.

Chloe was the one who was the most traumatised after she related what she had done, and what she had been through, David came over and put his arm around her, Chloe thought to herself "I wish this was for real, she felt so safe in his arms," David related what they had been doing, and Abdul put the video of what Arnold the bird had captured on the large TV screen, Sean asked if Joe was okay?

"Yes! He's fine, and you have a very brave and clever Grandson there Sean!" Sean felt proud of his boy; he was growing up to be the carbon copy of his father, Sean Junior. The video started with the full sweep on the perimeter fence, "We were a bit puzzled about the lack of security," stated David, and they all saw, there was not one sign of any of the guards patrolling,

"I see what you mean," exclaimed Sean

"Stop!" shouted Darren, they all jumped by the loud shout, Abdul stopped the video, "Go back a little," said Darren, Abdul did what he was told "Stop there! Do you see it?" they all looked at the screen,

"See what?" asked Chloe, Darren got up and walked over to the screen, and pointed to a spot,

"There," he said "Just near that tree," they all looked again until David spotted what Darren had seen,

"I can see it too now," he exclaimed, with excitement in his voice,

"What?" asked the others with one voice, Darren again pointed to the spot just near a tree, and then all of a sudden they all could see,

"It's a Drone," exclaimed Scott, who along with Darren had quite often been out with Joe flying his drone,

"Now we know why there are no guards patrolling," said Abdul, Abdul pushed the start button again, this time it was David that shouted stop,

"Go back!" Abdul pushed the rewind button again, until David told him to stop once again, what David had saw was one of his sheep resting against the perimeter fence, he knew that his sheep roamed far and wide, his fence had a lot of holes in it, and his farm was only about two miles away, "There, one of my the sheep,"

"It looks dead," stated Chloe

"But can you see why?" Asked David, "Abdul can you zoom in please," Abdul pushed a few more buttons and the picture increased in size "See that the blackened area on the sheep," David exclaimed

150

"The poor thing has been electrocuted," they all looked a bit more closely,

"Your right," said Sean "They've electrified the fence,"

"And also have a security drone patrolling the area," stated Abdul,

"Carry on," said David, Abdul pushed the start button again, and all were really surprised when they saw the three trucks come out of the small dilapidated building,

"How on earth could that be," said Sue, this was the first words she had uttered during the whole meeting, plus the meeting before, she had no idea what was going on, after all she was just an office girl, and had no knowledge of guns, killings, or drugs and the like,

"I think it's a secret air base, put here by our Government during World War Two," said David, not believing one word of what he just said.

Ned who had been noticeably quiet during all what was being said and what they had all been watching, finally spoke up "Your right," they all turned round at the sound of Ned's voice, most of them not realising that he was actually in the room, Ned carried on "In World War Two, after the Japanese bombed Pearl harbour, our Government was not sure how the war was to play out, so made provisions in case the Japanese did manage to get this far,

"No way!" exclaimed Darren, "How could anyone build a secret base on an Island like this?" Ned put his hands up,

"The Island was inhabited by about 50 people back in 1941 when Hawaii was attacked, a small fishing community, and a few land owners, one of them my Father, and his father before him, and as San Juliet is also the farthest from the Californian coastline, it seemed the ideal place to build," Ned paused for a moment,

"And you know all this, how?" asked Chloe

"My Dad helped to build it,"

50
The same day Columbia

Juan Luis Cordova was making himself comfortable in the jump seat of their cargo plane, ready for their take off, the pilots having managed to get the earlier slot they had asked for; the time was 8pm local time, the flight time was going to be around eight hours, but with the time difference of two hours it was estimated that they would land on San Juliet at approximately 1am Tuesday morning, the plane taxied along the runway, Juan feeling very nervous this was a very crucial moment, would they get away with the largest quantity of cocaine ever smuggled into another Country, ever, or would at this vital moment be stopped by the authorities, but the fears Juan Luis Cordova had, disappeared as the DC8 lifted into the sky, towards a pay day in excess of one Billion Dollars.

Earlier back in the Columbian Capital, Bogota, Captain Morella and his team were no nearer finding the airport from where Cordova's flight was departing from; he rang the DEA men "No, we have not heard anything that could pinpoint the airport either,"

Morella went over to his computer man "Tell me something's showing up on all this expensive equipment, Please," the man shook his head,

"Sorry Sir!"

A shout came from the other side of the room, "Sir! Captain" a woman was holding up a phone, he could see that the call was going to be important, as the phone she was holding was his private one, and only a few people knew the number, he ran over snatching the phone from her hand,

"Yes" he shouted down the mouthpiece unable to contain his excitement, he listened for a few minute his heart rate going up bit, by bit, he slammed the phone down and ran back to his wall chart, and studied the maps, "We've found the airport," he called out "I want all flights from the Barranquilla airport stopped as from now," Morella looked at the clock the time was 6pm, the whole of the basement room went into frantic mode, one operative on the phone to Air Traffic Control at Barranquilla, the others, directing agents from across the area to converge at the airport, Morella himself was talking to the chief of police in Barranquilla, asking him to dispatch as many men as he could muster, and carry out a full search of all hangers, planes, and storage areas in the airport, plus the surrounding areas adjacent to the airport, the police chief was not forth coming with the plea, but when Morella mentioned the name of the President, the man went into overdrive, and promised men were on their way as they speak.

Morella picked up his coat, strapped on his pistol, and with a look of triumph on his face, run out of the basement to the now, waiting helicopter.

The two DEA agents received the same message the Captain had, and were now on their way to Barranquilla, having a fully fuelled plane ready at a moment's notice, always. Robert looked across at James and asked "What happened? Who was the call from?" James was going through all the flights leaving Barranquilla today, also any that had already left, "It was from the Captain's Sgt, Durrell." James paused for a moment as he noticed something on the sheet in front of him, "Sorry, the Sgt remembered something that Cordova had said whilst talking, it was an off the cuff remark, and at the time did not mean anything to him, so he forgot all about it, but all this excite-ment and the family reunion he has just had with his Wife and kids, triggered something from the back of his mind,"

"What?" James caught his breath

"His Wife said something like, (It's good to see you!) That was when Durrell remembered the thing that Cordova had said,"

"Come on, spit it out," Robert was getting fed up with the time his partner was taking,

"It was when he was talking to Cordova about the Barranquilla docks ruse, when we were being sent around in circles, he said "I can see him," now thinking about it, the only thing he could think of was that Cordova was in Barranquilla himself, and now that has been confirmed by a sighting from an anonymous call," James turned to the pilot "Can't this thing go any faster!"

Back in Virginia at the DEA headquarters, a frantic scramble was taking place, to reassign agents who were covering the docks, to all airports able to accommodate a large cargo plane, and there were quite a number, so the acting head requested the help of FBI in the mammoth task of covering the large number of airports, hoping that this could be shortened when and if, the two agents on the ground could figure out what flight is being used, and what airport the final destination is?

Over in the CIA at Langley, the head of operations had his own headache to contend with, "How is this assassin thing going?" he asked two of his agents, the two agents looked pleased with themselves,

"We have good news Sir, we have tracked down the connection between the two officers who have been murdered they were both commanders in an operation in Afghanistan, three and a half years ago, when an op went wrong," one of the men held out a file,

"It seems that the operation to take out a Taliban leader in a village near the border of Pakistan, ended up with the now confirmed murder of 100 children, and a number of teachers of the local school that El Jaffa had taken refuge in, EL Jaffa was the Taliban leader. There were also two men who were sent out to carry out the actual sighting, one from Delta and one from the British SAS, these men all took a part in one of the worst atrocities that we have been involved in, the murder of innocent Children. The two commanders were reprimanded, and have since left their respective forces, but it now seems that this assassin is targeting the men responsible for the killings," the man nodded to his partner who took over the debrief,

"We have now sent agents to this village to find out if anyone there have lost Children, and who could have reason to hate the United States so much that they have been on this vendetta for three and a half years, at the moment, we are trying to identify who the two men were that were directing the hit,"

51
Monday

No1 received the call that the package was on route, and would land approximately between Midnight and one in the morning, No1 looked at the clock seven hours before they land, he called the site manager and informed him of the time scale, "Everything is in place Sir! We will be ready," putting the phone down he picked up another one, this was a direct line to THE MAN, ringing the man was not a thing he liked doing, but this was vital to the operation, as THE MAN had all the codes for the main money transfer, and he was the only one who could complete the transaction.

Finishing the call was the best part of whole thing, "Hopefully this would be the last time I would have to deal with him personally," he thought to himself.

The site manager called all his men together, and went through all the procedures that would require the runway to be ready for the imminent arrival, and that the trucks were ready to unload the plane and the distribution protocol is prepared.

Stuart the generator man, Gen1, was not invited to this meeting as he was considered an outsider, Stuart was the only man on this drug operation that was not involved in the drug trade, he was just a brilliant engineer, that No1 had found while trawling the internet for an expert on old generators, and he turned out to be just the right man, at just the right time, broke, and owing a lot of money to the bookies, he was easy to recruit.

Stuart went down to the canteen for a coffee, he always sat by himself, but was also able to hear what was being discussed by the rest of the men; he could not believe what he was hearing, Drugs! Stuart had an inbreed disgust for anyone involved in this deadly trade, as it reminded him of the Sister he lost four years ago, due to a drug overdose. At the time he was still at collage, and felt he should have helped his elder Sister, how he was not sure, but he could have tried, he blamed himself for not being there, and not looking after her, as she had done many times for him in the past. "I don't know how but that plane is not going to land at this makeshift airfield," he vowed to himself.

52
Monday

After the bombshell that Ned had exploded in the pub the others did not know what to say or do, so Ned continued his story, "I was just ten years old when all the men left the Island, I had no idea what was going on up there, my Father forbade any talk in the house about the secret site, but we knew it was for military purposes, as the military trucks had to use the only road we had on the Island at that time, and most of this was built by them, although the trucks didn't have any military writing on them, or any sort of camouflage colours, I knew what they were,

"What did your Dad do?" asked Scott,

"He was just a labourer I think," David butted in

"Carry on Ned," Ned settled himself down,

"These papers have been in the basement for all these years just collecting dust,"

"If he was only a labourer how, could he get secret papers?" asked Scott, they all looked at the box noticing the big letters TOP SECRET,

"I don't really know," he replied, "But I never not looked inside the box as my Father said that if anyone ever talked about the secret base up there, they would all go to prison or be shot, it scared me then, and it still scares me now, and as I was only ten at the time, it has stayed in my mind to this day, and I have not thought about it until now, even when my dad died the box never entered my head,"

"But now you think it could help us," said Sean, they carefully opened the box, and just as carefully, started to read the papers, there were a lot of sheets that had the top secret writing on them, David held up a folder,

"This is what we need," he cried out, they read through the whole folder and were surprised to find that not only were there under-ground facilities, that were very much like you would find on a aircraft carrier, there was also a underground submarine pen,

"Well we know about that one," said Chloe,

157

"But look at this!" exclaimed David, what they were looking at was a separate folder in the main folder, setting out a network of tunnels that connected to other parts,

"That's what we saw in the water cave," said Chloe excited, "And do you remember we saw those pipes that seemed to go through the wall, there must be a tunnel that leads to the main facility," looking at David

"Your right but it would be impossible to enter the place through there, there must be other ways in," they pulled out all the papers and went through them one by one, looking for another entrance.

"It's getting a bit late said Darren, shall we continue this after we have eaten, I'm starving," they all realised that most of them had not eaten a thing, since breakfast,

"That sounds like a very good idea," said Scott rubbing his tummy; Sean went out to find Mary his wife. And before long they were tucking into one of Mary's steak pies.

They resumed their deliberation once they were all well fed by one the best pies on the planet, "You start Ned," said David. Ned tried to remember something from the back of his brain, something that had been niggling him for years but now it was all flooding back to him, the image's that had laid dormant were coming back at an alarming rate.

"I've got it!" he shouted they all looked at him,

"Got what?" asked Chloe,

"I have just remembered something that happened back when the Island was being used by the government in 1945," the others crowded round him in anticipation, "I was ten years old and playing in an old barn near the coast road, when a large fleet of trucks came by heading for the dock, the military had build a large dock in the harbour, but when they left they blew it all up, now no part of it is visible, but then again even though it was big, it was also invisible, even then, if that makes sense," they all looked puzzled by this statement,

"I think what he's saying that it was camouflaged to not look like a dock," remarked David,

"Yes that's right it was well hidden," Ned went Back to the story, "Well as the trucks came past the barn, I was in the loft at the time, and below me was another truck that had been parked there the day before, it was a bit strange at the time, as this barn was my secret place, and I was a bit peeved that someone else was using it, I looked in the back of the truck to see what was inside, but all I could find was some old scrap metal, I never took much notice of it at the time, then one of the trucks from the convoy broke down and some men got out, I never saw what went on, but one man came into the barn and drove the truck out, the other man drove the truck that was in the convoy to a place in the woods, and the thing just disappeared," If the others looked baffled before, they looked even more so now, Abdul had a look of understanding on his face,

"It was a switch," he exclaimed

"What's a switch?" Asked Sue,

David took up the story, "The two men were stealing a truck full of, we don't know what, and switching it for another full of old iron,"

"I would imagine for the weight to be the same," Abdul chimed in again,

"Yes and it sounds like they were coming back at a later date to recover what was in the stolen truck, once the war was over," they all agreed that it did sound plausible,

"But how can this help us?" asked Chloe

"Well my Dad mentioned that the military at the time, were removing all their armaments from the Island, so I assume that this truck could have some sort of weapons hidden inside,"

David and Abdul nodded in agreement "I think you could be right," said David "A lot of weapons from those days are still in circulation, my Dad had an old webley pistol, plus a 303 rifle from his days in the army in 1945, and they still work, I propose we start looking for this truck first thing in the morning, as it's getting a bit late now," looking at the clock 6pm, they all agreed it has been a long day.

David went out to his buggy followed by Abdul "I think I'd better come home with you tonight," he stated, David looked a little surprised by this statement,

"Why's that?" he asked,

"Well seeing what happened the last time you was at your place, those people will be wondering what happened to their men, they may come back, and you do need protecting," saying the last part with a grin, David laughed,

"I guess you're fed up with the hotel then!" Abdul held up his hands.

"How dare you think I have an ulterior motive about saving your life," again David laughed,

"If I recall, I saved your life," they both laughed "You go and collect your things from the hotel, and I'll collect my dog from Joseph.

Chloe still hadn't got over her ordeal at the marine Lab, so Sue asked if she would like to stay with her, at her place, Chloe jumped at the chance, she went upstairs to collect her things thanking Sean and Mary for their hospitality, the two girls went off down the road giggling, Chloe's ordeal quietly fading.

Darren went back to the garage to find a man who he did not know, waiting for him, "Can I help you?" he asked, Stuart held something in his hand,

"Yes I hope so, we need one or two of these," holding out the generator part, Darren could see that it was a circuit breaker from a generator,

"I'm not sure, but think I might have one, come through," leading the way into the garage, the guard started to follow,

"It's okay," said Stuart "I won't be a moment,"

53
Monday

Earlier, back at the airfield site, Stuart the generator man was wrestling with his conscious, he knew, that what he had got himself into was highly illegal, but the circumstances he found himself in at that time, were so severe, that he just jumped in with both feet, not bothering with what the illegal things were, but know Drugs! Remembering his Big Sister he looked at the massive generator in front of him "How can I make this beautiful machine go wrong without damaging it, and without the bad people killing me," he thought to himself, he had come to love his baby, and had come to love his life, so it would have to be something simple, something that would appear not to be his fault, It took him a long time but in the end had come up with an answer, and a plan, the removal of the generators circuit breakers, once he had formulated the whole plan in his head, he started to implement it.

He removed one of the vital circuit breakers, and immediately the light went out in the main area, he heard a lot of shouting, putting the breaker back in, the lights came back on, at the same time removing the breaker that controlled the landing lights, No1 came running in "What happened?" he cried

"One of the circuit breakers blew out, I've replaced it with a spare it should be okay now," replied Stuart, trying to control his voice,

"We don't want any more scares," said No1, with menace in his voice, turning and walking out with one last look round, his eyes firmly looking into Stuarts, Stuart looked a bit afraid as No1 said these words, but decided to carry out the plan he had formulated in his mind.

The breaker he had removed from the circuit that controlled the main lights he deliberately blew, and put this one in the landing light circuit hoping that no one would notice until they had to use the landing strip, blowing two more that he had as spares, he put them all back in his work box, and went to the canteen for a black coffee, needing something to calm his nerves, also knowing that if by any chance they did check the landing lights, he had a solution.

In another part of the site No1 was talking to the site Manager "I want to go through and check everything right now!" He said "The lights going off like that has troubled me," the two of them went to where the trucks were getting their new logo's painted on, and the site manager made the men start up each truck, they left there, satisfied. Then made their way to where X1 was finishing up the last of the charges, the one that would be the one for the cases switch.

Travelling in the lift they came to the preparations for the actual landing, "Is everything in order?" asked the site man,

"Yes Sir!" Came the reply "All the movable boxes can be cleared in twenty minutes," these are the boxes that look like trees and bushes to conceal the runway,

"Good! And the landing lights?" the man replied

"We checked them about an hour ago Sir, and everything was in order," No1 was not satisfied

"Check them again; we had a power cut below, so check them again now," The man went over to a small shed went inside pulled a switch, nothing happened, switching it off, he tried again, still no lights came on,

"I don't understand it," he said with a look on amazement "We checked it only an hour ago and they worked perfectly,"

No1 and the Site rushed down below as fast as they could, shouting into a phone at the same time. Stuart was still in the canteen sipping his coffee, when he heard his phone ringing, right away he knew that the landing light had been checked and were found not to be working, but he was not unduly worried as he had planned for this when making his hurried plan.

Once back in the generator room No1 and Site were waiting for him, No1 with a look of thunder on his face, "What's happened to the landing lights?" he demanded

"I don't know but it could be the circuit breaker again, I'll check," taking the breaker out, Stuart checked it over, and around the edges it was black, "It's blown," he exclaimed, "Similar to the other earlier one Sir," He went to his tool box and removed a replacement breaker, and inserted it into the now vacant compartment, nothing happened, taking this one out and inspecting it he found that this one was faulty as well, taking the last one out and on inspection found it was the same as all the others "I'm sorry Sir! It seems as if we may have purchased a dodgy batch," without a single word No1 hit him, Stuart fell to the floor,

"Get up you useless bit of shit!" he shouted, Stuart stayed where he was on the ground, Site stepped in-between No1 and G1 stopping the man going for G1 again,

"Whoa! That's not going to help," looking down at G1 telling him to get up, still blocking the way of No1 one getting to him, "Can you fix it?" asked site, Stuart went over to his baby once again, and looked at the breaker, and making sure they were taking notice of him really trying to repair the fault,

"I can remove a breaker from one of the other circuits and put it in this one, but that would mean no lights somewhere else," he said, the Site Manager looked at No1,

"That will have to do, once the plane has landed we will not need the landing lights, so he can change the breaker back," G1 stepped in,

"Sorry but that may not work,"

"What do mean?"

"Well, if we do that and the another breaker blows, we will be in total darkness, and nothing will work," No1 was getting more and more up tight,

"What do you suggest?" asked No1 glaring at G1,

"The only thing I can think of, is the garage in town, when I was here before I had a look at the place, and found that he had a repair shop for all types of generators, I'm sure he would have the sort if circuit breakers I need, we could maybe buy some off him?" No1 was not too happy about this, there was too much going on outside the site area, what with the teacher and his friends making noises, and his men going missing, he was unsure if the so called garage owner was part of the conspiracy against him,

"It does seem the only way," said Site,

"Very well," said No1, take one of the cars, and see what you can do, but be careful, and do not mention a word about what is going on up here," Stuart picked up one of the faulty circuit breakers, and made for the door, "Wait" No1 shouted "I'd like you to look at this," holding up a computer tablet, G1 looked at the screen, and saw his little Sister and her family playing on the front lawn,, "That is a live shot, they look like a lovely family, let's hope nothing happens to them," Stuart shuddered and knew this was a veiled threat, Stuart walked out towards the parking area, No1 turned to site, "Make sure you send one of the guards with him, I don't fully trust him, and remember, he is not one of us,"

54
Monday

Darren led Stuart into the store room knowing that this was one of the men from the Marine Site, he felt a bit nervous, but decided he maybe could learn a bit about the site itself, Stuart looked behind making sure the Guard had not followed "I'm from the place up north, the Marine facility," said Stuart, again looking behind,

"I thought that," replied Darren "What do you really want?" Stuart looked a bit stunned,

"What do you mean, what do I really want?" Darren took the piece in his hands,

"You know as well as I do these are not vital to a generator working, you could have easily by-passed them," Stuart again checked to see if the guard had followed,

"I need help," they talked for ten minutes before the guard came in, Stuart thanked Darren, and with the guard in tow got back into their car, Darren watched them go with a hint of knowing on his face, this man had given them some valuable information and all he had to do now was to share it with the others, but it would have to wait until tomorrow as the phones were still not working, he turned to go back inside when he heard a call , looking up he saw Scott walking towards him,

"Who was that?" he asked,

"He was from the Marine site up there," pointing to the north,

"What did he want?" Darren started for his door

"Come inside, I'll fill you in," they both went inside, Darren made some coffee, they sat down and Darren told him what had been said, and how this man, who had not told him his name, was going to help them get into the restricted zone.

55
The same day Columbia

The two DEA men arrived in Barranquilla before Captain Morella, and they went straight to an address where the rest of their men were stationed, "Have you been to the airport," asked James, looking at one of the men,

"Yes it's crawling with police and army, we could not gain access," James picked up the phone and dialled a number, after talking for a few minutes he put the phone down "Let's go," he said to his men "We have a green light," they all rushed out and jumped into their SUVs, and shot off towards the airport.

The police chief of Barranquilla met Captain Morella's plane, "Good afternoon Sir!" giving a salute "We have started the search but found no trace of drugs so far," they walked towards the main terminal,

"Have you spoken to the airport Manager and checked what flights have left in the last few hours, or are due to leave in the next hour or so?" walking hurriedly, the Chief answered,

"Yes, he is compiling a list as we speak; we are to go straight up to the control tower where he will be waiting with the full schedule of flights,"

Morella turned towards his computer man who he had brought along with him, "You go to the communications centre, and be ready to inform all relevant agencies, and airports, once we find out what flight this shipment is on," the man went off with an airport worker to show him the way. Morella, and the Chief, burst into the control tower, and were confronted with an entourage of officials, having been called by the Manager, this included Lawyers and legal representatives, the airport Manager had called these people in, in case the airport was in breach of any laws, concerning the export of drugs.

The control tower already full to the brim, was a hive of activity, everyone trying to do their jobs as well as being asked stupid questions by the police, when the two DEA agents walked in "What's happening," James asked, his voice being lost in all the noise, finally getting to Morella he asked the same question

"We are still going through the flights, so far forty odd flights have left to day, twenty of them to the US," James looked at the flights sheet given to him by Morella,

"Most of these we can discount, no way would they be able to land at any recognised airport, there is too much security," Morella took back the paper, and started to eliminate the bigger airports with the help of James. They were left with no airports at all, once they had contacted all the airports on the list, "They do not intend to land at any recognised airport, they have found one out of the way, and one large enough to be able to land a large plane," exclaimed Robert, who had been looking at the paper as well,

"Go down to communication, and alert Virginia and the FBI, and ask them to make a list of any airfield that could be capable of a cargo plane landing," Robert left the tower.

"How can I be of help?" asked the Manager

"Thank you Sir! You have already been a great help in letting us use your facilities, and with all these flight details, and be assured there will not be any comeback on you, or the airport due to your cooperation on the matter," replied Captain Morella, shaking his hand, the Manager left the tower, taking his legal entourage with him,

"I'm glad that lot have gone, they were making me nervous," commented James.

Out on the tarmac police vans were running around everywhere, from one hanger to another, until a shout came from one of the hangers near the perimeter, Morella's phone rang "They've found it," he cried, running towards the stairs "And they have also arrested three men," Morella could not keep the excitement out of his voice. James was trying to keep up. They jumped into waiting cars, and shot off to the hanger the search party had discovered, on inspection, it was found to contain traces of cocaine and even a broken container that had coffee beans printed on the side, with traces of cocaine still in it, they contacted the control tower to find out what plane had been using this particular hanger, the interrogation of the three men could wait for now.

Once back in the main terminal, they made their way to the Air Traffic Control Centre where a flight controller was looking up the details of the plane, and of the company using the hanger, and hope-fully the planes details and destination.

Morella looked a little pleased that the drugs had left his country, and these Americans would soon be leaving as well, inwardly he was thankful that all this was now out of his hands, is all he had to worry about now was the fallout of his Sergeant's betrayal, and his inability to stop this seemly extra large shipment of controlled drugs, being able to be collected, and exported from one of their largest and secure Airports.

They were told that the people using that particular hanger was a coffee export company called Clobia Coffee Exporters, but on inspection could not find any company with that name, the plane was a long distance DC8 cargo carrier with a squawk number7425, with this number Air Traffic Control can pinpoint any plane that has been given a squawk code, but is dependent on the plane itself having their transponder switched on, a transponder receives interrogation from the secondary surveillance radar, but a pilot could if wanted switch it off himself, but that could be dangerous and put their plane at risk of a mid air collision, James the DEA man stopped him "Forget about all that, can you tell us where it's going and where is now?" the man was not used to people being so aggressive, but went to his computer and started tapping keys, after about ten minutes of constant tapping and phone calls, the answer came back,

"HJ 1000B is bound for San Francisco Airport due 0100 hours, estimated to be over the Gulf of Mexico, but cannot pin it down precisely,"

The two DEA men ran out of the room to inform their headquarters in Virginia, Morella left for a friendly chat with the three men captured.

The flight control supervisor was talking to someone on a throw away cell phone.

On Cordova's plane the pilot was getting squawks in the headphones, but chose to ignore them, and Cordova received information, that the plane had been identified by the authorities. Juan Luis Cordova decided it was time to find out if the costly Military grade, anti radar and detecting system was worth the exorbitant amount it cost him, they were now coming towards the north of Mexico, it was time to disappear.

The interrogation of the prisoners was not as friendly as the Captain had wanted, but it did bring out one important thing.

Morella hastily picked up his phone as soon as he could, when James answered he gave the DEA man the news that Juan Luis Cordova was on the flight, James nearly collapsed when hearing the news. Cordova heading for the United States having only just escaped a prison term there, it did not sound possible, but the Captain had been adamant that the information was valid. James managed to get control of himself, although he had not been responsible for Cordova escaping from the FBI, he did feel responsible as a drug enforcement officer who was on the team that had led to his capture last year.

The FBI were going frantic once they heard the news that their most wanted prisoner was returning, they called in every available agent at their disposal, to find this plane, and recapture Juan Luis Cordova.

At Langley they were having a successful day, unlike their counterparts the DEA and the FBI, the CIA agents had found a young man in the village that the unfortunate killing of the children had taken place; the fifteen year old had been a pupil of the school in question, but on the fateful day had decided not to attend, he told us all about the incident and about his teacher Abdul Abdullah who lost his two boys, and he remembered on the day this teacher, Abdul, vowing to take revenge on those responsible, now quite often parents say these things without really meaning it, but it looks like this teacher who they now knew was an Officer in the Afghan Army, and a highly trained sniper who carried out several killings on behalf of the Afghan Government, he was not your normal parent.

The information becomes a bit sketchy after that, because one day, he just disappeared.

56
Tuesday

It was just after one in the morning, when David and Abdul heard a plane coming into land, the noise was tremendous, they ran outside to see this enormous plane going overhead, "It's happening," stated David, as they started to get themselves ready for their incursion into the site.

On the ground at the site, preparations had been going on for hours, the runway had to be cleared; the communications from the plane to their own communication centre, had to be encrypted, so no one outside could listen in, but all that had been designed well in advance, THE MAN and No1 had complete faith in the system they had put in place.

In the air the Pilot had managed to evade all detecting devises that the American Government had at its disposal, even the most advanced ones, that was due to the fact that they had got their hands on the best Anti Detecting equipment themselves, and the Pilot was an ex Air Force fighter Pilot as was his Co Pilot, the pair of them knew what to do to evade detection, and how to fly a large cargo plane avoiding the most sophisticated radar system, using technology gleaned from their respective areas.

(In the headquarters of Air Traffic Control "How can a plane just disappear?" Asked the man in charge, we have the best monitoring and detecting systems in the world)

(In Washington, FBI "We need every agent working on finding where this plane intends to land" said the agent in charge, "We cannot allow Cordova to enter the country again," only then can we put more men on finding this assassin Abdul Abdullah)

(Over at Langley, their top CIA agent along with a whole room full of analysts were going through imagines of security cameras from La Guardia Airport, where it is believed that Abdul Abdullah had entered the United States, "I've got him!" came a shout)

David and Abdul were approaching the fence hoping that due to the landing lights being on, the current to the electrification of the fence would be switched off, and they could quite clearly see the landing lights blazing from over the trees, "You touch it with your finger," said David

"You touch it," Came the reply, "It's your bloody Island," they both laughed they knew that just touching an electrified fence would mean instant death, David pulled out a large spanner from his pocket and threw it at the fence, it just fell to the ground without any sparks shooting out,

"It's as I thought, they do not have enough power to run the lights and the fence," the two of them moved closer and Abdul who had a giant wire cutter in his hand, gingerly pushed the cutters along the floor with a stick until it touched the fence, still no reaction, picking the cutters up, he started to make a big enough hole for the two of them to crawl through, but wide enough for their return even if the current was switched back on. For extra safety they covered the hole with rubber tubing to act as shield, and also to insulate the hole if the current is switched back on by the time they return, David put on the night vision goggles that he had taken from the guard in the submarine pen, Abdul was armed with the guards Sig hand gun, David still refused to handle the guns, but he was holding a wicked looking serrated bladed knife and he knew how to use it, many times this same knife, had taken quite a few lives.

They came up towards the landing strip keeping to the tree line, and seeing as the landing lights were so bright, the shadows were their saviour, David held the binoculars up to his eyes and related to Abdul what he was seeing, Abdul grabbed them out of his hands "Your useless," he said "With your descriptions no one could understand a bloody thing," after several minutes of taking everything in, they started to make their way back to their hole, when they saw a fork lift come round the side of the building carrying what looked like a bale of hay, but they both knew the bale was not what it looked like, before David knew what was going on, Abdul had started to run towards the building still keeping to the shadows, as the fork lift came round the next corner he calmly shot the driver, the sound of the shot was muffled due to the fact that previously Abdul had made a makeshift silencer using an old bottle, David came running up,

"What the hell was that?" Abdul just shrugged,

"It's a calling card, to let these bastards know that we can get to them," David could not see the sense in letting them know that they had got into the area, "Think of it like this, once they find the driver and their precious bale of drugs are gone, they will have to tighten up their security, and that will mean more men taken away from other duties, like unloading, and the loading of the trucks they have hidden in that underground cavern," David could see the logic behind it, but could not see the logic of telling the bad guys that their perimeter had been breached, David went to remove the driver of the fork lift only to find he was still breathing,

"What the hell!" he exclaimed "What did you shoot him with?" Abdul held up a dart gun "Where did that come from?" Abdul put the gun back in its holster and started the fork lift up, David jumped on and Abdul drove into the woods just as the landing lights went out,

"Give me your goggles!" Abdul demanded, David handed him the goggles and they drove to a ditch Abdul has seen as they made their way to the landing strip, they manhandled the bale of drugs, and the driver, who was slowly recovering from the forty thousand volts cursing through his body, down from the fork lift, then Abdul drove it into the ditch switching the engine off, he threw the keys as far away as possible, and after moving bushes and branches and oblite-rating the tracks it would make it harder for the bad guys to find it.

Getting the driver through the hole was not easy, but luckily the power had yet to be switched back on, once the driver and the drugs were through Abdul who was the one pushing, while David was the one pulling started to crawl through when a humming noise was heard "Be careful!" cried David "The power has been switched back on," immediately Abdul started to panic, David shouted to him "Stay still," Abdul did as he was told "Now take your time, just move an inch at a time remember the rubber will give you protection," Abdul was not impressed with David's reasoning, but carried on crawling ever so slowly, when at last he was through he gave a big sigh of relief,

"No problem,"

They made their way back to the farm; the driver who had recov-ered by now, was carrying the bale of whatever? but the writing on the bale said Columbian coffee beans, David read this out and said "At least we have enough coffee for the next year," they both laughed, and prodded the driver to get a move on.

57
Tuesday

The pilot of the DC8, was over the Pacific, when he did his final manoeuvre, in his bid to outwit the United States detecting systems, he suddenly switched on his transponder after speaking to his co pilot, immediately his headphones started squawking like mad, and the two of them knew that the Air Traffic Control had found them, and very soon fighter planes would be on their way to intercept them, they had all this planned, using the distress channel they put out a mayday call, then put the plane into a steep dive, as the plane dived, they switched off the transponder, and engaged the anti detecting system, once again they were invisible to all detecting devices, the pilot started to pull up as they approached four hundred feet, and steadied the plane at around two hundred feet knowing that at this height the radar stations would not be able to see them, this was quite normal for fighter planes, but for a large cargo plane was thought impossible.

But their plane was the exception, it had stealth capability due to the exorbitant amount of money they had invested in this operation, plus a second device, that enabled the plane to keep the two hundred feet height, stable, this had been perfected by fighter command, so both pilots, who were used to low flying using this gadget in their fighter planes, but they had to get to know how to use it in this cargo plane. They had practised continually for a long time, and were now confident that they could carry it off.

They flew for another hour before they came in sight of San Juliet; they had been in constant touch with the Island over a secure channel, and were now on their final approach. The landing light came on, and the plane landed perfectly, and taxied to the far end of the runway.

Juan Luis Cordova exited the plane with two of his bodyguards covering him, one each side. No1 went forward to greet him, not knowing how to address him "Hope you had a good journey," Cordova took the preferred hand, the greeting was similar to someone coming or going on holiday, but neither men knew how to greet one another, as they had never met, and not even talked to each other.

"Thank you; it's a pleasure to meet you at last,"

The formalities over, they got down to business. A fork lift truck came up to the loading bay of the plane. The main bulk of the cargo was not going to be unloaded until daylight, after the money transfer had gone through, and they had to wait for THE MAN to negotiate that, when the banks opened in the Cayman Islands, but No1 had been instructed to check the consignment as to the purity of the product.

The fork lift was one of only two they had at their disposal, No1 and No2 went on board to select one of the bales of coffee beans supposedly after selecting a random bale the fork lift driver drove it to the old barn building to transport it underground where it would be checked by a chemist.

No1 was satisfied, and led Cordova and his two guards to the buildings lifts, Cordova giving orders for the two pilots and the other two guards he had brought along, to guard the plane, No2 arranged for food to be supplied to the four men, and for cots to be available, if they wanted to get their heads down, the four had already decided who was to stand guard first, so both things were welcomed.

Cordova could not believe what he was seeing as they exited the lift, like other people who had seen the place for the first time, the sight was pretty impressive "This is fantastic!" he uttered in complete awe, "I've never seen anything like this in my life," still not taking the sight in. No1 led this legendary drug Lord to the sleeping quarters, and showed him the room they had made ready for him, they arranged to meet in an hour, to let the chemist No1 had brought over with them, to check the quality of the merchandise, the actual unloading of the rest would rely on the money transfer, plus the two suitcases containing the two hundred million dollars THE MAN had supplied,

"This would be the tricky part," thought No1, as he and No2 and a few others, were planning to switch these at some stage during the actual transfer of the money, No1 had all this in hand.

No1 went down to the makeshift laboratory they had set up, to find the chemist just sitting around "Where's the fork lift and the drugs?" he demanded, the chemist and another man just shook their heads,

"They have not arrived yet," the chemist replied.

No1 rushed out of the room shouting to anyone who could hear, "Everyone topside now, find that fork lift," No1 was beside himself with worry. No2 came running up,

"What's the problem?" he asked

"The fork lift, the drugs, and the driver, have gone missing," he uttered, in a very worrying tone,

"It probably just broken down or something, you know how un-reliable they have been since we purchased them,"

No1 was not convinced, he had a nagging feeling that something, or someone, had started to mess with an operation that had taken a year to put together, and was now slowly falling apart.

58
Tuesday

David and Abdul got back to the farm safely, and deposited their prisoner in the chicken coop, or on this occasion the geese coop, leaving the drugs with the tied up man.

Walking into the house they were accosted by the dog, David gave him a big cuddle and fed him, then set about cooking some food for the two of them. Once they had eaten, they went over what they had found out while on their holidays to the restricted zone, as Abdul had put it, "We know that the plane has landed, and the drugs are now in the country," said David,

Abdul chimed in "How come they had not started unloading,

David thought for a moment "The way I see it is the bale we stole was for a sample test, to see that the cocaine is of the right quality, and the main lot would be unloaded in the morning, once that had been proven, and seeing that it's so early in the morning I would imagine the drugs would not be transferred until the money transfer had taken place, and that's why we saw four men guarding the plane," Abdul was a bit taken aback by the knowledge David had of the drug trade,

"How come you seem to know so much about this drug thing?" he asked, David did not at this time want to go into too much detail, but said,

"In my previous life I had occasions where I had to deal with some of the scum that have blighted the lives of so many people," Abdul did not press the subject,

"So we have till morning before they start to unload?" David nodded

"Yes! But I cannot see us being able to do anything about that, we will have to concentrate on preventing them getting to the ferry," David's face took on a serious look "Also I saw something that has been troubling me since we got back?"

"What's that?" David's face screwed up even more

"A man got out of the plane that I recognised, a main Drug Lord from Columbia. Juan Luis Cordova,"

Outside the farmhouse, four men were approaching, having taken the long way round, they split up two to the front, two to the back, all were heavily armed, as they came up to the geese enclosure the geese started to make their normal racket, the two men who were approaching from the rear heard this, and with guns aimed, covered any escape by the man inside. The other two men went into the chicken coop and released their man who told them what had happened, and that there were two men in the house, one the teacher, the other, foreign looking, they were surprised to find the bale of cocaine in the shed as well, once they had confirmed that the man was okay, they contacted the men at the rear of the house, and without any qualms one of the men raised a missile launcher, and fired two missiles at the house, they watched for fifteen minutes, but no movement came from the now, on fire, and completely destroyed, farmhouse, "I don't think we will have any more trouble from those two again!" one of the men said, they all left taking the bale of cocaine with them, with one look back they could see that no one could have survived that utter devastation.

As they drove away two figures emerged from the ground.

David and Abdul were still talking about David's previous life when Abdul asked him about that day in the Afghan Village. David did not like talking about his life in the army especially that day, so he just avoided the question. But it surprised David when Abdul asked again, he was just about to answer when his ears picked up the sound of the geese once more, "I don't believe this," he exclaimed "We have visitors again," they both jumped up and ran towards the cupboard in the hallway, they had left their weapons in the gym, as they collected the guns David very reluctantly picked up the pistol but without thinking, dropped it on the floor and retrieved his knife, Abdul saw this and thought,

"He must have a real horror with guns since Afghanistan,"

They headed for the door at the back of the gym that led to a tunnel to the rear of the house, just as they entered the tunnel, the whole house shook, the ran down the tunnel as fast as they could, feeling the blast from up above, they managed to reach the exit to find the house totally destroyed, they retreated down the tunnel waiting for the intruders to go, "How on earth did they find us?" Whispered Abdul, David did not have an answer.

At last they emerged from their hiding place, not wanting to exit while the men were still there, and definitely not with there now quite evident fire power, David looked at his now utterly destroyed farm, "I built that place with my own hands," he said with utter sadness in his voice, "Me and Shep have lived there for three years and!!" all of a sudden David cried out, and screamed "SHEP!" David ran towards the now blazing building, "SHEP! SHEP!" calling out the dogs name repeatedly, Abdul came running and started to call out Shep's name as well, David was on the floor holding his head, tears flowing down his cheeks, Abdul sat down beside him and quite naturally put his arms around him, Abdul did not think for one moment that this was the man he had come to this Island to kill, "I'm so sorry!" Abdul got up and walked towards the burning building, "We may be able to hear him if he survived the blast," David came up beside him,

"You won't hear anything! Shep has not barked, or whimpered, ever since I saved him from people who abused him," Abdul again put his arm around his friend,

"I'm so sorry," is all he could say.

It was an hour later that Abdul was able to persuade David to leave, the man was distraught, his one and only friend he had in the world, was dead, Abdul had to practically carry David to the buggy, they drove off with David swearing to kill the men responsible.

59
Tuesday

The four men drove through the gate and went directly to the underground facility to give No1 the good news, No1 was ecstatic with the outcome "You're sure their dead," he asked,

"Yes Sir, We're sure,"

Cordova who had been waiting for the chemist to check the product was not impressed, "I thought you told us everything was going as planned and you had no problems?" No1 did not know how to answer,

"We did have a few minor things go wrong, but that has now been resolved," he said, not really believing it, there were still the others;

No2 took the four guards and the rescued man down to another room so they could have a proper debrief. Once he had analysed all the information, he checked the ankle strap the man was wearing, it was very similar to a released convict's security tag, they were able to confirm where they were at all times, all the men had been provided with these tags, they did not want anymore disappearances.

The chemist had finished his inspection of the goods, and confirmed that all was in order, the consignment was perfect and pure, Cordova and No1 shook hands and cemented the deal, "Now the money please!" said Cordova,

No1 said "It's early morning let's get a few hours sleep and do everything that needs doing in a few hours time," with that, No1 started to leave,

"I do hope you are not stalling for more time, or planning some sort of double cross!" said Cordova with menace in his voice, No1 just carried on walking.

No1 had noticed one of THE MAN'S guards had been hanging around quite a lot recently, and now thought that this was due to THE MAN not fully trusting him, and now Cordova had threatened him. "I had better be more careful in future," he thought.

No1 went into a large room where the money transfers were to take place, including the suitcases and the wire transfer. In the middle of the room was a large bench that just looked like a normal bench, but this bench was designed by himself, and was a bit special, the man who had put it together, a carpenter, was in the room with two suitcases, these were identical to the two cases THE MAN had given to him on the yacht, they were both metal, the man told No1 to put the cases on the bench, but out the corner of his eye No1 saw the guard who had been following him just behind the door, "You can come in and watch if you want to," he called out, the guard sheepishly walked onto the room

"I'm sorry Sir! I'm just doing what I'm told,"

"And what were you told?" the guard did not know what to say

"Just to report back if I see anything suspicious," he answered.

No1 pulled a gun out from inside his coat "And have you seen anything suspicious?" the guard could not take his eyes of the gun,

"No Sir, not a thing!"

"That's good, if you keep it that way there could be a large pay-day for you at the end, do you understand what I'm saying?" the guard was still looking at the gun that now had a silencer screwed onto it,

"Absolutely Sir!" he knew that his life was on the line here, and said "Sir! I have no allegiance to the man on the yacht, I have not even met him, and I was only recruited by G1 a few months ago, so if you need someone to be your eyes with the rest of the guards, I'm yours!" No1 did not know what to do, if he shot the man right here and now, it would cause more headaches, so he had no other option but to trust this man.

Once the guard had left, No1 and the carpenter who had made the bench were left alone, "Let's see how it works," said No1, the man asked No1 to pick up the suitcases and put them on the bench, No1 did this,

"Now take them off," No1 tried to take them off, but they were stuck firm, he pulled and pulled but they did not budge,

"I can't move them," the man pushed a hidden button in his pocket,

"Now pick them up!" No1 picked up one of the cases without any problem,

"Brilliant!" he exclaimed,

"Put them back on," No1 did this "Now these are our cases, if you look away for two seconds," No1 looked away, and counted to two, then looked back, the two cases were still there,

"What just happened?"

"These are now the money cases," pointing to the two cases,

"It works," he said with surprise in his voice,

"Yes Sir! It works perfectly,"

60
Virginia
Tuesday

The two DEA agents were now back in the United States and were in the communications room at their headquarters in Virginia, "I'll ask once again, how can a plane, just disappear?" They had been in touch with the USAF, but the only thing they could confirm, was that this plane had somehow purchased anti detecting equipment from an unknown source,

"Fat lot of good they are!" said Robert "I could have told them that," But the USAF Commander had promised them, that as soon as the plane became visible, they would deploy fighter planes to intercept, and force it to land. They had all their bases on full alert.

Virginia had also deployed agents to find any abandoned airports, airbases, or just any place they could think of that was capable of a landing of a large plane, but knowing that the DC8 would need at least a mile long runway, it did narrow it down quite a lot.

Over in Washington at the FBI headquarters, they were also in a state of panic. They had organised agents to cover airports in and around the southern states, and also to find this killer, but even with their army of agents they were still finding it difficult to maintain sufficient cover for all eventualities. The main agents looking for Abdul Abdullah the assassin, were getting nearer their quarry, they had all the images from La Guardia security cameras, and all the surrounding areas, including the car hire facilities that were dotted around, but the area was vast, and car hire firms were everywhere. It was going to be a long job.

The CIA at Langley had handed the finding of Abdullah to the FBI as they could not operate in the United States, but their investigation out in Afghanistan was taking a new turn, the young lad who had led them to Abdul Abdullah, had passed on new information about a prisoner taken at the time of the atrocity at the school, they now had more agents in the area, and were being helped by the Afghan army, and the British intelligence service, and were now on the verge of finding out if this new information was valid, but the agents on the ground were not convinced that this news was at all true, they had received no new knowledge of any prisoners being taken in the last few years, but they would keep looking.

The young lad had been taken to a secure place, as his life would now be in very difficult had he stayed in his village, but all the information so far had been proven correct, and they had no reason to doubt his account of this prisoner being taken, so they contacted their men who were now in the village, and the men who were on their way, to thoroughly investigate the lad's account.

61
Tuesday

Abdul and David arrived back to town with David still swearing vengeance on those responsible for his dog's murder, it was still early morning, the town was not yet awake, they went straight to the diner that was always the first place to open, luckily Julie was just opening the door, "What the hell are you two doing here at this time in the morning," she cried, David kissed her on the cheek, and Julie could see that this tough man had been crying "What's happened?" she asked with concern on her face, David took her arm and led her inside, once they were sitting down David started to cry again, Julie had never seen a grown man cry, so she knew it was going to be serious,

"He's dead!" Julie looked puzzled

"Who's dead?" David could not answer, so Abdul stepped in

"Shep, his dog," Julie hands shot up to her face,

"Oh! No," she cried, she knew how much David loved that dog, and how much he relied on him, she put her arms around him, trying to comfort him, but wards would not come out, Julie herself was close to tears by now "How can I help?" She asked, and then it hit her!, how on earth was she going to tell Joseph, he loved Shep even more than David, if that was possible, after several minutes David had calmed down and related what had gone on, Julie who had not been included in most of the talks about that Marine lot, could not believe what she was hearing, "I can't believe this is all happening on our beautiful Island," the door leading to the back opened and Joe walked in,

"Hi! Uncle David" he cried, running over to Cuddle him, he looked around for Shep "Did you leave Shep at the farm?" he asked, Julie took him by the arm and led him into the kitchen

"Leave David alone for a minute, I have something to tell you!"

Abdul and David heard a big shout come from the kitchen "No! No!" they heard the back door slam, Julie came back into the dining area, "We'll leave him for awhile, and I'll go and find him later,"

"No," said David, "I'll go and explain to him myself, now,"

Abdul was just finishing his breakfast when David come back into the diner, "Is everything okay?" he inquired,

"Fine," came the reply, they left the diner, David only managing a cup of tea.

Darren and Scott were already in the pub talking to Sean and Ned, as they walked in, they both sat down drained of energy David still suffering from the nights ordeal, Chloe who was staying with Susan, came in without her "Where's Sue?" asked Scott

"She has gone to work, she is trying to be as normal as possible" she replied.

David accepted another cup of tea from Mary, Sean's wife, and managed to eat a sandwich she had offered him.

Sean spoke to all at the same time after hearing about David's and Abdul's adventure, everyone was very sad to hear about Shep the dog. "Let's get down to business," said Sean going to the large board he had made, "Firstly we should have a look at what Ned saw that day back in 1945, and see if there in anything in that truck we could use, although I doubt it very much after all these years,"

David, Abdul, and Ned, were assigned the task of looking for the lost truck, and assessing the contents, Darren and Scott were organizing a raid on the site similar to David's, and Abdul's, David had not liked the idea of the two of them going into the lion's den, but they were adamant that they could do it, David told them where the hole in the fence was, and that before they left, they had tried to disguise it with some bushes, hopefully it had not been found, the good news was that they did not have to cope with the electric fence, the Generator man Stuart was going to turn off the power at 9 45 each hour, and would be off for 15 minutes each time, so they had plenty of time to do what they planned to do, and that was try to disable as many of their trucks as possible, they had a copy of the layout of the secret underground base, and were quite confident that they could get away with it without being caught, the two of them left to pick up the things they would need from the garage.

Sean had given himself the task of talking to the ferry captain, once the ferry had docked, they were on good terms, although he was not a very nice man, in fact he was hated by most of the Islanders, but Sean with his Irish humour, and general happy demeanour, had won him over to a point.

185

Chloe meanwhile was told by David to make sure the scuba gear she had got from her laboratory, was in good working order, they may need it at a later date, David was thinking well ahead.

David, by the time they all left on their different assignments, was starting to think a bit straighter, his mind had been taken off the killing of Shep, and now it was replaced with determination to put these killers, either in prison, or in a grave.

Darren and Scott had collected all their gear, and were now making their way to their greatest adventure, the destruction of trucks.

Sean was talking to his wife Mary on how to approach the ferry Captain, and asking for his help!

Chloe was down near the Mayors boathouse checking her Scuba gear when she heard a sound coming from inside, moving gingerly she looked through the dirty window, but could not see anyone, so she moved to the side door and as quietly as she could she opened it an inch at a time, inside she could she Peter Steinbach the Mayor fitting an outboard motor to his boat, Chloe walked in, "Would you like some help with that?" she asked, without an ounce of friendship in her voice, The Mayor jumped up so quickly he nearly fell into the water,

"What are doing in my boathouse?" he asked "This is private property," Chloe sat down beside the boat, and just looked at him without saying a word, eventually asking,

"So what's this, are you doing to a runner?" he carried on fitting the motor

"I don't see that it's any business of yours what I do," Chloe stood up and put her face right in front of his,

"Did you know that my two best friends in the world were killed by your friends, also did you know that millions of people are going to suffer due to tons of cocaine being smuggled into this country by your friends, and did you also know that David's dog had also been killed by your friends, and did you know that right at this moment due to your help, more and more people are going to die? Again by your so called friends," Chloe had said all this without taking a breath, but she could tell that Peter Steinbach their Mayor, had not realised how far his involvement in this operation on his Island, had resulted in so many people getting hurt, he sat down on the edge of his boat with his hands on his head,

"I'm so sorry about your friends, and David's dog, I know every-one loved all of them, it was a moment of weakness that I accepted their money, my one dream was to be able to return to my homeland, Israel, one more time before I die!" tears started to form in his eyes, Chloe at this moment in time felt sorry for him,

"We all have moments of insecurity and Peter Steinbach was no different from the rest of us" Chloe took his arm and led him outside "Go home to your wife and stay indoors, do not contact those peo-ple, we are going to stop them doing any more harm to the people on this Island, or the people of our great land," she said this with total conviction in her voice.

Once the Mayor had gone, Chloe rechecked the scuba gear, and stowed it on the Mayors boat, and set about finishing installing the outboard saying "This could come in handy later," not realising that this thought would become reality.

The Mayor walked into his house, to find his wife and a man from the site, holding her down, he just heard him ask where he was, "I'm here!" the man turned to confront him,

"No1 wants' you do something for him," Peter who was not a very brave man must have just developed a backbone, because he straightened his back and declared,

"You can tell your boss that I'm not going to do a single thing for him again," he said this with enough conviction to convince the man that he meant it, for the man grabbed his wife by the hair and pulled her down in front of him,

"Then I will just have to kill your darling wife then" said the man pulling out a knife, Peter did no more than pull a gun out of his pocket and shoot the man dead.

62
Tuesday

David, Ned, and Abdul were nearing the spot where he had seen the truck disappear back in 1945, he pointed to the now dilapidated barn that he had played in, all those years ago. "That was where I was hiding when the men from the convoy changed the trucks round," David remembered that this was the same old building that Chloe had seen the men that tried to kill her were inspecting,

"This is the same Barn that Chloe saw those men looking at," he said, Ned started to walk towards it "Leave it for now!" said David "Let's find this truck," they looked for an hour with no luck, Ned could not believe that they could not find a seven ton truck, it's not like it's a little thing,

"Are you sure that this is the place?" asked Abdul, without showing he doubted Ned's memory,

"Absolutely!" came the reply without any hesitation, they all took a step backwards,

"Let's think this out logically," said David, trying to visualise the truck, "It came off the road there," pointing to the spot Ned had remembered, "And disappeared over there," again pointing, they all pondered for a full fifteen minutes when a light bulb went on in Abdul's brain,

"It's in a cave or a man made tunnel," he stated, the others looked at him,

"Your right!" said Ned, "Do you remember on those plans, there was one part that you did not look at, but later I did, and there were papers that did not belong to the main building,"

"What are you thinking?" asked David not convinced that there were tunnels under where they were standing,

"Tunnels that connected to the main facility but were not included in the original plans, an escape route you might say," Abdul and David looked at each other and both nodded in agreement,

"Let's split up and look for a likely place a tunnel could be built," It was only a few minutes when a shout went up from Ned

"I've found something!" they were looking at a wall covered in greenery and large boulders, "Touch it," said Ned, David touched it and to astonishment the wall was made of something like plastic, they hunted around to find how to open a wall that had been shut for over seventy years, all of a sudden the whole wall started to move.

David could not believe his eyes "How on earth!"

Abdul called from behind a large real boulder, they could see that he was turning a large wheel as the wall moved, "I don't believe that something that has been left to rot all these years could move so smoothly," Abdul shouted.

The opening of the tunnel was now fully open, and they could see inside, but no truck was visible, with torches in the hands they ventured inside. Whatever the people who build the door had used, it certainly did its job. The inside was like it had only just been built.

They must have walked at least a hundred yards before the long lost truck came into sight, "WOW!" They all said at the same time, there it was, an old World War Two Studebaker US6 five ton truck.

Darren and Scott meanwhile, were just approaching the fence where David had guided them to, the hole they had made was still there, and the bush that was covering it was also in place, they gently removed the bush and waited for Stuart the generator man to turn off the power. Darren looked at his watch. Two minutes to go!

63
Tuesday

Earlier, No1 had called the exchange meeting for 7am. The people that were to be present were the computer man, the carpenter, No1, and Cordova with his two bodyguards; they had assembled in the main area, not in the room, but away from the frantic activity that was going on.

The actual money exchange was the most vital part in No1's plans, this was going to be his way out of the drug trade, a thing he had been trying to do for a long time.

Cordova had one of the guards fire up his laptop, and No1's computer man did the same, firstly they made contact with THE MAN who was to do the bank transfer, Luis had a quick word with him they had been friends for a very long time, the two men on their computers did the eight hundred million exchange without a hitch, Cordova and THE MAN said their goodbyes and the connection was shut down, "The money," said Cordova, No1 called his man over, the man was carrying the two cases, he gave the cases to No1 who put them on the bench and opened them both up, the guard who had done the money transfer inspected both cases, after taking bundles out from the top and the bottom, he announced that everything was in order, No1 shut the cases spun the locks dials, and gave Cordova the code,

"The code was for you only, and was chosen by your friend THE MAN" No1 stated. Just then a loud explosion shook the ground, the two bodyguards immediately turned at the sound, drawing their guns at the same time,

"What the hell was that," shouted Cordova,

No1 was all apologetic "I'm sorry," he said. "But that was the last charge for us to get to the surface without using the lifts," He looked embarrassed, Cordova and the guards had only taken their eyes off the cases for a couple of seconds, "Put them away," he said to his men, who holstered their guns, then he instructed them to pick up the cases and he walked off to his makeshift quarters telling his men not to take their eyes of them, Ever!

No1 was very pleased with the way his contraption had worked, it had worked perfectly. Firstly the two cases were made of metal; the base of the bench was also metal but was charged with a magnetic force. Once the cases were put on they were stuck until the magnetic force was switched off, so the cases that contained the money were put on the bench and the magnetic force was engaged, the explosion was timed by No1, the moment all of them had turned at the sound of the explosion, the bench top turned completely over, revealing the two identical cases No1 had acquired, this happened in a split second, and due to the magnetic force being switched on, the two cases that contained the money were now beneath the bench, stuck to the underneath of the metal top, the top and bottom worked independently, so no noise was heard of them falling, the whole thing had gone like clockwork.

The two cases Cordova had taken once the magnetic force had been switched off were filled with paper and an explosive device, so when Cordova opened the either one, both would explode, killing Cordova himself and anyone in the immediate area, and the beauty of this would be that THE MAN would get the blame.

No1 made sure that Cordova and his guards had gone back to their quarters, before pushing the switch to bring the cases with the money on top. He removed the cases swiftly, taking them up to his office and hiding them in a place he had already made available. He finally sat down drained of energy; this had been one of the most terrifying things he had ever attempted, and now there was two hundred million, just sitting in his office, He was so pleased with himself he reached for the whisky bottle he had hidden under the desk, this was strictly against his own rules, he had forbid any member of his team bringing any alcohol with them, or of trying to obtain any, as he reminded himself of this, He raised the glass and said "Cheers!"

64
Tuesday

Darren led the way through the thick part of the undergrowth, Scott keeping a watchful eye, and an ear out for the drone that was flying around, they had gone about two hundred yards when Darren called a halt, "It should be around this area," he said, they looked at the blueprint they had with them,

"There!" said Scott, pointing to a spot on the paper,

"I know where it is on the paper you idiot, it's where it is on the ground were looking for," they split up until they found what they were looking for, an air duct! "This must be it!" exclaimed Darren, trying to pry the grating open, "Pass me the crowbar," Scott handed him the bar, and in a few seconds they had the grating up, looking down they could see a metal ladder leading down, "This is definitely the right shaft," said Darren. Darren went first making sure the ladder was as safe, he gingerly tested each rung as he put his weight on it, when he was nearly half way down he called to Scott to start his descent, at last they both made it to the bottom both men were panting badly,

"I'm getting to old for this shit!" said Scott,

"How do think I feel, I'm older than you," they both smiled, "Come on! Let's do some damage," Darren said with a chuckle, they made their way forward using the plans once again, but it was quite dark in this area so they had to use a small flashlight so they were very careful, at the end of the tunnel they were in, they could see lights ahead, being more careful they gently edged their way into the main area,

"My god!" said Scott, Darren just looked, unable to take in, what he was seeing,

"It's ginormous," he exclaimed. Come on let's skirt round the outside and get our bearings, after what seemed like a five mile slow walk they came to where the trucks were parked, but to their surprise there were only five trucks parked up,

"Where are the others?" asked Scott in a whisper,

"I don't know, but it means we will be able to wreck these five without any problem," said Darren. After a bit more scouting around they was more surprised at the lack of people, there were no workers at all, "They must be unloading the drugs from the plane," said Darren,

"You're properly right," answered Scott, still whispering, "David told us they had destroyed one of the forklifts," Darren gave Scott two trucks, and took two for himself, after few minutes they had each disabled a truck each, but neither of them had noticed a camera panning round, and not noticing it had come to a stop with them the main focus, Darren first heard a sound as he disabled his second truck,

"Scott!" he shouted, Scott looked up and saw four armed men enter the motor pool,

"Time to go!" he shouted back, they started to retreat down towards the tunnel they had entered by, the four armed men split up guns covering every inch of the vast area, they could hear the men calling to each other "Over here!" they heard one shout, the entrance to the tunnel was now clear, they quietly made their way forward, as a bullet flew over their heads, "There over here!" shouted one of the men, Darren and Scott had no option but to run as fast as they could, hoping to get to the darkness of the tunnel without getting shot, bullets started flying around the two of them, but the men were still scattered around, so luckily only two of the men could see them, they had nearly reached the entrance when Scott went down,

"I've been hit," he cried, Darren turned round and started to go back, "You go on," cried out Scott "I'll follow you," Darren reached under his coat, and pulled out the gun David had given him, the same one he had taken from the man in the submarine pen, he loosed off a few shots, not knowing where the men were, but knowing they would now be less likely to rush forward, "Go!" Cried out Scott again "Get out and warn the others," but Darren had no intension of leaving another injured friend, he could hear shouts coming from the armed men and a couple of bullets came very close, Darren let off another couple of shots, mainly to encourage them to keep their heads down while he picked up his friend in a fireman's lift,

"Bloody hell!" he said "I think you ought to go on a diet when this is over!" panting like mad,

"It's not me being overweight it's you being a wimp!" came the reply, with both of them being over sixty it took a lot of effort to make it to the darkness of the tunnel, after running for a few yards both puffing like a steam engine, Scott said "Put me down," Darren could feel Scott's blood running down his side,

"Shut up and be quiet," but the burden was getting too much for Darren, in the end he lowered his friend to the ground, "Where are you hit?" he asked,

"In the shoulder," Scott replied "But I will be able to walk, but I think my playing tennis days are over?"

"So you're not going to do this year's tennis open then?" smiling to himself, Scott had not played tennis in all his life.

Darren heard the armed men enter the tunnel, so he loosed off a couple of more shots, he did not know how many more shots he had left, so he decided to wait until he could actually see something to shoot at, they travelled about a hundred yards trying to find the shaft they had come down, but knowing Scott would not be able to make the climb, it seemed a bit pointless, and Darren had said to himself that he would not leave his friend, if they were captured or killed they would do it together, Scott collapsed in a heap, Darren rushed to his side, "I'm sorry I can't go any further," he said though the pain that Darren could see etched into his face,

"Then we stay here together and surrender, and hope they don't kill us," as Darren was saying this last piece he felt a draught coming from the wall of the tunnel, taking a chance he turned on his torch and inspected the wall and to his delight saw a small opening, he shone his flashlight into the hole and saw it was quite long, turning back to Scott he said "Come on, we're going through here!"

"Through where?" the hole was very difficult to see, it was only Scott falling on the floor, that Darren was able to see it at all, Darren picked him up and manoeuvred him towards the hole, he could hear the men getting closer,

"Come on try to work your way through," Darren could see that Scott was in terrible pain, but despite the pain Scott did manage to worm his way through, Darren followed and they found themselves in another tunnel, this one a lot bigger than the other one,

"What's this place?" said Scott through gritted teeth; Darren had both the torches sweeping around,

"It looks like just another tunnel," as he walked he fell over, "Dam!" he cried, looking down he saw that he had tripped over a rail, "What the hell!" getting down on his hands and knees, he inspected the rail more closely and saw that it went down the tunnel out of sight, he was just going to walk down the tunnel a bit more when he heard a moan from Scott, going back to his friend he could see that the blood loss was getting worse, using a knife he had with him, he cut away Scott's clothing, and made a bandage with his own shirt, "Keep that pressed tightly," he said, "You must try to stem the blood flow," Darren looked at his friend, he was so white that he felt that his friend was not going to make it.

On the other side of the wall the four armed men could not understand where the two men had gone, when one of them found the shaft, "Here!" he said, calling the others over, when they looked they could see the footprints of the two men, the leader said "You two go up," pointing to the ladder, "We'll go topside, and hunt from up there," after a fruitless search for the two men, they had to report to No1 that the two had got away, how! They did not know,

"What damage did they do?" he asked

"Two of the trucks are beyond repair, the other is repairable and we have men working on it now,"

"Find those intruders! From what you have told me, one of them was injured, so no way could the other man carry a dead weight body up a hundred foot ladder, there must be another opening somewhere, find it!"

No1 walked away, feeling that this venture was going to crash down on top of him, he had to come up with something to bring it back on track, "You assured me that you had everything under control," a voice came from behind him, No1 turned round to confront Cordova, "It seems as if there are one or two Islanders who have a grudge against you!" said Cordova sarcastically, No1 had had enough of this jumped up Drug Lord, but bit his tongue in his reply,

"We did have a problem but be assured I will fix it,"

"I'm sure I've heard those words before." Replied Cordova

No1 left him, and made his way to the surface to check on the unloading of the plane, it had proven a bit more difficult having the one forklift, but the men had made good progress; he called No2 over "Have you heard from the man we sent to the Mayor's house?"

"No Sir, I'll try to contact him," No2 walked off talking into his phone.

No1 went down to his office to contact his people on the mainland, it took a long time to make contact, but in the end No3 answered, "Yes Sir everything is in order, and on time,"

65
Tuesday

David and Abdul could not believe, that 70 years old Studebaker truck was in such a good shape "It looks as if it was parked here yesterday," Abdul commented,

"I can't believe it myself," said David. Ned was already clambering over the tailgate to see inside, "I also can't believe that a ninety year old man could climb like that," he added, as Ned managed to haul himself over,

"Come on you two, don't just stand there," he called out, they could not see a lot, as it was very dark inside the tunnel, and they only had torches, but on their first inspection they could see that there were in fact, some usable armaments,

"We will have to come back with more light," said David, pulling a rifle from under a box,

"WOW!" exclaimed Abdul, "It's a sniper rifle," David handed it to him,

"I'll try to find some ammunition," Abdul held the rifle up, it looked in pristine condition,

"It's brilliant!" he exclaimed, after taking a better look, he could not wait until they got outside to inspect it further, David found a few rounds that would fit it, they got down from the truck deciding to find some more lights before searching anymore, they packed up the things they had brought with them and started to make their way out "What was that?" shouted Abdul, stopping and looking back

"What was what?" asked David

"I thought I heard a gunshot," they all stopped and listened, "There!" this time they all heard it,

"It came from behind that wall," said Ned, whose ears were as sharp as ever, He walked towards the wall, "I can hear banging," he cried out, they all went close and heard the banging for themselves,

"It's not just banging," said David, "It's Morse code," David who had learnt to use the code while in the army, told the others to be quiet as he listened and tried to decipher the tapping, "I don't believe it,"

"Don't believe what?" asked Abdul

"Its Darren and Scott behind that wall," Abdul and Ned looked flabbergasted,

"No way!" exclaimed Ned, "How on earth could they have got there,"

David went back to the truck to find some tools. Meanwhile Ned had found a crack in the wall and shouted through "Hello! Can you hear me?"

A faint voice came back "Yes! I can hear you," Ned pulled more stones away from the hole he had made,

"Are you okay?" he asked

"I'm okay, but Scott has been shot,"

Back in the tunnel Darren had not managed to stop the flow of blood leaking out from Scott wound, "We have to get you to a doctor," said Darren,

In a weak voice Scott declared that he was alright, "Go and find a way out of this place," he said, Darren looked at his friend,

"Don't go anywhere,"

"What! Not even to the toilet?" trying to crack a smile,

Darren went off to explore the tunnel, He came to a large cavern sort of place, and saw two hand pumped rail carts, looking at the railway tracks he could see that they went deep into the rest of the tunnel. Poking around, he was pleased to find some old kerosene lamps; The torch he had was slowly losing power, he shook the lamps and found there was still fuel in them, He lit one of them with a flint he found, being able to get a better idea of the place, he decided that their best option was to see where the tunnel went, it was bound to lead to the outside somehow, he manhandled one of the carts onto the track and with some old oil he found, managed to get the handle free and working, by this time he was nearly dead on his feet, but knew that his friend was relying on him to get them out, so gave himself a talking to and went to fetch his friend.

After pumping up and down on the rail carts for what seemed an eternity, to Darren's dismay they came to a solid wall "Shit!" he exclaimed, He looked down at Scott "Sorry mate but it looks as if we've come to a dead end," Scott did not reply, Darren went to his side and without having to check his pulse, he knew that Scott, one of his best friends, was no longer with them, "Shit! Shit! Shit! He called out, he held his friend in his arms tears streaming down his face "I'm so sorry mate," is all he could say, they stayed like that for ten minutes or so, until Darren heard someone talking, he gently laid Scott on the floor, and went towards the solid wall in front of him, he bent down and listened, and sure enough it was talking, he called out several times but did not get an answer, picking up a piece of rock started to tap out an SOS, he did this many times but to no avail, he pulled out the gun and checked if he had any bullets left, "Just two" he said to himself, "I might as well use them up," he fired one shot, bent down to listen once more, still nothing, he fired his remaining shot, the sound echoed around the enclosed area, Darren thought to himself "That's going to bring the bad guys down here," he carried on with the SOS signal until he heard a voice coming though the wall, he bent down near a small crack and was surprised to hear Ned's voice, while talking he heard men running towards him down the tunnel, "Tell David I'll do a Steve McQueen."

Ned related to David what had been said; "I can't believe that another Islander is dead due to those killers," said David with utter menace in his voice, "I'm going to kill each and every one of them," Abdul remembered the time in the gym,

"And how do you propose to do that, when you can't even touch a gun?" David picked up the rifle loaded it and fired a shot down into blackness,

"That's how,"

Going back on what Darren was able to tell them, they know thought that David and Abdul were dead, Darren had heard them talking, "What did he mean when he said I'll do a Steve McQueen?" asked Ned,

David smiled "The great escape film, he said he would escape,"

66
Tuesday

On the Mainland at the ferry port there were only three vehicles ready to be loaded, and they all belonged to No1.

No3 three had a word with his six man squad, "We do this quick and silently," he said, No3 had already put out a bulletin saying that the ferry due to circumstances beyond their control, had been cancelled for today's crossing, He had also set up a road block to turn back anyone who had not heard the news, so now the ferry that would take him and his men to the Island was theirs, and it would be made ready for the return journey carrying the largest drug haul ever seen, but he had one more job to do, he had already bribed the loading crew, but the captain who was a surly old sod, was not the sort to take a bribe, or anything else, so he had to be taken care of. The three vehicles were loaded onto the ferry, a van and two trucks, once the ferry was on the move, No3 sent one of his men up to the bridge to secure the Captain, the Captain was already suspicious of the lack of vehicles being loaded, he was not told of the cancellation notice that was sent out.

The man just walked onto the bridge where the Captain was ordering the engine room to start departing procedure, he turned and asked "Can I help you?" The man went straight up to him and hit him with an improvised blackjack,

"I'm the new Captain," he said.

After tying the Captain up and depositing him in a locked cupboard, he proceeded to manoeuvre the ferry out of the dock, he was an ex ships officer recruited by No3. They would dock in San Juliet at around lunch time.

67
Tuesday

The guards at the site were exploring the tunnel thoroughly with halogen lights, "Look here," said one of the Guards, they could see blood splatters on the floor, they followed the trail until it disappeared in to the seemly solid rock, it was not until they were low down that they saw the small opening, then they heard the sound of two gun shots, after that It did not take them long to find the two men, but when they did they found one man dead, the other, an old man looking like death himself, Darren was just about on his last legs, and pretended to be a lot worse that he actually was.

Once they got him back into the main facility he was interrogated, but not to forcefully, Darren told them about the hole in the fence and that was the way they had got in, luckily he did not have the blueprints of the base on him, and did not mention the power being switched off, he told them that all they were going to do was to disable every truck they could find, and it was just blind luck that they found the shaft entrance.

After further interrogation, he was locked up in a cell, and was told that the boss would talk to him later.

No1 was pleased that the two men had been caught, but sad that one old man had lost his life, "They sound like a couple of brave old men," Angelo Romano, No1, applauded bravery.

But the disclosure of the Islanders knowing what was going on was very worrying to No1, as this was to be an in and out operation, they were not expecting any resistance from any of the Islanders, the Mayor had insisted that all the Islanders were of a passive nature, he called No2 over "What about that man you sent to the Mayors house?" he asked,

"We have not heard from him at all Sir," No1 looked even more worried than he did before,

"Send someone down there, and find out what happened to him, no better still, you go,"

The only saving grace that No1 could muster was that none of the people on the Island could call for help, and now that they had the mechanic guy in custody, the other intruder dead, (he felt sorry about that!) Plus the teacher and the coloured man also dead, the only people who were left were the girl and the big man, and he could not see how those two by themselves could possibly cause any problems, so all in all the day had not been too bad.

The news that one of the men that had managed to enter the facility and disable two of their trucks had been caught was being talked about in the canteen. Stuart the generator man, was drinking coffee and overheard some of the men talking, he asked one of the men who they had caught, "It was some old guy from the town," came the reply, with the knowledge that this man must have had to do that to the trucks, made Stuart immediately thought of the man he had met earlier the town's mechanic, the one who he had turned the power off for, but not in his wildest dreams did he expect this old man to infiltrate the facility himself,

"Where are they holding him?" he asked,

"In the old cells one floor above," answered the man, Stuart went off to his private room where all the plans of the facility were laid out, he had all these for the power switching he had to do on a regular basis, the generator was not powerful to run everything at the same time, once he had located the block that the cells were in, he set about working out how to enable Darren to escape without him being the prime suspect.

68
Tuesday

Peter, the town's Mayor, dropped the gun in his hand onto the floor, as he looked down at the man he had just shot, "What have I done?" he cried out. Being a very religious man he thought that he. Peter Steinbach could never do something so abhorrent as to take a man's life, but here he was looking at a man he had just killed with a weapon so unfamiliar to him, it just seemed like a terrible dream. His wife picked herself up from the floor and walked over to her husband putting her arms around him; he pulled away sharply, and without any warning was violently sick.

The wife gently led him to their bedroom, trying to avoid the dead man's body as she steered him through the lounge, she made him comfortable, and to her surprise found herself utterly composed, and thinking straight,

"I'm going to get help," she told him, although it did not look like he had heard her, his face had a blank look upon it.

She walked towards the pub where their one and only friend was the landlord, Paddy. They were the only people on the Island that called him Paddy.

Chloe was telling David what had gone on at the boathouse, when the Mayor's wife walked in looking agitated, "What's happened?" asked Sean, taking her arm and steering her to a chair,

"OH! Paddy, Peter has done something terrible," Sean, David, and Chloe looked at each other with a knowing look,

"What's he done that's so terrible," asked Chloe,

"He's killed a man!" Sean could not believe what he just heard

"What do you mean, He's killed a man?" thinking he had heard wrong,

"A bad man forced his way into the house looking for Peter, I told him I did not know where he was, and he threatened me with violence if I did not tell him, but really! I didn't know where he was," Sean gave her a drink of water,

"What happened then?" She took a sip and carried on

203

"I couldn't tell him something that I didn't know, he grabbed me and pushed me to the floor, still asking the same question," She took another sip "Then Peter came in, the man let me go and told Peter that No1 wanted him to do something for him, Peter refused, then the man grabbed me by the hair and threatened to kill me if he did not do what this No1 wanted,"

Chloe could see that this nice old lady was getting really upset, so went and sat beside her,

"You're doing brilliantly, what happened next?" she asked, putting her arm around her shoulder, the Mayor's wife calmed down and carried on,

"Peter pulled out a gun and just shot the man,"

They called Mary to look after her, and made their way to the Mayor's house. They entered through the open door and immediately saw the dead man on the floor in a pool of blood,

"It looks like what she told us was true," remarked Chloe; Sean went to the man and checked his pulse knowing that he was dead, "What do we do now?" asked Chloe,

"We take Peter to my place, and then we get rid of the body," they both went to the bedroom to get the Mayor, Chloe walked in first and almost collapsed,

"What's the matter?" called out Sean following her in, then he saw what had caused the near collapse, Peter Steinbach the Town's Mayor for umpteen years, was dead! Sean went over to his friend and removed the gun from his hand, "He was a good Man," Sean looked down at the now dead Mayor, "He got himself involved with something a bit too big, and then the killing of a human life he just couldn't cope with the guilt,"

They left the Mayor there and went back into the lounge, looking at the body they were trying to work out what they were going to do with it? When Chloe noticed something strapped to his leg,

"What's this?" kneeling down and lifting his leg, Chloe did not seem to be fazed about handling a dead body. After all, the last one was the one she killed herself,

"It looks like one of those things that prisoners have on when they are let out on parole," said Sean,

"It's a tracker," said Chloe, "A tracker so they know where each of their men are at a given time,"

Sean thought for a minute "Then they'll be on their way here soon if that's the case,"

Chloe went to get some scissors and cut the tracker off, then, stamped on it totally destroying the device,

"They won't be able to track it now will they," she said with a smile. They carried the body outside and hid it in a hut at the bottom of the garden, then made their way back to the pub for the unpleasant job of telling the mayor's wife,

"Hold on!" said Sean "I left the gun there, I'll go back and get it, we do not want his wife to see it,"

No2 had seen the two of them come out of the Mayors house, he had a tracking device in his hand, and it showed that his man was in the house, then all of a sudden it went blank, No2 let himself into the house and noticed the blood on the floor, and the broken tracker, he searched the house for his man, but only found the Mayor, "You useless bit of shit," he said to the body, then he heard a noise come from the other room, he hid behind the door, and as Sean entered he hit him with a terrible blow to the back of the head, but with Sean being six foot six, the blow did not have the power as it would have for a smaller man, Sean turned round and surprised No2 with his speed, even though he had hit him with all his power, Sean picked him up and threw him across the room. But this so called fat man was not fat at all, he was all muscle, the man jumped up, and started to pull a gun from under his coat, Sean charged him and forced him back against the wall. No2 hit him full in the face with the power that would have felled an ordinary man, Sean retaliated with an elbow to the side of his head, No2 reeled back unsteady on his feet, Sean pressed home his advantage, and landed a full blooded blow to solar plexus that doubled the man up, but the man still did not go down. He swerved his body to the side and with a side step that he shouldn't have been in a fit state to do, kicked Sean just below the knee, Sean went down his leg unable to hold his weight, but again something inside of him said "Do not go to the floor," Sean pushed himself up using his good leg and caught the man under the chin with the top of his head, the man underestimated this big Irishman, he had thought that he was down and out so came in a bit too close trying to finish him off, the man went down like a sack of potatoes, Sean positioned himself to finish it with a kick to the man's head, when Sean felt a heavy blow to the back of his head, then nothing.

69
Tuesday

Back in the tunnel entrance David had sent Abdul and Ned to Darren's garage to get a generator, while he explored the rock fall, the hole made by Ned was now a lot bigger, and bit by bit David had made it wide enough to squeeze through, pushing himself along he found he was standing in a tunnel that seemed to go on and on into the darkness, looking down he saw the train rails "It must have been a supply route not using the main road," he thought to himself. He shone the flashlight down into the darkness, but the beam did not go very far. His foot kicked something. Bending down he picked up the kerosene lamp that Darren had found, and to his surprise it was still warm, squeezing back through the hole he started to make the hole bigger having found some tools in the truck, by the time they came back with the generator he had made a big enough hole to crawl through with ease.

Setting up the generator the place came alive, the truck they could see was in pristine condition and by the looks of it they could possibly start it up, but that would come later, hunting through the back they found guns, ammunition, and explosives, David lifted a box containing packs of C4 explosives and carried them to out so as to examine them in a better light, Abdul looking over his shoulder said "They look dangerous!" David picked up a pack and threw it at him, Abdul ducked and the pack hit the far wall "What the hell are you doing!" David smiled

"It's perfectly safe in this state; you need a detonator to set it off," Abdul did not let on that he was well versed in explosives, but was not amused, David went back into the truck to find some detonators, but to his dismay there were none to be found, but plenty of other things like a box of hand grenades, David lifted these out with care, hand grenades were very delicate things and could be very unpredictable, but on a closer inspection, these looked in pretty good condition. Then he picked up something that looked like Frisbees,

"What are those?" Asked Abdul, David did not reply he just put them away for future use,

206

David showed them the hole he had made, and pulled one of the light cables through, now they could see the tunnel better they were convinced that this was the way they were going to enter the site, and now with their extra a bit of fire power, they were sure that they could scupper the plans of the drug smugglers. They even found the hand cart Darren had used, they heard Ned cry out in pain, both turning fast to see what Ned had done to himself, they found him looking down at something, and looking down David nearly threw up. David had seen many dead bodies before but this one was different, it was a good friend and someone who would not hurt a fly.

Ned took of his jacket and covered Scott's body up, "Whatever you two are going to do, do not think for one minute you are leaving me out, I maybe old but Scott was my best friend, and if I have too, I'll die getting the bastards who did this," after a lot of manoeuvring they finally got Scott's body through the hole and laid him in Abdul's car.

"I'll take him to the doctors she has a cold room," Ned said, with sadness in his voice.

They took an inventory of all the stuff in the truck, and laid them all out "These should come in handy," said David picking up what looked like Frisbees, Abdul looked at them but did not have the faintest clue as to what they were, old Ned touched one "Yes Son I think you could be right," they made some plans, then started out for the town to talk with the others, and to get their views on how to proceed.

After leaving Scott at the surgery, the three of them walked into the pub to be confronted with a scene of utter chaos, in one corner there was Mary and Susan comforting the Mayor's wife, while Chloe and the Doctor, we're dealing with a prone Sean, "What the hell happened here?" shouted David going over to where Chloe was treating Sean, he could see that Sean had a really nasty cut on the back of his head "What happened?" he asked, Chloe related the events. David asked the doctor how he was doing,

"He's one lucky man," she replied fixing the bandage, "He must have a head made of iron," she said smiling,

"Would you all bugger off and let me sleep," The doctor gently lifted his head,

"Bloody hell, you've got one big head," she cried out unable to lift him up,

"And you're an old quack," replied Sean

"I think the old goat will be okay," she said,

"Thank you!" said Mary "Thank you for saving his life." She gave the Doctor a huge hug. She left saying to call if you have any trouble. David followed her out and explained the situation concerning the drug people up at the restricted zone, she was very upset about Scott, and volunteered to help in any way she could.

Sean was sitting up trying to remember what happened; "Chloe went back to the Mayor's house to look for you, and found you on the floor unconscious," said Mary, Sean still looked dazed, but managed to tell them about finding the Fat man in the house, and about the fight, and when he was just about to finish it off with a kick to the head, everything went black,

"There must have been two of them," said David,

"Well done Einstein, I think I worked that out all be myself,"

"I'll put him to bed," said Mary, David and Abdul helped her upstairs with Sean moaning every step of the way.

After some lunch they all started to make plans on the assault of the marine site, by using the tunnel, "But surely the men at the site would have closed the entrance up by now, after all they did capture them in that part of the tunnel," said Chloe, David had not thought about this,

"The way I see it is that because the wall looked so solid they thought that no one could possibly get through, otherwise they would have sealed it before," in the end they decided to explore the tunnel first before making any other plans.

70
Tuesday

At the site No2 was giving his account of what had gone wrong at the Mayor's house, "Did you kill this bar owner?" asked No1,

"No, we left him where he was and made our way back here as quick as possible," said No2, "And thanks to G5 hitting him with the butt of his rifle, he probably saved my life."

"Well not too much harm has been done; we did not really need the Mayor anyway," No1 was feeling sadder each day as the death toll was building up, this was supposed to be an in and out job.

No1 went down to the loading bay to find the site manager, the site manager stated that everything was in order, and on target to board the ferry as planned, first thing, tomorrow morning.

"I'll need a car in about an hour," stated No1,

"No problem Sir! I'll see that one is available,"

No1 then went upstairs to where the prison cells were situated, looking through the bars he asked "Are they looking after you okay?" Darren got up off the cot and came over to No1

"Yes thank you, but there's no telly in here, I wonder if you could arrange for one to be available," No1 smiled.

"I'm sure that could be arranged, and I'm sorry about your friend," he said, sounding really genuine, Darren saw the look on this man's face and thought that this man was genuinely sorry,

"Thank you, he was a great friend, as were my other friends that you killed," No1 started to leave,

"I can assure you that you! Will not be killed, you will be set free when we leave, that I promise!"

No1 went down to his office where the carpenter man was waiting, "We can move the cases now!" he said, Cordova and his men are talking to the pilots of the plane, and all other personnel are busy, they pulled the cases out of the secret hiding place, the car he ordered was just outside his office, they had a good look round, and quickly put them in the trunk. Getting in the car, No1 took the wheel and drove out of the underground cavern, there was no need to use the elevator now as the passage to the top was now clear.

They came to the coast road where the old barn once stood; lifting the cases, they deposited them in the now rundown barn; No2 had already made a safe place for them, well hidden but easily accessible. Once they were done they made their way to town to meet the ferry.

No1 was not too worried about going into the town, as there was only one of the little gang he had witnessed left, The Marine Scientist, although he knew she could be a handful, she could not now prove to be a problem.

71
Tuesday

David and Chloe had got the job of inspecting the tunnel, and if possible finding Darren. Abdul and Ned were sorting out what fire-arms were usable, in the abandoned truck. Sean was recovering well. And Susan took over in the Mayor's office.

Mary, Sean's wife, was given the job of bringing the ferry captain to the pub, as Sean himself was not up to walking to the ferry port.

David and Abdul had to make sure they were not seen by any of the Marine lot, as they were presumed dead, Sean who had a small van parked round the back of the pub had given them the keys, David and Abdul got in the back with Chloe driving, with Ned beside her, on the way out they passed a car carrying the Tall man who they now knew as No1 heading for town, "I bet he's heading for the ferry," said David from the back of the van, "We should have covered that, I forgot it was due in," Ned turned round,

"You don't really need me at the tunnel, let me off here, and I'll keep a watch on what's going on at the port," they all thought this was a good idea, so Chloe stopped and Ned started his walk back, fortunately they had not gone that far.

They arrived at the tunnel entrance, David and Chloe made themselves ready for the rescue of Darren, Chloe had the blueprints of the site firmly in her mind, as well of all her other talents she also had a photographic memory, sometimes it was a godsend but at other times it was a burden. They were just about to enter through the hole when they heard someone calling, young Joe walked in, "I thought you might want these," he said, holding up two phones,

"How did you find us," asked David,

"I followed you the other day using Arnold," he said with a certain amount of pride in his voice, David took the phone

"Phones are no good," he said "There isn't any signal," Joe tapped in a number on the one he was holding, David's phone immediately started ringing, "How on earth did you do that," asked Chloe, Taking the phone Joe was holding,

"It's the two phones you took from the two dead men, I pro-grammed them to make calls and to receive calls, but only to these two, the bad men have managed to put their phones on a secure channel that did not need a Wifi signal," David put his arm around him,

"Well done! But will you please go home, or your Grandad will eat me alive if you get injured."

Joe jumped on his bike and peddled off, David and Abdul played with the phones for awhile, getting used to them, "We're ready to go," announced David,

"Good luck," said Abdul.

David and Chloe crawled through the now larger hole after mak-ing it a lot bigger, David looked at the spot where they had found Scott, and a shudder went through his body, and an extra resolve took hold, if the bad people had seen this look they would certainly have been afraid. They decided against using the cart as to making too much noise, so they jogged along the tunnel until they came to the wide open space, then they split up to find the hole Darren had told them about, eventually Chloe called out in a soft voice, "Over here!" they were surprised that the hole had not been filled in, "How come they did not block this hole up?" asked Chloe,

"I was thinking the same thing, but seeing as the wall we came through looked absolutely solid they thought it would be impossible for anyone to gain entrance to the site through that way, so did not bother, but again it may be a trap,"

Previously No2 had been down the tunnel to see for himself if it was secure, and decided that no one could enter the facility by this route.

David went first, then Chloe passed their gear through, before pushing her way through herself, they found themselves in a dark passage, but at the far end there was a glimmer of light. Making their way forward quietly and with an extra amount of care, they finally came to the large area; David had brought along his night vision goggles, plus army issue binoculars they found in the truck, they were not up to the standard of modern ones but on this occasion were adequate, he swept the area looking for any cameras. Darren had told them that he thought that there were cameras, and that was how they were discovered, David saw just one camera near the area that the trucks were parked in, "There's only one camera that I can see," he said in whisper.

Chloe was to lead off, using her memory of the plans, "Remember, Hop, Skip, and Cover" said David, this was a method used by David and Sean Junior while on missions, one hops forward, the other skips behind, while both cover each other, as testament of their method they both survived many successful missions.

They came to a staircase that led to the higher floor, after skirting round the Truck area, and an area that was filled with bales of what they now knew to be cocaine, luckily the lighting of the whole area was not that good, so around the perimeter it was in shadow, so they had no problem, moving without detection.

With their guns held out in front, they started to climb the stairs, David who now held a gun in his hand, after vowing never to hold one again, but with the image of his farmhouse destroyed with his beloved Shep underneath!!

They started to climb when they heard someone coming down the stairs, they positioned themselves in an alcove just below the staircase, Chloe moved in a bit closer and stood on a piece of metal, the metal bar rolled out, making the man look round bringing his gun to bare as he turned, David shot him in the head using the improvised silencer Abdul had made, it still made a noise, they listened for a few minutes but no sound came from the main area, in fact most of the other men were quite a long way away, they pulled the dead man into the alcove and with some old rubbish they found, covered his body.

They now had more fire power David now had his gun and a machine pistol, Chloe now had a pistol of her own, "I won't ask you if you know how to use it?" said David, remembering the submarine pen. At the next floor with Chloe directing, they moved with more caution as this passage was so narrow that if anyone came down they would be trapped, there were numerous passageways going off in different direction, Chloe using her memory unerringly led them directly to the place where the cells were. David had removed some of the clothes the dead man was wearing, it was not any kind of uniform but it did make him blend in a lot more, so without any hesitation he just walked straight into the room, the gun with the silencer held out ready to shoot anything that moved, the room was empty,

"It's about time!" said a voice from behind the steel bars, "Do you realise that I've been cooped up in here for hours,"

"Were sorry," replied Chloe "We missed the bus, so had to walk," Chloe tried to find the keys to unlock the cell door,

"As a Steve McQueen, your rubbish," said David "But as I'm Batman and this is Robin, we will help you escape," laughing as he shot the lock to pieces.

Darren gave Chloe a kiss on the cheek, and gave David a man hug, "That's enough of all that," said David feeling embarrassed, "We have to get out of this rat hole before you can go round kissing people,"

Chloe gave Darren one of her firearms, when they all heard the sound together, someone was coming down the passage, David positioned himself behind the door, and Chloe went into the now open cell with Darren. A man walked in, David was just about to hit him with the butt of his gun, when Darren shouted out, "No! He's a friend," David lowered the gun but pushed the man against the wall and searched him for any weapons,

"Who are you?" he asked, Stuart looked shocked to find outsiders in the facility,

"I'm the Generator Engineer; I'm not part of this drug lot,"

After explaining who he was, and how he helped Darren and Scott to enter the site earlier, he asked how he could help them escape.

With their plan agreed, they started to move back to the main area, David leading the way, but their luck was about to come to an end, as two heavily armed guards were approaching the prison cells, they ducked back in and waited to take the two of them out as soon as they entered, but their luck held out, the two guards walked right past, "They must be going to an exit near the main gate," Stuart confirmed.

David rang Abdul and told him they had Darren, and were now making their way back,

They all made it to the main area but there was a serious problem, with more men around, due to the fact that they were now loading the bales onto the trucks, so the route to their tunnel was to be more difficult, but as their plan evolved the lights being turned off. David had his goggles ready, they said goodbye to Stuart after talking about what to do next, David gave him the phone "This is connected to another phone that we have, so we will be able to keep in touch." They shook hands and Stuart left.

Looking at his watch David said "get ready!" just like in the water earlier, David, Chloe, and Darren were connected by a long rope, with David leading the lights went out. And they started their perilous journey to safety.

72
Tuesday

The tall Man waited for the ferry to dock, he could see the extra
trucks and van on the deck, and men standing next to them, "Good!"
he said to himself, "We need their help," as the ferry docked the Tall
man went on board to find No3 , they shook hands "Did everything
go as planned?"

No3 smiled, "Like clockwork" he replied,

"What did you do with the captain?"

No3 led him up to the ferry's bridge and to a locked cupboard;
No3 pulled a key out from his pocket and opened it, but then could
not believe his eyes, the cupboard was empty,

"And the captain is where, precisely?" asked No1,

No3 could not believe it, he rushed out of the bridge and shouted
to his men to search the ship and find the ship's Captain,

"I'm sorry Sir! I put him in there myself,"

No1 started to bang on the walls "There there must be an explanation!" the far wall sounded hollow, after several seconds they
found what they were looking for, a secret compartment that ran
down to one of the lower decks "So much for your locked cupboard," said No1 with distain , "Find him, and find him now!"

They searched the whole ferry without finding the Captain "What
else can go wrong," No1 thought?

The Captain could not believe that someone would hijack a ferry
that only made journeys to this remote Island, but here he was tied
up on his own ship, in his own cabin, in his own cupboard, but he
smiled to himself, one of his great passions was doing magic tricks
for his grandkids and for his friends, not that he had any, but he did
have one trick that always astounded people the ability to extricate
himself after being tied up, so getting out of this little problem was
Childs play. Once he had freed himself, again he smiled, "What a lot
of idiots," fancy locking me in a place that had a secret compartment
from the ferry's smuggling days; he made his way down to a lower
deck and waited for the ferry to dock, knowing that the only way off
was over the side once it had docked, he was getting ready to jump

when all the men around the ferry's ramp run back onto the ship after being shouted at by the man on the bridge, using this uninspected opportunity, the captain just casually walked off.

The Captain made his way to his friend, Sean the pub owner, Sean was the only man on the Island who gave him anything like friendship, but he knew that he was his own worst enemy.

No1 was furious at No3's inability to contain one old man, but to say anything at this stage and in front of his men would be foolhardy, so he decided to wait until they were back at the site.

After leaving two of the men on the ferry, they made their way to the site where the last preparations should be underway for the loading first thing in the morning, but the Captains escape was worrying?

The Captain was a bit unsteady on his feet by the time he arrived at the pub, he was not a young man anymore, and now it was showing, "That's it," he said to himself, "If I get out of this alive I'm retiring," he smiled to himself, "And if I don't, I'll still retire,"

73
Tuesday
Columbia earlier

Captain Morella was congratulating himself on a job well done, he had convinced the President of Columbia that Sergeant Durrell was a good officer, and under the circumstances he had found himself in, like most people, they would have acted in the same way. To start with it had fell on deaf ears, but after what they had achieved Durrell was reinstated into the police force be it at a lower rank.

The day after Cordova and the drugs left his Country, things had started to unfold very fast, the three prisoners after a little persuasion, talked as if their life depended on it, and quite probably it did.

The security cameras dotted around the airport showed numerous coming and goings of the people and the vehicles that were being used. Following up on all this information along with the army, they had by this time two hundred suspected drug workers locked up, along with three Drug Lords. Between them they had managed to break up three large drug cartels, and that was only in 48 hours, what the next few weeks would bring was very exciting.

Smiling to himself he sat down at his desk raised a glass of whisky to his lips, he looked at the amber liquid, "This is much better than our own rum," he remarked; as he raised the glass high and downed the rather full glass, in one go!

In Virginia at the DEA headquarters James and Robert were waiting for an update on the plane that had sent out a mayday signal, "It must be theirs," said James "And it must also be a well organized ploy, no way would a plane with the most wanted man practically in the world, and Billions of dollars worth of drugs, just disappear due to a technical fault, and crash into the sea, it's a decoy, they have landed somewhere on the west coast," Robert who was looking at the screens scattered about in the room, said while still looking,

"It's impossible to land a large plane like this, on a small runway, and any large runway is being covered by an army of agents, police, and even the FBI, they want their man back, so no way are they landing anywhere, unless there's an airport or landing strip, we know nothing about?"

The call came in; no trace of the downed plane could be found?

FBI headquarters had received the same news as the DEA, no trace of the plane could be found. "No way is anyone going to buy the story, that the plane that Cordova was a passenger in, crashed into the sea, just like that, they must think we're stupid?" cried out one of the agents.

In another part of the building the hunt for the assassin was making good progress, they had traced him hiring a car outside the airport, and the tracker on the vehicle had traced it going to somewhere in Maine, but could not identify the exact area, "That confirms that he was the one that carried out the murder of the Officer up there, and now confirms, also the murder of the Officer in London."

The FBI had agents all over the United States, and after a few hours more information came in, "Can you believe this guy," said one of the agents manning a computer terminal, "He booked the car under the name of Assas Abdullah El Sin," the other agents could not see the connection, the agent explained "The first name Assas, the last name Sin" all of a sudden the others got it,

"The cheeky bugger!" they chorused,

"Not only that, he even used part of his real name Abdullah," said the agent.

We have a recent sighting and a booking on United Airlines, for an Assas Abdullah El Sin from Maine to San Francisco International Airport, and we have just received confirmation from the Airport, that Assas was on the flight, and exited the Airport in a Taxi to the City centre; we are checking all hotels and car hire firms.

THE NET WAS CLOSING IN ON THE PROLIFIC ASSASSIN!

In Langley, all agents were busy coordinating a strike on the village where the unfortunate incident happened three and a half years ago, the CIA had their own army of well trained operatives who were not averse to killing, but on this operation they needed help from various factions, including the United States Delta force, plus the British SAS and the Afghan Army.

After checking the information the young lad in the village had given them, and from another sources, they were able to confirm that an American was indeed a prisoner in the Taliban compound in the north of the village, and also that it was manned by a large force of armed Taliban fighters, this was news to the authorities in the area, including their armed forces, they were not aware of any activity in that area at all, so this joint force were deployed at great speed, but with precise coordination only made possible due to the fact that it was an American that was being held prisoner.

It was to be a three pronged assault; the British SAS would attack a high ranking Taliban leader in a neighbouring town, and draw some of the Taliban fighters from the target village.

The Afghan Army would then lay an ambush on the road and take these out, leaving Delta and the CIA agents to deal with the remaining fighters and the Taliban leader in the compound, the estimated strength of the compound was twenty five fully armed men, not including the leaders personal guard.

All elements of the plan were in place and the okay to execute was given.

74
Tuesday

Ned had walked back to the town just in time to see the ferry dock, and positioned himself so as to have a good view of the going and comings; it was not long after he saw the Tall Man go on board that Ned saw the ferry Captain Walk off, "That's strange!" Not understanding how a Captain would walk off his ship just after docking, he put it to one side for now and carried on watching.

Sean his bump on the head forgotten, as he heard what had happened on the ferry crossing, "They must be getting ready to transport the drugs to the mainland tomorrow" he said

"What drugs?" said the Captain, not really understanding what was going on. Sean filled him in on what was happening, "I just can't believe that an army of crooks have invaded San Juliet," said the Captain with absolute astonishment in his voice.

Ned meanwhile saw the men on the ferry running around as if they had lost something, at long last the Tall Man and four of the men got into their car and drove off, Ned could see that two guards were left on the ferry to presumably guard it from any intruders like us.

Ned made his way to the pub to meet up with the others and was surprised to find the ferry captain there, "How come you're in here, and your ship's in the port?" he asked "And this is the first time I have ever seen you leave the dam thing!" he said noting the captain sitting talking to Sean, "And why were there no vehicles on the thing?" Sean got up and poured Ned a nice pint,

"Sit down and we'll fill you in" After all the information was passed on Ned told them how David and Chloe were going to rescue Darren.

75
Tuesday

David, Chloe, and Darren waited for the lights to go out and bang on time the site was in total darkness, David switched on the night goggles and led the way, using his unerring sense of navigation, night vision goggles gave a strange green look at the world around you, but they do the job. They were making good progress when David came face to face with one of the men in the darkness, he thought of killing him, but just said sorry, the man said it back, and the trio carried on, they arrived at the tunnel entrance and started down the long passage until David realised that they were in the wrong tunnel, quickly retracing their steps, they carried on until they entered another tunnel desperately hoping that this was the real deal, Darren who was bringing up the rear of their line was just about to enter, when the light came back on, he ducked down, the two in front stopped and the three of them crawled the rest of the way in, the men who were loading the bales of cocaine were not looking in their direction, they were also disorientated by the sudden brightness so did not see them, they just carried on what they were doing, not taking too much notice of the light failure as it was quite common occurrence.

Making their way forward was now a lot easier for the three of them, as they made their way towards the opening, as they could now use the little light that was coming from the main site, plus they could now use their torches.

Abdul heard a noise coming from the other side of the wall, and immediately picked up one of the guns and covered the hole, ready for the first bad man to poke his head through, but a soft whistle from the other side let Abdul breathe a sigh of relief, David, Chloe and Darren came through and the three of them one by one hugged Abdul, Abdul was not used to this show of affection, and quite visibly looked out of place, "I do believe he's blushing!" said Chloe laughing.

After filling in the hole they had made in the wall so as it looked untouched, and impregnable, they collected their gear and climbed into the van to make their way back to town, very relieved that the rescue had gone down so well, but without the help from Stuart the generator man it could have gone horridly wrong.

76
Tuesday

No1 drove through the gates of the site noting that the guards were a bit agitated "What's going on?" he asked,

"The lights have gone out in the main area," replied one of the guards, No1 did not take too much notice of this as it was happening more and more often, he knew that fuel was at a premium, and the generator was not always up to the job,

"I wouldn't worry too much," he replied "

Driving down into the underground cavern to the main area, everything was as normal, most of the bales of cocaine were now loaded onto the trucks that would transport them to various parts of the Country, and No1 could see that Cordova was overseeing a lot of the work; this did not please No1 at all, and reminded himself to have a word with the site manager,

He went to his office to check that the men he had on the mainland side, were in place for the crossing tomorrow, all was well.

He looked up as Cordova came in, "I've been in contact with THE MAN," he said, "And he, like me, is more that a bit worried that you are losing your grip on this operation," No1 got up off his chair and slowly walked over to this jumped up prick, and without any warning, hit him so hard that Cordova fell to the floor gasping for breath, "Please can you get back in touch with THE MAN and tell him everything is on schedule," he said in a nice pleasant voice picking Cordova up of the floor, "And next time you want to enter my office please make an appointment," then threw him out the door.

No1 sat down not fully realising why he did that, he had enough enemies of his own without making another one.

Cordova made his way back to where his men were helping the loading of the bales, in all the years he had been in this game he had never been treated with such disrespect, "Whoever you are Mr No1 you are about to die," he said this out loud but out of earshot of any of No1's men.

No1 had pulled himself together and decided to talk with their prisoner the mechanic, he made his way up to the cells and was surprised that the guard that was supposed to be on duty was nowhere to be seen, but not as surprised as the sight of the cell door fully open and their prisoner not in it. He grabbed his phone and shouted down it, a newly installed siren started wailing, No1 bolted for the stairs and ran into the main area shouting orders, most of the men had picked up their guns not knowing what was happening, "Find him!" shouting at the top of his voice "He must still be in here somewhere."

After an exhausted search no trace of the escaped prisoner was found, "Did you look in the tunnel where we found the other men," one of the guards answered

"Yes Sir that was clear," the siren was still going

"Turn that bloody thing off," he shouted to no one in particular, "I want all personnel here in half an hour including Cordova and his men,"

"What about the guards at the gate?" asked No2?

"Those as well, just get everyone here; I want to find out who helped this man to escape,"

Cordova was already on the phone to THE MAN and after a lengthy conversation Cordova smiled to himself.

77
Tuesday

They all gathered in the pub once again including Julie and her Son, Joseph, David had requested Joe to be there as he needed his help, they were all thrilled that Darren was now among them, after more hugs they got down to business but this time without Scott. Ned told about the extra men he saw the tall Man with, plus the two guards left on the ferry, "I could get back on the ferry and disable it," said the Captain

"No I have a better plan for the ferry if we get to a point where these men actually are able to board it, but hopefully we will be able to scupper their plans before that," Chloe yawned and covered her mouth

"I can't remember the last time I slept," she said yawning again, David and the others realised that along with Chloe, they had not slept for over 48 hours,

"Let's all try to get a bit of shuteye and start afresh in the morning, we'll meet in the diner at 7am," said David, they all agreed as it was now getting quite late, they all went their separate ways, David and Abdul going to the hotel, Chloe and Susan went back to Susan's house, Darren and the Captain stayed in the pub, Julie and Joe went back to their diner, Joe was nearly asleep on his feet as were the rest of them, Ned went to one of his lady friends in the town "Don't get up to any naughty business, we need you alive," shouted David, after having a quick chat with Chloe.

David and Abdul sat in the hotel bar eating a sandwich made by the owner, Abdul wanted to know more about what happened in his town on that fateful day, but did not know how to approach it, "That was a sad story you told us about Sean's son, the one in the village you were in," he commented as casually as he could,

"I try not to think about it now," David replied,

"Are you sure your friends dead?" he asked. David looked at Abdul, but could not see anything that might be suspicious in this question,

"Yes!" David replied, not embellishing on the answer, Abdul wanted to know more but thought better of it at this moment,

"I'll see you in the morning" Abdul said as he went up to his room, David finished his sandwich and drink, and walked out of the hotel.

78
Tuesday
Virginia

In the headquarters of the DEA James and Robert were going through reports from all over the country, and all the reports were saying the same thing, a large shipment of cocaine had successfully entered the United States, even lowly dealers were saying the same thing, "We have missed something, or somewhere," said James, Robert looked a bit sheepish,

"I don't see how, we covered every single airport, air strip, plus every large expanse of grass, no plane has landed," they went over to a large map of the West Coast and looked and looked but could not see how a large cargo plane could have landed without someone noticing, "If this plane did land then we are in for a nasty shock all over the country, the amount of drugs that are reported to be on board this elusive plane, the whole Country in going to be flooded with an excess of affordable cocaine,"

Washington

The FBI was closing in on Abdul Abdullah's whereabouts; they had traced him to the Palace hotel in downtown San Francisco one of the oldest and one of the best hotels in the town, they now knew more about this elusive killer, they knew that he worked for a Saudi Prince, as a horse trader, and that allowed him to travel all over the world without any hindrance, but they were not allowed to name this Prince for legal reasons. Local agents had traced him hiring a car just over a week ago, as of now; there has been no sighting, plus the car hire firm did not have tracking devises on their vehicles, "We now have a good picture of this man courtesy of the Afghan Authorities, pass it on to all agents and police forces on the West Coast," said the agent in charge, someone put a memo in his hand, "Hold on people!" he shouted "We have a new sighting," the agent rushed over to one of the computer terminals, "What can you tell me?" he asked.

"It turns out that the car hire firm that Abdul Abdullah used in San Francisco has had the car returned to their Santa Barbara office, local agents raided the hotel Abdullah had booked into, but he only stayed for one night, but we did find out where he hired his next car, and he was heard to say at the car hire firm, that he was heading south, all CCTV cameras were at this moment being looked at, we now have the registration of the vehicle," the agent in charge tapped him on the shoulder "Keep at it

THE NET WAS GETTING TIGHTER!

Langley

After the okay had been given for the rescue operation, all units were now in place, and the reports coming in were very encouraging, the British SAS were in situ, and on standby, the Afghan Army contingent were positioned on the road leading to where the SAS were due to attack the Taliban camp, and the combined force of agents from the CIA and Delta were in sight of the compound where the supposed American prisoner was being held, they were now waiting for

YOU ARE GOOD TO GO!

79
Tuesday

At the site Stuart was talking to X1 the explosive man, "How are you getting on?" he asked, X1 could not understand why this engineer nerd was even passing the time of day with him,

"Fine thanks," he replied "Can I help you?" he asked in not a to pleasant voice, Stuart was in the area that X1 used as a workshop,

"I'm sorry!" he said "But we had a power blip a few moments ago, and the fault seemed to come from this area, so I'm just checking the wiring," he said as an apology, X1 took no more notice as Stuart carried on looking around as if he was checking, he found what he was looking for, detonators, "Is it okay for me to move this crate?" he asked "I need to reach that junction box" pointing to a box in the ceiling,

"Sure," came the reply, a bit more friendly this time, Stuart lifted the crate and accidently dropped it, some of the contents fell out, X1 did not notice Stuart putting a handful of the detonators in his bag,

"Sorry about that," he said, he carried on with his inspection thanked the man and walked out.

Making his way back to his part of the complex, he was going over his head what the man David had asked for. He now had the detonators, now he had to get another couple of phones. Going to the communications room, he again made the excuse that he was checking why the lights had gone out. He left there, with two extra phones, now the hard part, getting out of this place. He had surmised that it would not take No1 to long to figure out who had helped the mechanic man to escape, as he was the only who had had any contact with the man. Back in the generator room, he grabbed what he needed, and made his way up the stairs to the outside where he knew he was going to be vulnerable to being seen by the armed guards patrolling the area, plus the guards at the gate. He started up one the electric bikes that he had stashed earlier, he had chosen these for the quietness of the engine, and he started to make his way to the gate a plan in his head to allay any suspicion by the guards. when he got there, he was surprised that the gate was unmanned, he looked around thinking it was a trap meant for him, "Had someone found out he was missing?" he thought to himself, after several seconds everything seemed to be normal, just no guards! He opened the gate pushed the bike through, shut the gate behind him and roared off down the road.

All the men were in the main area, except the man who was flying the security drone patrolling the fence, and the gate. No1 had insisted that at least one man should be on guard. They did a roll call and found that two men were absent. One of the guards, the one who was supposed to be guarding the prisoner, and G1 the generator man, all other men could prove where they were at the time of the escape, including Cordova, who No1 suspected of having a hand in it so as to discredit him, but him and his men were all accounted for, the only two who could have helped the escape were they guard or the generator man. The generator man was the one he had always been a bit worried about as he was not one of us, "All of you, spread out and cover the whole place, find these men,"

It did not take long to find the body of the missing guard; the generator man was nowhere to be found, one of No1's men told him about the encounter he had with some people while the lights were out, "I knew I should have done something about that man!" he said out loud. His phone rang, "Yes!" he shouted down it, a look of utter surprise and a feeling of failure, he had called all the men down here including the gate guards, and now finds out that the generator man just walked straight out of the site, taking one of the two bikes, "Idiot!" he said to himself,

"You do seem to be making a few mistakes," uttered Cordova from behind him,

"Maybe you should hand the running of this operation over to your No2," he said with a smirk "He couldn't do any worse," No1 wanted to hit him again, but held back this time.

Putting the men back to work he went back to his office with a look of hate on his face for this supposedly drug Lord, "when I get the chance I'm going to kill him," he said to himself, but then remembered that he was going to kill him anyway with the bomb he had planted in the two cases, he smiled to himself his face taking on a more pleasant look.

80
Wednesday

David got back to the hotel at 1am after using Joe's workshop, he was well satisfied with the job he had done. Now he had to put his plan into operation?

They all met in the diner at 7am sharp, even Sean, who still had a sore head, "Here comes thick head!" said Chloe laughing,

"Enough of that young lady," he said "I'll have you know I'm a fully paid member of Mensa, they told me that my IQ was above the average person," now the whole diner roared with laughter, it sounded good, but it did not take long to get down to business.

"Now we know that this man No1 still thinks that Abdul and I are dead, we can use that to our advantage," said David,

Chloe who looked more tired than the rest of them asked,

"How can we use it to its full advantage?"

David told them what he had been doing with Joe's help late last night "I'm sorry Julie," he said with a resigned look at Joe's mum, "But Joe and I were working on Arnold most of the night, Joe had done most of the work by the time I got there,"

Sean piped in, "Where is where?" he asked,

Joe carried on the story "David asked me to fit Arnold with a device for dropping bombs," Julie nearly had a fit,

"You did what?" she said in a voice that was filled with astonishment and utter disgust, David cut in once more

"We can fly Arnold over the site and hopefully drop some of the grenades we found in the military truck," the whole room sat there their mouths wide open,

"I've never heard such a stupid idea in my whole life!" remarked Julie going over to put her arm around her Son, Joe gently removed her arm,

"I'm not a kid Mum, it's a good idea," the others were all mulling over the revelation David had just come up with,

"I think it's a brilliant idea," said Sean with all the others now nodding their heads, Abdul was looking a bit puzzled, and David asked him what he thought,

"It sounds perfectly feasible except for one thing," David knew this was going to come up,

"You're going to ask how we are going to pull the pin out. a good question, we all know that to detonate a grenade you pull the pin, wait a few seconds then throw it!" they all nodded once again,

"And how do you plan to do it?" asked Abdul again, David looked at Joe,

"We don't know!"

Darren the mechanic used his knowledge of explosives he learnt whilst in Vietnam, in his time there he had thrown quite a few of these devices, "The way I see it is," he stopped to think for a minute "Got it!" he exclaimed.

Joe and David went to the workshop to work on the solution Darren had come up with, it had sounded like good idea, but how to put it into practice was going to be a problem, but Joe had an idea how it could be done.

The door of the diner opened although Julie had put a closed sign up, Darren could not believe it when Stuart the generator guy walked in, Julie called out "Sorry we're closed!" Darren got up and walked over to the man who had just walked in, and put his arms around him,

"Ladies and Gentlemen this is the man that saved our lives," the others all went up and shook Stuart's hand,

"Thank you for what you did," said Sean, Stuart who was only about five foot five looked up at this big man and in a weak voice thanked him back,

"Don't be put off by the big lump of lard, he's a pussy cat really," said Darren, all of them laughing.

David and Joe came back into the room wondering what all the fuss was about; when David saw Stuart he too went over and shook his hand, "Well?" asked Sean, Joe held Arnold the drone in his hand,

"We now have a, San Juliet Bomber Command Plane," he replied with pride in his voice, David turned to Julie,

"You have a very bright boy here," he said, tapping Joe on the head,

"I know," she replied "Just like his Father, he'll see that when he comes back to us," Sean Senior smothered her in his enormous arms, he wanted to say that his Son was dead, but did not want to shatter his Daughter in law's dream.

Stuart related what had gone on after they had made their escape, and why he had to get out fast, "I found these laying around," handing the detonators to David,

"Brilliant, we can hopefully put these to good use," Darren had a woeful look on his face,

"If Scott had been here, he would have known what to do with this lot, he was a brilliant destroyer of buildings!" they all raised their coffee cups and toasted their absent friend, Scott.

Stuart carried on "After I stole these from the explosive man, I went back to my room, picked up my belonging, not that I had much; and made my way outside, stopping at the small fuel depot, we did not have a lot of fuel left, but now they have even less, after a made holes in every fuel barrel, and as I walked away the oil was running down the path, so by this time they would have run out of fuel completely," Stuart stopped, looks of admiration on their faces, "Then I stole one of the bikes we had and made my way to the gate hoping to bluff my way through the guards, and to my surprise the gate was unmanned," David looked puzzled,

"What do you think happened?" he asked

"I don't know I was just thankful that I was able to just walk straight through with the bike," Stuart took a sip of his coffee, and a bite of his sandwich, that Julie had made for all of them, "But one thing I did hear was the drone flying overhead, but by that time I was well away,"

Chloe who was still yawning, asked "How long do you think the lights will stay on?" remembering how dark it was whilst they made their escape,

"Until about now I should say," looking at his watch.

They worked on their strategy trying to come up with a plan that would prevent the drugs getting to the ferry and onto the mainland, after an hour of difficult choices, they came up with a plan that they all agreed on.

Abdul and Joe were to go out to the farm, then to their hiding place where they last flew Arnold the drone.

David, Darren and Stuart were to set up an ambush on the road leading to Darren's garage, now they had the detonators that Stuart had obtained, they could use some of the C4 they found in the abandoned Studebaker truck, plus they now had weapons.

Ned was put on ferry duty again, while Susan was to continue running the Mayor's office.

Chloe had her own job to do.

Sean was not given a specific task as to his injury, everyone was happy except Julie she was not in favour of her Son Joseph being put in arms way, "I'll be fine Mum," pointing to Abdul "I have a body-guard all to myself," they all smiled.

Everyone was ready to go. Abdul jumped on the buggy with Joe, Arnold the bird, safely in Joe's arms.

David and the others left for their ambush.

Chloe went off.

Ned went to the port.

And Sean back to bed.

The only one who did not have a job to do was Julie, is all she had to do was to worry about her Son.

81
Wednesday

No1 did not get any sleep. He was still made at himself for not dealing with the generator man earlier; looking at his watch it was time to put the finishing touches to the loading of the trucks, and to get them topside ready for the drive later on today.

He went down to the main area to find Cordova and his men getting into one of the vehicles, "What the hell are you doing?" he shouted, running over to stop the truck, Cordova leant out of the trucks side window,

"We are going to do something that you and your No2 forgot to cover properly!" he called out in a very patronising way,

"And what might that be?" replied No1,

"The safety of the ferry," came back the reply,

No1 had thought about it at one time but then dismissed it, but now with all the disasters that were happening he should have revaluated it, "I should have thought of it myself," he said,

"You only left two men on the ferry, and they were not proper guards," said Cordova,

No1 just started to reply, when the place was plunged into darkness, "What now?" No1 pulled a torch from out his pocket; most of his men were given torches due to the fact that this had happened so many times, The driver of a truck put his headlights on, other trucks seeing this put theirs on, but all the drivers knew that they could not have them on for too long as the trucks did not have a lot of fuel in them, No1 did not want to much fuel below ground, the trucks were due to be fully fuelled up once outside, "Get the trucks topside now," he shouted to the drivers, turning to Cordova, "Get to the ferry as quick as you can, I don't know why I did not think of it earlier," Cordova smiled as the driver started for the opening, luckily he had already fuelled up his truck, so they drove straight out of the site towards the town, and the dock.

No1 went up to the generator room with the site manager and one of the men who was a mechanic, after a quick inspection the mechanic found that the thing was out of fuel, "There must be some

236

sort of air lock, the things empty," he stated "I'll go topside and see what I can do,"

No1 went back to see the last of the trucks make their way to the top, when the lights came back on, looking around, he was surprised that the underground area was so big now that the trucks and cars were out, he quietly congratulated himself. Then he heard an explosion from the far end of the vast area, "What the hell was that!"he shouted, running down the length of two football pitches, he found X1 pushing his way through a large hole he had made in the last of the tunnels, No1 remembered that this was the one that X1 one had told him about, No1 crawled his way through he also was curious to what those people sixty years ago were hiding, No1 and X1 just stood there mouths wide open unable to comprehend what they were seeing, "No way," said No1, X1 fell to the floor his hands on his head "I just can't believe it!"

Cordova and his men lost no time in heading for the port, without the ferry their precious cargo was going nowhere, they were travelling along the coast road and saw a motorised buggy coming towards them, Cordova could see that one of the people on the buggy was the foreign looking man, he turned round as they passed, still looking, "He's supposed to be dead?" he said to no one in particular, he carried on staring in the rear mirror.

As they entered the town the truck had to stop to let the school children cross the road, the truck carried on towards the ferry port, the two men guarding the ferry were blocking Cordova from boarding, "I'm sorry we do not know you," said one of the men pointing a gun at Cordova,

"I'm Juan Luis Cordova your passenger," he stated walking towards the man ignoring the gun pointing at him, the man lowered the gun and was just about to say sorry, when Cordova pulled out a gun of his own and shot the man dead, looking down "I do not tolerate people pointing guns at me," giving the man a kick, "Throw him over the side," he told one of his men, turning to the other man,

"Welcome aboard Sir," the man said hurriedly, Cordova walked past him, giving orders to his men to secure the truck, and to secure the ferry,

"Who else is on the ferry?" he asked, the man replied

"Just two loading crew and the ferry's Captain,"

"Bring them to me," he ordered walking into the main seating area, "And find me a drink,"

After giving more orders Cordova was satisfied that all precautions were now in place, he settled down to wait for the loading to take place, later that afternoon, the ferry was planned to dock on the mainland just as the light was fading, they did not want their trucks to create too much attention.

82
Wednesday

Danielle the school teacher was not privy to all that was going on but knew that something big was happening, due to the fact that the mayor had not been seen for a number of days, and David her colleague, had not turned up for the school day.

Danielle made sure the school Children were settled in their classroom then went to find Susan, On the way to the Mayor's office she saw Susan coming out, "Sue!" she called, "I was coming to see you," Susan stopped, "I don't know what's going on, but I do remember you saying the last time we talked, that if I see anything out of the ordinary, to tell you," Susan steered her into the office, she did not want to discuss things out in the open, once inside she asked what it was,

"Just a few minutes ago whilst helping the children cross the road, this large truck came along, it stopped to let us cross, but it was the driver and the man beside him that looked out of place, I had never seen them before, and the passenger gave the children a funny look, when the truck went past I noticed men in the back as well, I just thought it a bit odd?" Susan thanked her and said not to worry, they knew who the truck belonged to, and they would find out what they were doing.

Danielle went back to the school with a worried expression on her face; Danielle was not a stupid person, and immediately knew that her friend Sue was not telling her the whole story, "She's defiantly holding something back,"

Susan went to find Sean and told him what Danielle had seen, when Ned came running in. The 90 year old was out of breath, "They've increased the guards on the ferry," he managed to get out, Sean and Sue looked at each other now knowing where the men Danielle had seen where going, to beef up the security on the ferry,

"When you think of it, it's a wonder they did not leave more men on the ferry in the first place, without that ferry they would not be able to get off the Island," remarked Sean, they knew that they could not do anything about it, but would inform David, when he returns.

Chloe had finished her chore, and was returning to the diner, she still had not woken up, so needed another strong coffee, on the way she passed the ferry, and she too, noticed the increased activity, "David and I knew that would happen," she said to herself, walking on a bit farther, to the other side of the dock, she was surprised to see the fishing boats sailing into the harbour, "That's strange," she carried on to the diner.

The fishermen had decided to return early from their trip, worried that they were unable to contact the harbour master or any of their family, after mooring the boats, one of them went off to see what he could find out, while the others, set about unloading the fish they had already caught, the trip had not been successful however, so the unloading did not take them too long, they had just finished putting the fish in the cold storage warehouse, when their wife's and young ones came running down, all talking at the same time, the whole fishing community only amounted to about fifty, once everyone had calmed down the men made sure their boats were secure, and as one, marched up to the Mayor's office looking for answers.

83
Wednesday

Abdul and Joe parked the buggy at the now ruined farmhouse not being able to comprehend the damage caused, seeing it in daylight the place looked deserted and empty, Joe went up close to the once lovely farmhouse, and went down on his knees and prayed for the loss of his best mate Shep, wiping away the tears he and Abdul made their way to the same place where they had flew Arnold from before.

Arnold the pigeon drone, flew like the bird it was supposed to represent, but this time he had a live hand grenade fixed to his undercarriage, David and Joe had constructed a simple release system after Darren had given them the idea, they had already tried it out around the back of the farmhouse, and it had worked perfectly, but working with live grenades that were over sixty years old was not a good idea, but Abdul who was quite adept in all armaments, felt confident that after Darren had given him a crash course in the handling of these very dangerous objects, he felt he was capable of not blowing the two of them up.

Arnold flew straight and true, and was hovering above the area where the trucks that had come up from below, were parked, Abdul who was in charge of the laptop, and was the one giving the orders of where to fly, could see that there was a lot of gesturing among the bad men, all were milling around not knowing what to do, Abdul thought he saw the man called No1 the tall man issuing orders but could not be sure, with Abdul directing, Joe released the bomb, the release went according to plan but the target, one of the trucks carrying the drugs was not hit, and as Abdul could see the explosion had missed anything of importance, but it did have a great influence on what was going on, all the bad men ran for cover.

Joe brought Arnold back and Abdul quickly reloaded another grenade, this time Abdul told himself to be a better bomb aimer. Once again Arnold flew beautifully Abdul was studying the screen with utter conviction, "Release he shouted!" Joe pushed the release button, Abdul could see the Grenade fall but once again just missing one of the trucks, but this time he could see that it exploded far to the left of a truck, where some man was kneeling down fixing something, the explosion this time was absolutely massive, Abdul looking at the screen jumped back, "What the hell was that?" he shouted out aloud, Joe came over to look at the screen himself once Arnold was safely home,

"Wow! What was in that one?" not believing the power,

"We will have to be careful with the next one Joe," said, Abdul, "We do not want any accidents we all know how unreliable these things are." Abdul attached another grenade but seeing as the other one was so violent he took his time, this time Joe released the bomb but it exploded well before it reached the ground, Joe had difficulty keeping Arnold flying the blast had affected the flight, but Joe had got really good at this flying lark, so safely brought Arnold home once again, "I think we should get out of here!" said Abdul "They will be looking for us," to prove his point, they heard the enemy's drone overhead, they both ducked down lower, as the drone flew over, but as it did so, it suddenly turned back,

"He's seen us," whispered Joe, Abdul put his hand on Joe's shoulder,

"Stay still," he said, the drone came back and started to hover just near them, all of a sudden one of David's sheep ran out from a thicket, it made Abdul and Joe jump, the drone turned and carried on its search.

"That was close," they both said together

"Quick grab your things, and let's get out of here,"

84
Wednesday

No1 pushed his way back out of the last tunnel followed by X1, "I can't believe we are going to blow this whole place up," said X1,

No1 looked back "I'm sorry myself, but it has to be done," he said with a certain amount of sadness, just then the lights went out again "What now!" He exclaimed, using their torches, that by now were no more than just a glimmer, they started to make their way out of the underground complex that had been home for the last week, No1 thought "Has it only been a week since we set foot on this tiny Island?"

They made it to the outside to find all the men were just milling around, "What's going on, why haven't you started fuelling the trucks?" shouting to no one in particular, his No2 took him over to where the fuel drums were kept, and showed him that all of them had been vandalised, oil was running down the slope,

"We do not have enough, for even, one truck, to make it to the port," said No3 who had come over, No1 walked off to ponder this latest upset, then one of the guards came over with a suggestion.

No1 gave the order to find enough fuel to enable one truck to make it to town, and fill it with all the undamaged drums, they would then fill them with the Islands garage fuel tanks, the guard who suggestion it was the one who had accompanied Stuart to the garage earlier, all the men were running around finding small amounts of fuel, and trying to siphon some out of the trucks that did have some left.

X1 was busy joining all the different wires to terminals on his detonator box when the first explosion happened, "What the hell!" he turned round quickly to see what had caused the explosion, to find men running around in confusion, No1 came up to him,

"Was that one of yours?" he asked, X1 held his hands up,

"No way," he replied, looking at the explosives on the floor behind him. Everyone was looking skywards but no one saw anything,

"Carry on," shouted No2 to the men, the guards had their guns trained on, they did not know what? The men were very wary about

243

being out in the open when they did not know where this explosion had come from. They carried on working, X1 had just finished his setting up, and was just asking No1 for approval via his phone, for he was well away from the trucks and most of the men, No1 looked around, all the men were out of harm's way just in case the underground explosion that X1 had set up affected them on top, but X1 has assured them that the explosion would be contained to the lower levels, No1 was just about to give the signal when the area X1 was in, exploded in a huge fire ball, No1 and all the men around him were thrown off their feet, No1 immediately thought that the underground destruction had somehow affected up here, after the flames had died down and the dust had settled No1 discovered that the underground explosion, had not taken place.

No1's men had taken cover under the trucks as another explosion above them went off, but this one had exploded before it hit the ground, No1 used his phone to the man in charge of the drone that was supposed to be patrolling the area, "Someone is firing at us, find them!" he shouted down the phone, the plume of smoke was seen by the man, and the drone was already scouring the area.

No1 called over the communication man "What about the Wifi signal blocking?" the man assured him that the signal would be blocked for another 24 hours, it had its own Power Pac that would last for 24 hours at least, "At last a bit of good news," turning to another man "Do we have anymore explosives left?" "No Sir! X1 had what was left with him when he got blown up,"

They all stayed under cover for the next fifteen minutes but no more bombs dropped from the air above them, No1 stood up and cajoled his men into action, "Hurry up we must get to that garage before they blow, that up," his phone started to ring, "Hello," he shouted,

"This is Cordova, what the hell happened?" Cordova had seen the plume of smoke from the port,

"We have been attacked from the air, someone has a grenade launcher somewhere, but the bombing has now stopped," No1 explained that they would be a bit late getting to the ferry, as to the fuel being dumped, and the constant threat of another bomb attack, Cordova listened to all this with disdain for this useless man,

"It was probably those men you told me were dead," he said,

"What men?" he asked

"The ones at the farm, the ones you told us your men had killed," he replied,

"What makes you think that it was them?" he asked again,

"We just saw one of them, the foreign looking one driving the teachers buggy, with a young lad," No1 cut the call, not knowing what to say, and what to do about this latest revelation, things were only about to get harder from this day on.

85
Wednesday

Meanwhile David, Darren, and Stuart, were waiting for one of the trucks from the site to come down the road that they had dynamited, with the help of Darren, and what he had learnt whilst in the army, they now had a supply of explosives themselves, but as the explosives came from the back of a sixty year old army truck, they were not taking any chances with it, and only had a small supply, when they heard the explosion from the site and saw the plume of smoke soaring into the sky, "What the hell!" said Darren, "That couldn't have been one of Abdul's grenades, it was too big," he exclaimed, the others agreed, "It looks as if we are wasting our time here," said David, not knowing what to do,

"They must still need fuel," said Stuart, "We wait, they have to come to the garage at some time, and it now seems that any fuel that they did have has just gone up in smoke," they all agreed to wait it out.

David had one of the phones Stuart had stolen, and was waiting for Abdul to give him an update on what was going on at the site, and whether Arnold's bombing raid was successful. They could see the column of smoke getting bigger, "Arnold must have done a lot of damage," said Stuart smiling, David was not so sure, no grenade he had ever used could be capable of that sort of power, he started to worry, he did not want to use the phone to ring Abdul in case they were in a tricky situation?

At long last his phone rang, "Did you hear it?" David felt a great weight lift from his shoulders,

"Yes we heard it, and we can see the plume of smoke from here, what happened?" Abdul could not explain the size of the explosion, but did confirm that they were lying low at the farm, and would be heading to town when the time was right,

David told the others that Abdul and Joe were okay, and would make their way to town later when the coast was clear.

They settled down to wait for the trucks to come.

Back at the farm Abdul was scouting the ruins while Joe tried to sort out Arnold's body, the blast had damaged a few panels, he had managed to fly him home, but to his eye it did not look as if he would be flying again, for a very long time, Joe put him in his box and started to walk towards Abdul who was busy sifting through the rubble, when he heard a faint sound, walking back he again heard the sound, "Abdul!" he called out, "Over here!" Abdul came running thinking something was up,

"What's the matter?" he asked,

"I don't know, I heard a sound but I don't know where it's coming from," they both listened, the sound came again,

"I think it's coming from over there!" said Abdul pointing, they moved a bit closer to where they thought the sound was coming from, and both listened with their ears cocked to one side,

"There!" shouted Joe, pointing to a place Abdul knew quite well, it was the entrance or in Abdul's case, the exit from David's tunnel,

"I know where it's coming from!" he said running over to the place he remembered exiting just a few hours ago, he lifted a wooden trap door, Joe looked down the shaft, and the look on Joe's face was the most wonderful thing Abdul had seen in his whole life, for there at the bottom of the shaft was Shep!

Joseph lost no time in climbing down to his friend who looked in a bad way, his coat was all matted and he looked dreadful, but it did not stop the dog licking Joe's, face happy to see him, Abdul climbed down and between them managed to get Shep out of his what could have been, his grave, David had a water well on the farm, so they were able to give the dog a drink, after a few mouthfuls Shep started to be the wonderful dog he was.

Joe was crying tears of joy the tears running down his cheeks, "Don't ever leave me again!" he said, Shep seemed to understand and started licking his face over and over again,

"I think he's happy to be alive," remarked Abdul stroking the dog, Joe who had been given some food by his Mum, fed Shep what he had left, the dog seemed to come alive like magic, and started to jump about with Joe encouraging him, the two of them went off, and Abdul picked up the phone to let his friend know that his beloved dog Shep was alive and well, this was going to be one of the best phone calls he had ever made.

Back in the town the fishermen had gathered outside the Mayor's office and they were bombarding Susan with question about what had happened to the phones and the internet, and mainly what has happened to the Mayor. The Doctor, who had treated Sean, was not told the full story about what was going on. David had just told her just enough to allay any fears of the town's people. But now they wanted the full story, but Susan did not know the full story herself, only being on the outside of talks, in the end, she managed to calm them down, and promised that all the problems they are facing at the moment, should be resolved in the next 24 hours, but in the mean-time please be calm.

Susan went to see if Sean was able to give her an update. Walking into the pub, she was confronted with Mary coming down from upstairs trying to make Sean go back to bed, "He's still not right," she said as they sat and had a coffee, but to Sue's dismay Sean's wife could not tell her anything about what was being done.

Ned was still on duty at the ferry but not a lot was going on, and he was now getting a bit bored until Chloe came up, "What's going on?" she asked,

"Nothing!" he replied, Chloe trained the binoculars she had brought with her on the bridge of the ferry, but could not see anyone moving, swinging down she could see the guards patrolling on full alert,

"Senor Cordova must be really worried," she thought to herself, she moved the binoculars down the side of the ferry and was pleased about something, Chloe give a small smile, "I don't think anything is going to happen until they start boarding the trucks," she said "So you go and get something to eat, I'll keep an eye out here," Ned was grateful for the break, and headed for the diner, Chloe again trained the glasses on the ferry.

86
Wednesday

Unbeknowing to Ned one of Cordova's men had seen Ned spying on them, and told Cordova, "Don't worry about it yet, let's wait until we need to neutralise him,"

The phone Cordova had given to him by THE MAN rang, "Hello" he answered "What's going on down there," shouted THE MAN, "I can see smoke coming from the site," Cordova told him what was happening and how he was now guarding the ferry that No1 had forgotten to do, he said all this making sure THE MAN knew that this No1 was a liability, "Once the product is on board and you have left the harbour, you have my permission to eliminate him, and his sidekick No2," he said, Cordova smiled remembering that he was already about to do just that, he was just going to say that he did not need THE MAN'S permission, when THE MAN carried on talking, "I'm sorry to tell you but your network down in Columbia had been dismantled by the police, and the Columbian army, all your three Cartels have been either killed, or are now in a Columbian prison," Cordova could not believe what he was hearing, all those months of planning, plus the difficult task of getting the three Cartel's to work together was now broken, and he knew that he Juan Luis Cordova could never return to his beloved country,

"How did they find out?" he asked

"From your informer a Sergeant Durrell and a Captain Morella, they alone were responsible for most of the arrests and the imprisonment of your own men," Cordova could not take all this in, it seemed impossible that his organisation could have been ruined by just two men,

"Can you get a message to my Brother, Pablo!" asked Cordova, "We still haven't got connections here,"

"Yes, what do you want me to do?" Cordova told THE MAN what he wanted done, and ended the call.

He went out onto the deck to make sure all the men were at their allotted posts, he had all corners of the ferry covered plus two roving guards, even No1's ferry Captain, was now on guard duty, along with the ferry's crew.

Chloe could see all this happening through her glasses "They do look a bit worried," thinking out loud, Ned came back feeling rested and full. Chloe said her goodbyes, and made her way to the pub to find out if the others had had any luck.

87
Earlier Wednesday
Columbia

Captain Morella, and Sgt Durrell, who was now just Detective Durrell, were putting the last touches to dismantling the Cordova Cartel, they now had more information on Pablo Cordova, Juan Cordova's brother, who in the investigations going on all over Columbia had disappeared, but the Columbia police force were at this moment closing in on his last known whereabouts.

Then they received a call from the Chief of the Columbian police, the Chief spoke to Morella "You have been requested to be at the Palacio de Nariño, to receive an award for your excellent work bringing down the Columbian drug Cartels," Morella nearly dropped the phone, he could not speak for a few minutes, he has been part of the police force for twenty five years but for this to happen? he called over Durrell to hear the last of the message putting the phone on speaker, "The President, Juan Manuel Santos, would like to congratulate the two of you himself, for your dedication and devotion to duty, not only for this successful operation, but for all the previous successes with one Columbia's highest honours, you are expected at the Palacio at 10am tomorrow and that will include your family members," Durrell could not believe that he a lowly Sergeant, was about to meet the President himself. He could not wait to tell his Wife and Children, Morella just took the news in his stride; he had met the President on numerous occasions during his career, even the one before Senor Santos, but this was a shock. His own Wife died last year and he had no other family, he thanked his Chief and put the phone down, Durrell was still in shock.

"We had better start getting ready to meet our president," said Morella, putting his arms around his Sergeant.

The phone rang again, "It's probably the Chief saying it's been cancelled," he said smiling, "Morella!" he answered, the captain listened for a few minutes before putting the phone down, "Cordova's Brother was not there, it looks as if he has gone to ground,"

DEA headquarters Virginia

James and Robert were getting more frustrated by the minute, the rumours were still coming in that the large consignment of drugs had in fact landed in the United States, "Bloody hell!" said Robert, "What if all these rumours are not rumours. We have all our informers saying the same thing, the drugs have entered the Country, so where the bloody hell, are they, and where the bloody hell, did they land?"

They were going over a report from a ship out in the Pacific about fifty miles from the mainland, of hearing a large plane go overhead, the plane in question was no more than two hundred feet high, just about skimming the waves, but as it was night time they could not see the actual plane, but various people on the ship heard the same noise of a plane flying very low, that report had now been verified by other ships in the area, and all reports stated that the plane without question was travelling northwards.

James had people searching for other sightings but so far no one else had seen or heard a plane flying low, they were consulting a large map of the west coast, just like they did on all the previous occasions, but still could not see how a plane as large as a DC8 could go missing, but one thing they did know that it did not go down after the mayday call.

They were staying in touch with their partners on this. The FBI who we're doing their own investigation on the whereabouts of their escaped prisoner Cordova, they had received some Intel that Cordova was in the Country and was scheduled to meet other drug dealers in a few days time, but that had not been confirmed.

They told the DEA that if anything came up they would let them know immediately.

Langley CIA headquarters

The British SAS had started their attack on the Taliban camp, using grenade launchers and mortar shells, but at this time no news as of the reinforcements from the village being on their way.

The Afghan Army unit were all ready to receive them.

The CIA and Delta were waiting for the bulk of the Taliban in the compound to leave, before mounting their own rescue plan.

88
Wednesday

David, Darren, and Stuart, had dynamited the road leading to the garage; the road was a private one, so no other traffic used it unless visiting the garage. They had also set charges in the garage itself just in case the men managed to avoid the first trap, David's phone rang, he listened his face taking on a big smile, and putting the phone away he punched the air in a sort of victory way, "He's alive!" he shouted, "He's alive!" Darren came over,

"Who's alive?" David could not control himself; he sank to his knees and thanked everyone he could think of including God, who he did not believe in, "Shep my Dog, He's alive!" Darren bent down and put his arms around him,

"That's the best news ever!" he said, both men quickly got up when they heard a truck coming down the road.

A truck with two men in the cab was slowly driving along the road leading to the garage, both men aware that it could be some sort of ambush;

David had the task of setting off the explosive device, just then the window David was looking out of suddenly exploded in a shower of glass the bullet just missing him, he ducked down quickly, David pushed the detonator he had in his hand and the explosion down the road shook the place, David risked a quick peek, the truck was un-harmed and still coming towards the garage, another bullet just missed his head, David knew that it must be a sniper up in the trees to the right of the garage, they could not afford to hit anything that was likely to blow the place up, so a full frontal attack was unlikely.

At the sound of the truck, Darren and Stuart made their way to a small hillock just behind the garage, with the other detonator in his hand for blowing up the entire garage, the garage was Darren's dream and the thought of having to destroy it, was paramount to blowing up himself.

David could not see where the shots were coming from, he had seriously underestimated this man No1, it looks like the truck was a decoy and armed men were surrounding the garage, in all the planning he had not thought this scenario through thoroughly, but like many times in his Army career, he always had some sort of get out plan in the back of his head.

Darren was waiting for David to make his escape before blowing his garage to pieces, as he thought this, his mind went back to his other life before he came to the Island, the things he was not proud of, the things he had done, he brought himself back to reality, when he saw David run out of the back door and jump onto the motor bike Stuart had misappropriated from the site, and quickly move off, the bike being electric it did not make a lot of noise, the sound of gun fire started again. David made it to safety, stopped so Darren could see him, and gave the signal to blow the garage.

Darren his hand on the detonator thought, I'll wait until the gunmen are inside then there will be less men to deal with later, he could see the gunmen angling down from the trees just to the left of the garage guns at the ready, the two men in the truck were approaching from the right both men had automatic weapons aimed at the doors, he saw the two men kick the door open and charge in letting off a stream of bullets, making sure they didn't hit anything vital, they came back out and gave an all clear signal to the other men who had now joined them.

Wishing he did not have to do it. Darren pushed the detonator that would destroy his dream. Nothing happened! Darren pushed it again, still nothing, "Shit! Shit! Shit!" He said out loud, Stuart tapped him on the shoulder "Come we should go," gently pulling him away, Darren gave one last look at his garage, "I was about to destroy my dream," he thought to himself, and now, deep down, he was glad the explosive device had not detonated.

89
Wednesday

No1 was pleased to see the truck come back with the fuel drums full, he anticipated that some sort of ambush or some sort of attack on the truck would be forthcoming, so sent one of the Range Rovers with four armed men including one of his best snipers to protect the truck, and to take out any resistance the Islanders could muster, he did not think that the threat would be that much, knowing that there were no real firearms on the Island, just a few farmers with maybe a shotgun or two, but hearing about the explosives used during the fight, and from the account his men had given him his worries were far from over.

He rang Cordova and gave him the news that the trucks would be rolling in about an hour's time, and to be ready for the boarding.

Cordova on hearing about the explosives these men had at their disposal, decided to put his own plan into operation, first he had to get rid of the old man that had been spying on them all day.

Chloe did not have any luck finding out anything about what was going on, Sean had not heard a word, and the fishermen had gone back to their homes for now. So she decided to go back to Ned's stakeout, she came up behind him without startling him too much, "Has anything happened?" she asked

"No, Nothing, but two of the men left a few minutes ago going towards the town," he replied, Chloe felt that something was wrong,

"Why would anyone need to go to the town?"

"Would you two like to get a better view of the ferry from on board," came a voice from behind them, Chloe and Ned turned round slowly, the two men Ned had seen going towards the town were now standing behind them, pointing guns to their heads,

"That's very nice of you, and thank you for the invite, but we're quite happy here thanks," said Chloe looking back at the ferry.

One of the men grabbed her by the hair and tried to pull her up; she turned so fast the man did not have time to defend himself, as the blow to his abdomen hit with the force of a hurricane, he went down Chloe was just about to hit him again, when the other man who had his gun pointing to Ned's head,

"I don't think that would be a good idea!" cocking the hammer, Chloe sat back down, the man she hit stood up, looked at Chloe with his intensions all to evident, his foot came back and the kick caught Chloe full in the face, she went down her world all black.

The man kicked her one more time, "Hope the bitch dies," spitting on her prone body, blood already staining the ground.

While this was going on, Cordova in a truck with two of his men, were making their way into the town.

Ned found himself in the ferry's main cabin tied to a chair, after being roughly taken on board by the two men, he still had the image of Chloe lying on the ground blood pouring from her head, he tried to get loose but the men had done a good job. He heard a truck come aboard the ferry but was too far away to hear what was being said by the men, the cabin door opened Ned could not believe what he was looking at "No!" he screamed "What kind of monsters are you people,"

Abdul and Joe and Shep were the first ones back from their bombing raid; all in all, it had been as good as the Dam Busters, as David would say! The three of them walked into the diner, Julie who had her back to them, heard the dog whimper first, then to all their surprise Shep actually barked! Julie nearly jumped out of her skin, turning she could not contain herself she came running from behind the counter cuddled Joseph first, then went onto her knees and let Shep lick her face, something she has never down before, "You Beautiful, Wonderful, thing you!" she cried, Shep barked again,

"I can't believe he can actually bark," remarked Joe, not even David had heard him bark before.

Looking out the window, they saw David pull up on the motor bike, seeing his buggy parked outside he knew that Shep must be inside, all of the sudden the diner's door opened, and this four legged monster ran up to him barking like mad, David was again taken by surprise and found himself on the floor being licked by this furry monster.

After the excitement of finding out his best mate was alive, David thought this was turning out to be a great day.

They were joined in the diner by Sean and Susan the Mayor's secretary, "Where's Chloe?" David asked, Sean looked around

"I thought she would be here by now," he replied,

"She was in here earlier, I think she went to find Ned to give him a break from his lookout station," said Julie.

The other two boys came in, Darren not really knowing how he felt about the explosive device not exploding.

Julie made them all something to eat, and they settled down to work out what they were going to do next, but no one could come up with a new plan of action.

"I'm getting a bit worried about Chloe, and Ned," said David "I'm going to look for them," he got up, and headed for the door, but before he could get there one of the fishermen burst in,

"There's been an accident," he shouted.

90
Wednesday

No1 was pleased that they were now ready to leave for the port, when THE MAN'S guard came up to him, No1 had not heard from him since they had that talk in the carpenters workshop, "I need to tell you something," they walked a little way from the rest of the men the guard looking out for his boss G1, "I heard G1 talking to another guard about the job they had been given, concerning you and No2," he said in a whisper,

"What about us?" No1 asked, the guard looked round again,

"They plan to kill you both once were on the ferry!" the guard was surprised that this information had not exactly taken No1 by surprise?

"Thank you," he said, "I figured as much myself, I always thought that THE MAN was a shitbag, and that Cordova and me where not the best of friends!" No1 shook the guard's hand,

"If you need my help, you've got it," said the guard.

No2 came over and told him they had one more truck to cover up, then they we're ready to go; they walked over to the last truck No1 telling No2 what the guard had told him, "We'll be ready," he replied, the two of them had already planned for this both thinking about a double cross.

The last truck had its livery still uncovered, the truck was now a FED X truck along with all the others, Fed X being one of the most recognisable trucks in the whole of the World, and would practically be invisible, they were planning to take the covers off once on the ferry, they did not want the Islanders to be able to tell the authorities what the trucks looked like, once on the mainland each truck had a different destination not one of them were going to the same place, then the drugs would be transported all over the Country, the whole of the United States would be swamped with affordable cocaine, and No1 would be a very rich man, providing he lived to see it, that was why he had hidden the two cases with the two hundred million in them in case something went wrong, believing that if anything did happen, he could come back and retrieve them at a later date.

Bob Ball

At long last they were ready to roll, No1 was very nervous about the trip; this is where it all could go wrong. With all the men and trucks ready, No1 gave to signal to move out.

91
Wednesday

David and the rest of them rushed to the medical centre, it seems that one of the fishermen found Chloe in a pool of blood, near the harbour, he did not know what it was at first, until he got closer, and found the woman who he did not know, lying there covered in blood, and managed to get her to the doctor, where she was now being treated. They arrived at the centre to find Chloe still unconscious, but she had been cleaned up, but she did not look as bad as she did when they brought her in, "She's a very lucky girl" the doctor said, remembering that she said the same thing just a day ago, "It will take a long time, but there should not be any permanent damage,"

The medical centre was just the house that the doctor, and her fisherman husband lived in, part of the downstairs had been made into an emergency room, plus a room that was used as a ward If anything bad happened, or anyone was really ill, they had a direct line to the hospital on the mainland, and an emergency helicopter could be there within the hour, but Chloe's injuries looked worse than they actually were, that was probably why the man who attacked her, left her for dead.

Chloe slowly opened her eyes, one of them black and blue and swollen to twice the size, David kissed her, "I'm not going to ask you how you feel? For that's the most stupid question that people always ask," he pulled away and asked "But how do feel?" they all laughed.

Outside the doctor's house, a crowd had gathered, each asking the question "What's going on?" Sean who had taken off the bandage, put on by the doctor the day before,

"It's about time we told the people what's going on," Sean decided it was down to him, to tell the people, as Deputy Mayor, it was deemed his duty. Noting all the people outside, he could see that it was not only the fishermen, but the shop owners, the few farmers that the Island had, even the pastor was there, he was delivering the horse that Abdul had purchased the other day as it was Wednesday, the day the ferry makes the return journey to the mainland. Once a month the ferry stays overnight to allow more business to be done, he told the crowd all will be explained in the hall, in half an hour's time, the crowd dispersed.

Chloe fought through the pain and related what had happened, but could not throw any light on the whereabouts of Ned, "I can only surmise that they have him on the ferry," said David out loud,

"Why would they take an old man hostage?" asked Darren, who was fond of the old goat!

"Maybe some sort of bargaining chip," said Julie, becoming more involved in this conflict they found themselves in.

The doctor came in, "I think you should all go, this young woman needs to rest," one by one they left, all giving their best wishes, David was the last to leave, the doctor seeing the way the two of them were looking at each other, she left the room.

"You look awful," he said kissing her,

"You didn't say that this morning," she replied a grimace on her face,

"That was a Titanic moment, me being Dicaprio, you Winslet," and this is now a David Cross moment, kissing her once more whispering "I love you!"

Sean looked down on the people of San Juliet from the raised stage; the hall was packed with worried Islanders. It took all the skills that Sean had as a talker, and leader. Being a Deputy Mayor, he had not envisaged this sort of scenario, but he did not hold anything back, he related everything that had gone on since the State Marine Survey Agency trucks rolled off the ferry, he answered all the question thrown at him, with as much honesty as he could, but there were so many unanswered questions, that the full picture was still to be seen.

The Islanders were all shouting at the same time when in walked Chloe, helped by David, you could see that she was in pain, but she knew they needed the help of the whole community to stop these men from smuggling truck loads of drugs into their wonderful Country, The United States Of America.

After she had spoken, the islanders asked how they could help, not just one, or two of them, but the whole Island we're behind Sean, David, and Chloe in stopping this dreadful thing happening on their Island.

Before they had gone to the medical centre, David had given the job of looking out for the trucks approach to the town, to Stuart and Abdul, as they did not know Chloe that well.

Stuart and Abdul were parked out of sight, on the coast road, with a clear view, but the view did not matter, they heard the trucks coming well before they saw them, Stuart rang David, "Fifteen minutes" he said. The trucks came into view, and they could tell by the way they were being driven, that all the trucks were fully loaded, having lost two of them thanks to Darren and Scott, once they had passed their position, they followed keeping a watchful eye on the last truck, they were not worried about being seen, the men in the trucks ahead, knew that this part of the operation, the boarding of the ferry, was not going to be easy and were expecting some sort of resistance, so them being visible to the people in front was a clear indication that the ferry boarding was not going to be a piece of cake.

No1 saw the teacher's buggy behind them, but he was not too worried about a single vehicle, he was more worried about what was waiting for them in the town.

In the town, they had come up with a plan, the whole community were going to block the ferry, the thought was, that no way would these drug smugglers try to get past two hundred people determined to prevent these drugs entering the Mainland.

The solidarity of the Islanders was something to behold, the talk by Chloe when she told them how they had killed her two friends, and how they had killed one of the Islands most popular characters Scott, and that they were holding Ned captive on the ferry, the whole community came together as one, so the plan was formulated.

David received the call from Stuart, "They're coming!" he called out, and as one they started to move towards the port, Chloe was helped back to the medical centre by the doctor, she was now in a bad way, David knew that it was not a good idea to let her go to the meeting, but she insisted, David kissed her, and said he would be there as soon as he dealt with this situation.

Cordova saw this tidal wave of people coming towards the ferry; his men were already positioned to repel any attempt of the Islanders to try to board, but to his surprise they did no such thing, they strung out blocking the entrance to the ferry, the entrance was not very large, so the barricade was three or four deep, and to his eye they looked quite formidable, he turned to the man behind him, "Get them ready! Plus the old man," the man went off, Cordova saw the first of the trucks enter the town and make its way down to the port coming to a stop just short of the people's barricade. A Range Rover came from behind the trucks and No1 got out, looking at the crowd trying to work out what he was going to say, and what he was going to do, no way was he prepared to harm these people, so he decided to bluff his way through, he shouted at the top of his voice "Get out of the way, now!" No one moved, "If you do not move my men will move you," six men with automatic guns came forward, and pointed them at the crowd,

"Stay where you are!" called out David, walking forward towards No1, David got to within five feet of the man who had threatened the people of his Island "We do not know who you are? And we don't want to know, is all we want is for you to leave our Island," No1 took one step forward,

"That's all we want to do, leave you're Island," he replied "So if you get these people out of the way we will do just that," David turned round to the expectant crowd,

"He wants to leave our Island," he shouted out, and one voice shouted back

"He can do that with our blessing, but the drugs in the trucks do not go with him," they replied!

"You heard the people, you and your men and your vehicles, can leave the Island once you, or us, have dumped the whole lot into the sea," David said in a nice calm voice.

No1 moved back to his car and made a phone call, he came back and stood in front of David and the crowd, and in a load voice said "I'm sorry we cannot do that," holding up his hands "So I suggest you just make a pathway for us and we'll be on our way," lots of shouting came from the crowd with all manner of profanity's,

"We're not moving," they shouted in unison,

No1 gave a signal, "I think you will have no choice in the matter," he called out, "I suggest you look behind you!" pointing to the ferry.

92
Wednesday
Columbia

Pablo Cordova put the phone down, after receiving the call from THE MAN. Pablo was enjoying the thrill of being the only Cartel Lord in Columbia, at the moment. But knew that all over the Country there were terrible killings, and torture, going on in the biggest power struggle the drug fraternity had ever seen, new Cartels were starting up, with small outfits trying to swallow other smaller outfits, the murders going on all over the Country, did not worry the drug enforcement agencies to much, as it was at the moment, drug gangs killing drug gangs, so Columbia was getting rid of a lot of bad people.

Pablo knew, that as the rightful chief of their Cordova Cartel while his bigger Brother was in the United States, he could control the majority of the other smaller units in the north of the Country, so had made plans to exert control on all known drug units in their region, as at this moment his control was invincible, he now had the north of the Country under his control, the next thing he had to do, was to arrange the killing of his devoted! Brother Juan Luis Cordova whilst he was still in America, he Pablo who was named after his hero Escobar, the greatest drug lord in the world, Pablo crossed himself "Rest in peace" before that he had more urgent things to do, the phone call.

DEA Headquarters Virginia

James and Robert still had not had any luck in tracing where the DC8 could have landed, but all reports show that it did land?

264

FBI headquarters Washington

"We have had a definite sighting" said an agent, coming over to report to the Agent in Charge of the hunt to find the Assassin,

"Where?" he asked

"South of Santa Barbara, a small ferry port that serves San Juliet an Island off the coast, about forty miles out, the ferry goes out on a Tuesday and a Friday only," the agent replied, they both looked at the map the agent had brought over finally finding it,

"It's tiny," said the chief, "What's on there?"

"Nothing," he replied, the agent gave him a rundown on the tiny Island of San Juliet,

"Who phoned in the sighting?" he asked

"We have agents all down the west coast asking and showing pictures of our man, and one of the ferry's operators recognised this man driving a small car last Tuesday going to the Island," the chief shouted out to everyone in earshot,

"Find out everything about this Island, who lives there? And what is actually on the Island that would interest our Assassin, and get my plane ready,"

Afghanistan

The CIA and Delta forces in the village were pleased when men in the compound started to run in all directions, three trucks came up to the gate, and about thirty fully armed men came out and piled into them, and roared off in the direction of the Taliban's Leader's Camp, The Commander who was the coordinator of the raid on the compound, gave the order to commence the rescue, their eye in the sky was a bird called Junior after the soldier who had invented it, they bird flew over and discovered about ten fighters still left in the compound, plus two guarding the front gate, and two more on the rooftops all heavily armed, but other security measures were not evident, as this particular compound was not on any forces radar, and not one of the Afghan's army's intelligence arms, were aware that the village had Taliban fighters in it, so there were no security cameras or any other kind of security measures.

The Commander had decided to attack when the men were at prayer, and that was going to happen in fifteen minutes, he spoke into his mike "All units check in," one by one the various units signalled,

"All clear and in place,"

The Commander gave an order, and an elderly couple started to walk towards the compound?

93
Wednesday

David thought that this man No1, was playing some sort of bluff when he heard a scream from behind him, then whole community started to shout and scream, David turned and could not believe his eyes, for there on the ferry in full view of the townspeople, were the Island's School Children, lined up with guns pointing at them, David did no more than launched himself at this barbaric man in front of him, but he was brought down before he could reach him by a rifle butt smashing into his skull, followed by a volley of shots over the heads of the Islanders by the six men surrounding the man who was doing the talking.

No1 had trouble being heard, "The Children will not be hurt," he shouted out, "You move aside let us through, and we will be on our way, and your Children will be released, we have no desire to hurt anyone especially young Children, but be assured we are going to board that ship," pointing to the ferry.

Darren and Abdul who had pulled up from behind the convoy, walked forward ignoring the six armed men, and picked David's prone body up, carrying him back within the crowd, putting him down they could see that the blow had not been as bad as they had imagined, David started to came round.

Earlier Ned was completely taken aback when the door of the ferry's main cabin opened, and Danielle with the School Children were quite roughly pushed inside, "What kind of monsters are you using children to further your ill gotten gains," he said with as much venom as he could muster, the guards took no notice of him, they left, leaving one man on the door, Danielle came over to him,

"What have they done to you?" she said starting to untie him. Once untied, they tried to calm the Children down, most of them had not stopped crying since they were abducted from their classroom, there were eleven in all, evenly split between boys and girls, they finally managed to calm them down, telling them, that everything will be okay,

"The bad men will let us all go as soon as they got what they want," she told them in a soft calm voice, Ned was amazed and very proud of the Island's teacher, the way she was handling this very tricky situation,

"What happened? How did they manage to kidnap a whole school?" he asked,

Earlier, Cordova and his men had pulled up outside the town's school, he could hear singing coming from inside, walking in he asked Danielle's if he could see the head mistress, Danielle replied "I'm she, what can I do for you?" her hand came up to face as she immediately recognised the man from the truck earlier in the day, she rose from her chair going towards the classroom where her assistant was taking the class, Cordova blocked her way

"What is your name?" he asked in a pleasant voice,

Danielle did not want to annoy this frightening looking man so just said, "Miss Humphries, and would you please stand aside I need to?" she did not finish the sentence.

Cordova forcefully pushed her back into her office, "I need you to tell the Children that today is going to be very special day, they are going to visit the ferry boat," Danielle sat down looked at this nasty looking creature and said,

"I will not!" defiance in her voice and on her face,

"Oh, I think you will," he said, pulling out a gun, and pointing, "And I would like you to do it now please, and without alarming the Children, just say it's a special treat," the Children were overjoyed at getting out of school early, and could not wait to visit the ferry as most of them had not been on it before, but things changed once they were told to get into the back of the truck,

"I don't want to go," said one little girl, one of the men pushed her towards the truck and snarled,

"Get in the truck," the others seeing this tried to get out of the truck, but the bad men locked the back door, when they were let of the truck and onto the ferry, the Children, and Danielle, saw other men who were carrying firearms,

"Why are those men carrying guns Miss?" asked one of the boys, some of the other Children refused to go on board after seeing the armed men, but were ushered along and pushed into a large room where a man was tied up, they all started crying.

Ned and Danielle got the Children singing the song they were singing back in the school before they were kidnapped, they did not tell the Children anything, but did assure them that everything was going to be alright

On the ferry Cordova was standing just in front of the Children while another man pushed Ned to front, in a loud voice he said "Would someone please come forward to take this man to a Doctor please," two of the fishermen went forward and carried Ned off the ferry, he was not in a good way, the strain of being tied up and to witness Chloe being killed, turned out to be a bit too much for him, he looked very pale, "Now would you please make way for our vehicles to come aboard," the crowd started to move closer to the ferry, Cordova nodded to one of his men, the man picked one of the little girls up, and dangled her over the side, the crowd instantly moved back, "I did not want to do that, but you gave me no choice," he shouted, "So would you now let my vehicles through,"

The townsfolk had no choice, they quietly moved aside, and the vehicles moved forward, the last one on, was the Range Rover containing No1 and three of his men. Once on the ferry No1 and his men moved closer to Cordova and his men, Cordova shouted out, "Thank you! Your Children will be returned to you once we are on the mainland, I promise I will send the ferry straight back," David who had recovered by now walked to the front of the crowd,

"You will let them off now, or we will storm this ferry and dump you and your men over the side along with your evil cargo," he said this in a voice that held so much venom that the townsfolk cheered, and again started to move forward, the man who was holding the little girl dangled her over the side again, with a second man doing the same with a boy, the Children were screaming, David raised his hand to stop the people moving even closer, "You are the monster everyone say's you are!" moving back himself "We will not come any further,"

It was then that Cordova had the shock of his life, as a instant recognition light came on in his brain, "I know this man?" he thought to himself, his brain could not work out where or how, but he said to himself "I will remember,"

David saw the eyes of Cordova and realised that Cordova had made him.

Then a strange thing happened, the man they knew as No1 moved behind Cordova pulled out a gun and pointed it at Cordova's head, David could not hear what he was saying, but did notice that other men on the ferry were also pointing guns at other men, "It looks like some sort of power struggle," he thought to himself.

On the ferry No1 who knew of the plot to have him killed, decided to act a bit sooner than he had intended, plus he did not sign up to kidnap Children, in fact he had no idea Cordova had this in mind until he rang and told him what he done. No1 had detailed his men to move behind all of THE MAN'S men, plus Cordova's men and await his signal, all his men had been armed although most of them were not gunmen, as most were engineers and labourers. Pointing the gun to Cordova's head he said in a quiet voice, "I did not agree with this, we let the Children go, and these people will be only too happy to see us leave this Island," Cordova turned his head slightly round,

"I have already killed a man for pointing a gun at me, so be assured I will kill you!" No1 smiled,

"You could always try," he replied, he called out, "Mr Cross," David came forward, "As you can see I am not in favour of harming Children, they will be allowed to leave if you give me your word you will let us leave?"

David knew what his reply was going to be before he said it, "You have my word, and the word of all the people," he called out, turning to the people behind him, they nodded in agreement. No1 gave the order. The Children came running off with Danielle trying to control them, whilst carrying the little girl who was dangled over the side, the girl was in tears, the little girl's parents came running forward, and Danielle put her in her Mother's arms.

On the ferry No1 took Cordova to the main cabin, they spoke and came to an agreement, they even shook hands on it, and although Cordova was a killer, he had never in his life betrayed on a deal made in good faith, so No1 was satisfied that the incident with the guns were now a thing of the past, and we could all carry on, and become very Rich. As No1 was leaving Cordova called him back "That man who was doing all the talking, was that the teacher?" No1 turned

"Yes, he's the one who has been organising the trouble we have been having,"

"Do you know who he is?"

"No! We tried to find out, but my communications man could not find anything on him, as far as he could work out, a teacher called David Cross does not exist," a secret smile turned Cordova's face into an unpleasant look of revenge,

"Do not worry about our teacher friend; I know exactly who he is,"

No1 rang the men waiting on the mainland, and was pleased to hear that everything was going to plan over there; No1 gave the order to set sail.

94
Wednesday

David and the rest of the Islanders looked on as the ferry left the harbour, the parents of the Children wishing them bad luck.

David could not believe that only a few moments ago, he was face to face with the man who he, and Sean Junior, nearly killed six years ago, whilst working in Columbia on an arms deal, that turned out good for Sean and Me, and a Columbian police captain, Captain Morella, who also benefitted from the deal, it was this Op where he first met Sean, David put the revelation to the back of his mind for now.

The crowd broke up, the Children happy to be free but excited, talking to each other as if they had been on a great adventure, as always. Children are a very resilient breed.

David made his way to the doctors check on Chloe, finding her sitting up in bed nearly back to her old self except for the cuts and bruises, "How did it go?" she asked, David filled her in with what happened, "So it went down as you had imagined it would," she said

"Yes and no!" replied David "I didn't figure in the School Children being held hostage, but everything else, as you said, went as I imagined it would," by this time Chloe was in David's arms and he was kissing her,

"So now do we do the next thing?" she asked, pulling away from David's amorous advances, David looked all serious and replied

"Yes!"

95
Wednesday

On the luxury yacht sitting off the coast of San Juliet, THE MAN was looking through binoculars, as the ferry left the harbour, happy that the venture on the Island was finally over, and the easier part of the operation, the distribution side, would be a lot easier. THE MAN picked up the phone that was ringing, "Your plan to have me killed; did not work," said a voice down the phone,

"I was not planning on doing that," replied THE MAN "Is all I said to Cordova, was, that we would have to something? As you we're losing control of the situation. But, as it turned out good in the end, we can look forward to our future together,"

THE MAN was still looking through the binoculars when the ferry went up in a sheet of flames!

THE MAN felt the shock wave and toppled over, he picked himself up, and Looking through the binoculars one more time, the ferry WAS NO MORE!

96
Wednesday earlier
5am in the morning

David left the hotel, and made his way to the boathouse carrying a large holdall, when he got there, Chloe was already there. David unzipped the holdall and took out what looked like Frisbees, "What are those?"

"These are World War Two limpet mines," Chloe picked one up, "They're heavy,"

"And they're very dangerous" replied David

"You still haven't told me what they are? Or where you got them? And what we are going to do with them?" David made sure the mines were safe and fixed one of the mobile phones onto one of them,

"They were used for blowing up enemy ships whilst at anchor, we found them in the truck in the tunnel, but surely you must have seen the film The Cockleshell Heroes!" Chloe had no idea what he was talking about, David explained, the film was a true story about British Commandos attacking a German fleet using collapsible canoes, and fixing these things onto them, these thing are called Limpet mines because they stick to the hull of a ship by magnetic force, and they go off with a big bang," Chloe still did not know what he was talking about, David gave up.

They donned their diving gear and swam out to the docked ferry, Chloe keeping watch; while David fixed the mines onto the hull, now normally the mines would be placed under the water line, but on this occasion David had to fix them above the water line, but made sure they could not be seen by those on board. With the mines fixed they swam back to the boathouse and changed in the cabin of the Mayor's boat, the whole operation had taken just 45 minutes, "That was exciting!" said Chloe stripping off her wet suit, David just sat there watching this procedure take place, "Are you enjoying the view?" she asked smiling, and slowly walking towards him,

"It's the worst view I have ever seen!" he replied, taking his own suit off, both their bodies were wet with perspiration, David sat down and Chloe slowly lowered herself onto his lap her legs encircling him, David kissed each of her breasts with their enlarged nipples as red as a berries, David felt the pain of lust and desire, flow through his body, Chloe gently moving her body forward and back with David feeling the weight of her now aroused feminine Adour sweeping through his senses, Chloe's face came down and David felt her lips against his her tongue searching inside, the sensation was not one that David had experienced in a long time, Chloe was now gyrating her hips so that David could feel her intimate parts pressing against his manhood that was now swollen to a such degree that David thought he was in danger of ending this feeling too early, he gently lifted her up and they sank to the floor, both were breathing in short sharp breaths, not one word passing their lips, David gently entered her and Chloe let out a gasp of pure pleasure her lips finding his, their tongues finding each other in a fury of sheer passion, Then David gave out a loud gasp and his body convulsed several times coinciding with Chloe's own convulsions, it was several minutes before they could talk or even catch their breath, their bodies now covered in sweat not related to the wearing of wet suits.

They got dressed both unable to talk, they walked towards the town David giving her a peck on the cheek before saying goodnight, Chloe went back to Mary's house, and David to the hotel, both with a smile, and a feeling of love, neither of them believing what just happened, but both glad it did.

97
Wednesday

THE MAN was still looking through his binoculars unable to comprehend what he had just witnessed, he scoured the area for any survivors, but the sea was empty, not that he was about to pick anyone out of the water if there was.

The yacht was too far out for him to see two people on the San Juliet cliff edge looking out to sea, David and Chloe had just done something they were not happy about, they had blown up a ship with over twenty people on board, "I hope we can live with this in time to come?" said Chloe in a whisper, David looked towards the smoke on the horizon,

"I agree, It was not a nice thing to do, but we could have saved many more lives by destroying that cargo of death," he said this with a certain amount of remorse, "Hold on!" he exclaimed looking through the telescope borrowed from Joseph, "There's a yacht out there," Chloe looked out towards where the smoke was rising,

"I can't see anything," she said, David let her look through the telescope,

"What's it doing?" letting David look through once more,

"It's just sitting there," he replied, David brought the yacht closer the scope having a very powerful optic, "There's some man looking at where the ferry went down," he said, "Whoops!" came a shout

"What?" asked Chloe, handing the scope back to Chloe she looked through; "Whoops!" she exclaimed copying David's remark,

"There are armed men on the yacht, and quite a few of them by the looks of it," she gave the scope back to David,

"It's leaving," he said with concern in his voice, "That must be the yacht that Scott saw down at the dock," turning to Chloe

"It looks as if there are more people out there for us to deal with," she said with a look of determination on her face. Once again David looked at this monster he had created, but was very proud of this beautiful scientist; they packed the scope away, and reminded themselves to ask Stuart about this man, and this yacht.

David had helped Chloe to the Buggy outside the medical centre, and travelled to the cliff edge on the coast road, the same cliff edge Chloe's friends Peter and Mike had died just a few days ago, now in this same place, she was to exact revenge, although Chloe did not think of it as revenge but as retribution.

Chloe had had a laptop with her, and was tracking the ferry due to the phone David had planted along with the mines; she was waiting for the ferry to reach an area above a newly discovered sink hole on the sea bed, the sink hole was about a mile in diameter and about a mile deep, the idea was that recovery of the ferry would be very unlikely, so the sinking and how it went down so fast would not be discovered.

The GPS signal on her computer beeped she turned to David, "Shall we?" they both hesitated not knowing if they were doing the right thing, they knew that all the souls on the ferry were bad men, but even bad men were not all bad, David remembered the man they knew as No1 letting the Children go. David said out loud to himself, this is like one of my favourite films (The Heroes of Telemark!)

"Will you stop with all this picture stuff, It's getting on my nerves," said Chloe, once again not knowing what the hell he was talking about, David was going to explain that in the film a ferry was blown up to stop the Germans getting their hands on heavy water, the stuff they made bombs with, but thought better of it.

They pushed the button together!

THE MAN told his captain to head for Santa Barbara, he did not want to be around when the authorities started asking questions, but he did vow to find out who blew the biggest amount of cocaine (his cocaine) to enter the United States in recent history, and to lose him seven billion dollars.

Back on the cliff David was driving the buggy back to town when Chloe shouted "Stop!" David slammed on the brakes nearly tipping the buggy over,

"What the hell!" looking behind him,

"Turn this thing around," David looked bemused,

"Why?" Chloe was looking over her shoulder,

"We've just passed the place where I saw those men that tried to kill me," she said, "And I would like to find out why they tried that, it must be something that they were hiding, or planting,"

David turned the buggy round and went back to the spot where Chloe had seen the men, David realised that it was the same spot that Ned had brought them to, the remains of the barn he hid in all those years ago, and where the WW2 truck was hidden.

They walked towards the rundown barn not knowing what were going to find, if anything, rooting around they came up empty, "There's nothing here!" said Chloe sitting on a broken chair, David was still looking. After a few more minutes they decided to give up, Chloe was drinking out of a bottle of water she had brought along, she sat down on the rickety chair again, but this time it collapsed under her, the water bottle careering across the floor, the life saving liquid spilling out and disappearing down between the floor boards, Chloe kept looking at the water seeping between the boards, jumping up she went down on her hands and knees, "It's under the floor boards!" she shouted. It did not take them long to find the two large metal cases, pulling them out they examined them trying to pry them open,

"We're not going to able to open them here," said David lifting one of the cases up, and then Chloe noticed a crow bar in the far corner,

"Will this help?" she called out after a tense few minutes the lid popped open, "WOW!" they both said in unison.

98
Columbia
Thursday

It was the morning Captain Morella and Durrell were going to meet the President, Durrell had invited the captain to stay with him and his family for the night so as they could travel together to the Palacio de Nariño. Morella did not have any family of his own and they felt sorry for him, although they would have never have said this to him, they had decided to drive themselves to the Palacio, not wanting the car the president was sending for them.

Durrell's wife and Children were running around unable to contain their excitement about meeting their President; they were all ready by 9am, by now, even Morella was getting nervous, he had been to the toilet about three times, already.

The Captain and Durrell were in their dress uniforms, Durrell's wife and kids were in their Sunday best, they walked out to the Durrell's car and one by one they shuffled in, the car was not really designed for five people, "I could always follow you in my car," said the Captain,

"Just get in," said Durrell, Morella climbed in the back between the Children, Durrell was just about to shut the door when Morella shouted out,

"Wait," Durrell looked inside and saw the look of pain on his Captains face, "I need to go again," he said pushing his way out of the car, "I won't be long," running up the pathway, this sort of thing had never happened to the Captain before, and he was embarrassed , Morella came out minutes after, and was walking back down the path when the car exploded in a sheet of flames, Morella was blown off his feet by the intensity of the blast, he picked himself up and looked at the spot where his best friend and his family were, Just a few minutes ago, the whole family were so excited about meeting their President, Juan Manuel Santos, now there was just a blackened hole, the car and four lovely people were no more!

Pablo Cordova received the news that the Police Captain and his Sergeant, plus the Sergeant's family had been killed. Pablo had carried out the message THE MAN had relayed to him from his Brother Juan. Pablo was just congratulating himself when the phone rang, he listened for what seemed like an eternity, he put the phone down and a big smile lit up his face, calling his second in command he told him that he: Pablo Cordova, was now the head of the only Cartel left in Columbia, due to the fact that his Brother Juan Luis Cordova had been killed.

Pablo was pleased that someone else had killed his Brother as it had saved him the job of doing it himself, but now he was the king. He could do things his way, and not be Juan's little brother anymore. Although he was pleased that Juan was dead, he still wanted revenge on the person or persons that performed this act, and along with THE MAN they had vowed to find them, and to punish them, and their families.

Virginia
DEA headquarters

James and Robert were getting conflicting information about the drugs that were due to enter the United States; one part was that the drugs were in the Country. The other, was that the drugs had been destroyed while in transit. "What do you make of it?" asked Robert, James looked at the reports coming in,

"I don't have a clue, but I hope it's the latter," he said, hoping that this large smuggling operation had gone dramatically wrong somehow, and his Country, the United States Of America was not going to be overrun with affordable drugs that could fuel drug wars and deaths.

South of Santa Barbara

The FBI were waiting for the ferry to dock, the Agent in Charge with a posse of agents had been waiting all night, "What time was the ferry supposed to dock?" he asked one of his agents,

"Just after midnight," he replied,

"Then where the fuck is it!" he asked using words he did not normally use. After the agent in charge had received the news that the assassin had boarded the ferry to San Juliet the week before, he had flown down to deal with the apprehension of the man himself, by now the sun had just come up "What's the time?" someone answered

"O seven hundred Sir!"

He shouted at one of the agents, "Find me a chopper, we're going over there!"

Afghanistan

The elderly couple walked towards the Taliban compound the two guards not taking any notice of them, one of the guards was smoking a cigarette the other sitting down on a stool both oblivious of the threat that was coming towards them, as the elderly couple came within a few feet of them two sounds were heard, plop, plop, like the sound of a champagne bottle being opened, the two guards fell to the floor, the elderly couple quickly relieving them of their weapons and checking that they were dead, the Commander gave the order to take out the two rooftop guards, a sniper perched on a rooftop some 100 metres away took the two shots both with a silenced gun, the two guards did not have any idea what had happened they just fell where they had stood.

The bird (Junior) flew below the roof line and hovered just outside one of the windows, and the Commander could see the men inside kneeling down in prayer; he gave the signal to move in.

Four men of the Delta unit scaled the right hand wall using grappling hooks, and four of the CIA men scaled the left, both units synchronising the attack, Delta dropped inside the compound without any alarm being raised, and moved silently towards the building where they had established the prisoner was being held, it was their job to make sure the Taliban insurgents inside the compound, were not able to kill him as the main attack took place, they were surprised to find no other guards protecting their prize, this particular compound was very lax, due to the understanding that this compound was not on any Afghan Army's radar, the Taliban chief having been assassinated the year before, who the CIA, have now connected, to their assassin, who is in America right now.

The CIA unit were outside the door leading to the room the insurgents were praying in, the Commander who was coordinating the attack gave the order.

The door leading to the cell block holding the prisoner blew at the same time as the door leading to the insurgents at prayer, the Delta unit quickly found their man and stood guard preventing any attack by other insurgents who were not at prayer, but the bird in the sky did not pick up any other armed men, and this was relayed to Delta.

The CIA unit blew the door at precisely the same time as Delta had; the four men rushed in, and without giving any warning, opened fire whilst the men were still on their knees, the whole operation taking just seven minutes from start to finish.

The Commander gave the order to stand down, the CIA unit making sure that all the Taliban insurgents were dead.

A Delta sergeant knelt beside a figure that looked like a human being, the man in front of him had a matted beard and hair that was hanging down his back, it looked as if he had not had a wash or any other kind of hygiene facility for months if not years, the sergeant could not believe that someone could have survived this treatment for as long as this man had been able too, in a gentle voice the sergeant told the man that they were here to take him home, "It's about fucking time!" came a reply. The sergeant was taken completely by surprise at this outburst,

"We're sorry, we got stuck in traffic," said the sergeant,

"You should have taken the turnpike," the man said, slowly standing up, with a small grin on his face. The sergeant took a good look at the man they had just recued, his eyes widened as recognition took place. The man's face also took on a look of recognition, "Charlie! Is that you, under all that fucking war paint?" the sergeant could not understand it; this man in front of him, was supposed to be dead!

"SEAN?"

99
Wednesday

David and Chloe made their way back to town, not knowing what they were going to say, or do, about the two of them blowing up the ferry with all those on board. After sitting outside the town for what seemed hours, they came to a decision. They entered the pub, but the place was empty except for Mary, "Where is everyone?" asked Chloe,

"They're at the hall," she answered, "Sean who is now Island's Mayor, is trying to calm everyone down, they were very angry and were demanding answers, so he decided to talk to all of them, and try to explain why they were kept in the dark about what was going on for so long,"

It took all of Sean O'Rielly's oratory skills, to pacify the Islanders in the hall, and he was glad when David and Chloe walked in. It took David with Chloe's help, a long time to explain why and what was going on and how it could all be resolved with the help of the money in the suitcases, but they did not reveal all, some things had to remain strictly secret, the meeting broke up with everyone walking away with a smile and a feeling that the past week had not been so bad after all, the cases helping to pacify them, but the sadness of the deaths of three of their own clouded the euphoria they could have shown.

Once back in the pub Sean, David, Chloe, Abdul, Darren, and Ned sat down to discuss all that David had promised the Islanders, plus the funeral arrangement of Scott their partner in crime, "Did someone inform Scott's Mother?" asked Chloe, Darren said he had spoken to her. Stuart sat apart from the rest of them, not knowing how he fitted in being one of the men who invaded their Island.

Chloe left it up to David to tell them what they had done. All five of them were astounded by the manner that David related the facts of one of the most audacious acts they had ever heard of, "How on earth did you come up with the idea?" asked Darren "And how did you do it? And what did you use?" Chloe stood up

"That's easy!" she exclaimed "It's from a film called The Heroes of Telemark," Sean immediately knew what she was talking about,

"The film with Kirk Douglas in it," he shouted, Ned came up to David and put his hand on his shoulder

"Well done son, did you use those limpet mines?"

Stuart who was standing a little bit away from the others also came over, and said,

"Good, now they won't be able to kill thousands of people, with their drugs, like they killed my Sister,"

David expanded a bit more how he and Chloe had fixed the charges, and how they had detonated them. David stood up, and with a serious look, and voice, said, "Now this must never ever leave this room; no one must know that the ferry was actually blown up; as far as we know it just went missing. Are we all in agreement?" all six of them nodded.

They talked and made plans when all of a sudden Abdul got up and started to walk towards the door, "I'm sorry but I must bid you farewell," he said in a sad voice, "I will be leaving on the next ferry with the horse I purchased for my employer," David got up and put his arms around his new friend, this man who he had only just met a few days ago, and was now like a brother to him,

"Why?" he asked "We," pointing to the others "Don't want you to leave,"

"You are like a brother to me, and a true friend, as are all of you," the others came up and tried to persuade him to stay, Abdul was not able to control his emotions for the first time in three and a half years, his one purpose in life was to kill the people who had taken the life of his two boys in his village that day, so control of his mind and body were the only thing that kept his emotions in check, but now, the man who he had come to this Island to kill, was now offering him freedom from the long and hard quest, to bring his boy's killers to justice, he broke down in front of these people who in this very short time, had come to love, and admire.

Abdul pushed his new found friends away, and sat down unable to continue with the lies; I need to tell you the real reason why I came to your Island.

"A long time ago I was a teacher just like you," pointing to David "When my two sons were killed by a missile fired upon my village by the Americans," he stopped and looked at David, David could not believe what he was hearing, Abdul carried on, "For the last three and a half years, I have been hunting the men responsible for that slaughter of my two sons, and of those innocent children that day, so I came to this island to complete that task," David jumped up ready to defend himself, "You do not have to worry," said Abdul pointing to the chair, "I'm not going to kill you today, in fact, I'm going to thank you for your explanation of events on that day, and how you tried to stop the bombing, if I had known then, what I now know, I would not have wasted my life on this three and a half year vendetta, as I now know that it was the Taliban leader Ali Masood El Jaffa, who was to blame, by using innocent children as a shield," Chloe had tears in her eyes, and David just sat there his hands on his head, eyes shut, unable to comprehend the confessions of a man like Abdul, who seemed a decent man, who has had this Burden on his shoulders for so long, David got up and went over not really knowing what to say, so he simply took both of Abduls hands into his,

"You're now a free man, you can stay here for as long as you like, you are now one of us," the others all murmured in agreement,

"Abdul Abdullah you must stay with us and make a new life for yourself here! On this island," said Chloe with assent from all the others,

"Alas! That will not be possible," he replied "The things I have done in the past are slowly catching up with me, and I would imagine the authorities have already found me, and are waiting to take me into custody as we speak," Abdul had resigned himself that this last killing would be his last, that was why he had used his real name in this trip to the United States Of America, he just sighed in defeat,

"Then we will find a way to make you disappear," said Chloe, "We will not give you up to the authorities."

They persuaded Abdul to sit down, and talked for the next hour, trying to find a solution; at long last David came up with a plan, they all agreed that the plan was faultless. It was quite late now, so they all planned to meet the next morning in the diner, as before. They all went off their different ways, except Chloe, who stayed around a bit longer, and then she left.

David was just about to go to bed in the hotel when he heard a faint knock; he opened the door to find this beautiful house maid standing there? Grabbing her hand he pulled her inside, and put the Do Not Disturb sign on the door.

100
Thursday

They all met very early at the diner, to work out what their story would be, when the authorities visited the Island, they knew that the coast guard would be by now, scouring the seas around the Island, looking for the ferry that did not dock on the mainland last night, so they had to get their story straight.

The meeting broke up with all the participants having specific jobs to do.

All the boys went up to the restricted area, to make sure the runway that the drug smugglers had made, was not visible from the air. When Abdul and Joe had flown Arnold yesterday on their bombing raid, they had noticed that all the movable plants and bushes had been put back in place so that the airstrip would again be invisible, and hopefully, be FORGOTTEN once again!

They found that the No1's men had done a good job in covering up the airstrip, and they just made it a bit better by cutting down a few more trees, the one problem they did have, was the plane, How do you make a DC8 disappear?

They entered the underground base, with Stuart leading the way, Stuart knew his way around much more that all the other men who had been here, as this was his second visit, having been here months ago to set up the generators.

They could not believe that back in 1942 after the attack on Pearl harbour in 1941 by the Japanese navy, that the authorities could have built this place in complete secret, and then leaving it to be FOR-GOTTON "I wonder what secret things they were concocting back then," said Sean to know one in particular,

"One thing we know for certain," said David "Is that, whatever it was, they did not want the ordinary people to find out, and that's why they wiped all knowledge of the place of, all the documents relating to it, that's how it became FOROTTEN."

Walking into the large main area with just torches to light their way, they were amazed to find that the place was so big, their torch

286

beams only showing up a short distance, but what they did discover was explosive devises all over the entrance, and here, below ground,

"It looks as if they were planning to blow the whole place up," said Darren, bending down to inspect the charges,

"Maybe the grenades you bombed the place with, stopped this place going up?" said David to Abdul,

"Well the last grenade we dropped did have a bit of a kick in it," grinning,

Stuart interjected, "Maybe that's why the cargo plane is still intact, you must have killed the explosive man before he could set the whole thing off," Stuart explained, that all the men that were here did not have names, just G1 for the guards, or as in this case X1 for explosives, they had noticed explosives around the plane, ready to be blown up as well as this place,

"It certainly looks as if your bombing raid was a success," commented Sean, they all laughed. "We will have to come back once the inquest on the ferry is over, and to see what we have here in a more relaxed way. What we do know is, that we have a World War Two Submarine on our island, and goodness knows what else, and I'm sure we can make a bit of money from all this, as long as we can keep it hidden from the authorities, remember this place has been FORGOTTEN for over sixty years, so let's not remind them!

101
Thursday

The Captain of the ferry was now laying in the bed that Chloe had been in the day before, with an undisclosed illness, he had been told of the fate of his ship, but the details had not been disclosed to the Islanders, as far as they were concerned the ferry had just disappeared, the Captain was in the medical centre, so was not able to command his ship on the return journey, that had been left to the first mate.

Susan the late Mayor's secretary was sitting at her desk when her phone rang she nearly fell out of her chair, "Hello!" she answered, it was the coast guard cutters Captain, he asked a lot of questions about the ferry, but Susan acted surprised that the ferry had not made port, so was unable to give them any information to its whereabouts, as the phones had been down for a long time.

She put the phone down, and immediately picked it up again, and rung Sean, to tell him that the phones were now working, but he had already received calls himself, as did half the Islanders.

Chloe was at the Marine facility, where she once worked, and lived, the authorities were bound to ask about the Marine trucks that had come over on the ferry, just over a week ago. She and Danielle were moving things around so as it looked like they were packing things up, they had decided to say that the marine trucks that came over last Tuesday, were only here for the day and went back on the return sailing, other than that, they did not know anything about them. Both Chloe and Danielle's phones started ringing; Chloe went off to talk to her Mother who had been trying for days to get in touch, Danielle's call was work related.

Chloe, after putting her Mum's mind at rest, called David's phone he answered straight away not realising that the phones we're back on, "We're just finishing of up here, and we'll be back in town in about 30 minutes, is everything okay where you are?"

Chloe answered "Yes," then she and Danielle started back to town themselves.

102
Thursday
Columbia

Captain Morella was mortified, at the unwarranted murder of Durrell and his family; the local police had been quick on the scene, and had whisked Morella away to a safe house, leaving whoever had planted the bomb, that Captain Morella of the Bogotá police force, and Sergeant Durrell had both been killed by a car bomb, along with Sergeant Durrell's family, and the whole of Columbia's police force, were now investigating the whereabouts of Pablo Cordova, who they believe carried out this horrendous act.

Virginia
DEA headquarters

The news that the drugs that were supposed to be entering the Country, had been destroyed, was circulating across the whole of the drug world, and news that the supposed drug lord, Juan Luis Cordova had been killed, was also being bandied around, but at this time James and Robert had not verified the rumours, although they hoped it would turn out to be true, and this whole sorry mess they had found themselves in, could be put to rest.

CIA headquarters Langley

The whole of Langley were celebrating the success of the operation in Afghanistan.

FBI headquarters Washington

The Agent in charge of finding their lost prisoner, Juan Luis Cordova, was hearing the same stories that the DEA were hearing, that Cordova had been killed, and the drugs were missing, and now from their informers down in Columbia, the killing of Cordova had been confirmed.

They also reported that Cordova's Brother, Pablo Cordova, had taken over the running of the Cordova Cartel, and was now starting to flex his muscles in other areas of Columbia, trying to bring the whole of the Country under his control, "We get rid of one Cordova, then we get another!"

An agent sitting at a computer consol reported that Intel coming in suggested that the killing of Juan Cordova was carried out by his little brother Pablo.

FBI Santa Barbara

The Agent in charge of the FBI unit chasing their Assassin, were on their way to the Island in a FBI chopper, having commandeered it from the local office in Santa Barbara.

103
Thursday

This time they met at their usual headquarters, the pub, they all had their stories fixed in their heads, but Sean made them all go over it, again! And again! David smiled "What are you smiling about?" asked Chloe "You're not going to come out with another one of your film excerpts, are you?"

David said "No I'm not, but it did remind me of the Dirty Dozen film, where Lee Marvin was going over the plans to attack this chateau in France," they all booed, and he was told to sit down and shut up, he gave a look of deep hurt, and sat down.

David called Stuart over, "I forgot to ask, when we were on the cliff yesterday, we saw a large yacht it looked as if it was keeping an eye on the ferry, and when the ferry went down this man did not even go over to see if there were any survivors, then he just sailed away, do you know if there was a Mr Big?" Stuart searched his memory,

"I did overhear one conversation when I was eating in the canteen between two of the guards that had joined us after a few days, and they spoke of, I'm not sure if I got this right, but they called this man THE MAN, not the boss! They referred him just as THE MAN, and I also heard No1 refer to someone as THE MAN, I suppose that there could be a Mr Big,"

David left it there and for the moment, and put it out of his mind. Then they heard an unmistakable sound of a helicopter coming overhead, "We have visitors," said Sean

"Where's Abdul?" asked Chloe,"

"Ned took him to his place, out of the way until all this is over" replied David,

"Good!" Chloe exclaimed.

It did not take long for the FBI Agents to find Sean, the interim Mayor, Susan had rung and asked him to come over to the Mayor's office, Sean walked it to find two smartly dressed Agents talking to Susan, all FBI Agents looked the same, they say that you could always tell the FBI, by the way they dress. "Morning gentlemen," said Sean, holding out his hand, the Agent shook the preferred hand,

"Good morning Mr Mayor," he said, Sean sat at his desk and asked the agent to sit, and "I prefer to stand if you don't mind,"

"How can I help you?" asked Sean.

Back in the pub, two other FBI agents walked in, they had been going round the town asking question, "Do any of you know this man," one of them asked, showing round a photo, David looked at the photo,

"Yes I've seen him before, he was staying at the hotel," the Agents eyes lit up, this was the first positive ID he had heard,

"Can you tell me what he was doing on this Island? And where we could find him now?" David made believe he was searching his memory,

"I did talk to him once, in the hotel, he told me he was a horse trader, I had no idea what that was, but it turned out he was here to buy a horse, we have a wonderful racing stable here on the Island," the Agent was looking pleased with himself,

"Do you know where we could find him?" he asked

Chloe piped in, "Yes! I saw him leave on the ferry last night," she said, "I'm sure you could find him he was towing a horse box," the Agent's face took a turn for the worse,

"Did you talk to him?" he asked

"I did once in the diner," she replied "We talked about horses, I have always loved them, he told me he worked for some sort of Royal Prince, at first I didn't believe him, but as it turned out he actually did, the Pastor who owns the stables, told me, that this man, I think he said is name was Abdul something? Was a horse trader for a Royal Prince, so it was true," the other Agent was taking notes,

"And you say you saw him boarding the ferry last night?"

"Yes, If you go over to the hotel they will tell you when he checked out, he seemed like a nice man," she added.

The two Agents left "Well done!" said Darren "Do you think they believed you?" Chloe sat down,

"What do you mean did they believe me? Of course they did I'm a very good actress, I was recently in a remake of Titanic!" looking at David, David hid his face.

Sean came back in "How did it go?" they all asked at the same time,

"Fine, I told them that the ferry left a bit later than usual, due to the fact that the ferry's Captain had taken ill, and the first mate took it out, I never gave any indication that I knew the ferry had not made it, and told them that as far as I knew, this Abdul person they we're looking for, was on the ferry," Mary Sean's wife who had not had any dealings with what was going on, but she was a very shrewd woman and knew more that she let on, she brought them all a beer and a sandwich, once again they realised how hungry they were.

The FBI Agents, after speaking to the Pastor, at his racing stables, and what they had gathered in the town, it was now evident that their man, Abdul Abdullah, had indeed been on the now lost ferry.

Darren went off to find Ned and Abdul, David and Chloe went to David's farm, to feed the sheep and geese, stopping to pick Joe and Shep up on the way. On the way David turned to Chloe "Did you notice that nothing was said about the trucks coming over," Chloe was herself a bit bemused about that,

"The only thing I can think of, is nothing was known about them, and no one mentioned them to the authorities, especially the FBI," David fell silent again, "You know we may get away with this," he said, touching Chloe's hand. David felt like he was in heaven, he had not had a woman in his life "like forever" He had always been a loner on the relationship stakes, due to his commitment to his regiment, being in the SAS, was paramount to being at risk of death every single day, you never knew what was round the corner, it was always possible, that the next day would be your last, so romantic liaison were for him a No! No!

They carried on until they saw the once lovely farm house, now a complete ruin, David gave Joe the job of feeding the geese that were going mad. David fed the sheep, whilst Chloe just looked around. She found the entrance to the tunnel She and David had found so useful all those months ago, remembering, It was in fact; just a few days ago, but it felt like months, she decided to go down and have a look.

"David! David!" She shouted, running over to where he was just finishing off the feeding, Joseph and Shep came running over as well, "The gym, its intact!" She cried out, they left Shep on guard duty, and made their way to the gym, David often kept a change of clothing in there so he grabbed them and a few other things, Joe was busying himself on the different contraptions, they collected a number of things that might be useful, including David's right hand glove that he missed? Then they made their way back to town.

Darren, and Abdul, we're at the cave, going through what they had found in the 70 year old Studebaker, "Look at this" said Darren showing Abdul a long tube,

"What is it?"

"It's a bazooka,"

"I've heard of them but never seen one before, do you think it will still work?" Darren looked for the rocket propelled grenades and found a box containing six grenades, looking over the M1 launcher and the grenade's, he declared that this ancient gun, was ready to go into action at any time. They found lots of other things, but the main priority was to get the truck working, Darren, with Abdul's help, got the truck working in record time, the engine fired up after an intensive two hours, of hard work,

"Thanks Abdul," said Darren, "Without your help I could never had done it in two hours," Abdul looked pleased, "It would have only taken me one hour," he cried, running away laughing, Abdul caught him up and gave him a playful slap,

"That's the last time I help you to get a 70 year old truck working!" he replied,

"I'll hold you to that," he replied, still grinning, they prepared to leave. Making sure, the huge door was closed properly, and made their way back to Ned's farm, to wait until the authorities had left the Island, especially the FBI.

The Agent in charge of the FBI unit was still conducting their inquiries into the unexplained disappearance of the ferry, but they were now convinced that their man, Abdul Abdullah, was definitely on the ferry along with a very valuable horse that the unnamed, Saudi Prince, would not be too happy about. The Agent decided that all the inquiries about the disappearance of the ferry could now be made from the mainland, so he and his men made plans to leave the Island, making sure that Sean the acting Mayor be available for further talks, Sean told them that he was not planning to go anywhere soon.

At the Island's harbour, the coast guard cutter was just pulling in, the Store owner, who acted as the harbour master, was there to greet them, he knew that the ferry had somehow disappeared but could not provide any reason why, he told them that the ferry's Captain was in the medical centre in town, and maybe he could throw some light on how, or why, his ship could just suddenly disappear?

The sea around the Island was alive with ships searching for any sign of the ferry, or if there were any survivors, but no sightings of wreckage, or any sign of survivors, had been found.

The coast guard Captain went to see the ferry Captain, but the Captain could not give a plausible explanation as to the whereabouts of his ship, except that, one of the boilers was playing up, but to his experience, not to the extent of causing an explosion, or anything else.

The coast guard Captain seemed satisfied with the ferry Captain's Explanations, and concluded that he had no idea what was going on, and why the ferry he had sailed for the last thirty years, should just suddenly disappear, it just did not, make sense?

Back in the town, the Coast Guard Captain asked the harbour-master, how many people were on board and what cargo it was carrying, but as the ferry had not made it's normal crossing on Tuesday, the ferry just had the crew and one vehicle a car with a trailer, the coast guard Captain had got the names of the crew members from the ferry's, Captain, and the details of the car and trailer, from the harbourmaster, Sean had had a word with him, but he was not told the full story, just that he was to say, the car and trailer were on board.

After talking to the FBI who we're also investigating the disappearance, he decided that any further talks on the Island, were not going to turn up anything new, so joined the other ships and planes in finding the lost ferry.

Chloe was standing on the cliff edge, looking out to sea thinking to herself, that the area where we had sunk a ship with over twenty people on board, was never going to be found, and that troubled her, she knew, that they were all bad men, but as she said before, not all bad men were bad all through, her body shuddered and she thought to herself "It's going to take a long time for to get over this and for this to be FORGOTTEN, if ever,"

The FBI and the coast guard had left; San Juliet was going to be their Island once again.

They all met in the diner, David had called them the magnificent Seven, but now they we're a lot more, Darren, Chloe, Sean, Ned, Susan, Danielle, Joseph, Stuart and even Julie had joined this Merry

Band, "Goodbye Yul, hello Errol," said David, they all looked at each other,

"What the hell is he talking about now?" asked Sean,

"Don't ask," said Chloe "I lose track of all this film jargon," Sean took charge of the meeting; they had been joined by some of the Islanders, who still did not know how the ferry went down, and hopefully would never find out.

The explanation they had been given, about the drug smuggling operation, was just that these men, had made an airstrip in the north of the Island, and had used this to bring in the drugs from Columbia; he did not at this time tell them about the entire underground infra-structure. That could wait for later. The thing that worried them was the lack of inquiries about the trucks belonging to State Marine Survey Agency; they knew that this particular company did exist, but this part? They thought someone would have had mentioned it at some time, about the trucks on the ferry, but in all the inquiries so far, no mention of the trucks had been forthcoming, so they in the diner, decided not to mention it to anyone ever!

104
Columbia

Captain Morella was getting restless, cooped up in the safe house they had put him in, he wanted out of this place, and start the job of finding Pablo Cordova, the man behind the murder of Durrell and his family, but his superiors had told him to stay put, until they find out if the Cordova Cartel believe they had not only killed Durrell and his family, but Morella as well. But the Captain was not your normal policeman, he had a code of his own, and that code did not correspond with his superiors, or the police code, but it did follow some of the Militaries code, get information anyway possible. He was not a prisoner, but he did have bodyguards around the clock, so he formed a plan to escape, as soon as the news came through that he was dead, hopefully that would come through soon, as a dead person, you could do a lot of things a person alive, could not? You were invisible.

Virginia

James was sad to hear about Captain Morella's death, and that of Sergeant Durrell. But one good thing has come out of this, the drugs that were supposed to flood the country, had indeed been destroyed, and that was good news, his partner Robert had been assigned another case, and as he was due some leave, he thought, all this good news and the destruction of most of the Cartels in Columbia, he was due a break, so he decided to get his swimming trunks out of the wardrobe, and get himself down to Florida.

Washington

The operation to find the Assassin, Abdul Abdullah had been closed, as was the hunt for Cordova, both now thought to have been killed, but the operation to find out how the Islands ferry went down was still ongoing.

Afghanistan

The SAS had halted their assault on the Taliban camp, without sustaining any casualties, but they informed command about the series of underground tunnels they had spotted, and suggested a bunker busting bomb be used as normal bombs would not penetrate the deep tunnels, command had in their armoury a bomb they called the MOAB, the mother of all bombs, and decided when the time was right to obliterate this camp for ever.

The Afghan Army had successfully ambushed the reinforcements that had been sent from the village, and killed or captured all the insurgents.

Delta and the CIA had successfully rescued the prisoner the Taliban were holding, again with no casualties, and had been taken completely by surprise as to his identity, the Delta Sergeant had known Sean (Junior) O'Rielly for a very long time, they had been on ops together in the past, and he was now over the moon to be reunited with a comrade, he thought was dead.

But their euphoria changed, when both sections got warnings from their eye in the sky. That insurgents were approaching their position, "Where the hell did they come from?" asked the Sergeant. The Commander still in position up high, saw the open top truck approaching the village, with armed men in the rear, on a quick count he reckoned about fifteen insurgents were on board, they were approaching fast, but this time from the east, the reinforcement that had left the compound had headed west, so this lot had to be a contingent from another compound they had no knowledge about,

"You have approximately fifteen minutes to get out, or to wait until they enter the compound, then take them all out!" the Commander said to his leader,

"We'll wait and until they enter," came the reply.

The bird called Junior was still flying, so the Commander flew the bird over the incoming truck, and advised the men in the compound, that the incoming insurgents had no knowledge that the compound had been taken, and were coming in without any degree of alarm.

The Commander was still tracking the vehicle when to his surprise it stopped, and the fighters disembarked fanning out, and started to enter the village heading towards the compound picking up more men as it approached. The Commander again contacted his men, "Be advised: The enemy have now swollen to forty fighters, and there's no time for you to exit compound, make ready to defend prisoner, we will do what we can from up here, but our position in precarious,"

Inside the compound the Sergeant who was the team leader, gathered all his men, and related the information that a large force of insurgents were approaching their position, and we have been ordered to hold until help can arrive, and he intended to do just that. The prisoner Sean Junior said "Get your men out Sergeant, that's an order," the Sergeant looked at the once Captain,

"I'm sorry Sir, but as you are dead, I'm not allowed to take orders from you," gently pushing him down onto a chair, Sean looked at the Sergeant and the men, and said,

"This is the Alamo all over again, welcome to the party Davy Crocket," as the Shepherd would say.

The sergeant smiled, he had been a friend of the Shepherd, David, and knew he was always liking situations to old films, "Your right!" he said, "So shut up and let us do our job," Junior stood up unsteady on his feet,

"Give me a gun," he said "I can shoot the bastards before they can shoot me," the sergeant gave him his pistol,

"Try not to shoot yourself with it? And definitely do not shoot any of us," he said, walking out still smiling.

"Be advised the enemy are now within your perimeter, do not open fire until I give the order,"

The sniper on the other building, called the Commander, "Sir! There's a man walking towards the compound's gate, and he's carrying a white flag," The commander looked through his binoculars, and saw the man, instantly recognising him as the father of the young lad who gave them the information about the prisoner the Taliban held, then he saw his sergeant walk out the compound's gate and walk towards the man holding to flag, the Commander told his sniper to draw a bead on the man, and shoot at the least sign of trouble.

Then to all the men inside the compound, and to the commander on the rooftop, the sergeant shook the man's hand, and put his arms around him.

105
Saturday

Friday had been a day of rest for the Islanders, David and Chloe had spent the day up at David's farm, trying to salvage what was left after the missile attack, they did manage to save some things and made the entrance into the gym a lot easier, they had water thanks to David's excellent water well, and Darren had given them a generator, so they had light and water, what more do you need?"

The whole ten of them met outside the gate leading to the restricted area, now looking abandoned, Stuart and Darren had been up to the site yesterday to get the main generator working, and Stuart was still in awe at this piece of machinery, it was so advanced for its age. They made their way to the main building that still looked derelict, Stuart made them stand in the middle of the floor, pushed a button and the whole floor started to descend, "This is fantastic!" they all said at the same time , they descended four decks down, until they came to the main hanger,

"This is really like an aircraft carrier," said David, who had been on many before, his last visit to this place was not as joyful as this one, and they split up, each wanting to explore the whole place.

David and Chloe teamed up together, and finally found the tunnel that looked as if was the one leading to the submarine pen, "See these electricity cables they must be the ones that gave the light in the submarine pen," remarked David, pointing to some overhead cables, Chloe was inspecting the end of the tunnel where they had dynamited,

"It doesn't look to thick here," she said, "It looks about the same thickness as the other one, the one we excavated," picking up a rock and hitting the rock face to hear the echo.

They backtracked to the main area where most of the others were standing around all talking at the same time, about what they had found. Stuart led them to the place he had last seen X1 the explosive guy, "This is the last place he was working on," he said "I saw him just before I stole the detonators from his workshop," they approached a tunnel that led down to where Stuart had last seen X1,

"This tunnel is about three times the size of all the other tunnels," remarked Chloe. Looking around they could see that you could have got two trucks down this one, side by side. Then they came to another wall,

"This one looks a bit more formidable," said Darren putting his hand on the wall,

"Over here!" came a shout, Danielle was over the other side looking at a large hole that had been punched through, "It looks as if they managed to get through just here?" she said pointing,

"Who's going through first?" asked Julie, they all looked at each other,

"I suggest the youngest member of our merry band," said David, looking at Joseph. Through the hole you could just see that there was light in the space behind the wall, but it did not seem very bright,

"No!" Said Julie, "Someone else go," she had only just got the word out, as Joe slipped through the hole, "WOW!" he shouted out, "This is amazing," they heard Joe's voice coming from the other side of the wall; they all rushed at once trying to get through the hole,

"Form an orderly queue," shouted David getting ahead of all the others and pushing himself through. He just stood there mouth wide open. The others also pushed their way through, that is except Sean, he got stuck, and "I can't get through," he shouted,

"Come on you fat lump of lard," said Darren leaning through and tugging, at last Sean managed to get through.

They all just stood there, Mouths agape!

After what seemed a lifetime, they managed to pull themselves together, and start to explore, there were military trucks, Four Tanks, Six Folding Wing Aircraft that looked like Grumman F4F Wildcats, Darren had seen one in a World War magazines he read, there were also half tracks, bikes and even a fire engine, the whole lot looked in pristine condition due to the fact of the deepness of the cave and the air. "This is fantastic," said Sean; we could make a lot of money out of this lot.

Once back in their headquarters, the pub, Mary wanted to know, everything, she thought she had been kept out of the loop for too long. They had lunch and started to make plans for the development of the site, and how they were going to make a lot of money that would benefit the whole of the Island, and all the people who live on it. "The one big problem we have, is how we persuade the Government to sell us the land," said Sean, "It's quite clear they did not want anyone finding out they had built a secret airbase, so they would not be too happy to see it come to light, it has clearly been FORGOTTEN,"

Ned stood up

"I don't think we have to worry too much on that score," he said, looking pleased, and smiling, they all looked at him,

"What do you mean?" asked Sean,

"The government do not own the land," replied Ned,

"Then who does?" asked Chloe,

"Me!" said Ned.

It turned out that Ned did indeed own the land; he not only owned the restricted area, but also, the whole island, having been claimed by Ned's family as far back as 1864 after the American civil war, and to his knowledge the Island was passed down the line, and now belonged to the only surviving relative of his Great, Great, Great, Grandfather, in fact the Islands financial assets were all in Ned's name, controlled by a law firm in San Francisco, they had all the relevant deeds and ownership papers."So you have been our landlord for all these years," said Sean,

"I do believe so," as he walked out of the pub, with a wave and a smile.

Ned's lawyers had stopped any company from building on the Island, for the last fifty years, although various building company's had tried, but the Islands community is just how Ned's forefathers had wanted it, and Ned has adhered to this premise, he did not want the Island overrun by holiday makers.

106
Monday

After an exhausting search by the Coast Guard and other government agencies, the fate of the ferry was never discovered, and the search had now been called off, all relatives had been informed, and a memorial service was to be held, on the island, and on the mainland, in two days time. The replacement ferry had just docked in the harbour with a whole lot of traffic on it, including two nondescript sedans, each with two men inside.

The whole Island was in a party mood, they had been cut off from the mainland for quite a long time, and supplies were running out, so a big party was being organized for this evening. David and Chloe had made their relationship more permanent by declaring their love for each other, and were in the process of rebuilding the farm.

David came out of the hotel where he and Chloe had been staying, and was confronted by two men in suits; David immediately put them down as FBI agents "Mr Cross?" said the first agent,

"Yes," answered David, the man showed a badge,

"FBI Sir," David did not show it, but something was wrong, "We'd like you and Miss Barnwell to come with us," he said "We would like to ask you a few question, it will not take long," he said with a look of apology, "I know you have a lot on your plate right now but it is important," David nodded his head,

"Fine I'll just go and find Miss Barnwell," turning and walking back into the hotel, finding Chloe he said "Don't ask questions just do as I say, go out back and get the buggy ready, as we may have to leave in a hurry," Chloe, now being a veteran bad ass, did as she was told, without asking questions.

David walked back outside putting his glove on his right hand, "She's just getting ready, I didn't catch your name?" he asked, looking the agent in the eye,

"Agent Mulhern!" he replied,

"Pleased to meet you," David said, sticking out his left hand, the agent took the hand,

"Likewise," feeling a bit funny shaking with the left hand, David had anticipated this, the agent was off balance, David; with a twist with one hand, and a opposite twist with the other made the agent spin round, and collided with his partner, David moved in fast, and hit the first agent as hard as he could on the side of the head where it does the most damage, he went down like sack of potatoes, as he was going down David twisted his own body in a full turn and with a beautiful roundhouse kick, caught the second agent full in the face, the car doors opened and a volley of shots rang out, from the other two agents, David did not look at the damage he had done to the two agents, but he could see that it was not enough, they were both trying to get up, but it did give him time to run behind the hotel and onto the buggy Chloe had running, "Let's go," he shouted, Chloe gunned the engine and roared off.

On the outskirts of town Chloe eased off a little, turning round she asked "How did you know they were not boni fide FBI agents?" David had trouble talking with the wind in his face,

"The watch the man was wearing and the gun he was carrying," he answered,

"Thank you! That explains a lot," she replied sarcastically

"Sorry but this does not seem the right time to discuss this at the moment, seeing as the bad guys are catching us up," Chloe looked back, the two sedans were indeed catching up, Chloe gunned the engine, but the sedans kept up, and were slowly closing the gap, "We will have to go off road," shouted David, just as he said it the buggy left the road and shot through the undergrowth, "Wow! You're a quick learner," David shouted in her ear,

"I'm well ahead of you! Old Man," David gave her a friendly dig in the ribs, They were coming to a open area when the ground exploded in a shower of grit, as bullets flew all around them, looking up, they could now see a helicopter above them, they had been unable to hear it coming from behind with the wind in their face, Chloe swerved sharply trying to put the man who was leaning out of the door of the helicopter off, they shot in-between some trees that gave them a little cover, but it was short lived, bullets were still only just missing them, Chloe gave a mighty twist of the handlebar the buggy nearly turned over, as she changed course abruptly, David held on for dear life,

"You're making me all dizzy!" he shouted clinging on to the rail,

"Sorry, I'm not used to be being chased by helicopters shooting at me, I'll try to be a bit more thoughtful," laughing out loud, as another stream of bullets came close,

"We will have to find shelter, they're going to hit us soon," shouted David,

"Well done Einstein, wish I had thought of that," Chloe felt another dig,

"Over there!" he shouted, pointing to the left, "We can hide in the tunnel," Chloe realised that they were near the secret tunnel entrance, she gunned the engine and burst into the open, the helicopter pilot saw them and swooped down, the gunner trying to draw a bead on them, Chloe swung the buggy to the right then to the left, "This is worse than a Disney roller coaster," shouted David,

"Stop moaning," Chloe shouted back "You're like some old woman," David shut his mouth. Chloe swung the buggy into the trees once again; they could hear the helicopter hovering above,

"He'll be calling up reinforcement," said David opening the large door leading to the tunnel, he opened it just enough for the buggy to slide in, closing it behind him,

"What do we do now?" asked Chloe,

"We wait,"

"What do you mean we wait, wait for what?"

"You'll see," David replied, Just as he said it, part of the door exploded,

"They've found us," exclaimed Chloe,

"No shit!" replied David with a grin on his face,

"What the hell are you smiling at, were going to be killed," she cried punching him on the arm,

"Oh! You of little faith," said David, reaching into the back of the truck and coming out with a big long tube,

"What the hell is that?"

"This young lady is a Bazooka!" admiring it. Picking up a grenade he turned it over in his hands looking for any defects, he could not find any, then the helicopter fired another missile, they took shelter behind the truck while David fiddled with the missile launcher, "Ready!" he exclaimed,

"Ready for what?" she shouted over the sound of the helicopter hovering outside,

"I want you to do is to open the door just enough for me to see the helicopter, they knew it was just outside as they could hear the Whoop! Whoop! Of the blades, "Ready!" shouted David

"Ready!" shouted Chloe,

"Now!" shouted David, Chloe pulled back the door, David lined the sights up, and pulled the trigger, although the launcher and the grenade were over sixty years old, they both worked perfectly, the grenade flew as true as it must have done all those years ago, the helicopter exploded into a million pieces, the fire ball lighting up the sky, "Quick shut the door," as bullets pinged of the wall,

"I guess the FBI men have found us," said Chloe retreating inside, David rummaged around in the back of the truck trying to find something to defend themselves with, and found another box of hand grenades, "Let's lob a few of these out," said Chloe holding one up in the air,

"That's a good idea, I'll open the door, and you can lob them, as a hail of bullets hit the door,

"Maybe not such a good idea then," she said, they could hear a scuffling noise just the other side of the door,

"I think they intend to blow the door open, the door was already quite weakened by the missiles the helicopter had fired, "We may have to use these after all?" said David, taking a handful of grenades,

"By the way that was a great idea of yours, what was it again? Oh yes! Let's wait, and what did I call you before, Einstein; I think I did old Albert a dishonour,"

Outside the fake FBI agents were just getting ready for their last assault, after placing charges at the cave door, one of them was positioned behind a tree, when a hand came from behind, he fell to the ground his throat spurting blood, on the other side another one fell, with an harpoon spear sticking out of his back, another was already on the floor, his head at a funny angle, the forth man now had three guns trained on him.

"You can come out now, you two!" Shouted Sean in his loud bellow,

"The door won't budge," a voice from inside shouted. After a bit of pulling and shoving the door finally opened,

"Are we glad to see you," exclaimed Chloe with a look of relieve on her face, "How did you find us?" she asked, Abdul held up a phone, as did David,

"Modern Technology," he said "Isn't It wonderful!" she turned to David,

"You bastard," she said going over to kiss him.

David looked down at the man they had captured, "Who sent you?" he asked, the man said nothing Abdul walked over

"The man asked, who sent you?" giving him a kick, the man said nothing,

"I don't think he can talk," remarked David, "Abdul you come from a Country that does not condemn torture, I think you should ask him, politely of course," the others started to walk away,

"Wait," all five of them stood over him, "I was hired by THE MAN," David thought, that name again?

"What man?"

"I do not know, he is just THE MAN," he answered with fright in his eyes,

"Who do the others work for?" asked David

"I do not know that either; but I did hear one of them mention a Pablo something?" David looked at the others,

"Pablo Cordova, Juan's Brother."

They discussed what they were going to do about the bodies plus the two cars. "Abdul, You and Darren get rid of the two cars, and do something about him," pointing to their prisoner, we're going back to town, but I think we had better put these small fires out first, some of the helicopter was still ablaze.

Once the others had left, Abdul tied the hired killer's hands behind his back, and marched him to the coast road where their cars were parked, "Sit there and don't move," he said, Abdul and Darren had a quick chat and both nodded showing that they had come to a decision. Picking up the killer, Abdul dragged him towards the sedans pushing him into one of them,

"What are you going to do to me?" he asked, fear in his voice

"Nothing really," came the reply "We are just going for a short drive," Abdul got behind the wheel and started the engine looked back at Darren he gave a thumbs up sign, sticking the car into gear it started to move forward straight towards the cliff edge,

"What the hell are you doing?" shouted the man,

"Don't worry your trip to heaven is all taken care of," Abdul picked up a little more speed opened his door and jumped out, the car with its hysterical passenger screaming, careered down the 200 foot drop with its passenger, Abdul thought, what would David say? "I know! (Just a drop in the ocean) Darren, driving the other car with the three bodies in it, did the same, but his exit from the car did not go to plan, he left it too late to jump and rolled towards the cliff edge trying to grab hold of anything that could prevent him from tumbling over, just at the last second he managed to grab a tree stump, it held his weight for a short time, but the stump started to come out of the ground, desperately holding on, he grabbed another piece of wood, but this turned out to be Just a piece of wood. Darren was now shouting franticly for Abdul to help him, he started to slide more, the cliff edge getting closer, part of his body was hanging over the edge when he felt a strong hand grab his, looking up he saw Abdul's grinning face,

"Would you like a hand?" he asked

"No thanks," came the reply "I'm thinking of taking up cliff diving!"

David, Chloe, and Sean were back in the pub when Abdul and Darren came in, "Did you get rid of the cars?" asked David,

"Yes," replied Abdul,

"And where's our prisoner?" asked Chloe

"We lost him," said Darren,

"What do mean, you lost him?" Abdul put his hands up,

"He went over the cliff whilst driving his car, we looked around but couldn't find him?" he replied, with mock sorrow in his voice, nothing more was said, on the subject.

Chloe turned to David, "When I asked you how you knew those men were not FBI agents you said something about a watch, and a gun, what did you mean?" David stood up; he found it easier explaining things whilst standing,

"firstly I shook hands with the guy with my left hand, that was to put him off, also I wanted to look at the watch he was wearing, it looked like a very expensive a Rolex, secondly as he leant forward his coat flapped open and I saw his gun," the others were mystified,

"So?" asked Chloe,

"Well believe it or not, in my last job I had the pleasure of working with FBI agents, and all agents are issued with the same firearm, a Glock 26 9mm parabellum, this guy had a Sig Sauer p928," he explained,

"Thank you!" said Chloe "That was an awesome explanation," turning to the others "Did you understand a word of that?" they all looked confused except Abdul, he knew exactly what David was talking about,

"I've got a question?" he said looking at David, "What's with the glove?" Chloe nodded

"Yes I'd like to know that!" David sighed,

"I'm sorry, if I told you about my glove I'd have to kill you," he said smiling, Sean went up to him making himself look as big as he could, his six foot six frame overshadowing David's five foot ten, and in a menacing voice said,

"Show us the glove!" balling his fists in David's face, David cowered down on all fours,

"Okay please do not hurt me," he whimpered "I'll show you," Sean took a step back,

"I hope you all realise, that you have now signed your death warrants," David said producing the glove from his pocket, it was a strange looking thing, in the palm of the glove was a round ball filled with uncooked rice, across the knuckles was a strip of flexible titanium, "As you can see it's a knuckle duster," looking at Sean, "You can thank your son for this, it's his design," they all tried it on,

"It's brilliant!" remarked Darren, David snatched it back,

"And It's mine," putting it back in his pocket.

107
Monday

David and Chloe left the pub, and went back to the hotel where they had been staying while trying to bring the farm back to some sort of home.

Sitting in the room they sat down to analyse the events of the last few hours, "It's clear that those men were specifically targeting you and me," said Chloe,

"I agree, the only thing I can think of is that this person, who they call THE MAN, blames you and me for the loss of his valuable cargo," Chloe nodded in agreement,

"But how?" she asked, "And why?" David could not answer that,

"I have been targeted before," said David "It's scary, and your whole life is put on hold," Chloe kissed him,

"Was this whilst in the British forces?" She asked

"No,"

"Where was it then?" she asked

"You're not going to believe this; it was while I was at school," Chloe smiled,

"Can you remember things way back then," David gave her a pretend punch,

"Don't be so cheeky, I'm not that old,"

"I'm sorry Grandad," she said getting up and running round the other side of the bed, "But I did see your Zimmer frame while we we're at the farm, how old are you exactly?" David picked up a pillow and chased her around the bed, both falling on it in a tangle of arms and legs, "Now I'm about to show you how a decrepit old man like me, can still make love,"

Exhausted they lay in each other's arms for a long time neither talking about where they we're going, now that the Islands troubles were over, Chloe not having a job, and David not wanting to stay on the island now that people knew his past.

They got dressed and made their way down to the dining room, both realising that they were famished, "These last few days have been good and bad," said Chloe,

"What were the good bits?" asked David a devilish grin on his face,

"Definitely not what just happened!" she said, "That was pure torture," kissing him,

"Yes it was for me as well!" they both fell silent, neither one of them wanting to talk about the future. Finishing their meal, David went to the diner to see if Shep was okay and to tell Joseph something that was on his mind.

Chloe decided to ring her Mum to tell her that she was thinking of coming home for a while, she decided to ring first, as her Mum had a new boyfriend, and the last time Chloe had spoke to her, she had told her that plans were afoot for a wedding very soon, she tried several times but no answer, she decided to try a bit later.

David walked towards the diner the diner's door opened and once again this great big hairy thing came rushing out, David tried to get out of the way but he again found himself on the floor with this beast licking his face, "Get off me! You ugly brute," he shouted trying to get up; Joe came out of the diner,

"Shep here boy!" he called out, Shep immediately let David go and went straight over to Joe, David picked himself up and looked at the pair of them, Joe scratching Shep behind the ear, the worry of what he was about to tell him, not seeming so much of a problem now,

"Joseph let's go inside, I have something to tell you and your mum?" he said walking towards the diner's door.

Chloe meanwhile was still trying to get hold of her Mum; she rang the lady next door and asked her if she had seen her, and was surprised that she had not seen her for a couple of days, "Would you do me a favour please and call round for me? You can reach me on this number," the lady agreed, and promised to ring back.

David led Joseph inside and called out to Julie, there were quite a lot of people eating and Julie was very busy, "Hello! David," she called back "I'll be with you in a moment," as she dished up yet another plate of food, David thought to himself "This is not the right time," he bent down and whispered to Joe "Tell Mom I'll be back later," He met Chloe outside and the two of them jumped onto the buggy, and made their way to the farm, on the way Chloe asked him to stop at the cliff edge one more time, she had brought some flowers from the drugstore and with a short prayer cast them over,

"Rest in Peace My Friends," she uttered, "Let's go," she said, drying her eyes.

Darren, Stuart, and Abdul were working flat out at the garage, Darren having given Abdul a job, Abdul had told him that he knew nothing about cars, compressors, or generators, so he was the tea boy, while Stuart, had turned out to be a great asset to the place, Abdul's others jobs included picking up and dropping off, Abdul was the happiest he had been for the last three and a half years, but he longed for a return to teaching back in his own country, Afghanistan, but that he knew that was not about to happen anytime soon, he had recently told David that this is what he dreamed of, a return to Afghanistan, David had told him he might have a solution to his dream?

"(OI) You!, dreamer," shouted Darren, "Have you made the tea yet," a big torrent of abuse came back, they all laughed, things were getting back to normal.

Ned had made a move on his lady friend, and asked her to move in with him back at the farm, whilst also booking a place on the ferry for a trip to the mainland, then on to San Francisco, to meet with the law firm dealing with the ownership of the Island, this was his first to the mainland for thirty years or so.

Danielle and the Children seemed to have got over their spell as hostages, the classes taking place as normal.

Sean had been sworn in as the islands new Mayor, and that made Mary his wife Mayoress, she was overjoyed at the title. Today the pub was extra busy as the new ferry docking had brought more people onto the island, and seeing as the ferry will not return until tomorrow, trade for today and part of tomorrow, was going to do quite well.

The new Mayor had registered the death of Peter Steinbach as an accident, also registering the deaths of Professor Lomax and Mike Phillips due to a vehicle accident that will be investigated at a later date by the Coroner, Scott they decided, if anyone asked? Had just disappeared?

Susan the Mayor's secretary having taken a liking to Stuart, was in a good place at the moment, after the death of her employer, the Island's Mayor. She and Stuart had been on their first date, a meal for two at the hotel's restaurant.

The fishermen were out on their boats hoping to do a lot better than their last voyage, their wife's hoping for a better life once the contents of the two suitcases were decided on.

The late mayor's wife had decided to sell up, and move to Israel.

The ferries captain's mysterious illness had cleared up, and he was now back at sea.

108
Columbia

Captain Morella had finally been declared dead, killed by a car bomb planted by known drug dealers due to his dedication to the job, and the apprehension of hundreds of drug gang members, including the destruction of several Cartels.

It was early morning, and Morella decided to go out for his early morning run a bit earlier than usual, hoping the people keeping an eye on him were still not fully awake, the Captain had told the men that he did these runs every day, when in fact he had never ran in his life, this was his way to elude his so called minders, he went out telling just one of his minders that he was going, the man tried to protest, but Morella just went before he could do anything about it. "And never returned"

Later that day Morella was in a house he had brought several years ago unbeknowing to anyone in authority, this was his own safe house, one he had purchased with the help of two men over four years ago while breaking up an arms deal that Juan Luis Cordova was involved in, so the feud between the Cordova's and Morella goes back a lot longer that what just happened, the car bomb.

He went to a wall towards the back of the house and pushed a button on the remote, the whole wall slid sideways to reveal a large selection of firearms, machine pistols, a sniper rifle hand guns, grenades, even an missile launcher with missiles, in fact it could arm a small army Morella remembered what this man who called himself the Shepherd? Called him at the time, Arnie?

He spent the rest of the day calling in favours all over Columbia, until he had the location of Pablo Cordova's hacienda.

The next morning he set out with enough fire power to start a war?

Washington

The FBI after an extensive investigation came to conclusion that the ferry accident was just that, an accident no foul play was involved, and seeing that the search had been called off, the case was now closed. The islands ferry disaster was now FOGOTTEN as was the Island itself.

Afghanistan

The sergeant, after the initial shook of one of the insurgents walking out carrying a white flag, had gone out to meet the man without getting approval from his Commander, the man told the sergeant who he was and what they wanted, that was when he shook the man's hand. The Commander looking down saw his sergeant give the okay, then to his second surprise the rest of the armed force came out from the building's, shooting their guns into the air and cheering, it turned out that this was one of the armed brigades that have been springing up all over Afghanistan, to rid the Country of the hated Taliban, and when they heard that a large contingent of fighters had left the compound leaving just a small force, they decided to attack, and reclaim the once home to a leader who was against the strict laws imposed on the village, but then they were informed by the young lad's father of the taking of the compound by American forces.

The Commander pulled his men out of the compound and the brigade moved in, setting up a defensive perimeter until the Commander informed them that the Taliban had been killed or taken prisoner, and the village was now theirs.

Just outside the village a Chinook CH-47 helicopter landed, the Commander gave the order to the evacuation, making sure the medical facilities and medical staff were in place on the helicopter, and on the ground; their rescued army veteran was going to get the best treatment they could provide.

109

David and Chloe at the farm were getting on well with the chores they had set themselves, Chloe stopping every few minutes ringing her Mum to no avail, the phone rang; Chloe picked it up so fast it fell out of her hand, quickly picking it up, "Hello!" she said, Chloe put the phone down a look of pure fright on her face, she shouted for David, he came running over looking at Chloe's shaking body,

"What's the matter?" he asked, taking her in his arms,

"It's my mom, no one has seen her!" David sat her down,

"Maybe she has gone on holiday or just out," Chloe shook her head,

"No! Something's wrong, I can feel it,"

"What do you want to do?" Chloe got up and walked towards the buggy,

"We have to find a way to get over there. Now!"

David was making a few phone calls whilst Chloe sped along the coast road; He had to hold on for dear life, but didn't tell Chloe he was shit scared of her driving.

Three hours later they were flying over the ocean towards Santa Barbara.

"How on earth did you organise this so fast?" asked Chloe snuggling up to David in the back of the Helicopter,

"I have contacts,"

"But it must have cost an arm and a leg?" extricating herself from his arms, and looking at him waiting for an answer,

"I have a savings account,"

"But you're a school teacher and a small farmer, this must have cost a small fortune," David closed his eyes and pretended to go to sleep, as he did not want to answer any more questions.

(He remembered the time when he first met Sean Junior; they were both on an arms smuggling operation down in Venezuela, David was with the British SAS, Sean the American Delta force.

Intelligence had traced the arms, from Kurdistan, through to the port of Maracaibo, in Venezuela, where he met up with Sean who was leading the American side of it, and with the help of a Columbian Police Captain they halted the arms deal, made an enemy of a Columbian drug Lord who in his role of negotiator met a few times.

317

The end result, ended up with Sean and Me, and the Columbian police Captain finding and keeping a bag with fifteen million dollars in it, that now resided in a bank in Venezuela, under a company's name, with three directors having sole access.

After that successful joint operation, David was seconded to the American Delta force at his request, and he and Junior became like brothers and managed to be one of the most successful duos in existence, that was how he was able to help Sean senior purchase the pub, and for Julie to buy the diner, but never letting on it was him that supplied the money, saying that it came from the war office pension, and a one off insurance payout.)

Chloe poked him in the ribs, "We're landing," David had no recollection of falling asleep, rubbing his eyes,

"Sorry just dozed off for a second," Chloe smiled

"That second lasted one hour!"

Exiting the helicopter Chloe's fears came back, her body gave an almighty shudder, "Are you okay?" asked David, holding her tightly,

"I just had a terrible premonition," she answered with another shudder. "THE MAN has gone after my Mom?" They practically ran to the waiting car.

The driver an old army mate of David's, gunned the car towards the address David had given him. On the drive they were overtaken by police cars, with flashing lights.

"Something's wrong," Chloe, shouted, "Can't you drive any faster," David's mate who was ex Delta, drove like a racing driver and the short journey they did in record time. Turning into the road, there were no flashing lights to be seen, just a taxi letting out a couple of people, "That's my Mom," shouted out Chloe.

David's instructor whilst in the army always told him, "You do not to go after someone for revenge, for in your mind you cannot think straight, it's just too personal" but this time David knew that he was about to ignore the advice the instructor gave, the Man who was trying to kill them, was going to pay, so if you want to call it revenge, that's fine. But I would like to call it, ridding the world of a cancer.

After booking into a hotel David made a few more calls, one call he did not want to make but decided he had to.

"This is Shepherd," he said down the phone, the CIA man replied,

"That's twice you've been dead," a moments silence "You're on a secure line, what can I do for you?" He asked, "If you want to buy more sheep I can't help you, but if you want information I may be able to help!" he said in a cheerful voice,

"Damm it, I wanted to order two dozen woollies' to go with the two dozen I already have, can you put me through to someone who could help please," a laugh came down the phone,

"This had better be good," said the CIA man.

David got off the phone asking his once controller, to find out who this man the bad guys called THE MAN was, and if he could find out as much as he could about him, The CIA man said he would do what he could, but seeing as most of his work involved things outside the US, he did not know what he could find out, but he did have a good contact in the department of homeland security, he would give him a call and get back, David gave him the phone number of the throwaway phone he had just purchased.

He went back to the hotel asking the driver John, to get a team ready, they were going hunting. It turned out that Chloe's Mom had been on holiday to Las Vegas for two weeks, and that was why she could not get hold of her. But THE MAN was still trying to kill them. And the two of them decided that they could not live in fear of this man, so made up their minds to rid the world of him.

Back on the Island everything was returning to normal the ferry had returned to the mainland with the unlikely figure of Ned aboard on his way to San Francisco.

Sean and Mary after a few really hectic days, were trying to arrange some down time by organising a short holiday to Los Angeles.

The ex Mayor's wife left the Island on the ferry, to realise her husband's dream of going to Israel and she sold her house to Mary and Stuart who were now an official couple.

The garage was doing well except for Abdul who was getting restless.

Scott's funeral was due to take place in two days time, they were hoping that David and Chloe were going to be there, but it had been three days since they had left to find her mom,

Julie had been flat out in the diner for those few days the ferry and the Fishermen all contributing to her success. Joseph had confined himself to his workshop in between school lessons, perfecting Arnold, and had completed a drone of his own design, two in fact, one was a miniaturised version of Arnold designed as a flying bug, the other a drone powered by an engine but no helicopter blades, he was delighted with the results so far.

Danielle and the school children had forgotten about their ferry ordeal, and school lessons were going on as usual.

Julie was cooking breakfast in the diner for her Dad, Sean Senior when they heard a helicopter come over, Sean looked out of the window, It's landing!" he exclaimed, Julie came over,

"What do they want now?" she said "I thought this was all finished," Sean shook his head,

"It is, the last time I spoke to the FBI and the Coast guard, they told me that all enquiries had been dropped and the case closed," Julie went back to the kitchen, Sean carried on eating,

"Grandad, Look at this," shouted Joe, running over, and showing him the bug,

"What the hell is it?" Looking at the ugly beetle in Joe's hand,

"It's my latest flying drone, it's got a one hour flying time, a 4 megapixel camera that also has zoom, and it can be flown just by using a cell phone," he said, excitement on his face and in his voice,

"It's lovely," said Sean without any enthusiasm, just then the diner's door opened and two Military Officers entered, Sean looked up, and thought to himself "They've come about the secret base I'll bet?" he picked up his papers and started to walk out when he heard one of the Officers ask for Mrs O'Rielly, he went up to the officers,

"I'm Mr O'Rielly can I help?" the Officer looked around,

"I'm sorry Sir! I'm looking for a Mrs Julie O'Rielly," Julie came over,

"I'm Mrs Julie O'Rielly, how can I help you?" The two Officers took her to the far side of the diner and asked her to sit down; Sean and Joe were looking confused, when they saw Julie fall to the floor in a dead faint, the two Officers jumped up and gently lifted her back onto the chair, Sean and Joe rushed over, Sean barging into one of the Officers, and when you get a big lump like Sean O'Rielly barging into you, you know it! He didn't say sorry he just knelt beside his Daughter-in-law trying to comfort her, Joseph putting his arms around his Mom,

"What the hell did you say to her?" giving the Officer a look that said this had better be good,

"I'm sorry Sir, we did not mean to upset her," Sean looked into Julie's eyes the tears were flowing freely; in a whisper she said

"He's alive! Sean's alive!" Sean Senior nearly joined Julie on the floor; he turned to one of the officers,

"Is this true?" he asked in an unbelieving voice,

"Yes Sir, we rescued a prisoner from the Taliban in Afghanistan two days ago, and it has now been confirmed that the prisoner is in fact, Captain Sean O'Rielly" the two officers retreated to the far side of the diner to allow Julie, Joseph, and Sean Senior to have time to process the wonderful news.

The three of them were still on the floor unable to get their minds around the news, the tears were now flowing from all three of them, and Julie kept saying "I knew it, I knew it, I just knew it!" she kept repeating.

The officers came back over once the three of them had managed to get to their feet, Joe made his mom sit down, the Officers explained how Captain O'Rielly was rescued and where he was right at this moment, once they had given all the information that they possessed they handed Julie a phone, "This cell phone in encrypted, and is on a secure line, you will receive a call in exactly fifteen minutes time, I'm sure you will want to answer it!" the two Officers shook hands and left, after a short time they heard their helicopter take off.

On the Mainland, David picked up the phone and just sat there his face getting angrier as he listened. Putting the phone down his face took on a more determined look,

Chloe, who had been watching David's face change, asked "Well?" David put the phone down,

"We have a name," he replied,

Chloe jumped up "Come on then what are we sitting around here for," grabbing a coat, and starting to walk towards the door,

"Hold on!" he said pulling her back, "Where do you think you're going?"

Chloe pushed his arm away, "If you think; I'm staying here by myself," pulling a gun out from inside her coat, and cocking the hammer, "You do not know me at all; I want to be the one to pull the trigger, he's the one responsible for murdering Peter and Mike," she said this with so much anger that David once again looked at this once Marine Biologist, and wondered what he had created, but knowing, he had no choice, but to let her accompany them, to what to his mind was to assassinate a human being. David who had no qualms about the job they were about to do, but Chloe?

"Whoa! I said we had a name, "

"So?"

"We do not have a location, so far,"

Back on the Island, the diner had a closed sign on it, (closed till further notice) Julie, Joseph, Sean, and Mary were standing around waiting for the phone to ring, looking at his watch Joe said "It's fifteen minutes now!" just as he said it, the phone rang, Julie nervously answered,

"Hello?" she had the phone an speaker so as the others could hear what was being said, the phone came to life and Julie found herself looking at her Husband Sean Junior sitting up in bed, the image was something Julie thought would never, ever, Happen. But she always believed it would come about one day, and here it was. They talked for over twenty minutes each person taking a turn, at long last they said their goodbyes and the transmission was cut off, with a message "PLEASE DISPOSE,"

They could not stop talking about what they had just found out; Sean had been kept captive in that village for the three and a half years without anyone knowing about it. The rescue had gone to plan, and Sean was now in an American Military hospital in Kaiserslautern Germany and would be flown home in a few days time. And they were told that a helicopter would be made available, to take them to Captain O'Rielly, when he was back in the United States. They also wanted to know if we knew where a Major Collins could be found, by this time all the others had turned up all wanting to know the full story, but neither Julie or Sean could tell them much, at least not until they see Sean Junior and the Military to give them a few more details, "Major Collins must be our David?" said Julie,

"And a Major," added Sean, with pride in his voice, "I must try to get in touch with him," said Sean reaching for the phone.

The phone rang; picking it up David answered "Sean?" David put the phone down after several minutes his whole body shaking, Chloe came over, "What's happened?" she asked knowing that David had been talking to Sean,

"He's alive!"

"Who's alive?" putting her arm around him,

"Sean Junior, my partner, whilst in the army," tears came to his eyes "They rescued an American soldier in Afghanistan three days ago, and it turned out to be Sean my friend, and partner," David could not hold back the tears. The thing he could not get over was the fact that, he was rescued from the village they had been in three and a half years ago, where Sean's last words were

"I'm doing a Butch Cassidy," Chloe kissed him,

"We must clear this thing up as soon as possible, and get back. I must see my friend and partner.

110
Columbia

Morella had tracked Cordova to a large hacienda in Chiquinguira, north of Bogota; He was perched on a hill looking down on the hacienda, where he could see a small army of men, and a large quantity of drugs, being loaded onto trucks, armed guards were patrolling the grounds, Morella himself was nearly caught whilst getting to the position he was in now, looking through the glasses, he could see Cordova giving orders to the men loading the trucks, putting the glasses down he picked up the sniper rifle and trained the sights on his quarry, he took a large breath and held it, having been taught by the American soldier Junior;

His finger tightened on the trigger, when he felt the coldness of a gun barrel pressed against his temple, "Baja la pistola por favor" Morella put the gun down and raised his hands, he turned to find two armed men looking down at him, one of them gestured to him to get up and walk in front, another picked up the rifle, and all Morella's gear, Morella had started walking, when he realised that they had not searched him. They started to walk down the hill when Morella pretended to stumble pulling out a machine pistol from under his coat at the same time, quickly turning round he let of a short burst, swinging in a arc, the men were caught unaware by the sudden movement, and were dead before they hit the ground, but the sound of gunfire, had alerted the men in the hacienda. Men were scurrying around trying to find the source of the gunfire. Pablo Cordova had quickly taken refuge back in the house, surrounded by guards. Armed men started up the hill Morella knew he only had seconds before they found him, "How could I have been so stupid as to let someone creep up behind me?" he said to himself picking up the rifle and running, but it was whilst running that he decided that if he was going to avenge Durrell and his family, he needed help. He decided to make a call to the two soldiers who he had worked with in the past. The Shepherd and his partner, Junior.

After about half a mile he had to stop to catch his breath, "I'm too old for this shit!"he said, just as he said it he found himself falling down a steep bank crashing through undergrowth making one hell of a noise, at last he came to a stop blooded, and bruised. He picked himself up and looked around, he was in some sort of gulley, he could hear sounds coming from up above, "Hopefully they would not of seen me, or heard me fall," he thought to himself, he found a small opening and crawled inside covering it with branches, he felt safe for now?

Pablo Cordova looked down at his dead men, "Idiotus inutiles" (useless idiots) spitting on them.

Morella waited for darkness, before venturing out from his hide, all sounds of the pursuit having stopped some hours ago, picking up the rifle, and the machine pistol, he started the long journey back to the car three miles away, "Shit!" he said to himself "All this planning, running and walking all for nothing," he was not looking forward to the long trek home, he looked back at the cave, and stopped, what would the Shepherd and Junior have done? He ran through a few scenarios, thinking to himself "And what would Pablo Cordova be thinking now?"

Coming to a decision, he turned round, and started back towards the hacienda.

111

Back on the mainland, David was waiting for confirmation on the whereabouts of their quarry, a Russian, called Milos Kablinski, when his phone rang, but not the throwaway one, "Mr Cross, I understand you are looking for me?"

David nearly dropped the phone,

"Mr Cross do not bother looking anymore, as I'm now unavailable, but I would like to remind you, that I do know how to find you, and be assured, I will find out who you really are, you and Miss Barnwell are still in danger," The phone went dead.

David looked at the phone, "Mr Kablinski your days are numbered, I will find you?" He then destroyed the phone.

When David and Chloe returned to the Island, the others had just returned from seeing Sean Junior, "How is he?" asked David

"He's pissed off with you, for not waiting for him in that village," answered Julie smiling, not really knowing what it meant, "And he can't wait to see your ugly mug," she said giving David a kiss, "That's from him,"

Chloe who had never met him asked "When will he be coming home?"

Sean answered, "In two days time hopefully" Sean senior had never felt happier, since escaping from Ireland, all those years ago,

"How was your Mom?" asked Mary holding Chloe's hand,

"Fine" she answered, Chloe regretted not visiting her Mom more often, "I do love her you know, although I do not visit too often, she would always put me first," she remembered that her Mom had properly saved her life by moving them to California, all those years ago.

"What's been going on here then while we've been away?" asked David,

"The biggest news is Ned has just got back from the Mainland," answered Darren; David looked surprised,

"What! Ned left the Island?"

"And believe it or not, he has called a meeting in the hall for 2pm today,"

"What for?" asked Chloe

"No one knows" replied Sean.

They all stayed around until the time for the meeting, all trying to catch up on all the different news, David grilling Julie on Sean Junior's mental state, but it turned out that the enforced incarceration had not harmed him as much as you would have thought, David knew, that this was down to the training that he had had, with the British SAS, and Sean's training with the American Navy Seals, and Delta Force. They teach you to withstand torture, and solitary confinement.

The whole Island was assembled in the hall ready to learn whatever old Ned was planning to announce, Ned took the stage.

The meeting was over, and back at the pub, they couldn't stop talking about what Ned had done for the Islands community, "I can't believe he has given the Island to the Islanders," said Julie.

But that was exactly what old Ned had done. Whilst seeing his lawyers in San Francisco, the Island now belonged to the Islanders, Lock stock and barrel, and that included the restricted area.

112

David had come to the decision to tell everyone that he was leaving the Island. A decision he had come to a long time ago, ever since he had told people about his previous life, but now reality had kicked in, and he knew, that he could not stay on the Island, knowing that his, and the people around him, could be in danger knowing he and Chloe where still being targeted by THE MAN.

Sean Junior was due to arrive back on the Island the next day, and David had decided to leave as soon as he saw his old mate settled, but first he had to tell Joseph about his decision.

David found Joe in his workshop still messing about with Arnold, "I'm going to fly him over Dad, as he gets off the helicopter," he said excitedly,

"He'll love that," David said, "Joe! I need to tell you something?" sitting down opposite him, "I'm leaving the Island in the next few days," Joe was a bit confused,

"What for a holiday?" David leant forward;

"No!" he did not know how to say it, so just came out with it, "No Forever,"

After talking to Joe, David did the rounds, informing all his friends about his decision, they all tried to change his mind, but knew that the decision David had come to, was the right one for him, so they all wished him good luck.

David and Chloe spent the night at the farm; they had managed to turn the gym into a neat sleeping area, lying in bed the next morning, Chloe turned round, extricated herself from his arms, "I'm coming with you," she said, with as much forcefulness as she could muster,

"I know!" he replied.

113

The next morning, the whole Island's community were gathered in the town, bunting was everywhere, the whole place was alive. This was the day that one of their own was coming back to them, and they were all there to greet him, their hero, Captain Sean (Junior) O'Rielly was coming home.

Later that day David and Sean had time for a heart to heart, "What happened on that day after you said I'm doing a Butch Cassidy?" David asked, Sean who looked exhausted; the day had been a long one, replied,

"I had the gun ready, and just like the film rushed out the door shouting Butch and Sundance, I Pulled the trigger, but nothing, I had forgotten to turn the safety off," they both laughed their heads off,

"I knew you were an idiot!" they hugged, and started on their third drink, with plenty more over the next few days.

114

David and Chloe looked back at the island as the ferry pulled away, seeing Sean, the Mayor of San Juliet, standing on the jetty waving a certificate in the air,

Chloe looked at David with a glint in her eye,

"What?" David asked,

"Do you realise that we pretty good back there, busting drug Traffickers,"

"So,"

"I think we ought to go into it full time, and start a drug investigation agency," putting her arm through his, "What do you think?"

"I think I love you!"

They gave a last wave to Sean, who was still waving the certificate in the air. They turned to each other and kissed.

"Any regrets Mrs Collins?"

"None whatsoever, Mr Collins,"

THE ISLAND BEHIND THEM

FORGOTTEN

EPILOGUE
One year later

A convoy of military vehicles led by a 1941 Studebaker were heading for a restricted area on the Island of San Juliet.

San Juliet was now a major tourist attraction with the only World War two land based aircraft carrier in the world.

The vehicles were taking tourist to the WW2 site.

Sean O'Rielly and his Son, Sean (Junior) O'Rielly, run the attraction on the Island with the help of all the Islanders having turned San Juliet into the top tourist attraction in the United States.

USS SCOTT MEREDITH, named after their friend. Scott?

On show, WW2 folding wing planes, tanks, trucks, armaments and a submarine pen, with a WW2 Submarine in it!

With its usable flight deck, planes are able to land with no restriction on size, and the DC8 cargo aircraft they found on the Island they put to good use. But there was no mention of the laboratories, or their use?

The Island is now served, by a fleet of ferry's, manned and owned by the once fishermen of the island.

***

Joseph had a thriving business going, making and selling drones. Whilst feeding the sheep and geese on his farm.

Stuart and Susan were now married.

Darren was operation manager at the airbase attraction, plus a large garage facility.

Virginia

James now realises how the drugs he and Robert were chasing a year ago, had got into the country, a DC8 landing on San Juliet? And also had worked out that the drugs were now at the bottom of the ocean along with the ferry?

Washington

The FBI has had no sighting of their assassin Abdul Abdullah for over a year, and has now confirmed his death?

Columbia

A man lying on a sun lounger on the beach in "Isla de Baru, an Island just off the coast of Cartagena Columbia" was enjoying his cocktail, and raising it to his two best friends, The Shepherd and Junior.

The man's name was Manuel Rodrigo Diego?

Afghanistan

David Cross an English born Afghani, was taking a lesson in a village near the border of Pakistan, the school was formally a Taliban stronghold, the school was also one of the few in Afghanistan to allow girls to participate in school lessons, one of the girls, Jasmine, was the brightest of them all.

England

Daniel Collins looked at the little boy in his cot, Scott Peter Collins, while the little boy's mother, Chloe Barnwell Collins, looked at the both of them with pride and love, remembering how! And where! They found love. On the little Island of San Juliet,

The

FORGOTTEN ISLAND

25418073R00188

Printed in Poland
by Amazon Fulfillment
Poland Sp. z o.o., Wrocław